HER SENSE OF ISKANDER DEEPENED,
AND WITH THAT CAME THOUGHTS,
REACTIONS, AND EVEN MEMORIES
THAT DIDN'T BELONG TO HER.

Then he stepped between her legs and leaned into her, until they fell together, his body on top of hers.

Anticipation.

Need. Desire.

His eyes were a different color again. Not blue but a dark green-blue that moved and swirled and made her think there was something alive there that was more than human.

"I feel your magic," he said in a low voice. She felt . . . *something* flow from him into her. The sensation set off a vibration deep in her chest.

It was like a switch flipped inside her. The vibration turned into an electric hum that roared through her and when it ended, her skin rippled with gooseflesh as ice-cold fingers danced up and down her spine and along the back of her neck, her arms, and even her legs. His magic echoed in her and entwined with her. She reached for him . . .

Also by Carolyn Jewel

My Wicked Enemy

My Forbidden Desire

My Immortal Assassin

My Dangerous Pleasure

Carolyn Jewel

FOREVER

NEW YORK   BOSTON

This book is a work of fiction. Names, characters, places, and incidents are the product of the author's imagination or are used fictitiously. Any resemblance to actual events, locales, or persons, living or dead, is coincidental.

Copyright © 2011 by Carolyn Jewel

Forever
Hachette Book Group
237 Park Avenue
New York, NY 10017
www.HachetteBookGroup.com

Forever is an imprint of Grand Central Publishing.
The Forever name and logo are trademarks of Hachette Book Group, Inc.

The publisher is not responsible for websites (or their content) that are not owned by the publisher.

Printed in the United States of America

First Edition: June 2011

10 9 8 7 6 5 4 3 2 1

Acknowledgments

I'd like to thank the people who help make things happen: my agent, Kristin Nelson, I couldn't be in better hands; my editor, Michele Bidelspach, you have my back on this—thanks so much for making a better book; and the Grand Central art department for the wonderful covers. I have to thank my mother for taking me to ballet lessons for so many years; my ballet teacher, Mary Paula; and the late Harold Christensen of the San Francisco Ballet because I listened to every single story you told whenever Mrs. Paula talked you into coming to teach us. Ballet taught me that talent is never enough. You also have to work hard. It's a good life lesson. I'd also like to thank the people who provided valuable information. Any mistakes in the text are mine, not theirs. To Jared James for information about weapons and to Lisa Shearin and Katie Ford for their help with Southernisms. I must also acknowledge the Twitter community at large. If you need a quick answer, opinion, or just a really great joke, Twitter is the place to get it. Lastly, my thanks to my son for bringing such joy to my life.

GLOSSARY

blood-twin: A bonded pair of fiends who share a permanent magical connection. They may be biologically related and/or same sex. Antisocial and prone to psychosis.

copa: A plant derivative, of a yellow-ochre color when processed. Has a mild psychotropic effect on the kin, who use it for relaxation. On mages, the drug increases magical abilities and is highly addictive.

cracking (a talisman): A mage or witch may crack open a talisman in order to absorb the life force therein and magically prolong his or her life. Requires a sacrificial murder.

demon: Any one of a number of shape-shifting magical beings whose chief characteristic is, as far as the mage-kind are concerned, the ability to possess and control a human.

fiend: A subspecies of demon. Before relations with the magekind exploded into war, fiends frequently bonded with them.

kin: What fiends collectively call each other. Socially divided into various factions constantly seeking power over other warlord-led factions. The kin communicate with other kin via psychic connections. They typically possess multiple physical forms, at least one of which is recognizably human.

mage: A male who possesses magic. A sorcerer. See also *magekind*.

mageheld: A fiend or other demon who is under the complete control of one of the magekind.

magekind: Humans who possess magic. The magekind arose to protect vanilla humans from the depredations of demons, a very real threat.

sever: The act of removing a mageheld from the control of a mage or a witch.

talisman: A usually small object into which a mage has enclosed a fiend's life force, typically against the fiend's will. A talisman confers additional magical power to the mage who has it. Sometimes requires an additional sacrifice. See also *cracking* (a talisman).

vanilla: A human with no magic or, pejoratively, one of the magekind with little power.

warlord: A fiend who leads other fiends who have sworn fealty. Usually a natural leader possessing far more magic than others of the kin.

witch: A human female who possesses magic. A sorceress. See also *magekind*.

My Dangerous Pleasure

CHAPTER 1

A tingle shot through Paisley Nichols when she glanced up from the cash register and saw a tall man get into line. She recognized him because he was one of her regular customers, but also because he was strikingly handsome. Their gazes met, nothing out of the ordinary, just an accidental contact that was easy to pretend hadn't happened. She flashed a smile at him even though the morning rush was full-on and there wasn't time for flirting, not even if she had the nerve.

Weekday mornings were a madhouse, and anytime she was needed out front, well, she liked to think of the madness as a delightful way to make the rent on her hole-in-the-wall space. The tables were packed, and the line of hungry patrons stopping by on their way to work reached almost to the door. She worked the counter every morning to keep that line moving. Knowing the regulars helped a lot with that. By the time the regulars got to the counter, all they had to do was hand over their money, exchange a smile or a quick "good morning" and head off with their coffee and pastries. She prepped the hot guy's croissant and café au lait with three turbinado sugars while he tapped away at a cell phone.

She wondered if her interest in him meant she was ready to date again after her disaster of a relationship with Urban. The disaster part wasn't all Urban's fault; she was mature enough to acknowledge that. He'd met her mother—her tarot-card-reading, astrology-believing, psychic lunatic of a mother—and that only sped up the race to relationship death. She'd taken herself out of circulation for a long time after the crash. If she was ready to date again, this lovely, sexy man might be just the place to start.

He was handsome in a moneyed, elegant way that was subverted by long white-blond hair done up in dozens of braids with tiny red beads polished to a shine. The beads clicked when he moved his head. Very sexy. Today's suit was tailored, like all the others she'd seen him in. This one was a midnight-blue wool that turned his eyes an even more startling blue. His shirt was pristine white cotton with sharp collar points, his tie burnt-orange silk. An exquisite dresser. And then those beaded braids that worked with such ridiculous sex appeal. He didn't wear a wedding ring; that was something she'd noticed.

The line moved quickly because she had a lot of regulars now. The Financial District had discovered her, thank goodness. Paisley Bakery and Café was now a popular morning stop for people on their way to work. She got a lot of lunchtime traffic, too, plus a respectable number of orders for employee birthday cakes and lunch-meeting treats. Her catering business was picking up as well. Over the last three months, she'd had money left over after rent, payroll, insurance, and her loan. Profit.

The first dollar she'd made when the doors opened was framed on the wall behind the cash register. Whenever she looked at it, she just had to grin. This was her dream, and she was not only living it but was succeeding at it, too.

Today marked the fifth week of the man with blond braids coming into the café. He was three people from the front now, and she gave him a surreptitious once-over. He was watching her. Busted. She gave him a quick smile.

He smiled back.

Paisley smoothed her white chef's jacket and wished it was a little cleaner. A smear of chocolate ganache arced across one shoulder of the jacket. Occupational hazards of the bakery business included chocolate on your clothes and going home smelling like butter and vanilla.

"Good morning!" she said when he made it to the front of the line. She smiled, not too hard, and made eye contact.

"Good morning." He had a faint accent she couldn't quite place, but boy was his voice dreamy. She handed over his items, took his money, made change, and that was it. He hesitated, then said, "Thank you," in that faint and yummy accent before leaving with his coffee and croissant.

Rats.

Then she was on to the next customer with no time to think about her disappointment until after nine-thirty, and then it was time to start another bake and do the prep for the lunch crowd.

She was out front for lunchtime, and toward the end of the rush, he came back. Her heart leaped even while she told herself this meant nothing. She waved off the clerk and stepped up to the counter herself. He studied the various pastries and baked goods behind the glass display counter. Brownies, cupcakes, cookies, and pastries left over from the morning bake, as well as samples of the various cakes she sold, either whole or by the slice.

The beads in his hair didn't look like plastic. A few of them were faceted in a bezeled setting the color of rose-gold, but most of them were milky smooth. "Can I help you?"

He looked up and when their gazes met, she got a major rush of *whoa*. Her mother, if she had been here instead of in Georgia and if Paisley been crazy enough to tell her about the reaction, would have said it was fate. And then intone that fate came in three flavors: bad, worse, and disastrous. Her mother was a real ray of sunshine. Paisley had spent years trying to get out from under the habit of seeing doom everywhere.

"I would like to buy a cake."

There was no doom involved in a hottie who wanted to buy a cake from her. However, there was profit. And the possibility of a date, because if he showed the least sign of interest, she was going to ask him out to coffee.

"You're in the right place." She answered his questions about her ready-made cakes, how many they served and whether they could be personalized. But of course they could be personalized, she told him. He made his selection—a chocolate butter cake with a chocolate frosting decorated with white pastilles and white fondant daisies—and she took the cake in the back to pipe out the phrase *Congratulations on Your Success* on top of it.

At least he wasn't having her write *To my lovely wife* on the thing.

She brought it out, showed it to him, and he smiled his approval. What a smile, too. Serious with an edge of heat. That smile made her think her lack of a sex life needed to be remedied ASAP. As she boxed up the cake, she worked up her courage and said, "I'm Paisley Nichols. The owner and principal baker of this establishment."

His eyes jittered, which startled her enough that there was a brief and awkward silence. He closed his eyes for a moment, but she could see his eyeballs twitching underneath his eyelids. When he opened them again, everything was back to normal. "Yes," he said. "I know you are the Paisley of Paisley Bakery and Café."

He did? Did that mean he'd been noticing her the way she'd been noticing him? Mentally, she tried out a few more ways to ask him to coffee without sounding like she was actually asking him out. She taped a set of instructions for storing and serving the cake to the top of the box, wrapped it up with her murderously expensive paisley ribbon, slapped on a gold foiled sticker with the name, address, and phone number of her bakery on it, and set the box on the counter. All her prices included tax. "Twenty-five fifty."

"I am Rasmus Kessler." He said his name the way people did when they came from a country where they didn't speak English. He took a hundred-dollar bill from a slim wallet and handed it to her.

She grimaced at the bill. "I can't break a hundred." She could, but she was under strict orders from her accountant never to take bills larger than a twenty. Too much counterfeiting going on.

"Of course," he said smoothly. He returned the hundred and took out two twenties.

"Thanks." When she gave him his change, she steeled her nerve for her invitation to coffee. As she took the bills, the tips of his first two fingers touched her right wrist, and she got an electric shock. She laughed and shook her hand.

His eyes widened. They jittered again. "Are you all right?"

"Sure." Except her wrist burned where the static electricity had sparked off her skin. She handed him his change. "Enjoy your cake, Mr. Kessler."

"Rasmus, please." He picked up the box and stood there silently. Watching her.

Dang it, her wrist hurt. Enough that she had to concentrate on not crying. "Can I get you a coffee for the road?" Was that lame or what? But she felt like she was talking past a steel plate between her and the outside world. Inside, pain crawled into her head.

"Yes, thank you," he said. "That would be nice."

She made him his usual café au lait, remembered the three packets of turbinado sugar he liked, stirred the contents, and handed it over. The pain leveled out, but her wrist still hurt and her arm trembled as she held out the paper cup. "On the house, Rasmus."

He took the cup. She flinched to avoid him touching her again, which ended up being awkward. "Thank you again." He hesitated. "Perhaps I can buy you a coffee sometime soon."

"I'd like that."

"Friday evening?"

She nodded.

"Where should I pick you up?" Rasmus asked.

"Here." She pasted on a grin. "I should be done about five."

He gave her his cell number so she could call him in case something came up, and she watched him leave the shop with his cake and his coffee. The near certainty of her first date in ten months floated around her. She was practically giddy. Coffee wasn't a date, of course. Coffee meant you could bail if you found out he liked the Dodgers when this was a Giants town, or hated kids when you wanted a big family. Coffee was when you decided whether to never meet again or give a guy your cell number.

She'd have been more enthused about the uptick in her social life, except her wrist hurt like the devil. After he was gone, she pushed up her sleeve to take a look. A blister the exact size and roundness of a quarter had formed on the inside of her wrist.

Whoever heard of static electricity giving you a blister? She went into the back room and got out the first-aid kit. Burns were an occupational hazard in a kitchen, so she had the salve and bandages to wrap up the injury. A little later she popped a couple of aspirin for the pain in her wrist and the throbbing headache that went with it.

At home that afternoon, she replaced the dressing. The blister had popped, but another one looked to be forming where the first had burst. Her wrist hurt worse than ever, though the injury didn't look like it was getting infected. She half expected to see a red line heading up her arm. She felt crappy enough to have blood poisoning. The pain wasn't limited to her wrist anymore. Her entire arm ached all the way to her shoulder. Enough to make her sick to her stomach. She skipped dinner and sat on her cheap sofa with a cup of hot tea in her left hand because she was having trouble using her right arm.

She was sweating, too, and seeing double. Her head

felt like it was in a vise. The pain crawled around inside her skull and took over. A voice in the back of her mind said she needed to get to the hospital. Unfortunately, she didn't have health insurance. If she went to the ER, the bills would bankrupt her. Besides, who went to the hospital for a blister?

Sometime between coming home and sitting down, she'd gotten too weak to move. She put down her tea before she dropped it. Maybe the blister wasn't the problem. She staggered to her feet, intending to find her cell phone and call 911, because dead would be worse than medical bills she couldn't pay. She'd never been this sick in her life, and the really scary thing was that she was too sick to be properly afraid. Meningitis, she remembered reading somewhere, came on quickly, and it made you feel a lot like she felt right now. Killer headache. High fever. Stiff neck and joints. Meningitis was deadly.

The way she felt, she wasn't going to live long enough to have a date with anyone. *Fate*. She thought back to that moment of *whoa* when she and Rasmus Kessler locked gazes. Apparently, her fate was the disastrous kind.

Her phone was on the kitchen counter next to her purse. She lurched in that direction, but she saw three phones there. All of them looked real to her. She was shaking too hard to see straight, and the pressure in her head was unrelenting. Her stomach had other ideas about what to do next. She barely made it to the bathroom before she threw up. The first time. Every time she thought she could make it to her phone, she heaved again. Her stomach turned itself inside out until there was nothing left and still it didn't stop.

She could barely move. Her skin was hot enough to fry

an egg, her ears were ringing, and every joint in her body hurt.

The pain gripped her like a wild animal and refused to let go. It spread through her until she could no longer identify the source. She was nothing but agony. In the back of her barely functioning brain, she knew only one thing for certain: *If she didn't get to the phone to call for help, she wasn't going to make it.*

CHAPTER 2

9:15 P.M., *the same night*, Vallejo Street,
San Francisco

Iskander put up his feet and kicked back in his recliner for an evening of movies and junk food. First up, *Shaun of the Dead*. He was totally on for an hour or two of zombie killing with everything he needed at arm's reach. Root beer? Check. Pizza, just delivered? Check. Remote? Check.

Press PLAY and go.

Check.

And click.

He was in his house. By himself. He wasn't freaked out or thinking he needed to go get laid so he wouldn't be alone. He was just a normal guy hanging out at his own house, enjoying a night by himself. Chilling like nothing had ever been wrong with him or his life.

The movie hardly got past the FBI warning when every

goddamned alarm he had set on the property shrieked into his head like a subsonic bomb.

What the hell?

Iskander got out of his chair and headed for the back of the house. His skin prickled up and down his body while he did a perimeter check. Everything was in place along the fences. His garage, a separate building on the back of his lot, was secure. His house was secure. He looked up to the darkened windows of the rental unit over his garage and got hit by a wave of sick magic.

He walked into his backyard and stood at the bottom of the stairs that led to the apartment over his garage. This was not normal. The magic felt like some kind of low-level infection, and there just wasn't any mistaking the stink. Goddamned mages. He was more than a little miffed that one of the magekind had the nerve to come anywhere near his house to do magic like that.

Hell, no.

At the top of the stairs to the unit's front door, he stripped down to his bare skin. If he was going to shift into his other form, better if he was naked when he changed. The minute he dropped his shirt, the last of the magical wards he'd set around the rental unit gave way. He hadn't done anything major in terms of proofing his garage from the kind of creatures that might come looking for him. Maybe he should have. He was going to feel guilty as shit if it turned out he should have protected his tenant better.

In the meantime, he knew someone was inside there who probably didn't think someone like Iskander should continue enjoying his current freedom and good health. What the hell this person wanted with his pure-vanilla, not-a-drop-of-magic-in-her tenant was a mystery.

The faces in the medallions he'd placed on either side of the apartment door morphed from smiling woodland creatures to two silent horrors that blackened to ash before his eyes. Whatever was going on in there was heating things up magicwise, and now the occupants were paying for it. He hoped the power releasing from those medallions was putting a serious hurt on the fucker responsible.

The need for his proofing was twofold. First, it warned him about the presence of a magic user who wasn't known and welcome at his house. Second, if the intruder didn't take the hint and leave, the proofing set off a psychic scream capable of killing. The proofing he'd put around his rental unit was already well into the second use.

Obviously, some stupid fuck of a mage had gotten inside the apartment. About now, the mage or witch or whatever was in there wasn't feeling so hot. The demon warlord Nikodemus had his territory pretty well controlled. Everyone knew Nikodemus came down hard on anyone who broke his rules, and he had rules about messing with humans. There were transgressions from time to time, and since Iskander worked for Nikodemus, he was sometimes tasked with carrying out the consequences of breaking the warlord's rules.

His hand closed on the doorknob when it occurred to him that since the apartment was rented out, his tenant might be home. With a mage. She was a nice girl. Totally vanilla—no magic whatsoever, which was the reason he'd rented to her in the first place. A couple of other people who'd come by to see the apartment after he decided to rent it out hadn't exactly been normal humans. He'd made a good choice, picking her. She paid her rent on time, let him know if something needed to be fixed, and, up to now, lived quietly. He liked that she didn't bother him and never did much more than wave at him or say hello if they happened to see each other, which didn't happen all that often. Friendly, but not friends.

If his tenant, who so far hadn't done anything but mind her own business the entire time she'd been living over his garage, was getting assaulted or murdered because of what he really was, well, that just didn't seem right. Nikodemus would agree with him on that one. He didn't think he'd get in too much trouble if he kept his tenant from getting killed, even if it meant harming one of the magekind. He stared at the door and gave the doorknob an experimental turn. It was locked. It was possible she'd invited a mage over to her place. Maybe she was dabbling the way some humans did.

Or not.

What to do?

Coulda, woulda shoulda.

He could count on zero fingers and no thumbs the number of times she'd brought someone home with her. What were the odds that his tenant would have her first wild fling with one of the magekind?

On the other hand, if he went inside, he risked finding her getting it on with someone. Explaining why he was interrupting her booty time wouldn't be much fun. Particularly since he'd been informed that as a landlord, he did not, in fact, have the right to enter his tenant's unit without permission. Unless it was an emergency.

Was this an emergency? The lights were off in the apartment. He didn't hear a sound. Not one. Any normal person would think his tenant was either not home or in blissful slumber. Or having really great sex. On the surface at least, all was well. No human walking by would think anything was wrong.

He wasn't human, though, and every nerve in his body was on fire.

Whatever was in there wasn't kin. The kin were a species of demon also known as a *fiend*, which was what he was. What he was getting from the apartment was pure magekind. Rotten and perverted.

The front door looked undisturbed. No sign of forced entry. Which wasn't unexpected since there were plenty of creatures around who had no problem with human security. Like, for example, him. A locked door was no problem for him. Or the magekind.

His intention was to go in shielded from physical notice by a layer of magic, because if she was doing it with a mage, that was her private business. Just like it would be his private business to find a way to evict her for hanging with a mage whose magic felt like this.

Iskander sent a pulse into the door locks. If he hadn't dampened the magic, he would have heard the mechanical click of the tumblers moving. And so would the occupants. Paisley Nichols—if she was in there—wouldn't hear, but a mage? He'd hear something like that. And he'd know Iskander was here, too. If he didn't already.

He went in. The apartment was dark, but he'd shifted to his nonhuman form. He saw perfectly well in the interior gloom. All the hairs on the back of his neck rippled. The source of the magic was definitely here.

At first he didn't hear anything. No moans of sexual pleasure. No whispers or laughter. No squeaky mattress. Nothing. His tenant kept unusual hours; no nine-to-five job for her. It wouldn't be strange at all for her not to be home yet. Maybe she wasn't home, which meant he might have walked into considerable danger.

Someone dry-heaved in the bathroom.

One of the magekind broke into his tenant's place to throw up?

He pulled magic through him until he was confident he could smoke just about any mage or witch who happened to be here. Still hidden from sight in case Paisley was here, he moved through the apartment toward the bathroom, which was in the back. The whole unit was something like five hundred square feet, and most of that was the living room. The bedroom, kitchen, and bathroom were tiny.

The light in the bathroom was off, but he saw someone bending over the toilet. A woman who felt like goddamned magekind. She didn't react to his presence, so he let go of the magic that hid him from human eyes. Nothing changed. She didn't move, and the magic swirling around her didn't react. His tenant was about her size, but his tenant was normal. Not a witch.

She moved. The light reflected off her red hair.

His heart took a dive.

What if it was Fen? What if she'd managed to get herself out of her entanglement with Rasmus Kessler and was in there? The proportions of the woman's body weren't Fen's, but it was dark, he was changed right now, and he hadn't seen Fen without one of them being fucked up or fucked over in nearly two years. He took a step forward. Part of him was thinking she'd come back, and that hope and longing obliterated the rest of his emotions.

His feet refused to move.

How pathetically fucked up was that? He and Fen had been blood-twins. His kind—the kin—existed in two realms: the psychic and the physical. Their magic manifested in both planes and required both. Most of the time, the boundary between the psychic and the physical was seamless. His blood bond with Fen meant their physical bodies shared the same consciousness yet they possessed twice the magic of most of their kind.

Their blood bond had been severed, and everything they'd shared had gone to hell.

He thought about the years he'd had with Fen, the one and only woman he'd ever loved, and the signs that something had been going wrong for her and how he'd ignored the problems at first. Maybe he wouldn't have failed to help her if he'd done something sooner. If he hadn't waited until it was too late and there was nothing he could do because she'd already betrayed him to Rasmus Kessler. To save himself, he'd had to block himself off from his bond with her. His desperate act had slowly cost him his sanity. If it hadn't been for Nikodemus and his witch Carson, he'd be completely insane now.

His heart shattered all over again. He couldn't forget what they'd been like when they'd both been whole. What if that was Fen there in the bathroom? What if she was trying to come back to him? If he could go back to the days when everything was fine between them, he would. He still loved her. He loved what they'd had and what he'd been when they were strong and healthy and she had been the only lover he'd ever had or needed.

None of that was going to happen. He and Fen were over. Done. He hated that a part of him wished he could have it all back. The woman in the bathroom kept her arms around the toilet, but she turned her head, and he shifted back to human just in time.

Not Fen.

Not Fen.

And then his tenant, Paisley Nichols, sank to the floor, her rib cage heaving. His mental trip into the past ended with a jolt. His tenant wasn't anything like Fen, and he'd been stupid to be fooled for even a minute.

Shit, she was in a bad way. There wasn't any mage. All that sick magic was coming from her even though Paisley Nichols was not magekind. He wouldn't have rented to her if she weren't as unmagical as a human could get. Something had happened to change that. Something very, very bad.

"Ms. Nichols? Are you okay?"

She groaned.

"Hey," he said. He went in and knelt beside her even though she stank like bad magic. A layer of sweat covered her, and her skin burned to touch. Not normal for a human. "What the hell happened to you?"

She didn't move. He pressed two fingers to the side of her neck. Her pulse was erratic.

This wasn't right, not even in his world. His tenant was plain vanilla and here she was radiating magic. Sick magic. Enough that it had set off his proofing and made him think there was a mage in the apartment.

His proofing, the wards he set out to keep his property safe from intrusion, wasn't supposed to harm humans like his tenant. The protections were, however, designed to do maximum damage to mages and their magehelds. A mageheld was a demon unlucky enough to have ended up enslaved to a mage or a witch.

Paisley Nichols was now suffering under a double punishment: whatever the mage had done to her in the first place

and the effect of Iskander's proofing going off after whatever was wrong with her built to critical levels. Coming
home just might have killed her.

Some mage had broken Nikodemus's rules, and his
tenant was dying because of it. He'd seen this kind of thing
once before, and it was pure ugly what happened when
one of the magekind wanted to enslave a human. Ugly.
Very ugly. These days, of course, the magekind denied that
any such thing had ever happened. They saw themselves
as the protectors of humankind. Fucking hypocrites.

From what he could tell, Paisley had been resisting
the magic still working on her for a lot longer than most
humans could have managed. If she were any less of a
fighter, she'd already belong to whatever mage had done
this to her. That wasn't supposed to happen. They were
all supposed to be more civilized now. No fucking over
humans like this. Not anymore.

He did a quick check of her physically to see if he
could find a point of contact. He got lucky and found it
right away. He figured a mage was a more likely culprit
than a witch, and considering that Paisley Nichols was
a total fox, the mage wasn't going to mark her where it
would spoil her body. Iskander found the entry spot on
her right wrist, a round, angry blister, broken open and
oozing sera and blood. She whimpered when he touched
her wrist.

She lifted her head like it weighed a ton. "Don't want
to die," she said.

She didn't deserve this. No one did, but especially not
his sweet-as-sugar tenant who wasn't doing anything but
living the life she wanted.

To keep her alive, he'd have to break one or two of

Nikodemus's rules. Like the one about not going into a human's head without permission and not using magic on humans without permission. If he didn't, she was going to die, and wasn't that worse?

She'd said she didn't want to die. To him, that counted as permission. He tried to make a psychic connection with her, and, damn, it was like trying to dig through concrete with a spoon.

"Hey," he said, still crouched down by her. He pressed two fingers to her forehead. "I need in."

She didn't get it. Or didn't know what to do.

"Relax, cupcake." He tried again to get into her head.

She blinked a couple of times, and he kept his fingers on her forehead. No go. The second time, though, he made contact, but he had to sweat for it. Jesus H. Christ. Her agony about blistered the inside of his head.

He took as much of the pain away from her as he could stand. At the same time, he reached up and turned on the water in the sink so he could keep one hand under the running water while he siphoned off the magic boiling through her and let it drain away into the water. He kept his other hand on her damaged wrist. He growled and shifted forms again, because it was like running ground glass through his body and it was going to be a lot easier to take if he wasn't limited by being in his human form.

Before long, the room filled with steam from the water that was vaporizing almost as quickly as it hit his hand. But slowly, her breathing eased and the pain he was pulling through her and into him lessened enough that he could think about moving back to his human form.

Which, come to think of it, he'd better do because her eyes were fluttering open. He wasn't sure how much she was going to remember about tonight, though in his limited experience with humans, psychic and magical trauma at this level tended to get thoroughly suppressed.

After a bit longer, she lifted her torso off the floor and groaned. He backed off on the psychic link and *bam*. He was shut out. Locked out good. Paisley Nichols was one of those rare humans with a natural resistance to magic.

"I've got you," he said softly. He gathered her into his arms, and she leaned into him without protest, just a sigh of what sounded like profound relief. He didn't do the comfort thing well. The one time he'd been around a sick human, he hadn't been the one in charge, but he tried to take care of Paisley now. If this turned out badly and she ended up dead or damaged, he didn't want to spend the rest of his very long life knowing he'd let her suffer alone and in pain when he could have done something to help.

"Good grief," she whispered.

Iskander stroked her hair, running his fingers through the dark reddish brown of her ponytail. Not the fiery red of Fen's hair, but a darker red made up of what looked to his still-acute vision to be at least a dozen different shades of red and even gold. "How you doing?"

"Poorly," came the answer.

He kept his arms around her and leaned his back against the tub. He wondered if he was wrong about her not knowing anything about creatures like him. When a vanilla human got caught up in his world, it was most often because someone had been careless or the human had stumbled across something she shouldn't have. Sometimes, though, one of the magekind, or even one of his kind, did the deed and deliberately brought them into contact. "Who did this to you? Do you know?"

Paisley rested her head against his chest while he waited for the answer. She was doing better. Not much, but enough to hope she would pull through. "It must have been something I ate. Lord help me if I poisoned anybody at the bakery." She shivered. "Floor's cold," she said. "But you're not."

"Come on." He adjusted her in his arms. "Let's get you into bed."

"Okay." Her uninjured arm tightened around his waist, and she tried to get her legs under her. She couldn't. "I don't think I can stand up."

"I'll do the heavy lifting." Which he did. After he ran a wet washcloth over her face, he helped her brush her teeth. She had one of those electric brushes. He got her a drink of water, too. She was going to need a lot more liquid in her, he realized. The magic wasn't out of her system yet. It might not ever be. Paisley Nichols might not ever be the same again.

Understandably, she was too weak to do much but sprawl on the bed once he got her there. He almost didn't think about what he realized was a spectacular body while he helped her get her clothes off and then get under the covers. Normally he was all over naked women. Not this time. He wasn't quite that depraved, though she looked good enough to eat.

When he came back from filling a big pitcher with water, she was shaking, a teeth-rattling, bone-shivering convulsion. She was sinking fast. Everything he'd done so far had only delayed the inevitable. It pissed him off that someone had done this to her.

He got into bed with her after setting the water on the bed table. He made a cut in his forearm, pulled a little magic, and whispered what she needed to do to have a shot at making it through the night. She fit her mouth over the cut. And damn, the reaction rocketed through him. Unexpected, but then, unless he counted Carson, who was magekind and something else, too, he'd never taken blood from a human woman before. The experience was as new for him as it was for Paisley.

His magic boiled up, and oh, fuck, he was in her head and they had a link going, and he could feel the psychic draw of her—resistant or not, she wasn't vanilla. Maybe not ever and sure as hell not now. With her having some of his blood in her, he didn't have to work so hard to keep their psychic link going. After a bit, he slid off the bed and pulled the sheet over her. Her eyes fluttered closed. A little later, he gave her some water, and when she fell asleep and started dreaming, he dropped out of that level of her consciousness entirely. Shut out again. Huh. She was resistant even in her sleep.

It was after nine in the morning before he was sure she was past the worst of it and he could leave her to wake up with only a few memories of what she'd been through. If she remembered fragments, that would be okay and a lot better than her waking up with nothing but a hole where the memories ought to be. She was already going to feel like shit.

She wasn't the only one with aftereffects to deal with, though. He left her apartment, resetting his proofing on the way out and making sure he adapted the magic to the changes in her. Then he went back to his house where he had all day to think about the consequences of all that magic running through her. If she was a latent—a human whose magic was dormant—there was a strong possibility she wasn't latent anymore.

That's when the lightning bolt hit him. Her apartment had felt so strongly of magekind that he'd missed an obvious cause of her symptoms. The mark on her wrist had misdirected his attention, made him overlook the things that fit another cause of her condition.

An attempted indwell. A human would call it *demonic possession*, which was accurate enough from the human point of view. There were some humans, like Paisley, who were resistant to a demon trying to take them over. Resistant or not, there was always a psychic cost when one of the kin attempted to indwell, and Paisley was paying that price in a major way. There was no way to be sure exactly what had happened, but he could guess. The most likely scenario was that some mage had tried to take her over— that would explain the blistered point of entry on her wrist. The mage's attempt hadn't worked on account of Paisley being resistant. After that, the mage must have sent one of his magehelds, a demon slave, to do the indwell and get control of her. Resisting that had damn near killed her. Iskander must have arrived right after the mageheld gave up and left Paisley to die.

He was going to have to tell Nikodemus about this.

CHAPTER 3

Six weeks later, 2:10 A.M., Vallejo Street

Paisley had to juggle her groceries to make it through the gate that led to the back of her landlord's yard. Her apartment was a tiny one-bedroom located over his garage. She had her iPod playing the Greycoats too loud for the safety of her hearing, and she was singing along as best she could with her keys dangling from her mouth. She'd be dancing, too, if her arms weren't overloaded with canvas bags containing flour, Lurpak butter that had been on sale, and ten bars of high-quality, no soy-lethicin dark chocolate.

Her bra strap was falling down her shoulder, along with the sleeve of her sweater, and driving her absolutely batty. In order to free up a hand, she lifted a knee to trap one of the bags between her torso and the neighbor's wooden fence. Then she reached across her body, under the headphone wires, and hitched everything into place.

There. Now she wasn't going to arrive home with her clothes half off.

She got her bags rebalanced and headed for her apartment. Or she would have if the walkway hadn't been blocked by her smoking-hot landlord and a man she didn't recognize, who was also pretty darn hot. She hardly ever saw her landlord, despite the fact that she lived over his garage. The bakery meant she was usually sleeping or at work when most other people were home. The last time she saw him had to be at least three or four months ago when she'd noticed he was home and dropped by on her way to work to tell him her garbage disposal was jammed again. He'd told her he'd take care of it; in fact, when she came home, the disposal had worked just fine.

Her landlord quirked his eyebrows, grinned, and said, "Hey, Paisley."

With her house keys clenched between her teeth, the only thing she could say was "*Nnhh*." One of her earbuds fell out, and the tinny sound of music drifted on the air. It was plain her landlord and his friend had, like her, only just arrived.

No doubt about it, her landlord was the most beautiful man she'd ever seen. Ever. Including in the movies, in magazines, or on television. In real life, the man was a living god he was so beautiful. Right now, he had one hand planted on the wooden wall that separated his backyard from the one next door. He was leaning over a little.

In the dim light, she could see the flexing muscles of his upper arm. He had on a pair of worn jeans, leather flip-flops, and a dark green T-shirt. The tattooed side of his body was hidden in shadow, but she knew the ink covered more than just a portion of his face because she'd seen him in the yard a couple of times without his shirt on. Five narrow blue stripes went the length of his torso, too.

If it weren't so embarrassing that she'd obviously given both men an eyeful of her undergarment rearrangement, she'd swoon from the sheer perfection of his body. She lifted a knee to push the lowest grocery bag up enough that she could adjust her grip around it. The contents shifted. She savored the moment. For now, she could pretend she had a normal life. Lord, what she wouldn't give for that to be true.

The other guy smiled, too. Killer smile. He said, "Hello."

Oh. Voice to die for. She nodded. With sinuous grace, her landlord, Iskander Philippikos, stepped forward and stuck her earbud back into her ear. Then he took one of her canvas grocery bags. She had such an awkward grip on the bags that he had to come even closer to get one free without jeopardizing her hold on the other two. He smelled good. He took one of the bags with the flour, which meant she got treated to more flexing muscle.

"Hnks." Without question, this was already the longest encounter she'd had with her landlord, not counting the time she'd filled out the rental agreement and wrote him a check for first and last month's rent.

"No problem. This is Harsh Marit." He tilted his head in the other man's direction. "Harsh, this is Paisley Nichols." He pointed in the direction of the garage at the back of the property. "My tenant."

With only two bags to deal with, she was able to free a hand and shove her keys into her pocket. "Mr. Marit. Nice to meet you." She stuck out her hand in his direction and gave him her cheeriest smile. In the last few weeks, she'd gotten good at pretending everything was fine.

"Dr. Marit," Iskander said.

"Oh. Sorry. Nice to meet you, Dr. Marit." She smiled. "Are you a medical doctor or one of the other kind?"

Dr. Marit stood there, not saying anything at first. His eyes, a deep brown, fixed on her. Dang. Now that she could see him better, he looked more like a thug than a doctor of any kind. He was almost as tall as Iskander, beefier in terms of muscle, with eyes and skin that hinted at an East Asian ancestry in an extremely dreamy sort of way.

She took back her unclasped hand, feeling even more foolish.

"Medical," he said, like it was killing him to say anything to her. She had the feeling he'd taken an instant dislike to her, which was annoying and hurtful. "But I don't practice."

"Nikodemus is going to have something to say about that." Iskander gave Harsh a playful whack on the back of his head. "Come on, help her."

"Oh, that's not necessary." She juggled the bags she had left, but Harsh came forward and took one of the other two bags from her. When she got nervous, her mostly eradicated Georgia accent appeared. Like it was doing now. "Why, thank you, Dr. Marit."

"Harsh," he said, not at all friendly. "Miss Nichols."

"All right, then, Harsh. Please, call me Paisley." She had her hands free enough now that she could snag her keys from her pocket and head for the stairs to her apartment. Whatever Dr. Marit's problem was, her mother had raised her with the philosophy that when you had the urge to kill someone, you had to do it with politeness. And then consult the stars and tarot cards before you called down curses on their head. Her mother was bat-shit crazy.

Iskander led the way up the stairs to her apartment. His

friend stayed behind her. If you like big and rough, Harsh was hot. And unfriendly. She hoped Harsh stayed behind them. He did and his silent presence creeped her out. She decided she didn't like having him there. Not being able to see what he was doing bothered her. A lot. She dragged her eyes from Iskander's back and her thoughts from Dr. Harsh Marit. Harsh wasn't the one stalking her, for heaven's sake. He might be unfriendly, but he wasn't a psycho.

"What are you cooking tonight?" Iskander asked.

He knew she owned a bakery. Part of the rental process had included proof of ability to pay the rent, and that meant proof of employment. On the rare occasions when they ran into each other, he generally asked how business was going. A couple of times he'd been in the apartment to fix something when she'd been baking.

"Not cooking," she said. "Baking."

He looked at her over his shoulder. His shirt hugged his perfectly-put-together torso. She imagined herself running a finger down the narrow blue lines that ran alongside his spine, mirroring the lines tattooed on the front of his body. She would never be able to do that in real life, but she had an active imagination that helped her live a thrilling life in her head. Her real life wasn't anything like what she imagined. She closed her eyes for a bit. The sick feeling in the pit of her stomach almost never went away these days.

"Okay," Iskander said. "What are you baking tonight?"

"Birthday cake and chocolate mousse." What she wouldn't give for a normal life.

"Will there be extra?"

She laughed, and, Lord, it felt good to have a reason to laugh. "Sorry. No. They're a special order."

Iskander reached her door and held out his hand for

her keys. The light attached to the wall shone on each and every muscle. Her landlord was a chick magnet, and when he wasn't out doing whatever he did for a living, he entertained at home. With enthusiasm. A different woman just about every night. Or at least on the nights she was home to notice what he was up to.

"I can open my own door." She was standing several steps below him with Harsh behind her. She had to look a long way up. So what if he was a man of loose morals? He was still beautiful to look at.

"Or he could open it for you because he's standing there," Harsh said. "Please give him your keys."

She held out her keys but turned to give Harsh the iciest stare she could manage. "Thank you for your helpful suggestion. Bless your heart." Sugar dripped from her voice. Killing, murdering sweetness.

He gave her body an assessing glance. Was he being crude on purpose? His attention lingered. She turned her back on him—the simple solution. She used it as often as she could with men who were obsessed with female chestiness. At least Iskander didn't stare.

Iskander stood in front of her door with a hand up like he was a traffic cop. He placed her bag of groceries on the landing. "Harsh, my friend. Come here."

"What?" Paisley said. Her stomach dropped to her toes as a familiar foreboding prickled the back of her neck. *Please no*, she thought. *Not here.*

On his way past her, Harsh shoved the bag of groceries into her arms.

"Stay where you are, Paisley." Iskander made room for Harsh at her locked door. "You feeling that?" he said in a low voice.

Harsh nodded. He touched the two carved wooden circles on either side of her door. Even from where she stood, she could see they were deformed now. The faces that had been carved into them looked like they'd melted.

"Oh," she said. She managed to keep the fear from her voice. Maybe this wasn't what she thought, what she was afraid it might be. "What happened? I liked those! They're cute."

Iskander gave her a look she had trouble interpreting. Was he offended?

"Cute?" he said, eyes wide. *"Cute?"*

Definitely offended. She shrugged and kept pretending things were all right, because most days that's all she had. The pretense that her life was okay.

He addressed Harsh. "What do you make of it?"

Another chill went down her back. She tried to swallow but her throat was dry as dust. He'd found her. She knew it in her soul. Rasmus Kessler had found out where she lived, and the very last part of her life that belonged to her was about to go to hell.

Her heart dropped to her toes when Harsh reached for the door. She juggled the groceries, put down the heavier of the two bags, and dug into her purse. "Stop. Please. Just stop."

Iskander looked down at her from the landing. His eyes were the kind of blue that made people famous. The man should act or model or something.

"I know what this is." She wanted to cry, but she didn't. "Don't touch anything, okay?" She pulled out her phone and flipped it open, her stomach knotted up tight.

"What?" Iskander said.

"I'm trying to get a restraining order against him." She

looked down at her phone. Until Harsh snarled at her. He actually snarled. The sound made her take a step down, away from a man who could make a noise like that.

"Put that away," Harsh said.

"Restraining order?" Iskander asked.

She stared at the two men, phone in hand, aware she'd made a mistake. She wouldn't be the first victim of a stalker to get evicted. Or the last. She punched the number 9 on her phone. Her stomach hurt, but she didn't have a choice. She hated that her life had gotten so out of control. "Yes," she said. "A restraining order."

Harsh put his palm on the door of her apartment. "Stop her, Iskander."

Before she could press the other two digits, Iskander leaned down and wrapped his hand around her phone. His fingers were warm around hers. "Five minutes before you call, okay?"

"If he's been here, I need the police to know." Her arms shook.

Iskander's fingers tightened over hers. "Five minutes."

Her door swung open. Odd, because her keys dangled from Iskander's other hand. Iskander turned around and stared into her dark apartment. An odd smell wafted out the door. He shot out an arm when Harsh took a step forward. "No, Harsh. Let me."

The other man nodded. Iskander shoved her keys into his pocket and replaced Harsh at the door. Poised at the entrance, he did something graceful with his hand and slipped inside her apartment like a shadow. Harsh came down a step, took the bag she held, put it with the other, then grabbed the one she'd put down and did the same with it. He crouched at her door, staring through the opening with one hand on the landing, poised on three fingers.

She clutched her phone. Every nerve in her body screamed at her to get away. If Rasmus was inside, she didn't want to be anywhere near here. She ignored her fear and used her phone to snap a couple of pictures of the vandalized wooden faces. Three was all she managed before she was too creeped out to stay close. She backed away.

"Paisley." Harsh spoke softly, but she heard him. He made a downward motion with his other hand like he was telling her to be quiet. "Iskander can handle this."

Softly, she said, "You don't know what he's like."

"Iskander?" He laughed. "He's one of the most dangerous men I know."

She blinked. "Him? Dangerous?" That lighthearted, gorgeous, always-smiling demigod? A man who didn't even seem to have a job?

"Yes. Very."

"Well, I'm sure you're right. But I didn't mean him." Paisley shook her head. She meant to tell Harsh about Rasmus, but Iskander came to the door and she didn't get the chance. The odd, musty smell coming from her apartment got stronger.

Rasmus Kessler had been here. In her apartment. She felt his presence down to her bones. He was crazy. A nightmare that wouldn't stop. Their meeting for coffee had been a disaster to say the least. She'd politely declined his further requests for dates. After the sixth request on the same day, she'd told him as plainly as she could that she wasn't interested. Despite that, he called her at the bakery several times a day and lurked outside, waiting for her. She had to start leaving by the back door. Sometimes he waited near the bakery from opening to closing or until she called the police and had him rousted. He tricked someone into giving him her cell number, and now he called every day. Dozens of times a day in the weeks since the date from hell.

He'd threatened her male friends and employees and told anyone who would listen that he had a sexual relationship with her and that she was either the love of his life or a lying, cheating bitch. He sent her insane, threatening, and cajoling e-mails and left notes and gifts at the bakery every day. After the first package with a dead bird inside, she threw his gifts away without opening them. He'd called her bank and, posing as a bakery employee, convinced someone to transfer money out of her account.

In the doorway, Iskander's eyes slid to her for a minute. "Gone."

"How bad?" Harsh asked.

Iskander did his little flicker of a glance at her before he answered. "Bad."

Paisley headed up the rest of the stairs. "What did he do?"

Iskander's friend took a step back, opening the door wider. The lighting was all wrong, and at first she didn't understand what she was seeing. Something crunched under her feet, a fine gray sand. She gripped her phone when she saw what her tormentor had done.

That same grit covered the entire floor and drifted from the ceiling.

Other than that, there was nothing left. Everything in her apartment was gone.

CHAPTER 4

Iskander flinched whenever more than a few of the still-live particles landed on his bare skin, biting like tiny embers blown from a fire. The residue covered the floor and was inches deep in places. It slid down the walls and drifted from the ceiling with a malevolent life of its own and made the air smell like madness.

Every room in the apartment had been scourged. Utterly and completely. There was nothing left, and if that wasn't a statement of rage and retribution, he didn't know what was. Everything had been reduced to dust: furniture, the appliances, pictures on the wall, electronics, plants, books, dishes, and papers. The mage had left a message in the dust, which Iskander left intact since the words gave away nothing of their magical origins.

You belong to me.

"He did a number on her." Harsh had his back to the wall by the open front door. He brushed dust off his arms, but Iskander knew there wasn't any way to wipe away the rage that had shattered the apartment.

"Back in the States less than a week," Iskander said, "and things are already crazy."

Harsh sent a cautionary glance in the general direction of Paisley, who was waiting in the doorway. Somebody needed to make sure she didn't call the cops yet. "Any ideas which mage it was?"

He shrugged and, like Harsh, kept his voice low when he gave his best guess. "Kessler?"

They shared a glance that acknowledged Rasmus Kessler was at the top of the short list of mages who could scourge an entire apartment. If Kessler was responsible, there was a strong likelihood that Fen was involved. Not to mention his tenant was in a world of danger. Kessler didn't fuck around. If he wanted to screw with Paisley, he would. Hell, he already had.

As his oath to his warlord required, Iskander had told Nikodemus about what had happened with Paisley before and about the evidence that made him suspect a mage had gone after her. Per Nikodemus's instructions, Iskander had kept an eye on her, and for six weeks there hadn't been one single sign that Paisley was under another magical attack. There hadn't been any sign of her developing or using any powers or otherwise going witchy. She continued to go to work six days a week. She kept the same crazy hours and never brought anyone home with her. Except for that one night, none of the magekind or demonkind, excluding him, of course, had made contact with her—as far as he knew.

"What?" Harsh asked.

He told Harsh about the night he found her in her apartment with no idea what had been done to her. "She doesn't remember anything about what happened," he told Harsh. "I upped the proofing around her place, and since then, nothing. I figured whoever it was gave up, and that was that. Obviously not."

Harsh shook dust off his feet. "From what she's saying about a restraining order, my guess is someone's been messing with her a lot more than just one night six weeks ago."

Iskander nodded.

"If it's Kessler, it makes sense he'd try to avoid doing anything here. He knows you'd be on it in a minute."

"True, my friend. Very true. Except, one"—he began counting off on his fingers—"he did do something six weeks ago."

"If Kessler had been inside her apartment then, you'd have known. Whatever he did, he did it off-site."

He nodded because Harsh was right. "Two, something changed, because look at her place. He was here for this."

Harsh glanced into her apartment. "Sending you a message?"

"Great. Now I really feel like shit. It's my fault her life just got fucked up?"

"Maybe it's Kessler. Maybe it's not." Harsh slid a look in Paisley's direction. "Safest to assume the worst—that Kessler's after her for some reason."

"It's him," Iskander said.

"Using her to get to you." Harsh took the words right out of his mouth.

Paisley walked in, her shoes raising tiny clouds of gray dust, and looked with shock at the devastation. The dust that hadn't yet lost its magic gravitated toward her, though she was oblivious to the meaning of the undulations in the ashy grit that was in every corner and crack. He sighed.

There went any hope this was a warning directed at him. The still-animated particles were like iron filings, and she was a magnet. No question Paisley was the target. The message blurred, but she saw the words.

Her throat worked. "Oh my goodness."

Iskander watched her in the gray-tinted light. She was trying not to cry.

Damn.

If this was Kessler's work, they might all be in trouble. Including him. But especially her. She wasn't equipped to deal with a mage of any ability, especially not one like Kessler. Iskander walked into the center of the room, avoiding the message. The ceiling light fixture was gone, but dust trickled from the remnants of the electrical fittings. He'd already been inside long enough for a layer of gritty ash to cover him. Not good. The shit made him jumpy. He waited until he had Paisley's attention; then he put his hands on his hips and said, "*This* is going to cost me a fortune to fix."

Her eyes got big. Big, gorgeous hazel eyes filling with tears. Ever since he'd been severed from his blood-twin, he couldn't take it when a woman cried. He always felt like he personally had done something to cause the tears. Even when he knew he hadn't. That just wasn't right, a woman crying. Not that it happened much. Women seemed to like him. A lot. Usually he made them laugh or, best of all, scream his name while they held on tight.

She walked past him to the bedroom. He stayed where he was. At least he'd got her thinking about something else. He knew what she was going to see in there: dust. Pretty soon she was going to realize that everything she owned or had ever touched had been destroyed. This hadn't been a trivial bit of magic. Whoever the mage was, Rasmus Kessler or someone else, he had some powerful magic at his command. Kind of limited the suspects to a handful.

Harsh nodded at the floor. The particles were being pulled in the direction of the bedroom now, so the message was all but unreadable. He pushed the toe of his leather boot through the dust. "I think we can assume whoever did this is upset."

"No kidding," Iskander said in a low voice.

"What have you been up to while I was gone?"

He laughed. "A little of this. A little of that."

"Body count?"

"I don't know." He looked toward the bedroom door to make sure Paisley wasn't close enough to overhear. "Twenty or thirty, I think."

"You've been busy."

"Nikodemus isn't screwing around."

Paisley wandered back to the living room, passing through what was left of the message. He wondered if she'd done it deliberately. Whatever the answer, she stopped in the middle of the room, phone clutched in one hand, the strap of her purse in the other. Her eyes were wide and practically all pupil. The movement of the dust toward her accelerated.

"I know who did this," she said.

"You do?" Iskander said. He couldn't help noticing she was hot. Really pretty, and with a body to bring a man, or a demon, to his knees.

"His name is Rasmus Kessler."

Well, damn. He worked hard not to react. A glance at

Harsh told him he was doing the same. He wasn't sure whether to be relieved to know the answer or worried that Kessler was responsible.

"Let's get out of here," Iskander said. "This stuff can't be good to breathe."

She blinked and headed for the door. "I'm not letting him get away with this."

Out on the landing, he and Harsh stood there with no choice but to let her make the phone call. She was a normal human. Or mostly so. You could never be sure with humans and even less with her, considering fucking Rasmus Kessler was after her. The littlest thing could spark up magic in a vanilla human. Like a mage touching you with enough power to blister skin. Or taking a taste of blood from a fiend. Or both.

While they waited for the police, Iskander made a few calls of his own, walking a ways away so he could speak in confidence. Harsh was on the phone, too. The cops and the fire department came quickly. They stomped around the apartment, kicked up dust that was in the process of fading away, looked at IDs, took names and statements, and made fools of themselves trying to impress an oblivious Paisley.

Iskander watched the interaction and came to the conclusion that while his tenant, Ms. Paisley Nichols, was not unaware that she was hot, she was not stuck-up about it. She treated all the cops with the same polite respect. She wasn't using her looks or their reaction to her to get special treatment beyond what was going to naturally happen for a woman like her.

Someone gave him a card with a number he could call to get a copy of the police report for his insurance. One of the cops gave Paisley a card to contact the Red Cross in case she didn't have a place to stay. Iskander overheard him give her his personal cell number. Kind of annoyed him, the cop hitting on her like that.

A bit later, Paisley sat on the lower steps of the rental unit. Her eyes had lost some of the deer-in-the-headlights look. Two uniformed cops and one of the firefighters stood near her. There was another guy in a cheap suit taking notes while she told them about how Kessler was stalking her. Her voice broke, but she recovered quickly. "We had coffee once. It wasn't a date. We were never romantically involved, but he won't leave me alone. He's out of his mind and making my life a nightmare."

The guy in the cheap suit asked a question, and she answered, and Iskander figured things were about to get even more tedious. Except something about the guy bothered him. He had short hair. Not alarming considering lots of cops had short hair.

Only, a mage commonly shaved the heads of the demon-kind he enslaved, and Kessler certainly followed the practice. The cop was also talking to her boobs, and Iskander could tell from her closed-off expression that she didn't appreciate him acting like she didn't have a head. The pushy guy in the suit kept getting closer and closer to Paisley and edging out the cops in uniform.

Harsh got off the phone and walked to Iskander. They stood there, watching until Iskander said, "That asshole's going to hit on her."

"She's an attractive woman."

"Yeah. But that's totally not cool, hitting on her when she's all worked up." Iskander kept watching the man. He was tall and fit and looked barely old enough to have gotten off street patrol. Iskander lowered some of his blocks and took in the psychic state of the humans around him, which he didn't like to do. He didn't have as much experience with humans as most kin of his years. As far as he could tell, there was nothing abnormal. Nothing from the guy in the cheap suit but pure vanilla. The cops upstairs were finishing their investigation. Hopefully this would be over soon.

"Nikodemus would like for you to continue keeping an eye on the situation for him."

He gave Harsh a look. "No kidding."

They were quiet for a moment. "It was a formal request, Iskander. She's to be kept safe until we know more about whether the situation warrants bringing in Durian or Gray."

That got his attention, and not in a good way. Durian and his mostly human partner, Gray, both worked as assassins for Nikodemus. "He's going to sanction a hit on a human?"

"Or Kessler."

If Kessler got taken out, that would free his magehelds. Including Fen. He could tell from Harsh's too-controlled expression that he was thinking the same thing.

"She betrayed us, Harsh. For a goddamned mage." The blood bond he'd had with Fen meant that he knew, as Harsh did not and never could, that Fen hadn't been forced. She was never enslaved the way other magehelds were. She'd gone willingly to Kessler. There was no doubt whatsoever about that. Jesus, he hated himself for thinking for even a minute that he might actually go back to Fen if she got free of Kessler.

"I know," Harsh said.

"He can't hit Kessler." The fallout from a hit like that would be beyond nasty. Other mages. Other warlords. The whole damn peaceful coexistence thing would go *kaboom*.

"He could if we have proof he's targeting vanilla humans." Harsh glanced over at Paisley. "He wants to wait for Kessler to come after her again."

"I'm supposed to let her get killed? Is that what you're saying?"

"No. I'm saying if Kessler comes after her again and there's solid, incontrovertible proof he's moving on her, then we can act."

"Her word's not good enough?" He knew it wasn't. She was human. None of the other warlords or mages were going to take the word of a human in a matter like this. She didn't know the first thing about magic. The only thing she could talk about was Rasmus harassing her, and that wasn't the crime Nikodemus was going to have to prove. He stared at Paisley and the cop interviewing her. "Tell Nikodemus if anybody gets to kill that mage, it's me."

"Better that it's sanctioned." Harsh still had his phone in his hand and was texting while he talked. "Let Gray or Durian do what's needed. Or Leonidas, if Nikodemus thinks he can be trusted." Leonidas was a mage who'd recently sworn fealty to Nikodemus. There might be less trouble if another mage took out Kessler. "And that's only if there's proof."

Meanwhile, Paisley stalked away from the cop in the suit. The cop followed her.

"I know you're upset, Ms. Nichols," the cop was saying.

What the hell was that guy's problem? Iskander cocked

his chin in the direction of the cop still getting his jollies staring at Paisley's chest. "I don't like that one."

The cop waved off the uniforms. "I can take it from here." The two uniforms shrugged and moved away. The guy in the suit put a hand to Paisley's elbow and guided her closer to the house and farther away from the others.

Iskander watched the suit take her to the corner of his patio, near the covered hot tub. He listened to stupid questions about what she'd done during the day and afternoon and what she'd noticed before she went into the apartment. Nothing she hadn't been over already. The cop kept his notebook and pen out, but he wasn't writing anything. He asked questions about her personal relationship with Rasmus that got her agitated. Iskander heard the asshole ask her about the last time she had sex with Kessler.

She went totally stiff. "That," he heard her say in a tightly controlled voice, "is completely out of line." She jabbed a finger at him. "Are you saying that if I have sex with someone, whatever happens after that is my fault?" She pointed to her apartment. "That he's justified in doing something like that? I never had an intimate relationship with Rasmus Kessler, but it wouldn't matter if I had." She took a step toward him, shoulders tense, her finger jabbing the air like a bayonet. Iskander didn't blame her for being pissed off. "His attentions to me are not welcome. I have made that clear to him on many occasions, and he won't leave me alone. That's all I want. For him to just leave me alone."

The suit dropped his notebook into his pocket and touched her, a hand to her shoulder, not a big deal, but not standard cop behavior, either. Paisley backed way and the suit moved with her. This time he touched her temple.

Two seconds later, Paisley went into panic mode and the truth about what he was seeing hit him. The guy in the suit was a mageheld, and he was trying to take possession of Paisley's will.

CHAPTER 5

Iskander headed for Paisley and the mageheld trying to control her. He pulled hard on his magic. If there were sensitive latents among the cops and firefighters still hanging around, too damned bad. He wasn't letting this continue.

Paisley, however, wasn't going down without a fight. The mageheld was having trouble with the indwell, which made sense because she was a resistant. Before he closed the distance to her, she lashed out at the cop when he put one of his hands someplace rude. She drove the heel of her palm into his chin. The mageheld's head snapped back.

From behind, Iskander grabbed the fake cop's forehead. With one hand, he yanked back to make sure the mageheld's physical and visual contact with Paisley was broken and stayed that way, and then released all his pulled magic into the fiend's head. The free kin couldn't feel a mageheld's magic, so he had to work blind to what this one was doing. The guy dropped like a stone, or would have if Iskander weren't holding him up. The suit was immobilized physically and psychically from the force of the magical burn. Paisley reeled, the backs of her legs hitting the stone ledge around the hot tub. Her eyes locked with his.

"Thank you," she said. Her eyes flashed with anger. "I can't imagine what got into him."

Iskander kept the mageheld on his feet and spun him around. With one hand clutching the guy's shirt, he put a finger to the mageheld's forehead. One thing he'd learned since he'd been severed from Fen was that there weren't rules about psychic connections with his own kind, just customs about what was polite between the kin. Those customs didn't count with a mageheld. He couldn't feel the mageheld's magic, but Iskander had the guy's head locked down so tight his brains were going to start boiling in about thirty seconds. "Who sent you?"

The mageheld's eyes fluttered open. He shook his head. "Not permitted to tell."

Damn. It would have been nice to get the proof they needed, but he hadn't really expected the mage would have forgotten to cover his tracks in case things didn't work out with the indwell. Iskander grabbed two handfuls of the guy's jacket and yanked him off his feet, but then got a hold of his fury. The mageheld wasn't responsible for the attack. He was nothing but a slave who had to do whatever his mage ordered. He lowered the mageheld until his feet were on the ground.

"Listen up." He kept his voice low. "Nikodemus's witch Carson. Xia and Alexandrine. Remember those names. Find them, and they'll sever you. Give you back your freedom."

He nodded, but his color was getting chalky and his eyes were starting to bleed.

"Still listening? Good. If you get severed, you come find me and start talking. That's my reward for letting you live today. I want it all. Every goddamned detail."

The mageheld blinked, which smeared blood over his eyes. He let out a pathetic gurgle. Iskander released his psychic hold before it was too late and his brains really did boil.

"Get the hell out of here."

The mageheld pressed his first three fingers to his forehead and bowed. Blood dripped down his nose. He turned and walked away. Magehelds might be enslaved to their mages, but they weren't stupid. Whenever they could, they did exactly what they were ordered, to the letter, and to hell with what the mage intended. Iskander was sure the mageheld would do whatever it took to be in a position to get himself severed by one of the people he'd just listed. Sooner or later.

He looked up and found Paisley staring at him, eyes wide.

"Hey," he said. "You okay?"

"I don't know." She sat down hard on the ledge of his hot tub, looking up at him. "Oh my Lord," she whispered. Her long, dark red ponytail hung over her shoulder.

"Bad day, huh?"

"You said it." She stood up and Iskander tried not to enjoy the view of her legs. He made sure to keep his attention on her face. She looked around, forlorn.

They were alone. The streetlamps were just starting to go out. The cops and firefighters were gone, along with the curious neighbors. So was Harsh. The door to her apartment gaped open, and from where they stood, they could see her groceries on the steps. He shoved his hands in his front pockets. He was so busy trying not to stare at her chest that he inadvertently picked up a bucket-load of her emotions. Being resistant meant it was difficult, but not impossible, for a demon to pick up on her psychic state. He didn't have to try hard to get a sense of her fear. Denial. Resignation. A bit of helplessness overcome by determination. He pushed a bit, and just like that, he got cut off.

Paisley didn't seem to know she'd done anything. She dug her phone out of her purse and opened it, all business now. She flipped her ponytail over her shoulder and hit some buttons. He took the phone from her.

She looked up at him. "Excuse me?"

"Who are you calling?"

"My assistant baker."

"What for?"

"I have private orders to fill. I'm hoping she'll help me out. And let me crash at her place for the night."

That couldn't happen. "You're staying with me. I have four bedrooms, two and half baths, and I only use one of each. There's room in my kitchen for your groceries. Hell, you can even bake there."

She chewed on her lower lip and half glared at him, probably because she was too nice to do any worse. Without going into her head, Iskander didn't have any idea what she was seeing when she looked at him. Some women didn't like his tats. Then again, some did. The women he ended up taking to bed weren't sweet, polite women like his tenant. The women he fucked loved his tats. A lot.

He liked a little wild in his partners, and if Paisley Nichols had ever been wild, he'd eat his shorts. He said, "You're thinking way too hard."

"I hardly know you."

"I'm your landlord. You've been writing me checks for months." He laughed. "Cupcake, if I was a serial killer, I'd have picked you off ages ago. And if you're one, no offense, but I think I can take you down first." He grinned because he just now thought of a major plus to his invitation. "We," he said, "are going to be friends with benefits."

Her eyebrows shot up her forehead. "I beg your pardon?"

"Benefit for you—a place to stay and free run of the kitchen. Benefit for me—you bake extra."

She blinked a few times. Her lashes were dark red, too. "That's kind of you to offer."

"Yeah. I know."

She had cheekbones. A strong face, if you just looked at her without thinking about getting her naked and flat on her back. Sure, she looked sweet and talked sweet, but there was more at home upstairs than being a nice girl. "Just for the night." She waved a hand. "Day. Whatever."

"Until I get your place redone." He tossed in the deal sealer. "No rent until you're back in your apartment." He spread his arms wide, and in his peripheral vision, he saw dust drift from her apartment into the air. Some of it floated contrary to the breeze and headed for her. Rasmus wasn't joking about Paisley. "Come on. Otherwise you're sleeping on a couch in someone else's place. Here, you get your own room and your own bathroom, full use of the kitchen, and no rent. How can you pass up a deal like that?"

"I suppose I can't."

He handed back her phone, and she dropped it into her purse. "All right, then. Roomie."

"For now."

"Hang on and I'll get your groceries." He did just that. As he came down the stairs with her bags in his arms, he watched her. Too bad the benefits weren't going to include sex. His tenant was seriously, wickedly hot.

Five minutes later, they were standing in his kitchen, him with his arms full of her grocery bags and her with her mouth open. "Oh," she said, all soft and whispery. Her Southern accent got thick. Really thick. "I have surely died and gone to heaven."

He pretended she meant that for him, which led to some other images that stirred him more than was appropriate. "Is that so?"

"That's a Viking range." She walked forward, one hand extended. She caressed his stove. "A double oven?"

He walked to the counter and put down the bags.

"You have everything."

"I run a full-service facility here." He'd brought lots of women here, but this was the first time one was more turned on by his kitchen than by him.

She walked under the copper-bottomed pots and pans he never touched, staring up at them like she was getting a vision of bliss. He wondered if she looked like that when she came. He started mentally undressing her. Her top went first, and in his imagination, she wasn't wearing a bra.

"There's a bunch of other stuff in there." He pointed to one of the lower cabinets.

She went down on her knees and opened the door, taking out all sorts of pans, crooning, swear to God, to each one as she took it out. "I didn't know you cooked, Iskander."

"I don't."

She stood and he lost his prime view of her ass. He backed away. Human women were his thing these days, but it would be stupid to sleep with this one. Really stupid, for some reason he was having trouble remembering. She headed for the grocery bags and started unloading them. She opened the refrigerator and stood there staring in. "I guess it's been a while since you've been shopping."

His fridge contained two bottles of soda and a week-old box of pizza. He reached past her and grabbed the bottles. "Something to drink?"

"No, thank you. I don't drink Coke."

"Now, that is just plain insulting." He kept his tone light. "This here is root beer."

She waved a hand at him. "Where I come from, everything's 'Coke' until you need to be specific. Coke's bad for you. Nothing but empty calories."

"Whatever." He lifted one of the bottles. *Do not look at her tits.* "You sure you don't want one? I have two."

"Thanks, but no."

He concentrated on her eyes. Her big, pretty, hazel eyes. "Do you have flour?"

"What's that?" He took a long drink of his root beer and managed, just, to hold back a belch.

"You bake with it." She opened a few cabinets. They were all empty except for the ones with dishes in them. The groceries that were still good got divided between the fridge and the empty cabinets. When she was done, she leaned against the counter and crossed her arms underneath what had to be the most perfect, gorgeous breasts in creation. His favorite part of the female anatomy. He kept his eyes on her face. He deserved some kind of medal for that. "Mind if I ask you a question?"

"Sure." He wiped dust off his chest because it let him sneak a look at her rack.

"Why does someone with no food in his house have a kitchen like this?"

"I bought this place as a fixer-upper. I had to tell the contractors what I wanted to do with the kitchen. I don't know shit about kitchens, so I took them to see Harsh's and told them to give me one like that."

She blinked a couple of times. "You're not kidding, are you?"

"A good kitchen adds resale value to the house. It was a great investment." He brushed more dust off his shoulders. "So. What kind of cake you making?"

"None right now." She sighed. She sounded tired, and given it was almost seven in the morning, she probably was. "There's a few more things I need."

"We both have this crap all over us." He kept brushing at the dust. "Why don't we take a shower and then you give me a list, and I'll see about getting what you need." When he looked up, she was staring at him, her mouth open. "Showers," he said, realizing the problem right away from her stricken look. "Separate showers. Unless..." He was all for doing whatever he could to get lucky. "Do you want to share?"

CHAPTER 6

*About the same time. Broadway and Baker,
San Francisco*

Harsh watched Emily dit Menart walk into his office and sit on his red leather couch. The Baker Street house belonged to him, but in the time he'd been traveling for Nikodemus, the house had become a communal stop for several of Nikodemus's sworn fiends, including Emily. He didn't mind. There was plenty of room, and if he needed to get away, he had a smaller place not far away, as well as a farmhouse in Sonoma County. Nikodemus, aware that Harsh's place had become a halfway house for several of the strongest fiends loyal to him, had paid off the mortgage and transferred enough into an account for Harsh to pay the property taxes and his expenses.

Emily dit Menart was so beautiful he couldn't help but stare. That kind of perfection was rare in any human. She was tall, nearly six feet, and statuesque. Probably more so than usual since she was breast-feeding. Other than eyes that betrayed her exhaustion, she didn't look like a woman who'd just had a baby. If anything, she was a little too thin. The physician in him wondered if he ought to explain to her that she needed extra calories until she weaned her son.

Even Maddy, who was sitting behind Harsh's desk, stared at her.

Emily's blue eyes were made all the more striking by her inky black hair. She wore dark jeans, a pair of canvas slip-on shoes, and a cotton nursing top, and she looked glamorous in them for reasons he didn't understand but could not dispute.

She hadn't been a model, though there must have been offers. What she'd done instead was get a PhD in molecular biology. She'd been doing a postdoc at UC Berkeley before she got caught up with her late husband, the mage Christophe dit Menart. All that beauty and brains notwithstanding, she had more to deal with than motherhood. Christophe had wiped her past from her mind and substituted a false one. She had no memory of her education. Or anything else about her real life.

Harsh didn't envy Emily her present situation.

"Dr. Marit," she said. Her voice was as sexy as the rest of her. She crossed one long, slender leg over the other.

"Mrs. dit Menart."

She was a witch, quite a powerful one, but with almost no training. Magekind who didn't get training typically ended up insane or dead, so that made Emily unusual to say the least. According to Maddy, who made a point of studying these things, Emily had been spared either of those outcomes because her father, a mage who had burned out his powers, had managed to teach her enough to keep her alive and sane.

"Ms. Winters," she said with a nod in Maddy's direction. "Nice to see you again."

Harsh took a moment to reflect on the fact that he was in a meeting with not one but two highly intelligent women. Emily was breathtaking, but Maddy Winters was no slouch in the looks department, either. After all the months he'd been traveling for Nikodemus, it was about time his life had a benefit or two.

The demonkind were exquisitely sensitive to the mage-kind, and that aspect of his magic naturally responded to the two women. He was, however, equally aware that witches of their power were dangerous to him. Perhaps especially so to someone with his rare condition. Never trust a mage. Or a witch. Who knew that better than he did? And here he sat with two witches.

Maddy cleared her throat. "Thank you for meeting with us, Mrs. dit Menart."

"Please." She glanced at Harsh and then at Maddy. "Call me…" For a moment she looked lost, and Harsh had the absurd desire to find a way to make everything better for her. That, of course, was not his right. "Emily, I suppose."

Christophe's alteration of her memories had included giving her a new first name—Erin. Then he'd taken away her last name when he married her. She'd been told her real name was Emily, but she had no recollection of that. No wonder she was having a hard time adjusting.

"Dr. Marit, do please sit down." She leaned over and patted the other end of the couch.

Instead of sitting on the couch, he offered the women

water from the mini-fridge. Both nodded, and he poured the water into squat tumblers of sapphire glass. Only then did he sit, in the red leather wingback that, angled as it was, let him see Maddy behind the desk and Emily on the couch.

To his chagrin, he wished he'd worn a suit instead of jeans, a T-shirt, and his battered leather work boots. Behind his desk, Maddy was smirking. Yes, she must think it quite amusing to see him losing his cool over Emily dit Menart. Every inch of the woman represented white privilege, from her pale skin and blue eyes, to her childhood in the rich East Bay enclave of Piedmont, to her education, whether she remembered any of it or not. She'd probably never dated a man who looked like him.

"Thank you, Dr. Marit."

"Call me Harsh."

Emily nodded, looking like some kind of fairy-tale princess. In his peripheral vision, he saw Maddy pick up a pencil. He returned his attention to Emily but heard the soft tap of a pencil on a folder.

"I know Emily's my real name," she said. "But I don't remember it. It's foreign to me." She rubbed her arms. "Cold as ice." Her voice was calm and at odds with the emotions he was getting from her, even though he was blocking contact with both of the women. "Distant." She lifted a hand, and light reflected from the diamond in her wedding ring. "Vaguely repugnant. Which I supposed Christophe intended."

Maddy put down her pencil and folded her hands on top of the desk. "That's one of the effects of the magic he used to remove and alter your memories."

"So I'm told."

Harsh said, "I know it doesn't feel right to you yet, but I'm sure Maddy will confirm it's best if you use your real name."

"I know." Something akin to panic flickered in Emily's eyes, and he went back to feeling sorry for her. "I am trying. I've remembered a few more things since the baby was born. Little things. Mostly about my parents and Gray."

Gray was Emily's sister, now an assassin bound to Durian, who was, in turn, bound to Nikodemus, the same demon warlord Harsh served. As did Maddy. She picked up the pencil. The *tap, tap, tap* of the eraser on the folders in front of her started back up.

Emily sipped her water, then placed the tumbler on the glass coffee table in front of her. "I'm sure you two weren't expecting to talk about my personal issues."

"I'll let Harsh start," Maddy said. "He's been working with Nikodemus and can tell us both about the politics involved." She gave Emily a quick grin. "Luckily, that's not my area of expertise. I'm here to tell you about your legal situation and answer any questions you might have about that."

"Thank you," Emily said.

"If you stay here," Harsh said, "and you are welcome to do so, you need to make a decision about an oath of fealty."

Among the kin, swearing fealty to a warlord was customary. The kin aligned themselves with warlords in return for his, or in rare cases, her, protection. The warlord drew power and standing from his sworn fiends. While Nikodemus permitted unaligned kin in his territory and even worked with them on occasion, the magekind were another matter. If they worked for him or got involved with his sworn fiends, he required an oath of fealty from them. No exceptions.

Emily licked her lips. "My understanding is that the oath would be required. Is that not correct?"

"In your case, an oath would be required if you elect to stay in Nikodemus's territory, yes." Christ, she was beautiful. "But you don't have to swear yourself to Nikodemus."

Emily's eyebrows lifted, but it was Maddy who said, "What?"

He shifted so he had a better view of Maddy, but he addressed Emily. "Nikodemus has authorized me to tell you that he would find it acceptable if you swore yourself to Durian or to Kynan Aijan."

Maddy's pencil stopped tapping. Kynan Aijan was one of Nikodemus's sworn fiends, a warlord himself, sure, but one with issues. Huge issues. Not to mention some kind of history with Maddy that no one ever talked about.

Harsh cleared his throat. He wasn't sure how much Emily knew about the kin's practice of swearing fealty to a warlord. "He felt that since your sister is sworn to Durian, you might find that a more comfortable choice. However, Nikodemus is aware of your relationship with Kynan. If you swear fealty to Kynan, that would be acceptable to him, too."

"How soon do I need to decide?"

"Not immediately. A month, perhaps. Nikodemus is also aware that your son is quite young. He has young ones of his own. In case you're wondering, should you decide to swear fealty, the protection extended to you extends to your son so long as he is your dependent."

"What about Ian?"

Ian was the young boy her husband had abducted and who was, at present, still with Emily while they waited, and hoped, for his mother to recover from what Christophe had done to her. "Him too."

"Tell him I appreciate his patience." She put her hands on the couch on either side of her legs and leaned forward. "I'll let you know my decision."

"Unless you decide to swear fealty to Nikodemus, that won't be necessary. He'll know the moment you're sworn. Otherwise, I'll be happy to put you in contact with Nikodemus."

She watched him for a moment. She wasn't pulling any magic, but there was power in her gaze. "Thank you."

"I'll turn things over to Maddy, then."

Emily looked at the other woman. "Am I going to jail?"

Maddy snapped out of whatever funk she'd been in. "No."

"Why not? I killed my husband."

"I'm sure you're aware," Maddy said, "that your husband's death was a complicated matter."

Emily laughed, and God, what that did to her face. Harsh envied Kynan. "Murder isn't complicated."

"Nevertheless," Maddy said, "he was a mage, and your actions that night saved a lot of lives."

"I don't remember my husband as an evil man." She lifted a hand. "I've been told what he had planned for my sister and poor Ian, but that's not the man I thought I was married to." Her eyes teared up. Briefly, she put a hand over her mouth, and they waited for her to gather herself. "I'm sorry. Do go on, Maddy."

Harsh restrained his urge to stroke her shoulder. "With respect to the magekind and warlords, it was not possible to suppress your involvement in his death. It would have been a disaster for all of us if one of the demonkind had been blamed. There would almost certainly have been war." He met Emily's gaze. "It was beyond convenient for Nikodemus that you were the one to kill Christophe."

"If everyone knows, why haven't I been arrested?"

From the desk, Maddy said, "As far as the civilian world is concerned, Christophe's death has been ruled a murder that occurred in the course of a home invasion by a person or persons unknown."

"Not so far from the truth," Harsh said. As he now knew, Maddy and a few others, including Kynan, had been there the night Emily killed her husband. Durian, one of Nikodemus's assassins, had gone there to retrieve Gray, who had been taken mageheld by Christophe in a violation of the peace agreement Nikodemus had forged with the magekind living in his territory. Given the current fragility of relations between the demonkind and the magekind, whatever her personal justification, Emily dit Menart had done Nikodemus a favor by killing Christophe that night.

Maddy filled the awkward silence. "You're his widow, and you and your son are his only living relatives."

She didn't react to that. Harsh left her to her thoughts. Maddy did the same. Eventually, Emily said, "My son might not be Christophe's."

"Legally," Maddy said, "he is. You were his wife. The child is presumed his." She waved a perfectly manicured hand. "In any event, there's no one left to dispute paternity. Not that it would matter."

"Let me be clear," Emily said in freezing tones. "I have no recollection of having sexual relations with anyone but Christophe during our marriage. But, considering that he intended to have one of his magehelds impregnate my sister, why wouldn't he have done the same to me? And wiped my memory of it." Harsh heard the tiniest break in her voice, but her features were serene. "Why should I assume Christophe is my son's father?"

"If he wasn't," Maddy said, "why would he marry you?"

She answered quickly, which was interesting. "He liked beautiful things."

"Forgive me, Emily," Harsh said, "but he could have had you without marrying you."

Maddy glared at him before returning her attention to Emily. "Do you want a paternity test? I can arrange it."

"I don't care who his father is." She spoke with cold certainty. "Not for an instant. He's my son, and I love him. Whether any of you accept him or not. Whether his father was a mage or a demon or some stranger off the street."

Harsh glanced away until he was sure his face would reveal nothing of his emotions. "Nikodemus accepts you, Emily. You and your son. Ian as well. Neither Maddy nor I would be here with you now if the three of you did not have his full support." They would know, one day, whether the boy was magekind or demonkind or simply human. Harsh hoped to see him grow up in a world where the answer did not matter. In fact, he was counting on it. "Whatever the truth may be."

Maddy got the conversation back on track. "I can represent to you, Emily, that you are the only woman Christophe ever married. In this century or the last."

"Bully for me," she said.

Maddy and Harsh exchanged a glance. "From a legal standpoint," Maddy said, "you inherit everything. There is a substantial estate here in California. Harsh is still tracking down the European assets, but you should expect them to be substantial."

"Define *substantial*."

Maddy delivered the news with nonchalance. "Several hundred million at least. Euros."

Harsh knew that kind of money considerably changed her options. She wouldn't be dependent on Nikodemus's good will, for example. With Christophe's fortune, she could live anywhere she wanted to.

"Christophe had more than four hundred years to amass and preserve his fortune," Harsh said. "Legally or otherwise." Emily frowned at that, but he continued. "He was not a fool about his money or the manner in which it might be protected as the years passed and he continued to live."

"I want it in a trust for my son. And for Ian." She met Maddy's eyes. "Can you do that for me?"

"Of course. With a decent income for you." Maddy's voice softened. "I'm going to insist on that. You deserve that much."

She replied in a cool voice. "You can't make me spend it."

"You're right about that." Maddy sighed. "No one can make you spend the money. But either way, you need to designate an executor in case something happens to you. Someone needs the authority to administer and protect the assets in the trust and to care for your son and Ian. My recommendation is to have Nikodemus or Harsh or both administer the trust, as it's likely they'll outlive you. Depending on your son's heritage, they might outlive him as well. As for a guardian for the boys, I assume you'll want to name your sister or perhaps your parents."

She answered without hesitation. "Kynan."

Maddy opened her mouth to object but stopped herself. "Have you and Kynan spoken about that?"

"We have." From her stolid expression, Harsh surmised Emily was well aware of Kynan's reputation for mayhem. "I want him to be an executor, too."

"He's not...stable," Maddy said.

Harsh silently applauded the way Emily stared down Maddy.

"I trust him," Emily said. "Completely. It's not my problem if you don't."

"Kynan Aijan," Harsh said in a low voice, "has his issues. We all know that." He wasn't sure how much Maddy or even Emily knew about Kynan's past, and he wasn't about to discuss what specifics he knew. "But I assure you he would not agree to raise anyone's child unless he meant to do so honorably."

Maddy wasn't having any of it. "You don't know him, Harsh."

"But I do," Emily said. She was calm, but there was steel in her words. "At this point, perhaps better than you. In any event, it is not your decision." She closed her eyes, and while they were closed, her shoulders relaxed. When her eyes opened, she looked at Maddy. "I am aware of his past. I shouldn't say this, but I will. Kynan and I have talked about his feelings for you. He told me enough about what happened that I understand more than you think." She hesitated. "I'm sorry. On his behalf, I'm sorry." Then she threw Maddy a bone. "If you'd like to add Nikodemus to the trust administrators, please do."

Maddy didn't say anything right away. She stared at the folders in front of her. "I'll make inquiries, but I don't anticipate there will be any difficulties with that."

Emily stood. "Is that all?"

"I'll draw up some papers and send them to you for review." Maddy came out from behind the desk. "I think you should have another lawyer look over the documents that get filed in the human legal system."

Emily looked at Harsh. "Is there anyone you recommend?"

"I trust Maddy, but give me a day or two and I'll give you some names."

"Thank you again." She headed for the door.

"Emily." Harsh stood, too. "Do you have a few moments for me?"

Maddy looked up from the folders she was sliding into a maroon leather briefcase. Emily ignored her, and so did Harsh.

"Of course."

"Well, then." Maddy snapped closed her briefcase. "If you don't have any questions for me, Emily, I'll be on my way."

"None right now. Thank you. I appreciate your assistance."

"All in a day's work. Here's my card. Please, feel free to call or e-mail if you have any questions."

She took the card. "Thank you."

When Maddy was gone, Emily sat down again. "If you're going to take me to task for what I said to Maddy, don't. It was uncalled for." She smiled so sadly that Harsh's heart broke for her. She hesitated, and he waited for her to finish her thought. "Who knows?" She smiled, and this time it was not so sad. "Perhaps I'll get to keep him."

Harsh stayed on his feet. He acknowledged what she said with a nod. What could he say that would make any difference? "I have information about your life with Christophe that may answer some of your questions."

"Ah. I'd like to have Kynan here, if you don't mind."

"Of course."

"I need to feed my son, too." She slid a cell phone from the pocket of her jeans. "It seems ridiculous to call someone who's just upstairs, doesn't it?"

"Modern technology."

"It's me," she said after dialing. "How is he?" She waited. "He's hungry." She smiled softly, a smile that was meant for Kynan. "Can you come down with him? Harsh has something he wants to tell me in private, and I'd rather not hear it alone."

Ah. Yes. She was making sure Kynan knew Maddy wasn't there. Whatever had gone on between Kynan and Maddy, it wasn't over yet, and Emily knew it.

She put away the phone. "He'll be right down."

He didn't know what to say to that. She was with Kynan Aijan, for pity's sake.

She ignored his awkward loss of words. "Most of the time I know I don't love him. And then there are times, like now, when I think, if things were different, I could. It makes me sad to think I've met the right man at the wrong time in both our lives."

"Relationships take time."

She didn't answer because the door to the office

opened and Kynan Aijan walked in with a cloth diaper over his shoulder and Emily's son in his arms. Recognition robbed him of the words he should have had for Kynan.

Emily dit Menart's son was a genetic hybrid. Part demon and part mage, which was supposed to be impossible. Just like Harsh himself.

CHAPTER 7

Paisley laughed, but she was faking it because for the minute that she'd misunderstood what Iskander had just said, some twisted part of her had considered saying heck, yes, she'd take a shower with him. She couldn't, of course. And wouldn't. Not even with the most beautiful man she'd ever seen.

"Oh my goodness. Of course you meant separate showers."

"Sure."

She brushed gray dust off her arms. The stuff clung to her shirt and skin like there was glue in it. "I would love to take a shower. Thank you."

He grinned. "Sorry about that. That just came out wrong. I'm not really a perv."

"No worries." It was hard not to believe he'd been beautiful all his life, but maybe not. Maybe as a kid he'd been chubby or had a bad complexion, or maybe that incredible bone structure and musculature hadn't come together until after the horror of adolescence. She wondered if he'd been the class clown when he was a kid.

"You need to get out of those clothes."

"Desperately." She picked at her shirt. She liked the idea of Iskander having been imperfect once. It made him more human. "The stuff sticks like glue, doesn't it?"

How odd, though. There was a coating of the gritty stuff on the floor around where Iskander stood and hardly any around her. She scratched a spot behind her shoulder while she looked around. Some of the grit had gone down the back of her shirt and was itching something fierce. He kept his house tidy. There wasn't much clutter that she could see as long as you didn't count the trail of dust they'd left. "We're tracking it all over your house."

"I'll clean up while you're in the shower."

"There's only one problem." A chasm opened up in her stomach as the extent of her losses hit home. She couldn't run up to her apartment and get a change of clothes. "I haven't got any clothes but these."

He kept brushing dust off his torso but looked at her from under his thick lashes. She was used to men staring at her chest, and she was glad he wasn't. "Give me your sizes, and I'll run out and pick up a few things. Enough so you can go out in public and get new stuff."

Paisley stood there, her skin itching just about everywhere, and felt lost. Completely lost. Her stomach clenched as her thoughts flashed to her incinerated apartment. She'd lost everything. "I haven't got any money."

"Hello?" He waved his hands at her. "Plastic?"

She gazed at him. "My credit card was in the freezer, and the freezer is gone."

"The freezer?" He blinked and she caught a flash of

blue on his eyelid. "Why the hell would you put your credit card in the freezer?"

"My accountant put me on an austerity plan for the first five years of the bakery, and this is only year two. I'm not allowed to use a credit card except in dire emergencies. I read you should freeze your credit cards in a block of ice so you can't use them." She slumped against the counter and fought the urge to cry. "I pay cash for just about everything, and it so happens I just spent mine on groceries."

Iskander came over and patted her shoulder. "It's okay, cupcake. Jesus, don't cry. I promise everything's going to be okay."

She straightened and tried to brush off the dust that had accumulated in the crook of her elbow, but the stuff clung to her shirt and fingers. Tears jammed up in the back of her throat and burned behind her eyes. She was breaking up emotionally, and his being so nice to her wasn't helping her keep herself together. "I've got maybe ten dollars on me."

"Whoa." His eyebrows shot up. "No crying."

She swallowed hard. "Nothing except the groceries, the contents of my purse, and the clothes on my back." She was talking too much, she knew it, but Iskander was a sympathetic listener. If there was anything she needed right now, it was sympathy. "I have less than a thousand dollars in the bank, and I need that money for emergencies."

"You don't think this qualifies as an emergency?" He shook his head. "You're right. It doesn't. I've got your back."

She kept brushing at the grit on her clothes, but it just would not come off. The reality of her situation rolled through her. Her hands shook as she swatted harder at the dust. The stuff stuck to her fingers.

Iskander picked gray globs off her arm and fingers and shook his hand. The grit fell slowly to the floor, where he stepped on it like he was making sure it was dead. "There's no crying in this house." He put a hand under her chin and pushed up. She kept her eyes down, but a tear trickled down her cheek anyway. "Hey, Paisley," he said softly. "Cupcake. Listen to me. If you have to cry, I'll man up and take it, all right?"

"I'm fine."

He reached over the counter, grabbed a paper towel, and handed it to her. She dabbed at her eyes.

"Bless you for being so sweet."

"My insurance will pay to replace your stuff, so don't worry about money. I'll front you enough cash to get by."

"You can't do that." Her scalp was starting to itch, too.

Her landlord's expression turned serious. So much so that he looked like a different person. A frisson of arousal rolled through her. When he wasn't smiling, his features were a bit austere, and the tats made her think of gangs and street soldiers and the kind of man who got ink like that, which had surely been no trivial process to undergo.

"Yes, I can," he said. "What do you think insurance is for? Let me take care of this. At least until you're back on your feet, all right? You can save your emergency fund for when you're really desperate."

She had to swallow a lump in her throat in order to reply. "That's generous of you."

"Since you're staying here, give me your cell number. Just in case." She did and he entered in into his phone. He called her number so she could add his to her contacts. How odd and unsettling that he looked so different, so serious. So capable of violence. She backed away from him. "I'm texting another contact to you. If Rasmus bothers you, you call the police, but then I want you to call this number, okay?" He pressed a few buttons and then her phone beeped. "Put that in your favorites or on speed dial or whatever so you don't waste time looking for the number. If you do have to call, tell whoever answers that Iskander gave you the number and that you need help. It's going to be someone I work with, okay? If for some reason they don't know you're staying with me and that Kessler is after you, I promise you, it's enough that they know I told you to call, okay?"

She was having a hard time adjusting to the serious Iskander. "And just who is it you work with?"

He frowned. "People who know how to deal with shit like this."

"Like?"

"That's all I can tell you right now, okay? You call if you have to."

She nodded. Not that she would. He seemed to have guessed her reluctance to do any such thing, because he narrowed his eyes at her.

"Trust me, whoever answers at that number will have no trouble with Kessler."

Her heart lurched. "You sound like you know him. Do you?"

"Kessler?"

She hated that Rasmus Kessler had made her so suspicious. He'd proved to her how easy it was to fool people and what an illusion it was that life was ever safe or simple. "Do you know him? Has he been calling you about me, too?"

"No, he hasn't called me about you or anyone else." His sharp look wasn't anything like his usual cheerful self. He didn't smile at all, and his expression gave her a chill. "I wish I'd known he was bothering you."

"Why?" She was past wanting to cry. Mostly. But she was hollow inside. Bereft. "So you could evict me because I have a stalker?"

A guilty look flashed across his face and made her think that's exactly what he would have done. "No," he said.

She thought, *Liar*. Then he shrugged. She couldn't shake the feeling that she was looking at the real Iskander. What was it his friend Harsh had said? *One of the most dangerous men I know*. What if he was?

"Look, if Kessler shows up again, it'll take him a while to get past my pro—professional security, so I promise you, you'll have time for both calls."

Looking at him now, she believed Harsh was right that Iskander was dangerous. She took a step back. "He isn't right in the head. You and your friends, whoever they are, need to understand that."

"Believe me, we do." Somewhere in his private thoughts, a switch flipped, and he was back to the smiling, mellow specimen of male beauty she knew. His grin broadened. "You're getting all worked up over nothing. He isn't going to come back today. He's blown his wad for a while."

"He'll call," she said.

"How do you know?"

"It's what these sickos do." She'd had to explain this before to people who didn't get it. As she'd learned, there was a set of behaviors and psychological patterns involved in what Rasmus was doing to her. "He's going to call because he thinks that now that's punished me, I'll see the error of my ways and agree that I love him."

"That doesn't even make sense."

"Of course not." She threw a hand into the air. "Not to a normal person. But he'll call. A dozen times. Maybe twenty or thirty, and when I don't answer, he'll probably come here now that he's found out where I live." She felt the corners of her mouth twitch because, darn it all, she was about to cry. "I've been lucky up to now. He hasn't harassed me at home." She swallowed the lump in her throat that formed at the realization that her life had just gotten much, much worse. "He'll start driving by here. Leaving me presents of dead birds, and, God, I don't even want to think about it. You don't want any part of this, trust me." Her eyes burned with incipient tears. "It's a nightmare."

"Like I said"—he waved a hand—"professional security here."

"What if you're wrong?" She gripped the counter behind her. She didn't see anything but the worst outcome. "What if he burns down your place, too? Because I'm in it?"

"That's not going to happen." He sighed and brought out his phone. He pushed some buttons and while his call was connecting, he said, "Make that list of what you need and your sizes. Gray. Hey…uh, are you free? Good. Listen, I need you to do me a favor. My tenant…yeah, her. She's in a jam. She needs some stuff, and I don't want to leave her here alone. Exactly. I owe you. I'll e-mail you a list. Ten minutes. Fifteen tops. Me too. Thanks. Tell Durian I said hi."

While she was writing her list on the back of an

envelope she'd scrounged from the bottom of her purse, she said, "Your friend doesn't have to get me clothes. I can do laundry and be fine for later."

"She's getting you clothes. Up to you whether they fit."

"Fine." She wrote down her sizes and handed over the envelope. In her experience, most men understood bra sizes quite well, but there was no hint of a smirk when he glanced at it. Maybe her luck was finally turning. Her landlord was turning out to be a genuinely decent guy.

CHAPTER 8

Go take a shower," Iskander said. He used his phone to take a picture of Paisley's list so he could e-mail it to Gray. "But you might want to get your clothes into the laundry first."

Since her rental agreement gave her use of the machines in the utility room at the back of his house, he figured she could handle that without help. "Have you got a robe I can borrow?" she asked.

"I live here alone." He looked up from typing into his phone. "I don't need a robe."

"Oh."

Iskander looked up from typing into his phone. "I'm not going to run around naked, if that's what you're worried about."

"That's because you have more than one change of clothes."

"If you want to borrow something of mine until Gray gets here, that's totally cool." He sent his e-mail to Gray and returned his phone to his pocket. "I have to check on my security system. If you want something to wear, my room's upstairs. First door on the right."

"Thank you. I would really appreciate that."

"No problem." She'd had a really rotten day, and here she was smiling at him. He was ready to slay dragons to make things better for her. "See you in a few, okay?"

He went out the back, through the French doors that opened onto his patio, and checked the status of his proofing. He saw nothing unusual, but he made a quick circuit of the perimeter of the house and yard just to make sure. The morning commute was getting started. There were more traffic sounds now. Times like this, he missed the quiet of living in the middle of nowhere. All of his streetside proofing was in place and undisturbed. He swung around the rear of the house again so he could go back in the door he'd gone out. In the yard, his spine turned to ice. One of the medallions by the French doors was nothing but charcoal. Another one had broken clean in half.

Shit.

If Rasmus had come back, he would have felt it, and he hadn't. The thing was, he could see Paisley through the French doors. She looked fine. In fact, she walked over and opened one of the doors. "There you are," she said. Perfectly fine. "I was looking for you."

"Are you okay?" he asked. Had something tried to get in and failed? He went inside, reached behind him, and closed the door tight. Six of the wards he'd set around the inside of the door were broken. Paisley was fine this time because he'd reset everything to account for her presence in the house. That meant someone else had triggered them. He pulled his magic through him so he'd be ready for anything.

"I was upstairs looking for something to wear when I heard the most god-awful racket."

Iskander tried to keep his cool, but it wasn't easy, not with the way he was feeling all twitchy. "Was it just noise or did you see something?"

"Yeah." She laughed. "Your cat." She pointed at the French doors at his back. "Yowling and scratching to be let in."

"My cat?" Some of the kin could shift into shapes besides their nonhuman one. Kynan Aijan, for example. Back in the days when he didn't pay attention to much besides Fen, he'd heard there were a few mages who could shape-shift for short periods.

"Yes. I've seen it around before, but I thought it was the neighbor's. I didn't know it was yours. Anyway, I let it in."

His stomach dropped off the edge of the earth. "What?"

She cocked her head, at last uncertain. "Was that not okay? It acted like it lived here."

"I don't have a cat."

"Oh." Her eyes widened, and her cheeks flushed. "I am so sorry. Tell me you don't have a deadly allergy to cats."

"Where is it now?" *Please, please*, he thought, *let her have put it back outside*. But he knew she hadn't. There was a fucking mageheld in his house somewhere, and he was essentially blind to its location.

"I don't know." She twisted her upper body to look around. "It was here a minute ago."

"Shit."

"I'm sorry," she said again. She scratched the back of her arm. "It's just that it acted like it lived here, and I thought it was yours."

"No problem." He forced himself to smile. "I'll find it

and put it outside so it can go back where it belongs. Go get the laundry started."

"Sure." When she was gone, he stood in his living room, feeling like he might just jump right out of his skin. Where the hell was it? He cast around for more breaks in his proofing, but there weren't any so far. Could he be lucky enough that whatever was here was too injured to do anything? The laundry room door closed with a click. The mageheld had to be after Paisley, because even the dumbest mage alive would know he'd have to send more than one mageheld to kill him. He jogged down the hall in time to see the laundry room doorknob turn. He directed enough magic at the door to keep it from opening because he was pretty sure that wasn't Paisley trying to open the door.

Now that he suspected where his enemy was, he focused on the one thing he knew he was good at—turning himself into a weapon. He concentrated his magic, pulled it through him, allowed it to inhabit every crevice of his being. When he was like this, life was sweeter. More intense. The possibility that he might face someone stronger than he was hyped him up something fierce. He thought more clearly, moved faster, saw better. He fucking owned the world.

He sent more magic toward the laundry room door, and as expected, a soft *pop* accompanied the collapse of the magical constructs that kept the mageheld invisible. The air around the door shimmered and flashed blue. A mageheld fiend in its nonhuman form dropped to one knee, one fist arcing toward the door. The thing snarled, but Iskander had already secured the interior and exterior doors to the laundry room. No way was that mageheld getting in. He dampened this end of the house as best he could; with a bit of luck, Paisley wouldn't hear anything. If she tried to open any of the doors, hopefully she'd just think they were jammed.

The air got hot, and more and more of his proofing went off around them. Blood trickled from one of the mageheld's ears, but it twisted away from him and lunged toward the laundry room door. He grabbed it by the shoulders, but his fingers slipped in blood, now leaking from both its eyes, and that allowed the fiend's arm to slip free. Iskander danced sideways to avoid a vicious blow to his rib. The blow still landed, and it still hurt, but not as much as it might have. He got an arm around the mageheld's throat, cut off its air, and dragged it, kicking, down the hallway.

He had to juke to avoid a shot to his temple. With one arm around its throat, he caught the mageheld's fist before the asshole made a hole in his wall. His biceps screamed with the effort of holding the mageheld back. The bones in its hand broke, and even under a magical compulsion to get to Paisley at whatever cost, the enslaved fiend faltered.

Room to maneuver was precious here, hindering them both. He was holding back so he could keep the dampening going. The effort cost him more than he liked. The mageheld's other ear started bleeding, and as it flailed back, fighting to get out of Iskander's choke hold, it loosed a burst of energy that slammed Iskander against the wall, right into a closet door. The doorknob just missed his spine.

He took a breath and tightened his arm around the mageheld's throat while he fought for the leverage he needed to break its neck. The fucker shape-shifted to a mountain lion–sized animal. He gathered himself and slipped into the roar of his magic. He punched the mageheld; his fingers stiff and shifted into talons. His arm tore through the feline body and sliced through its spine. When he drew back his hand, the mageheld's heart was crushed in his fist.

Iskander had to let go of the dampening magic so he could safely bind the dead fiend's magic to his own. If he didn't, that magic, which made up a part of the fiend's life, might never rejoin the magical space shared by the kin, and its life force would never find peace. Nor would it ever really be dead. He didn't wish that agony on any of the kin. He said the required words and the energy crackling in the air diminished. The fiend's magic was now safe from the magekind, too.

He looked up from the body and saw blood everywhere. The laundry room door rattled. Magic raced through his body. He used the heat to scour away the blood and then incinerate it. The mageheld's body was still there, in human form now and not fading fast enough.

Paisley rattled the door again, then knocked. "Iskander? A little help, please?"

He opened the hallway closet, dragged the corpse inside, and shoved hard enough to close the door. He released the magic that had kept the laundry room door shut. The door flew open and there Paisley was. He could hear water sloshing around in the washer.

"Hey," he said. He straightened but kept a hand pressed to the closet door. "I forgot to warn you that door's tricky." He smiled at her, and hell, he was going to qualify for sainthood for all the time he spent not looking at her chest. "Now that you're here, I'll have to take a look at it."

She was wearing a faded black T-shirt of his he kept meaning to throw away. She had it knotted at the waist.

A pair of gray boxers, brand-new and still creased from the packaging, hung to about midthigh on her. She had on a pair of his socks. Jesus, her legs were long, long, long. "I was having visions of spending the rest of the day in there."

"Sorry about that." Delicious. That's what she looked like. Lickable. Totally fuckable.

"Did you find the cat?"

He leaned against the closet and crossed his arms over his chest. She was naked under those clothes. His clothes. "I took care of it."

"Thanks for letting me borrow your clothes, by the way."

"No problem."

"Did you hurt yourself?" she asked.

"No."

"Are you sure? You have blood on your face." She walked to him and brushed his cheek. Her fingers came away smeared with blood. He had to steel himself against touching her. He wanted to. "Did that cat scratch you?"

"Didn't even feel it."

"Do you have a first-aid kit?"

"No."

She grabbed his hand, and he sent a pulse of magic into the closet door just in case. It didn't come open, so it must have been enough. She hauled him to the bathroom a few feet down the hall, where he could see he did have a cut on his cheek that still oozed blood. Not horrible, but he could see why she was concerned. He let her wipe off his cheek and clean out the scratch with soap and water. He kept himself from healing too fast.

"Cat scratches can be dangerous, you know," she said, dabbing at his cheek.

"I'll live." The bathroom wasn't all that big, and, well, being good and not thinking about having sex with Paisley just made him think about it more.

She stepped back and studied the scratch. "I suppose you will."

For a minute they stood there looking at each other, and hell if it didn't feel like maybe she wouldn't mind if he put a hand or two on her. Half a second before he tested the theory, she backed away.

He cleared his throat. "You should probably get into the shower now."

"Yes. I probably should."

"Don't use all the hot water, okay?"

"I'll try not to."

He left and she closed the door.

Damn.

He listened to the water run in the downstairs bathroom while he cleaned up the dust. It didn't take long. He took the whole load into the backyard and incinerated it with a minor pull of his magic. After that, he went upstairs and took a shower himself. The whole time he thought about Paisley downstairs. Naked. In the shower.

Ten minutes later, he went downstairs in clean clothes. He checked the hallway to make sure he hadn't missed anything before, then checked the closet. The mageheld's body was only faintly visible. In the laundry room, he opened the washer and found about what he expected. Her jeans were little more than a mass of white threads held together at the seams. Nothing was left of her white chef's jacket except the metal snaps, which he picked out of the bottom of the washer. The shirt she'd had on underneath was dotted with holes. So were her bra and panties.

He set them on top of the dryer so she could decide for herself if anything was worth saving.

He threw himself onto his recliner and grabbed the remote from the table next to it. He started running through the cable menu. She came out of the bathroom a few minutes later, her damp hair slicked back and her skin smelling like the peppermint soap he kept there. "Feel better?" he asked.

"Yes." She sat on his couch, looking all adorable in his clothes and with his socks falling around her ankles. "I think that qualifies as the best shower I've ever had."

"That's good." He muted the TV, then wished he hadn't. Now it was too quiet. "Gray should be here pretty soon."

She nodded. "You have a very nice place, Iskander."

"Thanks."

"Have you lived here long?" She curled her legs underneath her, and he looked because, well, she had killer legs.

"'Bout a year." He kept his eyes on the TV. No looking at her chest. No looking at all.

"Really?" She ran her fingers through her hair, fluffing it a little. Her eyes were a really pretty hazel, more green than brown. "A year. That's so funny."

"Why?"

"I don't know." Could she be any cuter? He wondered why she didn't have a boyfriend. What idiot would ever cut her loose? She put her arms on top of the couch, and sitting kind of sideways so she could see him, she rested her chin on them. "You meet someone and you think they've always lived where they do or always had the same job. I thought you must have lived here forever."

"Nope."

"Where did you live before?"

He'd already figured out that she was nervous and that

she talked when she was nervous. He was the opposite. When he first got severed, he used to almost never talk. Different ways of coping with a fucked-up life.

"Are you from around here?" she asked.

He didn't take his eyes off the TV. He saw her just fine in his peripheral vision. "I moved here from Sonoma County."

"I'm from Georgia. I came here for college. Straight from home."

"Yeah?" He put down the remote and looked at her. He smiled. He could do this. He passed for human all the time. "I lived at Harsh's place up north. Way out in the boonies. I think most of my stuff is still at the farmhouse."

"Goodness. Why don't you just rent a truck and go get your things? Ten friends and free beer and pizza would take care of it."

"Because." He stared into the distance and tried not to think about the reasons why. He never really talked with the women he took up with, other than to give a few details about the normal job he didn't really have, sports, or maybe current events. Mostly, he got right down to business with them, and they were all fine with that. Paisley was easy to talk to, though. "Sometimes it's better to start over." He clicked off the TV and stood up. "She's here."

Paisley looked confused. Oops. She couldn't feel the magekind or free kin the way he did. "Who's here?"

"Gray. My friend Gray. With stuff for you to wear."

Paisley shot to her feet when he went to the door. He looked at her from over his shoulder. Her eyes were wide and staring.

"What's the matter?" he asked.

"How do you know it's her?"

Good question. He needed a plausible lie to answer her, and he couldn't think of one. His phone rang, and he reached for it. Caller ID said it was Gray. He lifted the phone. "Because she's calling to let me know it's her." Iskander took the call. "Hey."

"I'm right outside. I have this thing I have to do, and I'm late." Meaning, Iskander knew, she needed to take care of someone for Nikodemus. "Can you come out to the car?"

"No problem." He closed the phone and glanced at Paisley. "Be right back."

Outside, Gray tapped her horn.

As soon as Gray saw him come out, she opened her door and set everything on the street. She was driving off by the time he got to the bags. He trotted back to the house with three big shopping bags with twine handles. Paisley was standing by the window with her phone in her hand, ready to call the cavalry for him.

"Here you go." He put down the bags and made a big deal of locking the door and throwing the dead bolts. He watched her walk back to her purse and drop her phone inside. The two bulkier bags were full of bottles, boxes and cartons. He recognized sugar and chocolate and that was about it. He held out the last bag. "Enough clothing to get by, I think."

She peeked into the bag he handed her. She looked touched and grateful and, well, like she might break his rule about crying. "Honestly. I don't know how I'm going to repay you."

"You don't need to."

"Just bless you for all this." She swiped a hand underneath her eyes. "Please tell your friend I said thank you."

Iskander smiled. "Will do."

She headed for the bathroom to change, and while she was gone, Iskander checked the closet again. The body had vanished, as it should have. He returned to the living room when she came out in a pair of dark jeans that showed off her legs and a dark brown T-shirt that intensified the red and gold shades in her hair. The clothes fit like a dream. One of his dreams, but still. She'd brushed her hair and fastened it into a ponytail.

Paisley cleared her throat. "Everything fits."

"I'll say," Iskander said.

On cue, her phone started ringing.

CHAPTER 9

Paisley headed for her purse, tense out of habit now because these days, Rasmus was always the person calling her. Iskander leaned over, snagged the strap of her purse, and held it out to her. The muscles of his upper arm bunched and tightened, and for an instant she saw him as a complete stranger, a man of uncertain intentions who was bigger and stronger than she was.

The sheer masculinity of him took her aback, even aside from the plain fact that he probably outweighed her by a hundred pounds. Iskander Philippikos was a man, pure and simple. An image flashed into her head, him with some unnamed woman, naked and having sex, touching, entering. She resisted the urge to take a step back and instead took her purse. "Thanks. I think."

He shrugged.

She fished out her phone and flipped it open; then she did take a step back, until she was just out of Iskander's reach. She didn't recognize the number on the screen. That wasn't unusual since she got referral calls for catering or special-order cakes and pastries all the time. The unknown number didn't mean much. Rasmus was in the habit of calling from different numbers. "Paisley Nichols."

She knew it was Rasmus before he spoke. "I'm sorry I had to destroy your apartment."

Whether it was her expression or the tension that shot through her, something must have telegraphed her reaction, because Iskander jumped to his feet. She took a deep breath, trying to control the familiar anger, frustration, and guilt for not figuring out how to make the man understand she wasn't interested. "Leave me alone. Can't you just please leave me alone?"

"I cannot do that," Rasmus said over the phone. The hollowness in her stomach grew big enough to swallow her up. She recognized the manic undertone in his voice from all the other times she'd heard him when he was frustrated. He wasn't irrational yet, but he would be soon. "You must understand I'm serious. When we work through whatever prevents you from seeing that we belong together, when I've made you understand, you'll know I am right. My future depends upon you, Paisley. You must help me. We belong together."

She pulled the phone away from her ear to disconnect the call, but Iskander held out his hand. With a shrug, she dropped the phone onto his palm. At this point, she didn't care who dealt with Rasmus. Let the whole city of San Francisco try.

"Rasmus Kessler?" His eyes were practically glowing. She'd never met anyone whose eyes could look like that. Goodness, his expression was dead serious. He looked as angry as she felt, and that was strangely comforting. "She's in Nikodemus's territory."

He spoke matter-of-factly, as if he expected Rasmus to know what that meant. She sure didn't. Who was Nikodemus? What was his territory? And why would Rasmus care when he didn't seem to care about anything else that ought to matter?

She tried to recall her earlier sense of Iskander as a stranger, but this time it failed. He was just her landlord. The guy who cashed her rent checks and fixed her leaky sink. Maybe he was, in his own way, as deluded as Rasmus, because he was acting like he was some kind of übercop. Whether he was someone who lived off rental income or who had sold a software company for millions before he was twenty-five, he wasn't equipped to deal with Rasmus and his craziness.

Iskander caught her eye and rolled his as if he'd been reading her mind. He grabbed her hand and pulled her to him. With the index finger of his free hand, he traced some kind of mark on her forehead. He ended with a tap that felt hot when his finger landed.

She reeled back, off balance and dizzy from the contact.

"Paisley Nichols is under my protection now," he said into the phone. A smile spread across his face, like he was enjoying whatever Rasmus was saying. "You send anyone to my place again, and he won't come back, either." He waited a bit and said, "Mess with her, Kessler, and when I find you, which I will, I will rip out your heart." He disconnected and looked up with a grin.

Paisley took back her phone. Her forehead burned where his finger had tapped her. She'd heard about pressure points that, when triggered, could make a person collapse. Was that what he'd just done? She swallowed against a swell of nausea. "Not that I don't appreciate the sentiment," she managed to say, "but isn't it more effective if you make a threat you can actually carry out?"

Iskander laughed, and Paisley figured it was because he agreed with her. Then she saw his face and realized that wasn't it. He believed what he'd said. Her stomach rolled over again, and Iskander's face blurred. The stripes down his face seemed to be glowing. They weren't. They couldn't be. She blinked and rubbed her forehead. Nothing came into focus. No matter how hard she focused, she saw two Iskanders, both of them with glowing blue eyes.

"You okay, Paisley?"

The ocean roared in her ears. "I'm fine."

Only she wasn't. The room spun, and her forehead burned something fierce. Lord, she was going to heave.

Iskander said, "That should *not* have happened." He caught her before she hit the floor. The next thing she knew, she was sitting on the floor with her brain floating around in circles inside her head. Iskander crouched at her side, his phone to his ear. She was dizzy. Really dizzy, and her head hurt.

"Harsh? Situation here." He had a mostly whispered conversation that at times sounded like gibberish to her. Then he pushed on her shoulder. "Harsh says for you to lie down."

She lay back. Iskander grabbed her legs and put her feet on the seat of a chair. The spinning sensation slowed.

"She's a resistant," Iskander said into the phone. "I know." He took her wrist in one hand. His eyes, still an unreal blue, lost focus while he counted. "Fifty-three. Well, that's how many I counted." He looked at her. "Hypowhatsis. What the hell does that mean? Oh. Harsh says you probably have low blood pressure. It can make you faint if you don't sit down quickly enough." He gave her hand a gentle squeeze. "Any better?"

"I think so." His fingers were warm around her wrist. Her head stopped spinning.

Iskander let go of her wrist and listened to Harsh. "I can't ask her that. No."

"What?"

He actually blushed. "He says I have to ask you this."

"Go on."

He closed his eyes like he was hurting somewhere, then opened them and said, "Are you pregnant?"

She laughed out loud. Her thoughts were more coherent now. But not quite enough, considering the next words out of her mouth. "You have to have sex in order to get pregnant, and for that you need a social life, which I don't have. So, please, tell Dr. Marit that I am not pregnant. Bless his heart."

"No," he said into the phone. He listened some more. He ran a hand through his hair and avoided looking at her. His cheeks flushed red again. "No fucking way, Harsh. I am not asking her that. You ask her." He pressed the phone to her ear. "Harsh has a question for you."

She took the phone. What was worse than asking a woman you barely knew if she was pregnant? "Dr. Marit?"

"When was your last period?" Harsh asked.

Oh. She glanced at Iskander and found him staring at the side of the room. Great. Now her periods were going to be his business.

Over the phone, Harsh said, "It's a routine question for women of childbearing years. I'd like to be sure there's not an easy explanation for your fainting."

She turned her head and lowered her voice. "Maybe two weeks ago?"

"Are you on any medications?"

"No, sir."

He certainly sounded doctorlike now. "Ever fainted before?"

"Never."

Iskander was still holding her hand, she realized, even though they weren't looking at each other. And she was all right with that. His embarrassment was kind of sweet.

"How are you feeling now?" Harsh asked.

"Better."

"Think you can sit up? Let me know how it goes if you can."

"Yes, sir. I think I can." She swung her legs off the chair, and Iskander's hand tightened around hers. He helped her sit. Her head wasn't spinning anymore. "Sitting up now. I think I'm okay."

"Give the phone back to Iskander," Harsh said. She handed over the phone, and after he talked to Harsh some more, Iskander had her open and close her eyes while he stared into them. His eyes were the most amazing blue.

"Yeah, they're doing that." To her, he said, "How's your head feel?"

She touched her forehead. The spot where Iskander had touched her was sensitive, but at least she didn't feel like her brains where moving around in there. "Better, I think."

He relayed the answer and after some more listening, disconnected the call. "He says he thinks it was probably the stress of your totally shitty day and for us to call him if it happens again or you get worse."

She stood with another helping hand from Iskander. "I feel fine now." She touched her forehead. An echo of the burning sensation that had started everything remained in her head.

Iskander stooped for her phone. "You need to turn this off."

It rang while he was holding it. He checked the number, and an odd little smile curved his mouth. "Rasmus," he said to the phone without answering it. "Will you never learn?" He turned off the phone, then snapped open the back cover and removed the battery before she could stop him.

"Why'd you do that?" She grabbed for her phone, but he held it out of her reach. "Give that back! I own a business, Iskander. I need that phone. Maybe you can afford to sit around all day, but I can't."

"Relax, cupcake. I'm not going to cut you off."

"Then give me back my phone."

"You have this thing with you, he can use it to track you." Iskander took out her SIM card and tossed all the parts onto the table. "I'll get you a new phone, new number from Google Voice. Keep paying the bill on the old one, though. From now on, give people your Google voice number, not your new cell number. We'll work out what numbers forward where."

Paisley stayed where she was. There was something unsettling about his lack of hesitation about what to do. Like he'd done this sort of thing before. "Thank you. I suppose."

"No problem." Iskander gave her a to-die-for smile. "You've had a hell of a day. I'll show you your room, and you can get some sleep."

She didn't sleep well. The upstairs bedroom Iskander put her in got more light than she was used to without the extra-heavy curtains she'd bought for her apartment, and that made it hard to stay asleep. Her headache got worse, too, and the healing blister on her wrist ached enough to wake her up several times. Whenever that happened, she'd realize she'd been dreaming about Iskander. Disturbing dreams where he ripped Rasmus Kessler's heart out of his chest and then made passionate love to her.

The alarm on her cheap digital watch went off at one-thirty. In the morning. She was already wide awake, though. Definitely not the best morning she'd ever had. Her head pounded something fierce, and her wrist ached.

She rolled out of bed and got ready to go to work. Obscenely early hours were the norm for a bakery like hers. The morning bake took several hours to prep and start. Various doughs had to be taken out of the fridge and allowed to rise, batters needed to be mixed, inventories done. The ovens needed time to heat up. She was glad she'd given herself extra time to get ready, because nothing in the house was familiar to her. Not the bedroom, not the few clothes she had—nothing.

In the downstairs bathroom, she found Iskander had cleaned up and put out fresh towels for her. The new toiletries Iskander's friend Gray had bought for her were lined up on the counter. She showered and got dressed in her one and only change of clothes.

Iskander was watching television when she wandered into the living room on her way to the kitchen for toast and coffee—if there was any. But note to self, Iskander was a night owl. That meant she was going to have to be quiet on the days she did the late shift and was home in the morning. "Breakfast?" she said on her way. It seemed impolite not to at least ask him.

He hesitated, but only, she thought, because her question was unexpected. "Sure."

There was a high-end espresso machine in the kitchen. She found coffee beans among the supplies Iskander's friend Gray had brought over, and while she got the coffee going, she started making French toast. There wasn't time to let the bread thoroughly soak in the egg mixture, but, hey, good enough for going on two in the morning. She threw in a dash of vanilla, cream, and some cinnamon.

Iskander came in just as the first of the espresso was gurgling into the cups. Even with her usual morning grumpiness, she couldn't help but admire him. Gorgeous man. The worst part was, he knew. "Coffee?" she asked. "Or is it too late for you?"

He leaned over with his forearms on the counter. "Never too late for caffeine."

The smell of good coffee improved her mood considerably. Her lips twitched into an almost-smile. "Latté or capp?"

"Neither. Give it to me dark as sin and strong enough to straighten my hair."

Mornings were just not her thing. At all. "Your hair is straight."

He waited a beat. "Not that hair."

She turned away because she didn't want him to see her smile. "Good grief."

"Whatcha making?"

"French toast." She found demitasse cups and poured espresso into one. She slid a full cup to him, started another serving, then got the toast onto the griddle. Before long, the aroma of cinnamon and vanilla filled the air.

"That's good coffee, ma'am," he said.

"Besides good beans, the secret is in making sure the

water isn't too hot. Otherwise it tastes burned." She patted the machine. "This is a good one."

While she waited for the toast to cook, she made herself a foamy cappuccino. "Oh, God," she said when she had her first sip of her cappuccino. "Heaven." She closed her eyes and savored the taste and smell. "Almost enough to make me human at this hour."

"Me too," Iskander said. He drank more of his coffee.

When the toast was done, she served them both. The coffee, the butter, the sifter, and the powdered sugar stayed on the counter between them. She watched Iskander take his first bite, nervous the way she always was when someone tasted her food for the first time. While he chewed, he put down his fork and closed his eyes.

"This," he said when he finished his first bite, "is the best French toast I've ever had." He picked up his fork and knife. "Don't even talk to me until I'm done."

She snorted, and they ate French toast and drank their coffee in comfortable silence. God love a man who could be quiet at this hour. "All right," she said, taking her empty plate to the sink. "I have to head out pretty soon."

Iskander pointed at her with his fork. "Don't touch the dishes. I'll clean up."

"Thanks." Paisley scooped up her purse and the keys to her scooter. She couldn't afford a car, but her scooter was a cheap way to get around when public transportation wouldn't do. "How do I get back into the house?"

He threw a set of keys at her. "The one with the red rubber doohickey on it is for the top lock."

She remembered him talking about his professional security. "Alarm codes?"

He gave her a blank look. "For what?"

"Your security system."

"Oh, that." He waved her off. "It's automatic. Don't worry about it."

"Okay." She headed for the back door since it was closer to the garage, where she kept her scooter. "See you later."

He frowned. "Cupcake. Where do you think you're going?"

"To work?"

"From now on, I'm driving you. And picking you up."

"Oh." He was serious, and that made her feel . . . odd. And better. "You know if Rasmus sees you with me, he's going to start harassing you, too."

Iskander smiled like he had the winning lottery ticket. "I think I can deal with that."

"He'll tell you lies about me."

"I know that."

"Thank you." The words sounded completely inadequate. She walked back to him and touched his arm. "Really," she said. "Thank you."

"No problem."

He drove her downtown in a battered Chevy pickup with no radio and wire looped around the right side-view mirror to keep it attached. He parked so the truck blocked the alley near the back entrance of the bakery and left the motor running. Before she got out, he handed her a throwaway phone. "This is temporary until your new phone comes. I put my number in there for you. Give me a call when you're ready to leave. I can be here in ten minutes."

She slid the phone into her coat pocket. "Thanks. Again." Hand on the door handle, she said, "I appreciate everything you're doing for me."

"Have a good day." He glanced out the window. "Night. Whatever. Bring home something good to eat."

For half a second, she thought he was going to lean over and kiss her, and that set off a whole flock of butterflies in her stomach. He didn't, though.

"I promise," she said.

He waited while she walked to the back door. She didn't hear his truck leave until several minutes after she was safely inside. Thank goodness he wasn't looking for a serious relationship. If he was, she'd fall for him pretty hard.

CHAPTER 10

Ten hours later, alley behind Paisley Bakery and Café

Paisley closed the back door of the bakery and rubbed the nape of her neck. Her shoulders were knotted up tight and her legs were stiff, but today, the tension was just from working at the job. Rasmus hadn't shown up at the bakery, and since he didn't have the number of the phone Iskander had given her, she hadn't had to deal with any calls from him. The staff knew to hang up on him if he called the bakery, and they'd all learned the hard way to throw away anything he sent through the mail.

A day without Rasmus was...pure bliss. She arched her back to work out some of the kinks of standing for nearly ten hours and looked up at the sliver of blue sky that showed between the buildings. The wind, though, was blowing, and she was glad of the peacoat Gray had bought for her.

She walked to the mouth of the alley to wait for Iskander. The alley, just wide enough for a car, served several other businesses that fronted Kearney and exited to Clay Street, the nearest cross street to her right. She was looking in that direction since Iskander would have to come down Clay and either park there or drive down the alley.

A dark blue sedan was parked a few yards away near a set of stairs that led to the rear entrance of the Chinese grocer a few doors down from the bakery. The motor was idling, and the driver's side wheels were on the alley sidewalk so it didn't block access. She didn't think anything of it. People parked like that all the time. She thought about walking down to Clay Street and waiting there.

"Paisley." The all-too-familiar voice came from just ahead of her.

She jumped, heart slamming against her chest. She knew it was Rasmus even before he stepped from a shadowed area of the alley. Not far from the idling sedan. His suit was out of place, incongruously pristine against the dark, unfinished stone walls, Dumpsters, and broken-down crates and boxes. He moved into the center of the alley, blocking her way to the street. How the hell had she missed seeing him?

"You made your point with my apartment, Rasmus. Leave me alone."

He drew a hand through his braids, his fingers lingering on the beads that softly clicked. "I wish to talk to you. That's all. You have to understand me. If you'll just come with me, we can have a quiet discussion, and everything will be fine."

There was no point trying to convince him to leave her alone. His mind didn't work logically where she was concerned. She turned on her heel, fumbling to get her purse around to the front so she could grab her phone and call for help. And run like hell for the bakery. Rasmus followed her, and oh, Lord, he was faster than she expected. Too close. And she wasn't close enough to the bakery.

She sprinted for the bakery door, the phone clutched in her hand. Two more steps, but she could hear him breathing. She yelled at the top of her lungs, high and shrill over the sound of his shoes on the concrete, and felt the chill certainty that she wasn't fast enough to make it to the door before he caught her.

And she wasn't.

He reached around her and knocked the phone from her hands. It spun across the alley to land God knows where. She opened her mouth to scream again, and she saw stars as heat shot up her arm and, swear to God, ended up in her head.

His arm clamped around her waist and his other hand covered her mouth hard enough to pull her head back. She told herself not to panic, to pay attention to what he was doing. The pain in her head practically blinded her, but she went still, as if she were giving in.

"That's right," he said. He loosened his grip on her, and she struck out however she could, arms, legs, feet and hands. Rasmus swore and wrapped his arm around her throat, tight enough to make it hard for her to breathe. He was bigger and stronger than she was, and this was it. She knew he was going to kill her now. He dragged her backward, toward Clay Street, his arm tight over her throat. "You will come with me, Paisley Nichols."

The sedan's motor rumbled in her ears. Of course the car was his. She should have known. She ought to have been more suspicious. His goal was to get her inside the car. If that happened, she was as good as dead. At one point, she managed to get her foot tangled in his legs, and Rasmus stumbled. She whipped her head to the side, and his arm over her throat slipped. She sucked in a deep, blessed breath and screamed as loud as she could.

He recovered from his stumble in time to grab her by the jacket. He yanked her back. "Assistance, please," he called out. He put his mouth by her ear. "Scream as loud as you want. No one can hear you but me."

He had both arms around her now, and she realized someone had opened the rear passenger door of the sedan. The front passenger door opened, and a man got out and trotted toward them. His hair was buzzed short, and like Rasmus, he wore a suit and tie. She recognized him as the detective who'd interviewed her after the apartment fire.

She fought with everything she had. The other man reached them, and Rasmus pushed her toward the fake cop. She couldn't stop herself from falling. Falling. Off balance, stumbling, and painfully dizzy. He caught her, and her entire body exploded in pain. She could barely think.

The fake cop dragged her to the car. She choked on exhaust as he pushed her toward the back passenger door. The end of everything. This man was stronger than Rasmus, and he moved faster. Fear rattled through her, because the car was only three feet away. She kicked and screamed and hurt her fist when she landed a punch, but none of it made any difference. The man holding her grunted, then hauled her off her feet. If she hadn't kicked the car door and swung it partway closed, he'd have managed to get her inside. She had a glimpse of a dark interior and some-one in the driver's seat.

Ka-thump.

Something large and heavy landed on the roof of the sedan, rocking it on its wheels. Everyone froze.

"Tell him to let her go, Rasmus." Iskander stood on the roof of the car, knees bent, weight on the balls of his feet. His eyes glowed. "If you don't," he said, jumping to the ground without making any noise at all, "your guy is dead."

"This is not your business," she heard Rasmus say.

"Sorry. No second chances." Iskander drove the heel of his palm into the forehead of the man holding her. She felt the collision between hand and forehead, the backward jerk of the man's body; then there was a dull crack, and she was free. Iskander grabbed her upper arm, which was a good thing, because she was shaking. "Stay with me, cupcake."

Rasmus let out an inchoate sound of fury, and her vision still must not have been working right because the air around him shattered, as if somehow he'd turned it solid and then broken it into pieces.

"I wouldn't if I were you," Iskander said. The only sign that he was worried was that his fingers tightened around her arm. Rasmus said something that didn't sound like English. The man in the driver's seat of the sedan got out via the passenger door and headed for them. Iskander lifted one hand. "Oh, come on. I'll just take him down, too. You know that."

The driver kept coming.

When the man was within arm's reach, Iskander punched him the way he had the other, a hard strike to the forehead, and the driver just crumpled. Fast. So fast all she saw was the blur of Iskander's arm and then a body falling to the ground. "I wasn't kidding, mage."

Still holding her arm, Iskander walked past the idling sedan and away from Rasmus. She didn't believe for a minute Rasmus would let them go. But nothing happened except the air around them got hot. Five steps, then six, and the heat burned around them. Iskander sped up, a jog that widened the distance between them and Rasmus. She could see his pickup double-parked on Clay. She ran, too.

"In the truck," Iskander said when they reached Clay. He moved past a car legally parked at the curb, practically vaulting over the pickup to reach the driver's side. From inside, she opened the door for him, and he got in. The keys were in the ignition, and he casually started the motor, put the truck in gear, and headed into traffic like he killed people every day. No big deal.

A thousand questions whirled in her head, so many she didn't know what to say. Shouldn't he call the cops? Were those men dead? Where the hell had Iskander come from? She dropped her purse on the floorboard. "I lost the phone you gave me," she said.

"Your new one came today. I have it all set up for you, but it's at home charging."

"Oh. Thanks."

"Doesn't work if you don't charge the battery."

"I guess not."

"Next time," he said, reaching to briefly clasp her shoulder, "you wait inside until I call and tell you it's safe to come out."

"Okay." She felt numb, and that didn't seem right. He wiped his left hand on his jeans and left a dark smear behind. At one point on the way back, he drove over a pothole, and the window on his side rattled, then fell into the well of the door with a *thunk*. Wind rushed through the cab.

"I gotta fix that one of these days." He stretched his arm along the back of the bench seat, his fingers brushing her shoulder, and she didn't avoid the contact. Maybe she should have. He drove most of the way one-handed.

They didn't say anything until they were in the house and she'd dropped her purse on the floor by the rear door. Iskander wiped his left hand on his pants again, and she realized that was blood smeared on his jeans. She looked up and she just didn't have any words. Only emotions that got too big to hold in.

"Can I get you something?" he said. "Root beer? Water?"

She opened her mouth to say, *No, thank you*, but what came out was a sob she barely choked down.

"Hey," he said, looking appalled. "You know the rules."

She tried again, this time meaning to tell him thank you, but to her horror, her eyes burned with tears. She felt as if Rasmus had managed to get her into his car. That at any moment, she was going to wake up and find out she'd hallucinated the whole scene with Iskander and that she was a prisoner in Rasmus's car and about to die.

Iskander held out his arms, and she walked forward and let him fold his arms around her and hold her while she broke the only rule he'd ever given her.

CHAPTER 11

Two weeks later, about 7:00 A.M., Vallejo Street

Paisley always woke up five minutes before her alarm. She had a real alarm clock now and didn't need to rely on her watch. She lay in bed staring at the ceiling and absently rubbed her sternum. Her chest ached a little, almost as if there was a bruise underneath. The heavy curtains on the windows kept the room dark even when it was light out.

She looked across the room to where she kept her new alarm clock and didn't see the glowing red display. Strange. She blinked a couple of times and still didn't see it. Not knowing for sure what time it was sent a jolt through her. If the electricity was out, she might have overslept. She reached for the bedside light and clicked it on.

The light came on. While her eyes adjusted, she sat up and squinted in the direction of the clock. She deliberately kept it far from the bed so she had to get up to turn off the alarm. The table was empty.

She was halfway across the room, intending to find out where the clock had fallen, when the alarm went off with the usual jarring electronic buzz.

Eeh. Eeh. Eeh.

Behind her. The sound was behind her. She turned, a sick feeling in the pit of her stomach. The clock was on the floor by the bed, its red numbers glowing and the alarm blaring away.

She didn't remember moving it. It would be idiotic of her to move the clock there. She'd just turn it off and fall back to sleep. In fact, she knew the clock had been exactly where it always was when she went to bed last night. She turned off the alarm and returned the clock to the table.

Iskander wasn't home. She knew because...because she just knew. She walled off the incident with the clock. Maybe Iskander had come in to clean, and he forgot to put the clock back after he moved it. He was big on keeping his place clean. Maybe she'd only imagined the clock had been in its usual place last night.

The entire time she got ready for work, her chest ached. For a while, it hurt to breathe. She kept touching her sternum, expecting to feel a bruise, but the pain wasn't on the surface. She showered, dressed, and went into the kitchen to make breakfast. She took out eggs for an omelet and returned the carton to the refrigerator.

She still had her hand on the door when a familiar tickle in her chest started up. Without questioning her impulse, she opened the fridge again to get enough eggs for two omelets. As she closed the door, the carton slipped from her fingers. The eggs went splat on the floor. Egg whites and a slower stream of golden yolk oozed toward her shoe.

Drat.

She grabbed a roll of paper towels and knelt to clean up the mess. Or would have, except the center of her chest flexed; that was the only way she could think of to describe the sensation. She knew before she crouched down that there wasn't going to be a mess to clean up. The tiles were now dry, even though the cardboard egg carton was on the floor and listing to one side because the bottom had crumpled along that edge.

Her hand shook when she touched the carton. The top had popped open when the carton fell, and she pushed it wide. Of the eggs remaining, not a single one was broken. Not one. In her head, she could hear the crack of shells breaking.

She rose, the egg carton in hand. She wasn't crazy. She refused to be crazy. One at a time, she took out each egg, looking for breaks and cracks. There weren't any. Each and every egg was a perfect, unbroken oval. The bottom of the carton had caved in on one side, and it felt soggy to her.

Paisley put her hands on the counter and dropped her head. Deep breaths. She needed to get more air in her lungs.

This wasn't the first time something like this had happened to her. Those unbroken eggs were just the latest in a series of odd events that just kept piling up until she had to accept the truth. She was losing her mind. Her slide into madness was even more frightening because she understood she was losing her hold on reality. Better to go insane and have no memory of being normal. Or at least believe in her new, warped reality. But she knew what normal was. She didn't believe what was happening to her was in any way normal. Knowing made everything worse.

Strange things were happening to her. Impossible things. Things only an insane person would believe were real.

One time when she was making scones for Iskander in accordance with their agreement that she bake for him, she imagined she made her measuring cups move just by thinking about them. She knew for a fact the measuring cups she needed had been in the drawer. Fact. Incontrovertible. Except when she turned around to get them out, there they were in all their multicolored plastic glory. On the counter and within easy reach. Even though she knew she hadn't gotten them out.

Another time, at the bakery, the wooden handle of her spatula broke in half. A piece the size of her little finger catapulted onto the floor. She'd stooped down to pick up the splinter. When she stood, the broken spatula wasn't broken anymore. The handle was smooth, unbroken wood. She held the splinter in her hand, but there wasn't anywhere it could have come from. Yet, she'd seen the handle break and watched the fragment of wood fly through the air.

Then there was the thing with her knowing when Iskander was about to come home. Before she heard him walking to the back door or up to the front door. Before she heard his truck. Five minutes before he showed up, the center of her chest always gave a strange little hitch. By the time she heard the Chevy's motor, her chest would have been softly vibrating for at least a minute. The sensation always got bigger and bigger until he was in the house, and then, slowly, the vibration fell to a tolerable level.

A sane person knew that measuring cups did not move without physical cause. Broken spatulas did not repair themselves. There was no such thing as having ESP about when someone was going to come home. That sort of belief in the supernatural was her mother's provenance.

The scariest thing, however, the thing that woke her up when she needed to be sleeping, was the way she reacted to certain people. The phenomena had started a couple of days after Rasmus's attempt to abduct her. When she got close enough to certain people, she heard screams. Only they weren't physically screaming, and no one heard the sounds except for her. It was as if hell existed inside them and the screams from the souls of the damned went straight into her head.

The screaming didn't come from everyone she encountered—just a random few. It could be someone walking down the street or maybe a customer in the bakery. Sometimes the effect was low-key, like what happened with Iskander coming home; her chest got to vibrating, and almost always someone showed up who she knew had set her off. Sometimes the reaction was far worse. The screams deafened her; they slivered her nerves. She wanted to rush at the source, whoever it was, and reach inside them to make the awful sounds stop.

Compared to what was happening to her now, her mother was merely eccentric. She did her best to quarantine that part of her mind from the healthy part. If there were other people around when she had one of these experiences, she carried on as if nothing had happened—because, of course, nothing really had happened. The screamers were more difficult to ignore. Their wails broke through the mental walls she built. Her best defense, she learned, was to get as far away from a screamer as possible.

Right now, she concentrated on the part of her she

knew was sane and blocked off the rest. She understood who she was and where she was. Her name was Paisley Nichols. She knew the date and time and who was president of the United States. She owned her own business. Aliens didn't exist and, except for Rasmus Kessler, the world wasn't out to get her.

While she concentrated on her breathing, her chest vibrated in the same place that had flexed when the eggs fell. That meant that any minute now, she'd hear the rumble of Iskander's heinously old pickup. She stood, head bowed, while she waited.

Three.

Two.

One.

The sound of Iskander's truck was unmistakable.

She grabbed a bowl and cracked four eggs. This time they stayed cracked. While she chopped ingredients, the garage door motor revved up. That was him walking to the house. Coming inside. His keys clattered when they landed on the little table by the back entrance.

"You're home early," she said when he came into the kitchen. The first omelet was in the pan, bubbling away.

"Not much to do today." He never elaborated on where he went, and she didn't ask because his personal life was none of her business. She wanted to be a good housemate. Quiet. Respectful of his possessions and privacy. Sane. No one wanted a crazy roommate.

He opened the fridge and stared into it.

"You can't live on takeout," she said. The only thing he kept in there was root beer and leftover pizza or Chinese.

"Sure I can." As usual, he was casual in jeans and a navy-blue Cal Berkeley T-shirt. His dark hair was pulled into a ponytail. Their relationship was strictly platonic, of course. He never made a move on her. They were friends. Just friends. Sure, there was flirtation once in a while, but they both knew nothing would come of it.

"I'm making you an omelet." Her voice shook, but she covered it with a fake cough.

He wheeled around from the fridge, a slice of cold pizza in his hand. "You okay?"

"Why eat that crap when you can have fresh eggs from happy, dancing, free-range chickens?"

He stood there, grinning at her, and she felt better. Almost normal, just because he was smiling. Sometimes she remembered how she'd felt when she'd cried in his arms, and she wanted to feel that way again. Like there was someone who would hold her just because she needed the reassurance.

"Drop the pizza," she said. "You know you want to. Come on." She lifted the omelet pan. Iskander was a total pushover when it came to food. She used that against him as often as possible. "Hot, fresh cheese omelet? Yum."

His eyes followed the pan back to the burner. "What kind of cheese?"

"Raclette. Garlic, heirloom tomatoes, and basil. Plus, I'm cooking it in butter."

He threw his pizza into the compost she insisted on having. "It smells great," he said.

"I have a fruit salsa to go with it and butter cookies from the bakery. Grab a plate." He did, and she slid the omelet onto it, then arranged her fruit salsa garnish with a fresh basil leaf on top and a dollop of sour cream to the side. "Here. OJ in the fridge. Help yourself."

Iskander took the plate and breathed in deep. "I've never had anyone look after me like this."

Had he ever been in a relationship that lasted longer than eight hours? She gave him a gentle push in the back. "Eat."

He gazed at her over the steaming plate, and for a minute he looked sad. Like his heart was broken. Then the look was gone and he smiled. "It's nice," he said. "The way you cook for me."

"That was our deal." She put her hands on her hips. "I love cooking for someone who likes food as much as you do." That was absolutely true, too. Urban, her disaster boyfriend, as she liked to think of him, the man she'd loved to distraction and who had broken her heart, was a chef himself. Cooking for him had been a contest she could never win, even when she really did do better than him. "Eat before it's cold."

After he sat at the kitchen island, where they ended up whenever they happened to eat at the same time, she started another omelet. Behind her, Iskander groaned in delight. "This is amazing. You are amazing."

Lord knows those words had never come from Urban's mouth in any context. "Thank you."

A few minutes later, over the sound and smell of butter and garlic sizzling in the pan, he said, "How's the new phone working? Any problems with it?"

"No." She gave a quick stir to the garlic and butter sizzling in the pan. "I like it."

"You sure?"

She faced him while she whisked up more eggs. Iskander's arrangement with the phone numbers turned out to be clever. Brilliant, actually. "Yes, I'm sure. Why?"

"You looked upset when I came in." He had excellent table manners, though he did use his knife and fork in the American manner, switching the fork between hands and keeping the tines turned down. "I thought maybe Rasmus was getting through somehow."

"No." If Rasmus was calling her, he wasn't getting through to her new number. She poured the eggs into the pan and raised her voice so he could hear her while she faced the stove. "I can finally leave my phone turned on without getting inundated with phone calls from him. So thank you, for your genius suggestion."

"If there's something going on, you should tell me."

"No." She turned around. Lord, but that shirt of his made his eyes look especially blue. "Nothing's going on."

"Not nothing." He lifted his eyes from his last bite of the fruit salsa. He had that strange, intense stare she found so unsettling.

"Just worried. About Rasmus."

"I won't let anything happen to you."

"Well. Thank you, of course."

"You don't believe me." He shrugged, finished the salsa, and took his plate to the dishwasher. "But it's true."

"It's not that." She got her eggs onto a plate, and she and Iskander did a little dance while she was heading to the island with her breakfast and he was heading for the fridge. "Bottomless pit," she told him while they adjusted their trajectories. Iskander slid his hands around her waist and pulled her close. Her stomach did a little loop-de-loop. She ended up near enough to him to catch the faintest whiff of a flowery perfume. "Ooohhh," she said, leaning in to sniff. "Who is she?"

His smile slowly vanished. "It's not what you think."

She took a step back, but he left his hands on her hips. "None of my business, Iskander. You need to have your fun."

"I was in a relationship once." He let go of her and shoved his hands into his front pockets. "A long one."

She recognized the wreckage left behind by a serious relationship that had crashed and burned. "Me too." She made a face in order to lighten the mood. "In fact, my ex is coming here. Urban Drummond. I've been meaning to tell you."

"You're getting back with him?"

CHAPTER 12

Iskander didn't understand what made him blurt out something like that. What a stupid thing to say to her. If she wanted to get back with her ex, that was her business. Not his. But strange that he would even think of objecting. Which he did.

"No," Paisley said. But she answered too quickly, and he wasn't sure she meant it. He thought probably she didn't. From the way she looked, he didn't think she'd been the one to end the relationship. "Believe me, we're over."

He didn't believe that, either. They gazed at each other for a while, and Iskander knew he should say something to break the tension. But he didn't.

"How long?" she asked. She carried her omelet to the counter and sat down next to him. "Your relationship, I mean."

Way to turn the tables. "A long time."

"Can I ask what happened?" She held up a hand. "It's okay if you'd rather not talk about it."

"What happened with your ex?"

"We were talking about getting married at the same time he was cheating on me." She took a bite of her omelet and then used her fork to make patterns in her fruit salsa. "I found out about her, and that was more or less it. Took a while to make it final, but if he meant it when he said he was sorry and that it was over, why was he still seeing her? You know?"

He poured more OJ into his glass and pushed it to her. "No cooties, I promise."

"Boy cooties is all." She drank some. "So. What about you?"

What could he say? The woman who had been, literally, his other half, betrayed him to a fucking mage. "We were together a long time, but it didn't work out."

She arched her eyebrows at him.

No one had ever asked him about losing Fen. Not even Harsh, and in a way, Harsh had lost her, too. "She left me."

"Urban and I lasted three years. Sounds like you were together even longer than that."

His chest got tight. He wasn't used to needing to figure out the right thing to do instead of doing whatever would feel good right now. "She left me for Rasmus."

Her fork clicked on her plate, loud in the silence. Her eyes flicked to his, and his gut twisted. "Are you serious?"

"Yes."

She pushed away her plate. Not hard, not like she was pissed off, but still. "When?"

"Couple of years ago now." He knew this was heading into dangerous territory, and there were things he absolutely could not tell her without explaining things he wasn't supposed to tell her. "She started up with him a while before we actually split."

"Is she still seeing him?"

He had no idea how to answer that, so he grunted. He'd just screwed himself where she was concerned. He didn't want to lie to her any more than he had to. "I don't know. Probably."

"Does him stalking me have anything to do with you?"

He met her gaze straight on. "Maybe."

"Does she know he's insane?"

"I don't think he was crazy when she met him. Maybe he was, though." He gave a rough laugh. "I didn't know him then. Even now, I only know *of* him." On impulse, he reached for her hand, folding his fingers around hers. His skin was several shades darker than hers. "It was a fucked-up time for me, and the truth is, I'm still fucked up over it."

They weren't sitting close, but they weren't far apart, either. He expected her to move away, but she didn't. She leaned toward him, leaving her hand where it was. With her head turned toward him, she gave a sad smile. "Falling in love with the wrong person is awful."

"Sucks," he said. He shouldn't be thinking of starting something with her. Things were complicated enough already.

"I'm sorry you got hurt," she said.

He shrugged. "It won't happen again." What mistakes had he made with Fen? She'd been his blood-twin. How the hell did you make a mistake when you were practically the same person?

"I wish I was as sure as you about that." She leaned her other arm on the counter. "Urban was...not who I wanted him to be. I should have realized that sooner than I did. Then I thought Rasmus might be a good place to start over. Bless my own heart. I went from one cheater to another. That doesn't say much about my judgment, does it?"

"Doesn't count. You didn't really date Rasmus. You figured out pretty quick that he's nuts."

"Not soon enough."

"Besides, from what I've seen, it's your ex who blew it. What kind of idiot would break up with a woman like you?"

She laughed. Oh, she was playing it cool, but her cheeks were pink and she gave him a different look. Thoughtful, even though she was trying to hide it. He stayed where he was. "I won't argue with you there."

"Better not."

"What about you?"

"What about me?" If he played this right, he could score major points.

"Starting over. I know you were dating a lot. You used to have women here all the time. Now you don't."

Well, fuck.

"Maybe we could work out a system." She lifted her free hand and waved it. Did she even realize they were still holding hands? "Secret signals so I know when to stay in my room or go visit friends. You know, a red cup in the window means one thing. A green one something else."

He didn't strike out with women very often. Practically never. "Number one, you aren't going anywhere without me until we deal with Rasmus. Number two, what if it's dark and you can't see what color the cup is?" He considered the fact that he could kiss her. They were close enough. He could just tug on her hand, and if she didn't let go, he could bring her around and see what kind of chemistry they had. He didn't, though.

"Okay, so not cups. Whatever. You know what I mean. Text me, for crying out loud. You won't hurt my feelings."

"Cupcake." He tightened his fingers around hers. "We don't need to work out secret messages. I'm getting what I need. Besides"—he rubbed his stomach—"I like having you here."

"Thank you. That's nice to hear." She looked at their hands and pulled her fingers free of his. "Speaking of exes, I keep forgetting to tell you the rest about Urban coming out here."

"What?" His turn to play it cool. No way was he going to make a play for her when she wasn't giving him clear signals that she wanted anything like that with him.

"Urban's coming out here to film an episode of his cooking show. Did I tell you he's a chef? Well, there's going to be a big party in the East Bay." She cocked her head. "I've been asked to do the desserts, and with all the press and attention, it's a big deal for me."

"That sounds great. When is it?"

"Two weeks from Monday."

"We'll work something out."

She slid off the stool. "We better go. I don't want to be late for work."

"Sure thing." Iskander took the dirty dishes to the sink while she grabbed her coat and purse. They didn't say much during the drive, but the silence wasn't uncomfortable. He parked in front of the alley, as usual.

And as usual, Rasmus was standing at the corner of Clay and Kearney so he'd know whether Iskander was going to take her in the front or the back. Three magehelds were directly across from the bakery's back door, and the mage probably had more at the front door. Two more were with Rasmus. "Front or back today?" he asked Paisley.

She shrugged. "Back, I guess."

He got out and pulled enough magic to keep parking control from noticing he was illegally parked, then enough for Rasmus to know he'd better watch himself. Today he was pissed off enough at the way the mage was screwing with her head that he draped an arm around her shoulder while they walked to the back door of the bakery. Rasmus followed, but he kept his distance.

When they got there, one of the waiting magehelds moved to intercept them. He didn't cover the distance quickly enough to make him think Rasmus had ordered an attack, but Iskander was in a mood. He took one step forward, grabbed the mageheld by the face, and released enough magic into him to make his eyes bleed. The mageheld dropped to the ground and didn't move.

He kept a hand on Paisley's shoulder while he whirled to face Rasmus. The mage walked toward them with his magehelds in tow. "You know the rules," Iskander said in a voice that wasn't nice at all. "Stay the fuck away from her." He nudged the fallen mageheld with his toe. "Next time I won't be so nice."

Rasmus stopped walking. "She's betraying you with me." The mage smiled, and Jesus, but he looked smug. Beside him, Paisley tensed. "We were together just yesterday."

Iskander put a hand on Paisley's shoulder. The tension in her shot through him. "I know he's lying, cupcake."

"She will belong to me soon. You cannot stop her from changing. It's already happening."

"That's enough, Rasmus. Nobody here believes anything you say."

"Before you came to get her last night, we made passionate love." He gave Paisley a rude appraisal that made Iskander fantasize about ripping out his beating heart. "Didn't you wonder why you had to wait for her?" Rasmus asked. "She told me she prefers me."

"In your dreams, asshole." Even Rasmus knew better than to interfere with him here, but he wished the mage would try something. He'd be within his rights to protect himself or Paisley.

Paisley grabbed his hand. "Ignore him."

She was right. He walked her to the door. A gust of frigid wind blew down the alley, scattering trash and creating eddies of dirt. The city could surprise you with bitter chill even in the depths of summer. Cold never bothered him much, but Paisley was human. She had a whole different set of tolerances than he did. She shoved her hands into her peacoat, hunching her shoulders against the wind. He moved so he blocked the wind and tucked a stray lock of hair behind her ear. "Pick you up about eight?"

"Sure," she said.

"I'll call you." He stayed close to her. His back was itching with the chill of whatever magic Rasmus was pulling right now.

"Okay."

He waited in the alley until she was inside, then took a few minutes to check the proofing he'd set. No major wards, just a few simple ones so if a mage or mageheld came snooping too close, they'd have some uncomfortable encounters. He walked past Rasmus without saying a word.

"She is mine, fiend," Rasmus said.

Iskander took Paisley's advice and ignored the fuck out of him.

In the truck, he called Nikodemus and asked him to send someone to watch the bakery front and back while he was taking care of a few things. Nikodemus agreed without even asking why. A few minutes before eight, he was back in the alley after dismissing the fiend Nikodemus had sent. This time when he walked past Rasmus's magehelds, they all kept their distance.

He called to let her know he was here and felt a surge of anticipation because he was looking forward to seeing her. She came out and smiled at him all sweet and pretty. He waited while she set the alarm on the door. "Good day?" he asked as they walked to the truck.

"Pretty good," she said when they were past the mage-helds. The fog was in, and she had her hands deep in her coat pockets. If Rasmus was around, he wasn't close enough for Iskander to tell. "The guy you had watching the bakery kept Rasmus away. Thanks for that."

"You saw him?" That was damn sloppy work.

"Yeah." She frowned. "What?"

He stayed by the passenger door. "Anybody I send to keep an eye on things, you shouldn't see him unless he wants you to. Not even if you were standing next to him. If Rasmus wasn't around, there was no reason for him to let you see him." He frowned. "What did he look like?"

"But he was one of you." Her eyes got big and wide, and he knew she hadn't meant to say that.

He said, very slowly and with a black hole forming in his gut, "What's that mean, *one of you?*"

"He was like you, Iskander."

He reached out and tapped her chest. "Did you feel something? Here?"

She went still.

"Paisley?"

"Yes."

"Shit." He took a step away from the truck and clasped his hands over his head. "Shit, shit, shit. How long have you been able to tell?"

CHAPTER 13

Paisley's stomach did a flip while Iskander stared at her like she'd just told him she could read minds. Or worse. "Tell what?" she asked softly.

He kept a steady gaze on her and something tugged at her. "Tell that it's me. Or someone like me."

"What do *you* mean, someone like you?"

"That's my point." He looked skyward, and his mouth moved in a silent prayer. Or a curse. "We have to talk."

"All right." She had to be misinterpreting this. Had to be. Right?

"There's a place not too far from here. We can walk there."

"You'll get towed if you leave the truck parked like that."

"No," he said, very firmly. "I won't."

"Whatever you say." They walked down the street to

Café deMonde, which, despite the name, wasn't competition for her bakery; deMonde served lunch and dinner, though there were tables for people who wanted only coffee. They didn't do a morning serve.

Iskander held the door for her, and she walked in only to stop dead because there was a screamer in here somewhere. The cries of agony that reverberated in her head made her sick to her stomach. She scanned the room, hoping to pinpoint the source so she could sit as far away from that person as possible. The sound ripped through her without ceasing. She shivered.

He put a hand on her shoulder. "You okay?"

"Tired."

He guided them out of a direct line with the doorway. "What do you want to drink? Anything to eat? They have great food and even better coffee."

"Americano, two extra shots." She had the screaming mostly blocked off, but her body quivered from the effort. "I'm not hungry right now."

"Find a table," he said. "I'll be back in a flash."

She did. There weren't a lot of free tables, and her choices were limited to the right half of the café since the screamer was to her left. This time the source was a slender woman with blond hair and brown eyes. She was sitting alone, a plate of food on her table and an e-Reader in her hand. She wasn't reading. She was staring at Iskander, a startled expression on her face.

Lots of women did a double take when they saw Iskander. The facial tats alone were striking, but the total package? Unbelievably sexy.

While he waited in line at the counter to order coffee and soup, Paisley found a place to sit near the windows on the complete opposite side of the room from the screamer. The sounds broke through again, wails of despair that ignited the now-familiar urge to walk over there and make it stop.

Only crazy people heard voices in their head. Only crazy people ended up convinced they had to attack complete strangers. The woman wasn't really transmitting the screams of the damned into her head. But, Lord Almighty, if this kept up, she'd be looking to make herself a tinfoil hat.

Out of habit, Paisley kept one eye on the street, watching for Rasmus. But she also noted how the café compared to hers. The effort helped her split off the part of her that was hearing the screams and get that awareness, real or not, walled off. She drew her wool peacoat tight around her and stretched her legs under the table while she waited for the chill of outside to fade.

The screamer was still checking out Iskander. No question her landlord was a prime specimen of man, beyond hot and into the realm of *could-this-be-for-real*? He was a big man, powerfully built with shoulders that were wide for his narrow hips. He had the body of a man used to physical activity, from his leanness to the size of the muscles that shaped his upper arms. She never saw him exercise, but maybe he worked out while she was at the bakery.

He turned from the counter, and she glanced away so she wouldn't be caught checking out his assets. Even though she had been. He brought over a plate with two cookies on it and went back to get her Americano and his Italian soda. With her schedule, she was pretty much immune to caffeine unless she went for quadruple shots. The Americano was nothing. When she got home, she'd still fall asleep. He sat across from her. The cookies looked good. He broke off a piece and gave it to her.

"Good," she said.

He took a bite, too. "Not as good as yours. They should get their cookies and desserts from you."

"Maybe I'll ask the manager if they'd consider it. I could bring over samples."

"Sounds like a great idea to me." He unclipped his phone from his jeans and set it on the table while he checked for calls and texts. It looked like he had several of each. He picked up the phone and responded to one of the texts.

She almost never got to go out to eat. If it weren't for the bizarre reason they were here, this would be a real treat. She had the screamer almost completely blocked, but that wasn't stopping her urge to walk over to the woman and rip out whatever was causing that noise. She focused on Iskander. He had something to say, and she wished he'd just get to it and put her out of her misery. Her mother, however, had taught her to be polite. She waited for him to get around to it.

He did after he'd finished his cookie. "Have you always been a baker?"

She leaned back, coffee in her hand. Her frustration came out in sharp words. "What difference does that make?"

"I need to know."

"Fine." She huddled into her coat. "No, I haven't always been a baker. My mom wanted me to go to law school. So did my dad, so that's what I was going to do even though I hated the idea of being a lawyer."

He sat up. "Your parents are still alive?"

"Not my birth dad. He died before I was born."

"Are you adopted?"

The screaming was getting louder again, and she was having trouble concentrating. Iskander misinterpreted her silence.

"I wouldn't ask if it didn't matter."

She rubbed her temples. Her head throbbed. *The sounds aren't real. No one is screaming.* "Actually, I am. Half adopted." Iskander made a face at that. "My stepfather adopted me two or three years after he married my mother, when I was five. And before you ask, yes, she's my real mom."

"What about her?"

"She lives outside Atlanta. Her favorite thing to do is send me star charts proving I should be a lawyer and married to a Taurus."

"Is your adoptive father still around?"

She sighed. "No. I mean, he's alive, but they divorced when I was seventeen. I don't really blame him. Sometimes she goes off her meds and things get strange. He lives in Florida with his new wife and new kids. We don't talk much anymore."

Iskander scratched his chin. "Why does your mom need medications?"

"Because she's loony."

"In what way?"

"For one thing, she thinks she can read minds." She laughed, because her mother's issues were just so absurd. Unless you had to live with her. "When I was little, she used to tell me what certain people were thinking. For a while I believed her. She was my mom, right? I was about ten, I think, when I realized she couldn't read my mind.

One day, when I was older—I didn't want to hurt her feelings back then—I asked her why she could read other people's minds but not mine."

"And?" He wasn't laughing. Or judging.

"She said she'd never been able to read my mind." She snorted. "Classic. Because I could have called bullshit on her and she knew it. After that we agreed to disagree about her supposed abilities." She waved a hand. "Anyway, I left home and ended up paying my own way through college working at restaurants and selling cookies and desserts to fellow starving students. And then to some people who weren't starving students." She smiled. "I could charge them more money. The summer before my senior year, I talked my way into the kitchens at Renegade in north Berkeley. Best thing that ever happened to me."

"Ashlin Lau's restaurant, right?"

"You've heard of her."

He smiled, and it was just such a cute smile, she couldn't help smiling back. "I like food."

"Urban's party is going to be at Ashlin's house. That's part of the reason it's such a big deal. Ashlin's a big deal in the cooking world. At any rate, I spent that summer in her kitchen, and Ashlin encouraged me, you know? She doesn't encourage many people."

"Smart woman."

"That's where I met Urban. He worked at Renegade, too. One of Ashlin's projects." Those days seemed so far away now, living on practically no money, learning how to run a restaurant, and cooking great food. "We all knew he'd be a star one day, and that's what happened. Now he has a restaurant in New York and his own cooking show. Much to my mother's dismay, instead of law school, I spent a year in France—Ashlin knew some people in the business. The rest, as they say, is history."

He nodded, leaning back in his chair in a careless position that did nothing but show off a perfect body. As far as she was concerned, the facial tats just added to his appeal. To her and probably every red-blooded woman in the room, those tats were drop-dead sexy. "You worked at Renegade for several years."

"Until I had enough saved up to open the bakery. I borrowed money, too. It's not cheap starting a business. Especially a bakery, with all the specialized equipment you need, and I don't cut corners on ingredients."

"Ashlin Lau is a major investor of yours."

Paisley didn't move. "You seem to know a lot about me."

"I did my due diligence before I decided to rent to you." His second cookie was just about gone. "She's backed a few winners. Including Urban Drummond."

"If you knew all that, why are you asking me?" She was getting that weird vibration in her chest again, and it was all she could do to keep from stroking her sternum. She glanced out the window, wondering if maybe she'd see Iskander's guy again. Nothing. Not even Rasmus.

"What's outside, Paisley?"

The ice in her Americano was melting, so she took a long drink before she answered. Lied, more or less. "Rasmus. Somewhere. He always is. You know that."

"I'd know before he got close enough for you to see."

His matter-of-fact delivery spooked her. He couldn't know something like that unless he was as crazy as she was. "What, you have radar for psychos?"

"Yeah." He held her gaze, and her heart folded over on itself because he was still serious. "Do you?"

She put down her drink because she didn't want him to see her trembling. It was hard enough keeping herself together with the screaming in her head. Add in a conversation that bordered on the absurd and she was right there at the edge. "Maybe you should tell me what you're after."

"You keep looking at that woman over there. Why?"

"She's staring at you."

Iskander looked in the woman's direction. "She's hot," he said after a longer time watching her than was polite. "I'd do her in a minute if I thought she was looking for a good time."

"Don't let me stop you."

"She isn't watching me because she's hoping I'll hop into the sack with her." He leaned forward and lowered his voice. "Tell me what you think is special about her, and I'll tell you if you're right."

CHAPTER 14

Just when Iskander thought she wouldn't answer, she did, in a low, soft voice that made him hurt inside because she sounded frightened, and he was pretty sure he was about to make things worse. The father she'd never known had likely been one of the magekind. The way she described her mother made him think there was something there, too. Reading minds was a very human way to describe what the kin could do when they had a connection going with each other or with a human. And what did that say about her mother's origins?

And if her mother could read minds, or whatever it was she could do, no wonder Paisley was a resistant. She'd probably developed her resistance in self-defense. Paisley's mother probably *couldn't* read her daughter's mind.

"You'll think I'm crazy."

"No," he said. He wanted to touch her, but he didn't want any of his magic to leak into her even inadvertently. He kept his hands to himself. "I promise you, I won't think you're crazy."

She looked at him from underneath her lashes and said, "She's a screamer."

"Well." He sat back, flummoxed by her response. "That wasn't even in my top ten most likely answers. A screamer? Like when she comes? Is that what you mean?"

"No." She curled her hand around her mostly empty coffee and looked at him from under her lashes. "That's what I call them. People like her. Screamers."

"Why?"

"Because that's what I hear when they get close enough. Screams. She happens to be particularly loud. Usually I have to be closer before I hear anything."

He got a chill when she told him what she was hearing. Jesus, no wonder she worried he'd think she was crazy. She wasn't, though. "Did you ever get that from Rasmus?"

"Yes." She nodded. "But it's completely random who's a screamer and who's not."

"It's not random." He scooted his chair in and kept his voice low. "Rasmus Kessler is a mage—that means he can do things you probably think are impossible. He's killed dozens of the kin, because if he does it just right, he can add a few years to his life. Tell me, how old do you think he is?"

She frowned. "Midthirties?"

"Try three hundred and thirty. Probably older than that." He wished he was better at reading human expressions, because if she thought he was full of shit, he was going to be in some deep trouble. "The kin are . . . people like me, and the way he kills them, they don't really die. Their physical bodies do, but a part of them doesn't."

She lifted her eyes to his face and studied him. "You believe that?"

Iskander took a breath. "Do you have a better explanation for what's happening to you? The screaming you're hearing?"

"Besides going crazy?"

"You're not crazy." He glanced at the witch over on the other side of the café and was reassured to see she was back to reading on her gizmo. "What I think is happening is when you get near one of the magekind, you hear the screams of the kin they've murdered." He pushed away his empty plate. Waste of money, those cookies.

She grabbed her Americano and drank about half of what was left. Her arm shook. "One of us is crazy, and until now, I would have bet it was me."

He set his hands on the table and bent his head for a moment. How much more to tell her? When he looked up, she was watching him with that careful blankness she sometimes got. "How about neither one of us is crazy? Would you go for that?"

"Yes," she said. "I surely would. But if you ask me, we're both..."

"What?"

She pressed a palm to her chest and narrowed her eyes as if she were in pain. "Is your psycho radar going off?" she whispered.

"No." He watched the hope in her eyes vanish, and it about killed him, it really did, but he'd told her the truth. He wasn't feeling what she was. What he didn't say—because he didn't have any idea how to say it yet—was that the witch over in the corner wasn't pulling any magic. If there were other magekind around, he'd know. Which meant she was probably reacting to a mageheld. Mostly likely one who belonged to the witch.

"I guess now we know which one of us is crazy."

"Not necessarily. Paisley, I—"

The café door opened, and Iskander knew from the look on her face that the cause of her reaction had just walked inside. He turned his head to get a look, and his stomach took a flyer.

Definitely a mageheld. But not one who belonged to Paisley's screamer.

Fen.

She hadn't changed at all. She was tall, ballerina thin, and the kind of beautiful that stole your breath. She was dressed to kill in straight-legged jeans, high-heeled fuck-me pumps, and a sheer white shirt over a black bra. Her long hair was loose and still a gorgeous fiery copper-red. Fen surveyed the room like she owned it, paused to check out the blond witch, then turned her head and looked directly at him. A familiar smile spread over her face as she headed toward him.

For half a second, it was like nothing had changed between them. Except he couldn't feel her. Their bond was gone, and magically speaking, she was a nullity to him because she'd willingly enslaved herself to Rasmus Kessler. Mageheld, but not against her will.

The shock of seeing her wore off, and he realized if Fen was around, Rasmus probably wasn't too far. He slid his phone into his pocket, set his hand over Paisley's, and pressed gently down. "Do exactly what I say, okay?" She nodded. "Don't say a word about who you are or that you're staying with me."

"Why not?"

"There's a chance she'll take the thoughts right out of your head, so if you can, don't think about me or my house. Recite a recipe in your head or something." He was counting on her magical resistance keeping Fen out of her head.

She started to laugh, but he gave her a hard look and she stopped. "You're serious."

"The less she knows the better."

Fen was halfway to their table, working the walk in those goddamned pumps.

"That's crazy."

He pinned Paisley with a stare. She needed to understand what she was involved with. No more keeping her at the far edges of his life or the truth. Ignorance might get her killed. "You knew she was coming before she got here, didn't you?"

After a moment, she nodded.

"That happens with me, too, doesn't it? Or something similar."

She nodded again.

"If I'm going to keep you safe, Paisley, you need to believe that." He touched her hand. "Do you trust me?"

"Yes."

Then Fen was at their table. She was even more beautiful than she'd looked from a distance, every feature perfect. Through the transparent shirt, he could see the five copper-colored bands around her forearms. They looked like tattoos, but like the markings on his body, they weren't. At one time, those copper bands had been analogous to the traceries on his body. Sensitive and a reservoir of magic they had once shared.

"Skander," she said.

He took his time acknowledging her. "What brings you to the city, Fen?"

Her eyes jittered the way they'd started to do shortly after she hooked up with Kessler, before she realized the cost of betraying her blood bond with him. He'd been the first to guess what was happening to them and had blocked himself enough to stop his descent into madness. She hadn't been so lucky.

She reached for his shoulder but he leaned away. Her smile faded. "I'm here on business."

"Good for you."

Her smile was more than a little predatory. He didn't miss her glance at Paisley or the flash of irritation when she saw his hand over Paisley's. "Can I sit down?"

"Sorry, Fen. We were just leaving."

"Only for a little bit. What's the harm in that?" She grabbed a nearby chair but kept it turned backward. She straddled the seat and crossed her arms over the top. "What are you doing, Skander?" She tipped her head toward Paisley. "With her?"

She said *with her* like she meant *with that skanky bitch*. Which she probably did.

"Not your business."

Fen looked Paisley over before she held out a hand. "Fen Philippikos. And you are?"

He tightened his fingers around Paisley's hand. "Don't let her touch you. And it's not Philippikos. She's lying about that."

Paisley looked from Iskander to Fen and back and did the wise thing, which was say nothing and keep out of reach. With her free hand, though, she massaged her temple, frowning.

"Fen," Iskander said sharply. He couldn't feel Fen's magic, so there was no way to be sure what was going on without getting into Paisley's head. But it was a fair guess that Fen was trying. "Whatever you're doing, stop."

"What will you do for me if I do?"

"If you have business here, why are you wasting your time with me?"

"Maybe my business is with you."

He leaned back but kept his hand over Paisley's. "Tell Rasmus it won't work. He can't have her."

Fen studied Paisley. "Give up Iskander, and Rasmus will leave you alone."

"He isn't mine to give up."

"Then leave him." She leaned closer. "He belongs to me."

"I have a feeling he disagrees with that."

"We don't have any business, Fen. If you want to talk to Nikodemus, I can make a call for you."

"Oh, please." She made a face and stared at Iskander. "Did you mean to tie yourself to him?" She swept her thick hair behind her shoulders. "Wouldn't you rather be free?"

"Wouldn't you?" Seeing Fen again wasn't as bad as he'd been dreading. He wasn't tempted to go back.

"You could work both sides," Fen said. "My way, there's no rules."

He shifted his chair closer to Paisley, which was only smart, anyway, and slung his arm around her shoulder. Paisley's shoulders tensed under his arm. "Go home to Rasmus, Fen."

His former blood-twin pushed back so she was sitting straight on the backward-facing chair. "Don't be difficult, my love."

He played with a strand of Paisley's hair, trying to fig-ure out what the hell Fen wanted and deciding whether it was worth the risk of staying to find out. All those times he'd thought he'd go back to her if the opportunity arose, and it turned out he was wrong. He and Fen were done. "I'm not your love."

"You should be. I'll always love you, Skander. Nothing will ever change that. You should be free. As we were meant to be."

"If it weren't for Nikodemus, I'd still be fucked up and probably insane." His voice came out flat and cruel. "What you did to us, that wasn't freedom. And what you have now, that's not freedom, either." He stood, not letting go of Paisley's hand. "Nice to see you. No, that's a lie." He leaned down. "Stay away from me and stay the hell away from Paisley."

"We want you back." Fen jerked her chin in Paisley's direction. "With or without her."

He kept his voice low, but he knew Paisley heard every word. "You touch her, you do anything to her, and I will crush your beating heart in my hand."

"I could love her, too," Fen said as if he'd been talking about the weather. "If I had to. I would let you have children with her."

"With all due respect, Fen. Fuck you."

Her eyes locked with his. "You used to," she said. "And very well."

He pulled Paisley to his side. "If you or Rasmus want to meet with Nikodemus, I can arrange it."

Fen snarled, and though he couldn't feel the magic she pulled, he knew she'd done it because Paisley flinched. On the other side of the café, the witch stood up fast enough to knock over her chair.

He whirled to face the witch. *Her* magic he could feel. So could Paisley, who went completely stiff at his side.

He pointed at the woman and in a voice loud enough to carry said, "Stay out of this."

The witch, however, couldn't leave well enough alone; her kind never did. She stopped pulling, but she also walked over to them because the magekind thought they were the protectors of the poor harmless humans, and she obviously thought Paisley was in need of protection.

"Make it stop," Paisley whispered. She swayed against him, but her eyes were on the witch, not Fen.

Iskander remembered what she'd said about the witch being a screamer. He needed to get her out of here, and that damned witch was between them and the door.

"This is not wise," the witch said in a low voice. "A confrontation in front of so many normal humans."

"We were just leaving," Iskander said. He didn't like having Fen behind them, but there wasn't anything he could do about that.

"Stop," Paisley whispered. "Stop the screaming. Please."

"Let's go, cupcake," he said. But she didn't move with him. Instead, she took a step toward the witch. A chill rolled through him. Holy Jesus, that was magic coming from Paisley. Not trivial magic, either.

"The screaming has to stop." She stretched out her hand, her face a mask of agony, and she just kept going until her palm made contact with the witch. The witch's eyes got big, and she howled. High and piercing.

Fen had her hands on her hips, her eyes on Paisley, doing nothing. He dampened the sound of the witch's screams so they wouldn't end up calling Harsh to bail them out of a mess with the police. Then things got worse.

Paisley made a fist and yanked. Hard. The air around them shifted as power left the witch, ripping away with the motion of Paisley's hand. The remnants of dozens of lives—the psychic lives of murdered kin that the magekind took in order to extend their human years centuries beyond normal—left the witch with the movement of Paisley's hand. All that energy swirled around her.

Her face relaxed, and she opened her hand, palm up, fingers taut but shaking like a leaf in a strong wind. Those dozens of lives were free. Somehow, Paisley had taken away the magic the witch had murdered for over the years. What was left of those psychic lives whipped around her. Already in contact with them, Paisley was the obvious refuge. Something very similar had nearly killed Nikodemus's witch, Carson Phillips. Paisley's resistance was the only reason the energy didn't simply flow into her.

If he didn't do something, the entire café was going to erupt in chaos. He put their half of the café under a dampening cover of magic that would make just about all but the most resistant humans simply look the other way. He shoved the still-screaming witch onto the chair Fen had been sitting on and spun the chair to face the window. The witch had her hands pressed to her chest, tears streaming down her face. At the same time, he muttered the words that would keep the magic Paisley had released safe from the witch taking it back, safe from other magekind, and safe from Fen. One after another, the lives Paisley had freed were absorbed into the psychic realm.

He grabbed Paisley's hand, and he hauled them both out of there. Outside, he released his magic and took vicious satisfaction in leaving Fen to deal with the aftermath of the screaming witch. On the street, Iskander kept moving. His heart banged hard in his chest. What Paisley had done to the witch was miraculous. Amazing. She'd freed kin they had believed were forever lost. Jesus, he had to get them out of here. Now. Because she'd also broken one of Nikodemus's rules.

"Slow down!"

He kept walking.

She yanked her arm. He put a hand on her back and pushed her forward. They were not safe right now. Not at all. "Keep moving, Paisley." He kept them moving. "We've got to get the hell out of here until I know if that witch intends to come after you or if Nikodemus is going to sanction you for what you just did."

"Slow down."

He did slow down, a little. But not much. They were nearly to his truck. "What that witch could do to you is nothing compared to what's going to happen if Nikodemus comes after you. I can keep you alive if that witch tries something, but not if it's Nikodemus."

"Who's Nikodemus?"

"My boss."

His phone rang, and he almost had a heart attack when he saw Durian's number flash at him. Nikodemus's goddamned number-one assassin. He turned off the phone and dropped it into a mailbox. He didn't want to make tracking him any easier than necessary. When they made it to his truck, he practically threw Paisley inside. "We do not go home," he said. "We do not pass Go. We just get the hell out."

"All I did," she said as he put the truck in gear, "was make the screaming stop. It wasn't real, Iskander." She was shaking, pale as chalk, and still leaking magic. She covered her head with her hands. "I'm not crazy. I'm not. Not completely. It's just my brain, telling me how to compensate for whatever is wrong with me. Nothing happened."

"You aren't crazy." He took deep breaths until he had himself under control. He pointed them down Clay. "What you did was real. It happened."

She lifted her head, calmer now. "What happened? Because I surely do not know."

"What you did was harm a witch."

"There's no such thing as witches."

"Wrong. Listen to me." He squeezed the steering wheel. "I don't think your mother is crazy. I think she probably can read minds." He wasn't sure how she was taking this. Not as bad as she could be, but she wasn't sitting there agreeing with him, either. "She couldn't read your mind because you're a resistant."

"A what?"

"Resistant. To magic. And trust me, what you did back there was magic. For all I know, that witch will die from what you did. It's bad even if she doesn't. We're not allowed to harm the magekind. Nikodemus can't afford for anything or anyone to screw things up for him. He'd be within his rights to sanction you for what happened."

"What's a sanction?"

He looked at Paisley. "It's what we call it when someone needs to be dead."

CHAPTER 15

Iskander stopped in Novato, in Marin County, to stock up on supplies at a supermarket. Paisley came along, which he would have insisted on in any case. He wasn't going to leave her unprotected. She didn't say anything while they walked into the store, and he didn't know whether to be worried or relieved. So far she hadn't demanded any of the answers she deserved except for, "Where are we going?"

They were heading north into Sonoma County to the farmhouse where he used to live. In the store, she pushed the grocery cart while he dumped in food. Every so often, she looked at his selections and put them back when she thought he wouldn't notice. She threw in plenty of the fruits and vegetables she stocked in the house and tried to get him to eat instead of pizza or leftover takeout, but she also cleaned the store out of Swiss chocolate and loaded up with a bunch of other cooking supplies he wouldn't have known to buy.

When they got to his favorite aisle, the cookies and chips,

she didn't make the turn. He shot out a hand and bodily pulled the cart left. She pulled back, but he was stronger and forced the left turn. She planted her feet. "No way."

"Yes."

"This aisle is evil."

He dragged the cart down the aisle and grabbed a bag of chips.

"Evil," she said. "Pure evil. Trans fat. Carbs. Salt. Partially hydrogenated vegetable oil. Chemicals you can't even spell let alone pronounce. Don't put that stuff in your body."

"Evil tastes even better than chocolate." Iskander tossed in another bag of Doritos and headed for the baked goods.

She gasped, laughing. "Blasphemer."

"We should get doughnuts." He was glad he could make her laugh. "Those little powered ones. I love those."

"No. No. Absolutely not." She jerked the cart backward so his doughnuts landed on the floor instead of in the cart. "I'll make you doughnuts."

He turned around and arched one eyebrow at her. "Powdered ones?"

"Yes, powdered ones."

"Really? You're not just saying that?"

She sighed. "Really. I will make you powdered doughnuts."

"Awesome."

They finished the shopping and got in line. He also won the argument about who was going to pay by refusing to notice her digging in her purse and being faster than her to take out his plastic. She, of course, did not have plastic with her. He handed over his and smirked at her. "I'd let you pay, cupcake, but you didn't bring your block of ice."

"You're lucky, because I'd hit you with it."

Damn, she was pretty when she smiled. "I love it when you threaten me. Do it some more."

She made a face at him.

They put the groceries in the back of the truck. While he had the chance, he fished the driver's-side window out of the well and duct taped it to the top of the door frame. "This is why you should never travel without duct tape."

"That's not enough tape," she said. The weather was colder here than in the city, and she buttoned her peacoat against the chill.

He studied his handiwork. "Sure it is."

"No, it isn't."

"This here is the AC." He tapped the window with a knuckle. "If I put more tape on it, I'll never get the window down when it's hot. Not the normal way."

She shivered. "Right now it's cold."

"It's not much farther. We'll be fine." He opened the door and she slid in, scooting over to the passenger side.

She looked at him sideways while he started the truck. "Bet you a dollar that window falls."

"Done." He wiggled his fingers at her. "Show me the green, Paisley. I'm not taking plastic or IOUs from you."

She rooted around in her purse and came up with three quarters, two dimes, and five pennies. "There. Now you know I'm good for it."

"Sucker."

The window stayed up for the twenty minutes they were on the freeway, but five minutes after they were on the back road, the duct tape failed. She crossed her arms over her chest and stared at him. He pulled a crumpled dollar out of his pocket and handed it to her.

"Thank you very much." She shoved the dollar into her jeans and made a show of buttoning her coat.

He stuck his elbow out the window and kept driving. Back roads meant street lighting was nonexistent except at rare intersections. He knew the way well enough that his lead foot wasn't a problem even on these narrow, twisting roads in the hills between northern Marin County and southern Sonoma County. Before long, he turned the truck down the long rutted gravel driveway that led to the farmhouse. Paisley braced a hand on the dash.

He parked the truck in the barn and got out. Paisley did the same, stretching while she looked around. This was where his life with Fen had fallen apart. They'd moved here after Fen hooked up with Harsh, when the guy still believed he was a normal human doctor and was stashing his money in real estate that hadn't yet gotten insanely overpriced. Harsh had come into his power here, with Iskander and Fen to get him through the confusion of the change.

For a while, things had gone well. Harsh was in the city a lot, but he came up whenever he had time off. Once in a while, Iskander and Fen had driven to the city to meet Harsh, but that was rare because back then neither he nor Fen dealt well with other kin or crowds of humans. Then Fen had betrayed them with Rasmus Kessler, and his life and Harsh's had become a nightmare.

Not all the memories were bad, though. Nikodemus and Carson had saved his life at this house. In the driveway behind the house, he motioned to Paisley and tapped his chest. "Do you feel anything?"

She stayed where she was, on the gravel area between the barn and the house, hands shoved deep in her coat. In the dark, her hair was a shadow of its usual color. "No."

"All right, then." As they walked up the steps to the back porch, he resisted the urge to take her hand. He said, "Whoever Harsh got to look after the place is doing a good job." The house had been recently painted, there were no cobwebs, and the yard was weed-free. In rural Sonoma County where native grasses could easily hit six feet high, that was an accomplishment. The proofing was solid and remained in place. He wondered who Harsh had found to take the dog.

He held up a hand. "Stay here until I say it's okay to come in, all right?"

She nodded.

After dealing with the proofing inside the house, he hit the light switch. The lights came on. The first thing he noticed, besides the place being clean, was that all signs of Fen were gone. That had to be Harsh's doing, from whenever he closed up the house after Nikodemus established himself at the Tiburon place. Harsh had just as much reason as Iskander to want to eradicate Fen from his life. She'd cost Harsh his freedom and the life he'd built for himself among humans. He appreciated the follow-through.

Farther in, his spine tingled, but he recognized that as a reaction to the magical residue of his now-long-ago encounter with Nikodemus and Carson. He'd been so close to giving in to the insanity, but instead he'd ended up severed from Fen and sworn to Nikodemus. Best two things ever to happen to him. He took a deep breath before he walked back to where Paisley waited, leaning against the porch railing. He motioned to her. "Come on in."

"Nice place," she said when they were in the living room. She looked around while she took off her coat. She was still wearing her work clothes, which consisted of black pants, chef's jacket, and rubber-soled clogs. She looked good. "It's cute."

"Thanks." He cleared his throat. "I'll get the groceries."

"I'll help." She help up a hand. "Don't argue. Please."

They put away the groceries, and when that was done, he said, "Can I borrow your phone? I have a couple of calls to make to find out where we stand. Then we'll talk."

She handed over her cell. "Are you hungry?" she asked.

"Starving."

"I'll make us some dinner. Go make your calls."

He went into the living room and set up the phone to connect to his e-mail. While the messages downloaded, he dialed his voice mail. He had twenty messages, three more than the last time he checked, and disconnected without listening to any of them. If Durian came after them here, Iskander figured his chances of taking down the assassin were fifty-fifty at best. He called Nikodemus.

Nikodemus answered on the first ring.

"It's Iskander."

"Talk to me."

The tension in his chest eased. If Nikodemus had sent Durian or Gray to track them down, he'd have told him so up front. He sat on the couch and talked for a long time, keeping his voice low. He told Nikodemus what had happened at Café deMonde, about Fen showing up, what he saw Paisley do to the witch, and what he'd done to get her out of there.

"The witch in question," Nikodemus said slowly when Iskander stopped talking, "is plenty pissed off."

"I don't think Paisley knew what she was doing. She was protecting herself." His tension returned. He was telling Nikodemus the truth. But there were layers to the truth, and an oath of fealty tended not to flex with self-deception. He'd been sworn to Nikodemus for almost two years, and not once had his oath to the warlord ever been called into question. The tightness in his chest wasn't pleasant. He didn't like it. At all. But he wasn't going to throw Paisley under the bus. He couldn't, and that was a fact.

Who'd have thought there was a third person he'd die for?

"Did she really release the magic the way you said?" Nikodemus asked.

"She did."

"You don't have any doubt?"

"No."

Nikodemus didn't say anything for a bit. Iskander waited him out. Nikodemus wasn't stupid. He understood the implications of someone who could do what Paisley had done. "I need to meet her."

"No." The center of his chest contracted. It fucking hurt.

"There's not going to be a sanction." Nikodemus was more his normal, brisk self now, and the pain in Iskander's chest eased again. "The witch asked—don't get me wrong. She wants Paisley dead. We talked and eventually she got around to saying she wouldn't do anything about it."

"She was lying."

"No shit." Nikodemus laughed.

"How pissed off was she?"

"Enough to cause me a lot of trouble."

"She killed a lot of us, Warlord. There were dozens, and they were all in agony." Iskander waited out the silence.

"Before I let you go," Nikodemus said.

"Yeah?"

"I told her you were most likely to be at the farmhouse. I assume that's where you are now."

"Yeah." Throw the witch a bone by telling her where to find the people she wanted to off. As setups went, it was brilliant. Nikodemus knew exactly what he'd sent the witch to face.

"So." Amusement colored his words. "Pissed off witch headed your way."

"Uh-huh."

"Make sure nothing happens to that human of yours." Even through the phone, the warlord's imperative settled into Iskander's bones. Nikodemus didn't give orders like that often—the ones that obligated him to do what he was told. "Keep your girl under wraps until you hear otherwise, and keep her alive until I have a chance to meet her. When the witch finds you, do the needful. Harsh will take care of any cleanup."

Iskander smiled. He did his share of wet work for Nikodemus, but this was the first time the warlord hadn't set limits on what he could do. No limits was good. "Got it."

"I'll be in touch." He paused. "This the best number to reach you?"

"For now."

He stared at Paisley's phone after Nikodemus disconnected. The tension of believing he would be forced to break his oath of fealty to the warlord was gone, and in its place was anticipation. He stayed where he was until the smells from the kitchen reminded him that he was hungry and that he owed Paisley some explanations.

In the kitchen, he watched her cook. All her concentration was on the food. He set her phone on the counter. "What are you making?"

"Chicken with blood oranges. Rice." She glanced at him. "Chocolate soufflé for dessert. Almost done, if you want to set the table. Slice some of that bread, too."

"Sure."

It wasn't long before they were sitting down to the best meal he'd had since the last time Paisley had cooked him dinner. He savored every bite. The farmhouse was quiet in a way the city never could be, and he was okay with sitting here with Paisley, eating great food and not saying much. There hadn't been many women, none actually, who he was comfortable being around for long. He didn't spend much time with women when one or both of them weren't thinking about the sex to come or the sex they'd just had. He was good with women that way. But this... this went beyond his experience. He didn't know much about women like Paisley.

"Can we talk now?" she asked.

With a sigh, he put down his fork. "The woman you did that thing to is a witch."

She picked up a slice of the sourdough bread he'd cut and separated the crust from the inside. "You mentioned that."

"We call them *magekind*. Witches and mages. Humans who can do magic. Some of them kill demons, because taking their magic in a certain way extends their lives. The bodies of the demons die, but the magic doesn't, and we— Nikodemus and I—agree that's the screaming you've been hearing. The part of those demons that's still alive and trapped."

Her fingers pulled at the bread, rolling bits into tiny balls.

"You took back the magic she stole, Paisley. Magic she

murdered for. And now the demons you heard screaming aren't suffering anymore."

She met his gaze steadily. That's what he liked about her. She was calm until she had the facts even when the facts she had were turning her life upside down and inside out. "Demons?"

"The kin. Demons. A kind of demon."

"Who's *we*? You said 'we call them magekind.'"

"People like me."

"You mean the kin, don't you?"

"Yeah," he said softly. "I do."

Iskander heard the sound of the motor before Paisley did. He held up a hand for silence. The car was still far from the house but was coming closer. The motor cut off, but he heard wheels crunching over gravel as the vehicle coasted down the driveway.

He smiled.

Game on.

CHAPTER 16

The inside of Paisley's head got cold and the center of her chest thrummed. Everything seemed unreal—fleeing the city to avoid a possible assassination attempt, casually talking about magic and witches and, God forbid, demons. She must be crazy. But she was getting that strange feeling again, the one Iskander actually believed was real and that she felt when demons were nearby.

"She's here," Iskander said. "The witch." He picked up their dishes and took them to the dishwasher. "We should assume she's not happy with you right now."

"She didn't come alone," she said.

"No," he said. "She'd bring magehelds for something like this." He didn't seem to be panicking about an angry witch, so she didn't either.

"Magehelds?"

"Slaves. Demons who have to do whatever she tells them to do." Something dark flitted through his eyes, and her stomach hollowed out because it was like a door opening on an Iskander she knew nothing about. "We call them magehelds, but they're slaves."

"Then they're not friends of yours."

He turned around after he loaded the dishwasher. He wasn't panicked but he also wasn't smiling. "A mageheld follows orders because he has no choice. Even if he's told to kill all his friends and everyone he ever loved. So, no, her magehelds are not friends. If she gives them a kill order, you can bet they'll do it."

Paisley sat on one of the kitchen chairs. "How do I know any of this is true or that you're not just humoring me? Telling lies so the crazy lady doesn't go off the deep end? Because I have to tell you, all this is a little hard to take."

He put his hands on his hips. "I'm not humoring you."

"Everything that's happened since my apartment got wrecked pretty much defines insane." Her stomach curled into one huge knot. "I'm starting to believe in my insanity. How crazy is that?"

He glanced at her phone and held out his hand. Something tugged at her chest and then the phone wasn't on the counter anymore. Iskander was holding it. "Okay if I keep this for now?"

She nodded.

"You're doing fine," Iskander said.

"If you say so."

He gave her a quick grin. "I do say so." He put her phone in his pocket. "Wait here, okay? I'll be right back." When he came back, he had a gun in one hand. He held it shoulder height, barrel to the ceiling. "Effective against humans, not so much against us. Don't worry if you don't know how to use this. I'll teach you enough to fake it."

Paisley's eyebrows shot up. "Is it loaded?"

"Yes. So be careful—"

She took the weapon from him. "A SIG SAUER P232. Sweet." She flicked off the safety and moved the slide to chamber a round. She held out her other hand. "Spare magazine?"

Without a word, Iskander handed her two.

"Thanks." She stuck them in her back pocket.

"They're hollow points. That means—"

"The bullet makes a big mess inside. I know." She looked away from the gun and found Iskander watching her. "What does it do to witches?"

"They're human, so it depends on your aim."

"I'm a Georgia girl and my adopted dad was a cop." She flipped the safety back on. "Up until he left my mother, he took me target shooting and hunting all the time. When I was fourteen, he got me a gun like this. My little sister was jealous, bless her heart." She lifted the gun and familiarized herself with the weight and how it fit in her hand, then took a practice aim at the door so she'd know how the sights worked for her. After that, she dropped her arm and looked back at Iskander. "Best birthday ever."

He blinked. "Marry me, Paisley."

She grinned at him. "You're only saying that because weapons turn you on." She tipped her head to one side. "If I shoot the witch, what happens?"

"Dead is dead for the magekind." His smile made her feel like everything would be all right.

"You got anything for my ears? If I fire this thing inside, I'll go deaf."

"No one here ever needed them." The kin, she surmised from that, weren't affected by loud noises the way humans were. "If you have to shoot inside," he said, "I'll try to fix you afterward, okay?"

She shrugged. "Better deaf than dead."

Ka-thunk.

The sound came from overhead. The roof. Not loud, but loud enough. The vibration in her chest deepened. She clicked off the safety again.

"You feeling anything yet?" he asked.

She touched her chest. "Here. But I don't know what it means." Her heart was going a mile a minute. She knew her way around a gun, and the P232 was a great weapon, but that didn't mean she wanted to shoot anyone, witch or mageheld. On the other hand, she wasn't going down without a fight.

"If it's like what you feel when you know I'm around, then it's magehelds."

She thought about that. "Why? You're not a mageheld. Are you?"

"No. The free kin can't feel a mageheld the way we can each other."

She touched her fingertips to her breastbone and wondered if she was going to have some kind of attack. The speed of the vibration increased. "They're close."

One eyebrow arched. "How many, can you tell?"

"Three? I think. Maybe four?"

"No problem." He smiled. She could swear the tattoos on his face deepened in color. "If you shoot one of the magehelds, you're not going to kill him unless you get really lucky. Those hollow points will knock him on his ass for a bit, but don't take your eyes off him if he goes down. He might look dead, but he probably won't be. We heal from some pretty horrific stuff."

"Four of them," she said. "I think there's four."

His grin was back, and Paisley found that unsettling since if she was right, they were seriously outnumbered. "Four's no problem as long as you don't shoot me by accident."

She made sure the two spare magazines would slide easily out of her back pocket. If she had to reload, she didn't want to waste even a second. "It's dark out there, and I'm out of practice."

His smile flashed. "The witch. She's going to want you to put back what you took."

"No way," she said. "Even if I knew how, I wouldn't."

"She's looking for payback. That means she'll probably send one of her magehelds up the front steps to see if we're dumb enough to let him in. He'll have some bullshit story to distract you while the others sneak in looking to take me down." Iskander stood with his head cocked, like he was listening to something only he could hear. She didn't hear anything.

"What if it's not her?"

He snorted. "It is. I recognize the magic." His eyes flickered with more colors than were possible, all in shades of blue. "Keep your hands on that gun. Fire the minute you even suspect things are going south. Whichever one they send to the door, he'll be cautious and worried about you using magic. Keep him talking as long as you can. If he tries to get in, don't wait to see if he makes it past the proofing—that's the magic that keeps the bad guys out."

"Your professional security?"

"Exactly."

"Where will you be?"

"Outside."

Outside, where the odds were four to one. "Shouldn't you take the gun, then?"

"Don't need it." Iskander put a hand on her shoulder and squeezed. "This is going to work out. I promise."

"If you say so."

"I do." He bent and kissed her on the forehead. "I got your back, cupcake."

He left her with the P232 in one hand, her heart in her mouth, and her eyes glued to the door thinking of Iskander out there somewhere with a witch and at least four magehelds after him. She sat on a chair from the living room that she turned around to face the front door. She held the P232 on her lap while she waited. She was able to separate the familiar resonance of Iskander from the others—the magehelds he said were the witch's slaves. Maybe five minutes passed during which not much happened. Then the vibration in her chest got worse. She picked up the gun.

Outside the house, footsteps crunched on the gravel driveway.

She listened to someone walk up the steps. Slowly. She aimed the gun at the door. Whoever was out there knocked on the door. She was supposed to keep him occupied. She had to work up some spit before she croaked, "Who is it?"

"Hi there." The porch light created a human-shaped shadow through the curtained windowpanes. "I'm Ethan Leroy, from Cupertino? My wife and I are going wine tasting tomorrow. We're supposed to be staying in Sonoma, but I took a wrong turn. Can you tell me how to get back to the freeway?"

"Sorry. I have no idea." Which happened to be true.

"My wife's waiting in the car, and she's going to rip me a new one if I come back without directions. Have you got a computer? Can you MapQuest it or something for me? I can give you the address where we're staying." When she didn't answer right away, he said, "I'll pay you twenty bucks. We're lost. Come on. Have a heart, lady."

How long was it going to take Iskander to do whatever it was he intended to do? "Sorry. No computer." One of the presences vibrating through her winked out. Just gone. She kept the P232 trained on the door.

"What about a paper map?" He sounded human, and his story was a good one. If she hadn't known different, she'd probably have opened the door. "Do you have a paper map?"

"No, sir, I do not." She heard a sigh from the other side of the door. The porch creaked when he shifted his weight.

"What about your friend? Does he know which way to the freeway?"

She left her chair and walked toward the door, keeping to the side so the man couldn't see her through the door's glass panes. If he tried to get in, she wanted to be close enough that she wouldn't miss her shot. "What friend would that be?"

"The one who knows the way to the freeway." He had just the right amount of wheedling frustration in his voice. "I know he's around. Could you just ask him? My wife is going to be so mad at me for this."

"Sorry, sir, but I can't open the door."

A note of anger entered his voice. "Why not?"

"Because I can't."

There was a moment of silence. Another point of her awareness of the magehelds winked out, not softly like the last time but with a roll through her head and chest that hurt. That meant Iskander had eliminated another one of the creatures that were after them. The demon on the other side of the door sucked in a sharp breath. "Bitch. What the fuck did you just do?"

"Go away or I'll sic the dog on you."

"There's no dog here."

"Fine." She raised the gun to eye level and lined up the notch and ball with the dark mass that was the demon's torso seen through the window panes. She breathed in the smell of gun oil, and all those Georgia afternoons came back. Without thinking, her body settled into a right-foot forward stance. "Go away, or I'll shoot you through the door."

Someone else came up the steps. "What the hell happened to the others?" the first guy said.

"I don't know." This one's voice was low and thready. "They're just fucking gone."

One of them reached for the doorknob. It rattled.

Shit.

She didn't know if the door was locked or it if mattered one way or the other, and she wasn't going to wait to find out. She squeezed tight with her left hand and pulled the trigger at the same time the door flew open. The recoil shoved her shoulders back, but she was ready for that. The muzzle flashed in a flower pattern that burned into her retina; then her ears hurt as sound exploded around her. All that data got processed while she lowered her hands and moved them back to the left so she was recentered for her next shot.

One of the demons went down with a crash that shook the floor, but she was already firing at the other one. He wheeled back but didn't go down. The sound he made wasn't even remotely human. She recentered again and her fingers were squeezing the trigger when Iskander dropped down into the doorway. She pulled away at the last second and her shot went into the ceiling.

Before she could even blink or come down from the terror of thinking she could have shot Iskander, the demon she'd shot first launched himself at her. She tumbled back, her spine hitting the wooden floor hard enough that she couldn't breathe. All she could think was that she had to get the gun back up. She had to fire again. Her left elbow smacked the floor and her entire arm went numb. The demon's mouth was open, but if it was making any noise, she couldn't hear it. She braced for the mageheld landing on her. But he didn't and she couldn't figure out why.

In the next instant, Iskander was in her field of vision. His lips peeled back from his teeth, and his eyes glowed an inhuman blue-flecked green. His hand blurred toward the demon's chest. A spray of red mist flash outward. The sharp scent of blood made her scuttle backward.

By then the other demon was up. From the floor, she aimed one-handed, squeezed, saw the muzzle flash again, and then a hole appeared in the left side of the demon's forehead. Iskander released the demon he held. The body fell to the floor and didn't move while at the same time, he grabbed the one she'd shot in the head. The demon's body quivered once and then again, even though he had to be dead. She leveled her P232 again, but Iskander had one hand up and his mouth was moving. She couldn't hear over the high-pitched ringing in her ears. She managed to lip-read the words *don't shoot him.*

He took a step toward her and made some sort of complicated motion with his hand. Scowling, he pressed his thumb to her forehead. Pressure built up in her head; then his eyes flashed a brilliant green and her ears popped. Just like that, she could hear.

The demon she'd shot in the head went from limp to quivering to alive in the space of about five seconds. Something clattered to the floor behind where Iskander stood with the demon—the misshapen bullet she'd fired into his brain. The demon's eyes opened, and while she watched, the hole in his head disappeared. Only the blood was left behind.

Iskander hauled the demon to his feet. "Call your witch and tell her to get her ass in here. If you don't, you're dead like your buddies. Come on," he said when the mageheld shook his head. "Choose to live another day. Call your witch. If you don't, I might take my time ripping out your heart."

Considering the reaction that got from the demon, the threat meant something.

She kept her P232 aimed at the demon's chest, but he shook himself once and nodded. She saw no reason to get off the floor. If the mageheld tried something, she had a better-than-decent shot from right where she was. The demon made the phone call. Two or three minutes later, the blond woman from the café walked up the front steps.

Iskander turned toward the shattered door, still holding the demon. "Paisley, make sure you're aiming at her."

"Got it."

He was back to his easygoing self. All smiles and friendly manner. It scared the bejesus out of her. "Nikodemus isn't going to like it when I tell him you sent magehelds after her."

"I was to have been safe, fiend." She put a hand to her chest and with the other pointed at Paisley. "She damaged me."

With a glance back at Paisley, Iskander said, "She still a screamer?"

"No."

The inside of Paisley's head froze solid. She took a breath and discovered there wasn't any air. The witch had figured out that she was resistant and was going for the simple solution of taking away the air around her.

"I want it back," the witch said. "All of it."

Iskander broke the mageheld's neck. The body dropped while he flowed forward until he had the witch by the throat. He squeezed. "Stop now or you're dead."

Paisley gasped, inhaling a shuddering lungful of air.

He released the witch to kneel over the dead mageheld. He'd left bloody fingerprints on the witch's neck. He did something with his hands that made the air around him shimmer. After a moment, he rose. "If it were up to me, I'd kill you right now and free every last mageheld you have left."

"You wouldn't dare."

"Try me. You have the magic you were born with." His voice went low and dark. "If you think I give a shit about you losing power you murdered my kind to get, you're smoking crack. You clear?"

The witch retreated. "Crystal."

"Good. Now, I'm not diplomatic like Nikodemus or Harsh, so you listen up. If you're not out of here in the next ten seconds, I'm going to take that as a threat and my girl will shoot you dead. There's thirty thousand acres of dairy around this house, and I know all the good spots to bury a body."

Paisley leveled the P232 at the witch. Now that the feeling had come back to her left arm, she could use a two-handed grip.

The witch blanched.

"Come near either one of us again," Iskander said, "and you're dead. That's not a threat. It's a fact."

The witch looked at the floor where the dead mage-helds lay and pointed at the one Iskander had just killed. "He has the car keys."

Iskander fished them out of the demon's pocket and tossed them to the witch. "Get the hell out."

The woman's mouth tensed, and she stared hard at Paisley. When she spoke, however, it was to Iskander. "You can't be trusted. None of you."

"Says the murdering bitch."

The witch turned and walked into the night.

"Cupcake," Iskander said into the silence. "You were fucking awesome."

About then, Paisley realized that Iskander's arms were red up to his elbows and he was covered in flecks of blood.

CHAPTER 17

A few minutes later, a motor turned over. Iskander listened until he was satisfied the witch was driving away. "Are the magehelds gone?" he asked.

"I don't feel anything."

He reached into his jeans pocket and pulled out Paisley's phone. He pressed the speed dial he'd entered so she could call Harsh. His fingers slipped on the case and left red splotches all over the keypad. "Damn."

He looked up and found Paisley, still on the floor, knees up and her gaze fixed on the phone. She held the P232 in one hand, muzzle pointing at the floor. At some point blood had dripped from his hands onto the floor between them in crimson splatters.

"Shower," Iskander said into the silence. Now that he looked, he saw he was covered in blood. A lot of it. The expression on Paisley's face, a combination of horror and, yeah, that was probably fear, reminded him she was human. For the most part, they got along so well, he just didn't think about that as something that separated them.

More like the opposite, really, given the affinity of male fiends for the human female. The mating instinct was there for him. "I need a shower."

"Yes," she said. She sounded normal. Maybe a little tired. "You do." She nodded in the direction of the damaged front door. "Do you think she's going to come back?"

"Nah."

"Good. Because I don't think we were ever going to be friends." She flicked down the P232's safety, then popped the magazine. The other two were still in her back pocket. She hadn't wasted a single shot unless he counted the one that went into the ceiling, which he didn't since otherwise she would have plugged him one.

He extended a hand and helped her up. Her fingers were icy against his, slippery from the blood now, too. She stood there, staring at the smears on her hand. Not good. Not good at all.

"This is what my life is like," he said. "This is what I do for Nikodemus all the time. He needs a monster like me. Ready to kill and fucking crazy—"

"You're not crazy." She looked up and her eyes were fierce.

"I'm good at it. The killing."

"You don't need to explain anything," she said. "I understand what you did and why you had to do it." She lifted her free hand like she was going to touch him, but then she didn't.

"You're a hell of a shot, Paisley."

She dropped her hand to her side. "Show me where you keep the guns and I'll try to clean up in here while you take a shower."

"Most of this will go away on its own."

"Then we'll see what's left after I've cleaned the gun."

He glanced at the bloody floor. A drop of crimson blood covered most of his big toe. "Right."

He showed her the cabinet where Harsh locked up the guns, then headed upstairs to the shower. He didn't bother with the lights. Paisley's magic echoed in the back of his head, and he didn't think he was wrong that his sense of her as a witch was stronger than it had been. He started the water, stripped down, got in, and started scrubbing.

He made his call to Harsh before he came downstairs, clean of the blood and dressed in some of the clothes he'd left behind. The leather tie he used for his hair was tucked into his front pocket. He found Paisley on the couch, watching television.

Over by the door, the floor was damp and now clean of the mess. He could still smell blood. Traces of magic lingered in the air, too. His. The witch's. Paisley's.

He sat down next to her and plunked his bare feet onto the coffee table. There was a strong aroma of chocolate in the air and underneath that the scent of the soap she'd used to wash her hands and face. "Anything good on?"

"The news." She handed over the remote. "Dessert's ready. Want some?"

"Sure."

She headed into the kitchen and came back with spoons and a tray with two containers of puffy chocolate things.

"That smells awesome. What is it?"

"Chocolate soufflé. Careful, the ramekins are still hot." When she put down the tray, he got a flash of her wrist. He grabbed her arm above her wrist.

"Let me have a look at that." The scar looked pinker

than he remembered. He brushed a finger across her skin. She hissed.

"Hurts?"

She bent over her lap with her head down. "Oh, sweet Jesus, yes, that hurts." She sat up and let her head fall back against the couch. "Give me a minute."

"How long has this been bothering you?" He made sure his fingers on her wrist didn't get anywhere near the scar. He didn't like this. Not at all.

"A couple of days." She turned her head sideways to look at him. "Lately I've been feeling like someone's trying to get inside my head. Like there's someone outside, pressing in, trying to break in. Is it Rasmus, do you think?"

"It's not something one of the magekind can do." He picked up the TV remote and turned off the sound. "I think it has something to do with that mark on your wrist. I don't know for sure if a mage can lay down a pathway that a fiend could use to indwell from a distance, but maybe that's what he's trying."

She studied him and leaned forward over the coffee table to pick up one of the spoons. "I keep forgetting you're not human."

"No," he said in a low voice. "I'm not."

Paisley stood up, opened her mouth to say something, and didn't. She sat again. "Mostly I feel you here." She touched her upper chest. But this"—she touched the side of her head—"it hurts. Like the inside of my head is about to go up in flames."

His heart kind of crumpled. "You're a resistant."

"Explain that to me so I know exactly what you mean."

"It means I had to really work to fix your hearing." He shifted on the couch so that he was facing her and explained what he knew and surmised about her resistance to magic and, more important, to an indwell, since that's what he suspected Rasmus was trying.

Her eyes went wide. "Possession like in *The Exorcist*?"

"That's an exaggeration." He touched her cheek and got a spark of arousal even though he hadn't been going for that. "You don't need to worry about me. It's against the rules for one of the kin to get into a human's head without permission. I won't do that to you. Not unless you say it's okay."

She picked up her soufflé and one of the spoons. She needed a break, something normal and familiar to her. He leaned forward, seduced by the smell of chocolate.

"Give me a taste of that?"

She held out the spoon. Instead of taking it, he ate the bite off the silverware. The taste spread over his tongue, rich with chocolate and smooth as silk. He closed his eyes for a minute. "Jesus, Paisley."

"More?"

"Oh, hell, yes." He took another bite from her and slumped onto the couch, eyes closed. He groaned. He wasn't faking it. He was in heaven.

"Better than sex, huh?"

He opened his eyes and looked at her with all the lust in his heart and soul and then some. "No. But it's a goddamned close second."

"I'm crushed." With a teasing smile, she held out another spoonful, and he sat up to take it from her.

He didn't sit back afterward. Instead, he swept her hair behind her shoulders and left his fingers at the side of her face. He enjoyed the hell out of the sizzle that went through him at the contact. She fed him another spoonful, then took a bite of the soufflé herself. He watched her lick her lips.

"Better than sex," she said.

"Cupcake, this is amazing." He slid closer to her. "Fantastic. But if you think it's better than sex, you're doing it wrong."

She lifted her head. "Prove it."

He put his arms around her and spent ten seconds contemplating what he wanted to do versus what he ought to do, and the good guy didn't win. "My pleasure."

He brushed her lips with his, and the anticipation just from that touch was like lightning. He pulled back enough to whisper, "Good?"

At first, she didn't move. Her eyes fluttered open and met his, and he held his breath. He prepared himself to be told no. Her eyes were soft when she looked at him, and so was her mouth, all soft and sweet. "You taste like chocolate," she said.

"You too," he said, and her smile made him feel strange. Like he'd do anything to make sure she always wanted to smile like that around him. He kissed her again. A real kiss this time. Softly at first and then not, and he still felt strange, because Paisley mattered to him in a way no one had since Fen.

They ended up stretched out on the couch with his body over hers, and while he was French-kissing her for all he was worth, he thought dirty thoughts about Paisley and sex, but he kept coming back to thinking up ways to make her want to stay with him.

CHAPTER 18

How long had it been since the last time she'd had sex? Too long. She hadn't slept with anyone since Urban, and that meant three years. Even she knew the sex had been bad in the last year of their relationship. Iskander kept kissing her, and Lord, he was good at kissing. All she could think was this was *Iskander* and he was beyond hot and he was kissing her right out of her mind.

To be fair, she was kissing him back. Her body had different ideas about what was good for her, and right now she felt very selfish. She arched up, one hand on his shoulder while she swept her tongue into his mouth, and he made this soft groan in the back of his throat, and she could feel his erection against her belly. His hand slid underneath her shirt, spreading out over her bare belly and slipping upward, and she wanted more, even though this was a terrible idea because she wasn't in any kind of control of herself.

She held his head between her hands, and she could swear her skin tingled where her flesh touched his tattoos.

His hair fell forward, and in the uncertain light she could see blue highlights, as if his hair was tattooed like his body. He drew back and she whimpered because she didn't want him to stop touching her. He put his fingers on the top button of her jeans and thumbed it open. He had one hand propped on the sofa just above her shoulder, and he was pulling down her zipper with the other. Was she going to let him do that? Just unzip her jeans like it was no big deal?

"This okay with you?"

"Yes."

"Good. Because there's things I want to do to you." He dropped his head and kissed the side of her throat. "Dirty things. Wicked things."

She grabbed his head and whispered in his ear, "You are a very dangerous man."

He laughed softly and slid his fingers down her belly. "As dangerous as they come." A shiver slid down her spine, and then the light just went away. She blinked. The room stayed dark.

"What did you just do?"

"Mmm." Iskander kissed her collarbone. "I took away the light."

"Why?"

"Because it's safer for you." He drew a circle on her stomach. "So. Can I keep touching you? Getting you hot?"

She threaded her fingers through his hair. The thing was, she wasn't so out of control she didn't know exactly what she was doing. She wanted to get laid, and she wanted Iskander to be the one she had sex with. "I will shoot you dead if you stop."

"Then I won't unless you tell me to."

"Good."

His hand slid around her to her shoulder blades, and without much effort, they ended up so that he was sitting with his back against an arm of the couch and she was facing him, straddling his lap, with her jeans gaping open. She gripped the back of the couch with one hand because it kept her oriented in the blackness. She could see only the barest shadow of him. He took her right wrist in his hand, which didn't hurt anywhere near as much as it had before, and traced a finger along her forearm. He was careful not to touch the scar.

A shiver followed in the wake of his finger moving along her arm. He reached for her blouse and started unbuttoning it from the bottom up. Her breath caught in her throat.

"Is it better than chocolate yet?"

"You'll have to try a little harder."

"Anything you want, cupcake. Want to maybe play a little? Here in the dark?"

She ached for him to touch her. She wanted his hands and his mouth on her and to listen to his breathing change, to hear that soft croon from low in his throat. The backs of his fingers brushed against her bare skin as he continued to push buttons through buttonholes, and for a while she thought she might just melt right here. She did want to play. A lot. He stopped unbuttoning her shirt and brushed his fingers along her bared skin. "Paisley? Tell me yes so I know you're okay with this."

"Don't make me get up and find that gun."

He laughed and undid another button. "After Fen," he said softly, "I found out I like having sex with humans." From the sounds and the way he shifted his body, she figured he'd just taken off his shirt. She reached out and discovered she was right. His skin was warm and smooth, and touching him made her long for more. He sucked in a breath when her fingers slid over his nipples. "You have a beautiful body, Paisley, and I want to see you naked and touch you all over and have dirty, kinky sex with you."

He shifted around again, unzipping his fly and taking off his jeans. She helped him with that. For a few seconds, when his clothes had been dumped on the floor and she was back to straddling his lap, she listened to the sound of them breathing. A chill slid down her back and sent her heart beating hard in her chest. He'd used magic—she'd learned enough to recognize that reaction—but she had no idea what he'd done with that magic.

"I'd love to have sex with you right now," he said in a rougher voice than she was used to hearing from him. "Like this."

"Like what?"

He whispered, "Not human."

She leaned over him, moving her hand forward to the arm of the couch near Iskander's head. The shape of his body had changed. He was larger; that was certain. She rested her palm on his chest, and his skin wasn't smooth the way it had been before. She slid her hand the length of his torso, over the ridged muscles of his chest. The texture of his skin was leathery but warm, so warm and supple. Her fingertips brushed over one of his nipples, and that elicited a soft inhale from him.

She bent closer. Her ponytail slid over her shoulder, and he pulled out the band that held back her hair. "I want to see you."

"Not a good idea." He pushed his fingers into her hair.

"Why not?"

"There's a rule about letting a human who isn't bound to secrecy see us when we're not human. Sometimes it happens by accident, but we're not supposed to let that happen. Not anymore."

Her heart stuttered but it wasn't in fear, exactly. "Weren't you always not human?"

He went back to unbuttoning her blouse. "I should clarify that, I guess. It's true—I'm not human. I am also not in my human form." His hands left her shirt as he stretched his body. "Want to break a few rules?"

"If I say yes, we wouldn't be breaking any rules, right?"

"True. So," he said after a heartbeat, "are you saying yes?" He went still while he waited for her to answer. He was serious about that, about needing an answer from her. "I won't do anything you don't say is okay."

She slid her hands over his face, finding the shape was different, his cheeks higher, more slanted. She stroked over his chest and down to his belly to his penis.

"It's dangerous this way," he said. "It's making me hot and not just because of where you have your hand."

"I don't feel like I'm in danger."

"You are. I can feel your magic, and it's working on me something fierce." He wrapped his fingers around her left wrist, stopping her from stroking his cock, except not really. His fingers tightened around hers, squeezing and then sliding up. Down. Slowly. "Listen to me, Paisley, there's more I need to tell you."

"Okay." She was more turned on than she'd ever been in her life, ready for whatever might happen.

"My kind don't reproduce with each other. Just with humans. And we're only fertile when we're like this."

"Not human, you mean?"

"Yeah. So I'm telling you now that if we do it when I'm like this, I can't come inside you. Condoms or birth control don't work well with us. I can't give you diseases because we don't get them." He touched her cheek with this free hand, and she shivered at the contact, at the faintest touch of what felt like a talon on her skin. "I want to have sex with you when I'm like this, but I won't tonight. I promise you that, all right? Because right now, we're playing. So you'll know at least something about me if it ever happens like that."

Her belly went a little loopy, and not in a bad way at all. He undid the last buttons of her shirt and pushed it off her shoulders. She drew one arm out of the sleeve and then the other, and he yanked and her shirt was gone. "Are you turned on?" he asked.

"Yes."

"Good. That's good. Me too." The cushions shifted when he sat up. He reached around to unfasten her bra. Oh, God, she just could not believe this was happening. She flashed back to Urban and the way she'd always felt so inadequate with him, and for half a second she was back to her old insecure, far-too-fragile self. As if he knew what she was thinking, he hesitated. "Okay?"

Her breath hitched, and her breasts felt heavy, and she was dying for him to touch her. What came out of her throat was a kind of choked, "Yes."

"Excellent." He pulled her bra away from her. He let out a low breath. "Paisley," he said in that same rough voice. "I swear if I was religious, I'd thank all the gods I can remember for giving me a life where I get to see you naked."

"I'm not naked."

"Not yet." He leaned forward and then his tongue flicked over her nipple. His mouth, hot and damp, closed over her, and his hand was warm as he cupped her breast, his fingers warm on the other one. Her body was committed to being aroused.

She buried her fingers in his hair while he suckled her. So soft, his hair was, like silk in her hands. After a bit, she tilted his head toward hers, and since she was still straddling him, she had to lower her head to kiss him. His mouth under hers didn't feel quite the way it should, but his lips parted and his tongue moved into her mouth, and she thought this kiss, so different from every other kiss she'd had in her life, was better than any of them. The heat was astonishing.

His hands curved around her rib cage, sliding over her, around to her back, sharp nails gliding down her spine, a light touch. She slid off him and as quickly as she could, she shucked her jeans and underwear.

"Thank you, Jesus." His voice was definitely rougher.

She went back to him, and he put his arms around her and kissed her shoulder. "I want you inside me," she said. "And I want to see you."

"Give me a minute."

She didn't, though. She kissed him, and he kissed her back, and one of his hands slipped between her legs, and she nearly came apart just from that. She threw back her head and moaned.

"We shouldn't do this," he said. "We should stop before it's too late."

"Bad idea."

"Stopping?" He laughed softly and circled his thumb

in the exact right spot. Coherent thought went flying right out of her head.

She bent down and kissed him, her mouth open, her tongue between his lips, touching his tongue, touching the sharp teeth, and when she lifted her hips, he moved, too, anticipating her, and then there was a moment of profound quiet. Neither of them moved.

"Yes?" he whispered.

"Oh, yes."

Then he was pushing inside her, and he slowed down for her because it had been too long since she'd been with anybody. Every nerve in her body seemed to be located between her legs.

And, God, this was just so good, stupefying. When he filled her, she arched her back, and he pressed in a little deeper and slid his hands around her waist and he was not human. She could see enough in the dimness to know he wasn't. Her breath hitched, hard and in time with the first tingle of orgasm. How could she do the right thing when she was about to come and she could tell it was going to be massively good? She looked up and saw the flicker of his eyes and the blue sheen of his skin, and their gazes locked.

His hands tightened around her, and for a while they just fucked. They didn't speak, and it felt beyond good. She ended up on her back again, and he gave her what she needed, which was this, to feel him moving inside her, to have him touch her and kiss her.

He supported his weight on his hands while she arched toward him, and then he pulled out of her and slowly drew his body downward, along hers, nipping at her legs, her thighs, and then between her legs, and he was wicked, so wicked. She screamed his name and called on God and came so hard she lost all sense of herself.

Then he raised himself the rest of the way up, and he was inside her again, thrusting, and she could feel muscles flexing beneath her hands. When he was close, he cursed under his breath and he froze, and then his body changed, and for some reason that made her shout again. She came again, and then he did, too.

Afterward, he held her close and kissed her and tangled his fingers in her hair and whispered, "Let's find a bed and do that again, Paisley."

CHAPTER 19

Paisley wanted to run but she didn't, even though the back of her head was cold and her chest hummed from a source deep in the center of her body. "He's here," she whispered.

Iskander had woken her from a sound sleep about an hour ago to tell her Nikodemus and Carson were on their way to the farmhouse. They'd showered and dressed, and she went downstairs to make a breakfast of eggs, dough-nuts, and muffins.

Both she and Iskander came to their feet at almost the same time, Iskander a bit sooner. From where she stood, she had a view of the hallway and most of the front door, with its boarded-over windows. Her pulse thumped in her ears.

Iskander opened the door and stepped aside, the first three fingers of his hand pressed to his bowed head. "Car-son." He repeated the gesture. "Warlord."

A petite woman with black hair walked in, a witch, judging from the way Paisley's head stayed so cold. Carson held hands with a tall man—a demon—whose sandy blond hair was a bit shaggy. A jade-green box about half the size of a brick was tucked under one arm. He held out a fist and Iskander bumped it with his.

After the men fist-bumped, Iskander bent to kiss the cheek Carson offered him. She had to be *the* Carson. The woman who had severed the bond between Iskander and Fen. Nikodemus's witch. She wasn't a screamer, thank God, and like Nikodemus, she didn't look very scary at first glance. Paisley liked her on sight.

Carson put out a hand and blocked the warlord's progress into the house before he and Iskander got out of the entryway. Paisley had the distinct impression Carson was the one controlling things right now. No one was going anywhere or doing anything until the witch said so.

The woman walked to the edge of the living room and scanned the room with a pair of brilliant green eyes. She paused at Paisley, who felt the merest whisper of something pressing in on her, but Carson did not acknowledge her in any way. The woman's attention moved on. She walked farther in while Nikodemus and Iskander waited by the door.

"I vouch for her, Carson," Iskander said, his voice raised. He propped one hand on the wall. "She's no danger to us."

Carson lifted a hand before she disappeared down the hall. She went upstairs next. Before much longer, she returned and addressed herself to Nikodemus and Iskander. "Clear."

Nikodemus strolled the rest of the way in. He wore

faded jeans and a red T-shirt that read *The Apocalypse was yesterday. Where were you?* His cowboy boots were scuffed, and he could use a haircut, but there was no denying he was a good-looking man.

Appearances were definitely deceiving. Nikodemus didn't look scary at all. Not until Paisley got a closer look at his eyes. They were a medium blue-gray, nothing special at first, but when his gaze meet hers, she felt like she'd been scoured clean. And that was with him smiling. He joined Carson, and the two linked hands again.

Iskander followed them into the living room. The demon warlord looked her up and down and at the end of his disquieting perusal of her, quirked his eyebrows. "Paisley Nichols," he said.

"Yes, sir."

"I've heard a lot about you."

Her mouth went dry. "Sir."

He walked toward her, letting go of Carson's hand to offer his hand to her. Carson came along, staying close. "Nikodemus," he said. "Nice to meet you." His shake was firm, his skin cooler than she expected. "This is Carson Phillips."

Paisley shot Iskander a look. His smile wasn't back yet, but he didn't warn her against touching the witch, so she clasped hands with Carson, too. Nothing happened to her. There wasn't any blast of energy, no pain, just a normal everyday handshake from a woman who looked too dainty to be dangerous. "Sir. Ma'am. Pleased to meet you both. Iskander's told me about you, of course."

"Please, call me Carson." She had a pretty smile, but it didn't make Paisley feel any safer. Her soft voice wasn't girly. "How are you?"

"Fine, thank you, and you?"

Like Nikodemus, Carson was wearing jeans, but the rest was less casual—a pink button-down blouse, diamond earrings, a matching bracelet, and a pair of bejeweled sandals. Her toenails were a frosty purple.

"Can I get you something to drink?" Paisley asked.

"Do you have coffee?" Carson asked.

"Yes, ma'am, I do. Regular or espresso?"

She gave Paisley a quick grin. "Espresso for us both, if you have it."

"I do. I'd be happy to make some for you. Iskander?" She kept her voice formal. "Coffee for you?"

He nodded, stretching his long body out on the sofa where, not so long ago, she'd been flat on her back and screaming Iskander's name. Better than chocolate. "The usual, cupcake."

Carson cocked her head and looked from Iskander to her. Great. Just great.

"I'll be just a minute, then." She wiped her sweaty palms on her jeans while she walked to the kitchen. She hoped to God there wasn't going to be trouble over him using that offhand endearment. She set herself to making espresso and setting up a plate with the muffins and doughnuts she'd made this morning, along with fresh butter and jam. She added the remaining soufflés.

Iskander came in while she was arranging the food and trying not to stress over all the horrible outcomes she kept imagining. He didn't say anything at first; he just stood close to her, one hand on the cabinet above him. Too close if they were just friends. Maybe not quite close enough for two people who'd been to bed together.

"It's not even seven in the morning." She snapped the

first serving of the ground espresso into place and flipped the START switch. Two hours of sleep. "Don't you people ever sleep?" she asked.

"No."

"Shit," she whispered. She didn't know anything. Not a darn thing about mages, witches, or demons, all of whom had, at some point, threatened her life. She rubbed the scar on her wrist.

"That bothering you again?" he asked in a low voice.

"Sometimes it itches."

"Now?"

"Yeah. A little."

He took her hand in his and rubbed his thumb over the scar. The streak of pain up her arm helped block the sensation of someone pressing on her head. "I know it's early for you, but Nikodemus needs to talk to us. He understands if you can't, but it would be better to get this done with."

"Fine." Her stomach hurt.

"I promise I'll get you to work on time."

"They can't fire me if I'm late. I'm the boss." She leaned against the counter while the espresso machine burbled. "Are you in trouble because of me?"

"I would be if you were dead." He snatched one of the doughnuts off the plate and ate it. "But you're not, so we're good."

"Am I in trouble because of what happened with the witch? Or because of Rasmus?"

"No." He leaned in and picked up the plate that held a haphazard jumble of food. "How about we distract them with this?"

"You can't serve them food like that. We need plates, Iskander. Napkins. Silverware, too."

"The food looks great. Nikodemus loves doughnuts almost as much as I do. You deal with the coffee. I'll take this and come back for the rest, all right?"

He'd been naked with her, inside her. Both of them desperate for each other. He'd made her come apart in his arms, and she would have done anything he asked. Anything at all.

Iskander didn't come back for the other things, so she stacked plates, napkins, and silverware on a tray with the coffee, cream, and sugar. When she came in, Nikodemus and Carson were on the couch, the demon with his arm around the witch's waist.

Serious inroads had been made in the plate of food, and the table was covered with crumbs. The soufflés were gone and so were the doughnuts. There was one muffin left. She put down the tray and handed out coffee, plates, and the like. Iskander scooted over on a love seat. When everyone had their coffee, she used one of the napkins to brush up crumbs.

"Not necessary," Iskander said. He put a hand on her shoulder and pulled her onto the love seat with him. "Your coffee's going to get cold." He stretched for her demitasse and handed it to her. "Relax," he said in a low voice. "Everything's cool. I promise you." He stretched an arm across the top of the love seat. His fingertips just brushed her shoulder.

Nikodemus added several sugars to his espresso. The green box he'd been holding was on the coffee table, and from here, it looked to her like it was real jade. Powdered sugar dotted the lid. Her reaction to them wasn't settling down the way she'd hoped, and it was disconcerting to say the least. This close, she couldn't imagine why anyone would ever think Nikodemus wasn't dangerous.

"So, Paisley—can I call you that?"

She nodded.

"Iskander says you own a bakery."

She had the feeling Nikodemus knew all about her, but she answered just the same. "Yes, sir, I do. It's downtown. Paisley Bakery and Café. We've been open about two years now."

The warlord fell silent, looking between Iskander and Paisley. He frowned, and it sent a chill through her to see that speculative look. "What I heard, Iskander," he said, "was that she was vanilla. What happened to change that?"

Iskander's fingers brushed the back of her neck. He told Nikodemus about Rasmus touching her and about the reaction she'd had that she barely remembered. She stretched out her arm to show them the scar.

"Well, shit." There wasn't any question he knew what he was looking at. Nikodemus's eyes speared her. "Where were you when that happened?"

"My bakery."

"Huh," Nikodemus said. "That's interesting. And it was Rasmus Kessler who did that to you?"

"Yes, sir."

"You can call me Nikodemus." His mouth curved up. "*Warlord*, if you feel the need to be formal."

"Yes, sir."

He picked up the last muffin. "This is really good. Where's your bakery again?"

"Kearney, near Clay Street, sir." She wished he'd get to the point instead of making all this small talk.

"The food was delicious," Carson said.

"Thank you, ma'am." She heard her accent coming on strong and closed her mouth.

With a glance at Nikodemus, Carson said, "We should go there, right, sweetie?"

"Sure." His attention swung back to her, and the tension ratcheted up. "Tell me about the screaming Iskander says you hear."

While she talked, Nikodemus finished his espresso. She described touching the witch and the way she'd just known how to make the screaming stop. When she finished, he put a finger on the jade box and pushed it toward her. "Do you think you could do that again?"

Paisley stared at the box. "I don't know."

"Would you try?" He rested his palm on the box and watched her. "Please?"

"How? There aren't any screamers here." She met Nikodemus's gaze. "And why? If I'm allowed to ask that question..."

"Because if you can do that again, I need your help." He tapped the box. His nails were on the long side for a man. Nothing outlandish. But was that a suggestion of a talon? "We need your help."

She noticed the dragon carved into the box. Stylized curls of smoke wisped from its mouth and nostrils. "Is it true? About the screaming I hear?"

Carson leaned forward. "It's true that some of the magekind murder the kin for their magic. I've seen it done. Personally. You have my word it's true."

"But are they really trapped like that? Alive?" She could hear the screaming in her head again, an echo of the real thing that tore at her soul. "They sound like they're in agony."

"They are," Nikodemus said.

Iskander was leaning against the love seat, quiet, no

sign of a smile. She knew, absolutely knew, what they were telling her was true.

Carson slipped her hand into Nikodemus's, and he squeezed her fingers. "Iskander says when you released that magic from the witch, he sent it safely home. Because of you, they are at peace. If you can do that for others, Paisley, we would be beyond grateful to you."

"Maybe I can't do it again."

Nikodemus met her gaze. "What if you can?"

She nodded. Iskander's fingers brushed over the nape of her neck again.

Nikodemus reached out with long, slender fingers and tapped the top of the jade box. "There's a talisman inside here," the warlord said. "One of the magekind killed a fiend—one of us—and trapped his magic in the carving inside. They used to do that before they learned how to take magic directly into them. The magekind still use them to augment their power." He picked up the box. "The fiend whose physical body died is trapped inside the talisman, going slowly insane."

"It can't die, can it?"

"No."

She stared at the box. "Oh, God."

"There's a risk to you," Nikodemus said. "It's possible what's in the talisman might tangle up with you. If that happens, you might not survive. When you went after the witch, you were damned lucky Iskander was there to prevent something like that from happening."

"Sweet Jesus," she whispered. She met Iskander's gaze. He winked at her.

Nikodemus tapped the top of the box again. "This talisman is stable, so everything should go just fine." The warlord's eyes flickered, and her chest hummed. "If you agree to try this, you have my word, Paisley Nichols, that I will do everything in my power to make sure no harm comes to you."

She nodded. "I'll try."

Nikodemus took the lid off the box, and she shuddered because the screaming started up immediately. Nestled inside was a gargoyle carved from a luminous white stone. The screaming in her head was a single voice, fainter than what she got from the magekind, but no less tortured.

Iskander stroked her shoulder and the back of her neck. She was glad for the contact. Whoever had carved the stone had talent. The details were startlingly lifelike. It wasn't hard to imagine that the stone creature might move of its own accord. There were signs of wear, too. The edges of the monster's folded wings had been rubbed smooth.

The wails of torment reverberated in her head, and when she picked up the carved stone, it was like having a firebomb go off in her skull. This wasn't the same thing as with the witch. The resistance was different. This was stone, not human flesh, for one thing. The center of her chest flexed as she closed her fingers around the carving and reached, if not physically, then metaphysically, for that soul-shivering sound and... nothing. She tried again. A tingle zipped along her arm, from her fingers to her shoulder. She reached the way she had with the witch, and this time she made contact.

It was as if the stone was no longer a barrier. The energy of what was inside clung to her fingers, and when she drew away her hand, the pulsing sensation came with her. Her heart beat once. The screaming stopped. Her heart beat again. Her hand burned and she fought to keep her stomach from turning inside out.

She was aware that Nikodemus, Iskander, and Carson were on their feet. The warlord was saying something, but whatever she'd done must have scrambled her brains because the words made no sense to her. The burning stopped, and as her brain settled down, she found herself staring at her balled fist.

She forced her fingers open. The talisman had disintegrated. Translucent sand spilled off her palm and trickled between her fingers onto the floor. She was horrified at the realization that instead of releasing the trapped life, she'd destroyed it. "I'm sorry," she said. "So sorry."

Iskander hunkered down beside her, and she lifted her eyes to his. "Hey, cupcake," he said. He pressed his palm to the side of her face, so warm. Such warm skin and, oh, God, she was lost in his eyes. Lost. He brushed the rest of the sand off her hand. "You did good."

"It's gone."

"Yeah." Iskander's smile was incandescent. "It worked, Paisley. You did it."

Nikodemus's eyes were on her, wide and a peculiar blackish gray. While she watched, still shaky inside, he went down on one knee, head bowed, with three fingers pressed to his forehead. She looked at Carson and Iskander, but Carson was watching Nikodemus. Iskander, too, had his head bowed, fingers pressed to his forehead.

The warlord lifted his head. His gaze made her feel like he was looking through her. "I won't ask you to give up your business," he said. "You have a life and you're entitled to that, but if you help us, there isn't much I wouldn't do for you." She opened her mouth to speak, but he held up a hand. "When the word gets out about you, and it's probably already started, some of the magekind will come after you. I'll make it clear you're under my protection. Even if you say no, from now on, if you ever need anything, anything at all, just ask." He made a peculiarly graceful motion with one hand. "My word on that."

Her head was still spinning, and it was sheer habit that made her say, "Thank you, sir."

"If you agree," he went on, "any of my sworn fiends will work with you. Whatever you need. Whatever it takes. We'll do what is necessary for you to bring them home."

Iskander took a step forward. "Warlord—"

"Settle down," Nikodemus said. "I'm getting to that." He returned his attention to Paisley. "Iskander has my full authority to call on whatever resources he needs to protect you. Make no mistake, he'll die to keep you alive. Any questions, Ms. Nichols?"

"No, sir."

The warlord smiled. "Then there's only one more thing we need to take care of in order to make it official."

CHAPTER 20

Iskander took his seat. Paisley looked determined, but that didn't mean she understood how her life was going to change if she went through with this. She'd be on the inside of the life he lived instead of outside of it. Not that he was thinking long-term about Paisley, except maybe he was. She already knew more than she was supposed to about the kin. More important, he'd now twice seen her free kin whose lives had been trapped by the magekind. Twice.

"What I need from you," Nikodemus told Paisley, "is an oath of fealty. It's not a normal promise. I'm talking about one that's magically binding on us both. There are consequences if I don't keep up my side of the oath, just like there are consequences if you don't keep up your side." He explained a warlord's duty to protect and deal fairly with those sworn to him and that she'd be required to support him and do nothing to harm his interests.

Paisley would be safer if she was sworn to Nikodemus. If something happened to him, she'd be taken care of.

"Make sense?" Nikodemus said to her.

She said, "Sure."

"Good. That's really good. Fuck me over—pardon my French—and your broken oath to me could end up seriously damaging you. I can't promise you'd recover if that happens. On the other hand, if I screw you over, the oath breaks and you're free of me and any consequences." He waited so she could think things over, then said, "Questions?"

Paisley looked at Iskander. This had to be her decision. "You're sworn to him?" she asked.

"Yes," Iskander said. "You don't have to do this, if you don't want to."

"I've heard the screaming." She turned back to the warlord. "All right."

"I need you to say you agree."

"I agree."

The blood exchange that cemented the oath was over quickly. As soon as it settled into place, Iskander's tension eased. He hadn't realized until now how much he wanted this result. Paisley was safe now. She had him and Nikodemus on her side. He put an arm around her waist and kissed the top of her head. "You're one of the cool kids now," he said.

She laughed, and that made Nikodemus and Carson relax, too. She grabbed Iskander's hand, her fingers tightening around his, and he squeezed back.

"Late last night," Nikodemus said, "Carson got an interesting call. Sweetheart, you want to tell them about it?" He winked at Paisley. "Better if she tells this part."

Carson sat straighter. "Rasmus Kessler called the number we give out so that other kin can contact us for help or let us know they want to swear fealty to Nikodemus."

"That number's everywhere," Iskander said. No more

worrying about what was okay to say in front of her or how much to tell her. Paisley was one of them now. "We pass it out like candy."

"Not the issue," Carson said. "The issue is that he called at all. Even more important, he was barely coherent. I've met Rasmus, and I almost didn't recognize his voice. The call didn't last long. Probably not even thirty seconds. About the only thing I understood was he was begging for help. We got cut off in the middle."

Nikodemus, who was now sitting down with Carson beside him, leaned forward. Paisley's oath to him was a weight inside her that was still settling into place. "What kind of help would a mage like Rasmus Kessler need? That's what I keep thinking. Not that long ago, he was after Durian's hide. Trust me," he said, with a look at Paisley, "you do not want to end up on Durian's bad side."

"I think I've heard something about that."

"An even shorter time ago, he was looking to take over Christophe's affairs—that's a mage no longer among us, Paisley—and was about ten inches from doing it, too. Now he can barely string two words together? What the hell kind of game is he playing now? That's what I'm wondering."

The room fell silent enough for them to hear the wind through the trees outside.

Nikodemus stared straight at the two of them. "See," he said, smiling that deceptive smile of his, "this is the part where if you know something, you have to share. Because it's in my interest to know what the fuck is going on."

The words had extra weight because they carried more meaning than mere words. Iskander didn't want to speak for Paisley, though he would if necessary.

"Jesus, Iskander," Nikodemus said. "Help me out here.

I don't necessarily expect the new girl to have a clue yet, but I know you do."

"Rasmus has been harassing Paisley. Stalking her."

He rolled his eyes. "I know that part."

"I think he's sending magehelds to indwell." He shrugged. "It hasn't worked so far."

"Our girl's a resistant." He couldn't have looked prouder if it were his own kid with that kind of ability. "'Course it isn't working."

"He also sent Fen to talk me into leaving."

"Shit." Nikodemus kicked out his long legs and threw one arm around Carson's shoulder. "How'd that go?"

"He said no," Paisley told him.

Iskander stood, hands on his hips, knowing all this was new to Paisley, the sensations that went with being sworn to a warlord like Nikodemus. "I'm done with Fen."

The warlord lifted both hands in a gesture of surrender, but his eyes were hard. "Just trying to find out what's happening."

"What's happening is Rasmus thinks I'm the weak link." It really, really pissed him off, too. "Someone needs to let him know he's wrong." He waited for Nikodemus to say something, and when he didn't, Iskander said, "The question I have is whether you're going to let me do that."

Nikodemus sat straight up, and Carson put a hand on his forearm. A warning? A reminder to restrain his temper? "Rasmus Kessler is not a legitimate target for sanction."

"It is if he's coming after Paisley."

Carson tapped her fingers on her knee. "As a political matter, Iskander, if Kessler dies, the magekind, and probably a few of the other warlords, will take that as proof that Nikodemus cannot be trusted."

"They think that anyway."

"Granted. But if one of us were to kill or injure Rasmus, they'd have proof." Carson sighed. "And they would be right, Iskander. Nikodemus has given his word."

"So we just hang Paisley out to dry. Is that what you're saying?"

"No," Carson said. "I promise you, killing Rasmus is a risk we're willing to take *if* Paisley is directly threatened at the time."

"In other words," Nikodemus said, "there's no being proactive about our issues with Rasmus."

"Fuck politics." Pain lanced through Iskander's chest because he was stressing his oath. Again.

Nikodemus wrapped one hand around his fist and bowed his head to his hands. Iskander's pain eased up. The warlord drew in a long breath, then let it out before he looked up. At Paisley. Not him. "Like I told Iskander here, you don't freelance. In my territory, you don't do your thing to anyone without my say-so, and you don't do it unless one of mine is there to back you up. Clear?"

"Yes, sir."

"You saw what Paisley can do," Iskander said. "And you're not going to use her whenever you can?"

Nikodemus stretched an arm along the top of the sofa. "I will take full advantage of her unique abilities when I've had a chance to minimize the backlash. If I use her now, the magekind will see it as a declaration of war. They might already. That said, if Kessler goes after you again, Paisley, and Iskander or someone else is there to make sure you don't get caught up in the blowback, you have my permission to defend yourself. That includes doing that thing you do."

"Yes, sir."

"Defense. Not offense. Not until I'm ready to manage the consequences." He stood. "Iskander. I need a word with you in private."

"Outside?"

"Sure."

They went out the back and stood in the open area between the house and barn. He expected Nikodemus to rip him a new one, but that wasn't where he started.

"You did good with the witch," Nikodemus said. "It's good you didn't kill her. I appreciate that."

He nodded. The sun was barely above the top of the barn, and the air was crisp and clean. They stayed quiet for a while, letting things settle between them.

"I take it I'm not going to lose you to Fen."

"Hell, no."

"That's good to know, because, between you and me, you're strong enough to survive breaking your oath."

Iskander gave a curt nod of acknowledgment.

"What about Paisley?" Nikodemus said.

"What about her?"

"Paisley Nichols is a decent woman," Nikodemus said. "It's easy to tell that about her. I like her. More important, Carson likes her."

"You have no say about who I get involved with." They stood there in the quiet some more. Nothing but birds and, farther off, a cow mooing.

"Are you involved?"

He nodded again.

"Are you thinking about binding her over?" He meant a permanent bond with her.

"Not yet."

"What she can do," Nikodemus said, "that's important to us."

"I know." He crossed his arms over his chest.

"But I still can't tell you it's okay to take out Kessler."

Iskander gave a vicious smile. "I'll kill him before I let anything happen to her."

Nikodemus let out a breath. "If it comes to that, I'll do the damage control."

Meaning if Iskander ended up killing Kessler, Nikodemus would try to sever his fealty oath to ease the consequences of breaking a direct order from his warlord. "Thanks."

Nikodemus gave him a quick grin. "Like you said, fuck politics."

"I'm fine with that."

CHAPTER 21

Paisley walked up the hill behind Iskander, on their way back to the truck after delivering a very large wedding cake. The pickup was halfway up the hill because there wasn't any parking near the house. Workmen blocked the driveway, unloading folding tables, chairs, and crates of dishes and flatware for the wedding of a cousin of a friend of a friend of hers. The couple had paid obscenely good money for the made-to-order cake. Good enough money for a personal delivery to the private home where the reception was to be held. With Iskander's help, the delivery was done, the cake safely in the house, assembled, frosted, and decorated, and now they were heading home.

They kept walking. Twenty or so years ago, this street had probably been rural. Now, any open fields there might once have been were filled with large houses on large lots. Mature firs lined the street on both sides so that even on a hot afternoon, there was a cooling shade. There wasn't any sidewalk, just a swath of pine-needle-covered soil between the trees, the ditch, and the road.

Things were a little awkward between her and Iskander, and she wasn't sure why other than plain bad timing. There hadn't been time to talk after they got home from the farmhouse, because she had to go directly to work, and when he picked her up later, she'd fallen asleep in the truck. She hadn't woken up until her alarm went off for the morning shift. In her own room. Alone. After her shift, she'd had the wedding cake to start on and Iskander was off doing something for Nikodemus and then too much time had passed.

Halfway to the pickup, the back of her head got cold, and she slowed down. Iskander kept walking. She was still adjusting to the nuances of her oath to the warlord. Now that everything was in the open, Iskander's otherness seemed even more intense. She was still coming to terms with a world where there really were demons and mages, and they were balanced at the brink of war.

The word from Nikodemus was that the mages were now officially aware of what she could do and had been informed that she worked for Nikodemus. As she understood it, that made her off-limits for retaliation. The warlord had given the magekind thirty days to either give up the magic they'd acquired through the murder of one of the kin or leave his territory. Starting on day thirty-one, magekind in his territory had no cause for complaint if his new girl took back what they'd stolen. This announcement had not been met with universal approval by the magekind. Iskander had been busy for Nikodemus. She didn't think that was a coincidence.

Her head stayed cold. Out of habit, she scanned for Rasmus, even though Nikodemus had warned her there would be magekind besides Rasmus looking to remove the threat she represented. About twenty yards away, she saw a familiar car parked on the pine-needle-covered ground on the opposite side of the street from Iskander's truck. She stopped walking.

The Mercedes was pointed downhill, the wrong way for that side of the street. While she stared, the rear passenger door opened and Rasmus got out. Two more men got out on the other side. She reacted to them as soon as they got out. Iskander stopped walking and looked at her. He smiled. "Company," he said.

"What do we do?"

"Nothing." He shoved his hands in his pockets. "Yet."

They started walking again, closer together now. About twenty feet from the pickup, she stopped walking again, because she was getting more chills.

"What?" he said.

She tipped her chin down the hill. Two men— magehelds, she knew now, were at the bottom of the incline, walking at a good pace. Two more men got out of Rasmus's car and stared at Iskander like he had a target painted on his forehead.

"Here." Iskander took his keys from his pocket and tossed them at her. "Get in the truck." He was smiling like he was about to see his favorite band. Live. For free. "If something happens to me, you get the hell out. Don't go home. Call for help and drive directly to Harsh's place. You know where that is, right?"

She shook her head, and he gave her an address in the heart of Pacific Heights.

By then the two men were running up the hill. In their suits. In the heat. Moving faster than any normal human. Heart banging away in her chest, she did as Iskander asked. She didn't make it.

Rasmus moved to intercept her. Screams reverberated in her head, deafening her, searing the inside of her head until she could barely think, and her stomach turned. He walked toward her, smiling as if they were old friends. This time, she felt him drawing on his magic. The sensation was a pressure between her ears. His lips moved, but if he was speaking out loud, the screams in her head kept her from hearing the words. More than anything, she wanted to see Rasmus brought to his knees.

She stood her ground. The closer he came, the louder the screaming in her head got. Rasmus, not expecting her to move toward him, collided with her. Off balance, she reached for the nexus that was the source of the screams. He caught her by the shoulder, and his fingers seared through her shirt. It was like sticking her finger in a light socket.

He threw his arms around her, preventing her from making the contact that would let her take back the magic that screamed into her head. He dragged her toward his car.

Paisley kicked and bucked, half mad from the screaming in her head and the painful burning wherever he touched her. Somehow she managed to trip them up, and they both crashed to the street. His arms popped free of her and she rolled away. When she realized he was momentarily dazed, she sprinted for the truck.

Rasmus lurched to his feet. He was fast. Hellishly fast. At the truck, there wasn't time to mess with the keys. She pounded on the driver's side door, and with a *thunk*, the window fell down. She threw herself inside, her skin burning where he'd touched her. Her shoulder slammed into the gearshift. By the time she had herself upright, Rasmus was almost to the pickup. His mouth twisted as he ran, a hand pointing at her. The air around him shimmered. Farther down the road, Iskander was straightening from two bodies. She saw him look in her direction. Rasmus hadn't come unprepared. Six more magehelds raced toward them from the top of the hill.

She shoved the key into the ignition, turned it, and put the truck in gear, all the while sitting on the edge of the seat in order to reach the pedals, because Iskander was quite a bit taller than she was. Which meant she had an unimpeded view of Rasmus and Iskander.

Iskander ran for the truck. The six magehelds flashed past her, converging on him. They were big. Too big for him to handle alone. His name tore from her throat. The truck shuddered, and she yanked hard on the steering wheel and let the truck roll into the street. Two of the magehelds caught up with him. Or maybe he caught up to the fastest of the six.

She hit the gas and aimed the truck for Rasmus. He stood motionless. Their eyes connected, hers and Rasmus's. The bastard didn't believe she'd actually run him over, because he didn't get out of the way until it was almost too late. She braced herself for the impact. The side of the truck hit him and spun him away. She kept going.

Four magehelds and Iskander, and she wasn't going to get there in time. At what looked like the last second, Iskander whirled, stepped to the side, and slammed one of the four in the forehead with the heel of his palm. He got the second one with a strike to the back of the head. They both went down and didn't move. He shouted her name and sprinted toward her.

The remaining two caught up with him. She saw the blur of his hands and an arc of red mist and the first one went down. Then the other one. Iskander veered off for Rasmus, who was only now standing up. Without a doubt, Iskander intended to kill the mage and a part of her wished he would. But the thirty days weren't up, Rasmus's mage-helds were dead, and he was so unsteady right now, she didn't think either of them was danger anymore. She knew Nikodemus was serious about the consequences for her and Iskander if Rasmus died like this.

Paisley turned the truck toward Iskander and jammed on the brakes. The truck shuddered to a stop. She leaned out the window and shouted as loud as she could. "Iskander, no!"

He turned and she locked eyes with him.

"Get in." She threw the truck into park and practically kicked the door open before she slid over. In five strides, Iskander was there. He wasn't even breathing hard. He slid in, took a look in the rearview mirror, and put the truck back into gear. She twisted to look.

Rasmus stood in the middle of the street with his mouth open in an angry snarl, blood pouring from a gash on the side of his head. Even from here, Paisley could tell his eyes were jittering.

She stuck out a hand and braced herself against the dash as Iskander gunned the pickup down the hill. He took the first corner and they fishtailed hard. He slowed, took a few more turns, and ended up on a shaded residential street. He parked underneath a tree. "Are you all right?"

"Of course." A lie, but Iskander didn't need to know that. She wasn't all right. Not even close. She hurt wherever Rasmus had touched her, and her head felt like someone had set her brain on fire.

"Let's see your arm." Blisters covered her arm wherever Rasmus's fingers had come into direct contact with her skin. He pushed up her sleeve. There were red welts everywhere. "Where else did he touch you?"

"Shoulders. I don't know. It was hard to keep track."

"Shit, Paisley." He yanked at the shoulder of her shirt.

"Ouch." She sucked in a breath when he touched her shoulder.

"Not as bad as the marks on your arm. You're already healing."

"I tried to take back his magic." Now that she wasn't running for her life, she was feeling sick and shaky.

"You shouldn't have."

"Like you should talk." Inside, she was a void. Empty. His eyebrows drew together, and he touched her forehead. He didn't use any magic, but the contact rocked her all the same.

"Good trick with the truck."

She could still hear and feel the thud of the truck hitting Rasmus. Maybe later she'd worry about not caring that she'd wanted him to die. "I wish I'd killed him," she said.

He cupped her head between his hands. "You were amazing back there."

She put her hands around his wrists, figuring she'd disengage from their embrace in a minute. Her stomach went all loopy from remembering what he was like in bed. *Better than chocolate.* Her mind turned to mush when he lowered his head.

God, it was a mind-blowing kiss. Slow and tender but wild around the edges. Then he had his tongue in her mouth and she was doing the same right back, and she had a hard time thinking at all, even once she realized his hand was underneath her shirt and halfway up her back and that her bra was unfastened.

She watched his eyes get dark, and he moved his hand, and she didn't budge; then his hand was cupping her breast and her mind just slipped away entirely, and she didn't even care. He unfastened his seat belt and leaned down, and his mouth opened over hers, and it was hard to think much at all because his fingers were on her bare breast and it felt good, so good. She returned the kiss—with all the heat racing through her, how could she not? Iskander was lovely and she liked him more than was safe. Besides, he made her laugh, and he was never mean about anything. Oh, Lord, could they do it in the truck?

His other hand got underneath her shirt, too, and he pushed her down onto the seat, or maybe she lay down and he just followed; it didn't matter to her which it was. Her belly exploded into shivers when he pushed up her shirt, and his mouth was on her breast, on her nipple, and his other hand was just as gloriously busy. She wound her fingers into his hair and kissed him hard. She got her hands busy, too. He was warm and his body was so amazingly male, all that delicious bare skin right next to hers. She wanted more. Much, much more.

They were both breathing like racers at the finish line when he pulled back, and his eyes were doing that flickering thing again. "Hell," he said on a whisper. He pulled her shirt down.

"No." She grabbed his arm and squeezed. "Don't you leave me like this."

"Paisley, I am absolutely not going to do you in the

truck where anyone could come out of their house and see my naked ass."

She closed her eyes. He was right. Of course.

"Because I do not want to explain to Harsh why he has to bail us out of jail and then stand in front of Nikodemus and explain the same damn thing."

She wriggled around and got her bra fastened, and he reached over and pulled down her shirt again. They got their seat belts on, and then he stretched an arm along the back of the truck's seat, almost but not quite touching her. "Later," he said, and he sounded determined. "We'll pick up where we left off later."

CHAPTER 22

About 11:30 P.M., Rasmus Kessler's house on Wildcat Canyon Road, the Berkeley Hills

Rasmus Kessler sat in his office, a room that over-looked Wildcat Canyon Road and acres of open space. There wasn't much traffic at this time of night. Through the open window, he could hear owls and the ever-present dull roar of distant traffic from down the hillside where there was never any quiet. For these few minutes, he had his sanity, and he could pretend his life belonged to him. His body was sore and he had a bruise on the side of his head. Most nonmagical wounds healed quickly. The cut on his head and the surrounding bruise remained tender enough that he wondered how he'd gotten it.

Footsteps echoed on the steps that led to his refuge. His heart thumped. Maybe she would turn right at the top of the stairs instead of left, and yet, at the same time, Rasmus hoped she would come to him and that things would be as they had before. Like him, she had her moments of sanity.

At this moment, he was lucid, and that was a rare mercy. He knew he didn't have much time to enjoy his solitude. Fen had roused herself from her sulk over the debacle of her confrontation with Iskander, and if he was lucky, she would fail to recall that he had advised her against contacting him in any fashion just yet—for more reasons than just the plain fact that few men cared to have their current lovers thinking of past ones.

"Rasmus!"

Her voice carried up the stairs. He knew from the light tone that she was at least marginally in control of herself and that, thank God, he had a moment or two longer of solitude before he had to deal with whatever she was right now.

Before him on the desk sat a black notebook. It was his habit at such times to make quick notes of whatever snatches of memory remained to him. He closed the notebook, the pages of which were filled with Danish. His native language was not one that Fen had troubled herself to learn to read. He slid it underneath the desk, back into the corner where even the housekeeper wouldn't find it.

His right hand still didn't work correctly, not since the day his daughter Alexandrine Marit had managed to injure him. Badly. That should never have happened. She was magekind, yes, but with so little power as to make her insignificant. Since that day, his slow recovery from the damage had forced him to write left-handed.

Once, he had loved Fen so deeply he would have done anything for her. Anything. Even offer his life to her. He'd done so, and she had accepted. There had been a time when he wanted nothing more than to see Alexandrine dead along with every fiend who'd ever helped her. Tonight, all he had left were memories of the woman he'd loved. Tonight, he knew that if he was to survive this, he might need to beg for his life. An unlikely outcome.

"Here," he called, because if he did not, Fen might misinterpret the reason for his failure to respond. They both knew she could find him no matter where he was, but that wasn't the point. He used the toe of his shoe to make sure the notebook was out of sight. He'd been speaking English for three hundred years, the last fifty here in America. It was his hope that if somehow Fen happened across the journal, she would not recognize the language as something relevant to the present. His entries were, of course, undated. They might have been written anytime during the last seventy or so years.

Fen made it to the top of the stairs. She had yet to traverse the length of the hallway to reach his office. A few moments more, then.

On this night, when he had awakened, sore and stiff, to find himself in rare possession of his wits, he'd slipped out of bed and come here to write what he could recall of the events since the last time he'd been in his right mind. His memories were ragged and incomplete, but when he'd finished writing what he could call to mind, he had, as usual, scanned back through the entries, looking for patterns, anything that would help him guess what was going on during his blackouts. Anything that would help him save his life. Or Fen's, if such a thing were possible.

The pages held names he recognized. Harsh was one; translated literally from English to Danish. Harsh Marit had been Fen's gift to him, or so he had thought. Rasmus now believed Harsh had been Fen's first attempt to stabilize her deterioration by bringing in someone from her old life. The decay in her mind had likely begun before he ever encountered her. Her deterioration had accelerated the moment she'd betrayed Iskander for him and found herself cut off from her blood-twin.

The knowledge that Harsh had regained his freedom remained clear in his memories, since those events predated the point at which his recollections became fractured or missing altogether.

He'd translated *Iskander* as the Danish equivalent of Alexander. Oh, he recognized that name. Like Fen and unlike Harsh, Iskander was a full demon. He was a former lover to Fen, bonded to her, in fact. *Blood-twin* Fen called it. Had been bonded. But no longer.

There was a time when Rasmus had been as in love with Fen as Iskander must once have been in love with his blood-twin. Desperately in love. Without subterfuge or reservation. Without coercion. Fen was beautiful and carefree and breathtaking in bed. When she had still been in possession of her sanity, she had been the delight of his life. Despite what she was. Despite what he was.

He would willingly have died for her. To have watched her descent into madness and now to bear witness to the wreckage she had become...that was agony, a kind of living death.

She was walking down the hallway now, her steps light, and he could no longer pretend that she would ever be all right. The damage to her was not something she could recover from. Not now. She was humming to herself, some melody without any real tune. Rasmus had learned the humming was a precursor to a cycle of madness, each worse than the one before. Each more heartbreaking than the last. And with each, his loss of memory extended from hours, then days, and now, sometimes, weeks as he learned from the calendar on his phone.

Rasmus turned on his chair so that he faced the door. The ruby beads worked into his braids clicked softly. He needed the power that could be drawn from the gems. He suspected that during his blackouts, Fen was entirely in control. She allowed him to keep the gems because the additional focus the rubies gave him helped when she controlled his power.

She was here.

After all this time, after all that had happened to them and between them and no matter how much he hated her now, his pulse still raced when he saw her. She was mad and dangerous and as beautiful as ever. Every time he saw her, he remembered the days when he had loved her beyond anything. He still did.

She carried a tray on which sat a French press, two cups, and two plates, each with a brioche. "Good morning."

"Fen." He knew better than to tell her it wasn't morning. He'd left their bed and come here. For her, that meant morning. He cleared a place on the desk for her tray. "You've brought us breakfast." He watched her face as he took the tray from her and set it down. Her blue eyes were normal right now. A smile curved her mouth and even reflected in her gaze. His heart turned over in his chest to think she was, if only momentarily, in possession of some corner of the sanity left to her.

It wouldn't last. The word *mercurial* could have been defined with her in mind. While he had the time, he shoved all thoughts of his journal into a deep corner of his mind. And locked it away.

"I bought the brioche from that girl's bakery." She sat sideways on his lap and picked up one of the brioche from the tray. She held it while she looped an arm around his neck, underneath his braids.

"Did you?" He wasn't sure what bakery she meant, and he didn't dare think about anything he'd written down. If she indwelled again, those memories would be close enough for her to examine.

"She wasn't there. The girl."

"Ah."

"Mmm." She took a bite of the bread and rolled her eyes in delight. "Pour the coffee?"

"Of course." He did so for them both. There was no scent of coffee in the air, because the French press contained cold water and coffee grounds, and there was no convincing her that coffee should be made any other way. Fen drank hers as if it were delicious.

He sipped his coffee, trying to leave the grounds behind, and took a bite of the brioche she held out to him. It was stale, but he could taste the butter and imagine that if fresh, it would be lovely to eat. Whoever the baker was, he was talented. But Fen had said *that girl's* bakery. Therefore, the woman was talented.

"We have a lot to do today," she said. She swung herself around so that she sat facing him, with her legs on either side of his. The bitch was insane and no longer the woman he'd loved. *Unfair.* Unfair of him to blame her madness for what was happening to him now.

The truth remained, however, that he and Fen had indulged in some dangerous practices. Besotted as he was, so deeply in love, he had allowed her access to his mind. The result, at first, had been beyond anything he could have imagined. He'd had a similar bridge to hers, but not in the way of the demonkind. Unlike Fen, he had no ability to control her mind. He could only touch. He had trusted her with his life. More than his life. He'd trusted her with his free will, and he was now paying the price for thinking he could control a creature as volatile as Fen. His magic was compromised, no longer his to pull. The last few times he'd tried to regain his control over her, she'd nearly killed him. He'd become what he'd dedicated his life to preventing.

Her madness broke his heart, but he had no one to blame but himself. The magic that bound Fen to him had never been meant for equals. What he'd done had likely broken her as thoroughly as the severing of her bond with Iskander had done.

"Do you love me, Rasmus?" she asked him. She put her hands on either side of his face. Her eyes jittered, slowly for now.

"I'll love you forever." It was true. If he had the choice to make again, he could not see a different outcome. He had loved Fen then and he loved her still, even though in his moments of lucidity, he understood the woman he loved was gone.

Her hands slid down his chest, and he touched the five copper stripes on her forearms. Her magic pulsed there, so close to the surface. Her eyes flashed from blue to orange. She lowered her head to his so that her lips hovered over his. "Rasmus," she said. "I'm better now."

"Yes, my love," he said. "I can feel that you are."

Fen worked at the buttons of his shirt. Rasmus felt the first push of her will against his. He knew better than to resist now. "You'll make love to me?" Her hand was on the top button of his trousers and then the zipper, touching expertly.

"Of course," he told her. He helped her out of her pants, removed her shirt and bra, and at the same time they removed his clothes, too. Her body was perfect, and he didn't mind at all taking this extended moment of being almost alone in his head to allow his sexual instincts to come to the fore.

When they had sex, which happened less and less often now, they forgot everything but the satisfaction their bodies brought them. He moved the tray to the top of the desk and put her on the writing surface. She arched her back and opened her legs for him. There was nothing, nothing like sliding inside her. Nothing better than being the instrument of her sexual release. He denied her for as long as he could deny his own release. God help him. They ended up on the floor, with him grinding his hips against her pelvis, holding back his orgasm while she twined her long legs around him. She whipped her head to one side and levered up enough to sink her teeth into the meat of his right biceps.

He cried out at the first slash of pain. His elbow gave and he took more of his weight on his other arm. Her mouth fixed on his upper arm, and in the back of his head, he felt the echo of her pleasure at the taste of his blood. His braids swung in time with his hips. Since he was open magically, he drew from the rubies and, yes, his magic surged through him at the moment of his release. Fen shouted and fell over the edge with him.

"I love you," he said, and he knew she felt his despair because she was in his head.

Fen repeated the words back to him, wiping a finger along his eyes. "Don't weep," she said. "Don't weep.

When we have Iskander back, everything is going to be better."

"As you say." If she succeeded in this, he intended to kill Iskander as soon as possible.

Fen kissed him on the mouth. "You'll see. I've found a witch who can finish what we started with that girl."

"What girl?"

She snarled softly. "Paisley Nichols. He'll come to me if I have her."

He felt he ought to know that name. A woman's name, but he could not remember everything that mattered in connection with that name. Among the snatches of memory left to him, he thought perhaps Fen had wanted him to bind this Paisley Nichols, whoever she was, with his magic. Doing so required a significant use of his abilities, but such was well within his power even now, damaged as he was.

Another memory floated up from somewhere in his brain. Paisley Nichols rented an apartment from Iskander. She was a human woman—the very sort it was his long life's calling to protect. A face to go with the memory clicked into place. She was a lovely young woman, which was why Fen thought to use her to get to Iskander. As his tenant, she was in close proximity to the fiend, and a fiend's affinity for the human female was well known. With even a little encouragement, so Fen believed, Iskander could be seduced. With the human woman under Rasmus's control, and therefore under Fen's control, Paisley would become the conduit that would get them to Iskander and make everything right.

So Fen thought, though it sounded now as if she planned a simple trade. Paisley for Iskander.

He wondered if he really had touched Paisley and

sent magic into her or if that was something that came from Fen's disorganized thoughts and wishes. It would be clever of him to do that. Fen wouldn't understand the significance of sending his magic into someone else. The fact that it was Paisley Nichols was all the better.

"We need to make this work soon," she said. Her eyes quivered, and, linked as they were at the moment, he knew she was losing her grip on reality.

Pressure built up in his head. "Fen, no. This is not necessary, I promise you."

"I love you, Rasmus. You know I'd never hurt you." She vanished from his sight and became his mind. His will. What little he experienced of the world was through Fen.

When he was alone in the room, he stood and drank his cold coffee, gritty with the unbrewed grounds, and he and Fen left to find the witch.

CHAPTER 23

A couple of days later, 9:30 P.M.,
Paisley Bakery and Café

Paisley closed her phone. Iskander was busy tonight, so he'd sent another of Nikodemus's sworn fiends to get her safely home. Her private taxi had just called to tell her he was waiting outside. She locked up, then had to go back for some papers she wanted to go over at home.

Purse slung over her shoulder, she set the alarm and stepped into the alley. She didn't see anyone, which was odd. She also wasn't having a reaction to one of the demonkind. Odd. She should. Maybe her ride was waiting on Clay Street and therefore too far away for her to sense. She took a step forward to check and slipped in something wet. She flailed about to keep her balance and ended up stubbing her toe. On a body.

She about jumped out of her skin.

What she'd slipped in wasn't water. It was blood, and

it pooled around a man she didn't recognize. His hair was medium length, and he'd probably been good-looking. Now, a black shuriken protruded from his left temple. Another body lay a few feet away, this one a man in a suit, his hair shorn close to his skull. She spun, heading for the bakery door.

Rasmus dropped straight down the side of the building, from higher than any human could have survived. By the time she had a physical reaction to his presence, it was too late. He landed on the ground with hardly a sound, between her and the bakery door. He tugged on his suit jacket and smiled. "Paisley, my love."

"Go away." Screams reverberated in her head. She tried to shut out the horrific sounds.

"Is something wrong?" His eyes had that fevered look that meant his hold on his sanity was precarious, and now he didn't even sound like himself. The accent she'd found so charming when they first met was gone. "It's dangerous to be out this late at night. Allow me to give you a ride home. We can talk things over on the way."

She slid her cell phone out of her pocket. Her fingers trembled. The device beeped as the screen lit up.

"No phone calls."

She scrolled for Iskander's number. Right as she touched the contact, her phone died in her hands. Then it got so hot, the screen cracked and the back of the phone burned her palm. She dropped it with a yelp.

"I said no calls." His voice sounded funny. Too high pitched for a man's.

She made a dead sprint for Clay Street. Behind her, metal groaned and the next thing she knew, a Dumpster was flying over her head. She skidded to a stop as the

Dumpster crashed to the ground and skidded several feet down the alley, the sound of metal against stone blasting at her ears. Refuse flew everywhere.

"Paisley." Rasmus walked toward her. Behind him, three magehelds plummeted to the alley from the side of the building. High enough up that they, too, had been out of the range of her ability to sense them.

This was it, then. Even if she managed to take back Rasmus's magic, there wasn't anyone here to deal with the aftermath. Besides, that wasn't going to kill Rasmus, and even if he was disoriented, she could count on his magehelds subduing her. She grabbed her keys and held them in her fist with the individual keys sticking out from between her fingers. The metal heated to the point where she was forced to drop them.

"You need to listen to me," Rasmus said. "You must be with me. If you don't do as I say, innocent people will die, and it will be your fault."

He walked toward her. She grabbed a length of wood that had broken off a delivery pallet and wrenched it free. She faced him. "Don't come any closer."

Rasmus kept walking. She hefted her piece of wood, and then the back of her head turned to ice.

Someone else said, "You heard her."

Paisley didn't recognize the voice, and she didn't dare take her eyes off Rasmus to find out who it was.

Rasmus, however, was just as surprised as she was by the interruption, because he whipped toward the mouth of the alley so fast the beads in his hair clacked and clattered.

A tall man she didn't recognize stood framed in the light at the mouth of the alley. He wore a suit, and given her reaction to him, he was a mage. He picked his way past the ruins of the Dumpster and the scattered garbage to stand beside Paisley.

"Look," Rasmus said in his normal voice. An indisputably masculine, accented voice. The change sent a chill down Paisley's spine. "I do appreciate your concern. If I were you, I would do the same. Rescue the damsel in distress. But this is not what you think. I'm here to give my girlfriend a ride home."

She didn't know who the hell the other guy was, but thank God he showed up. "I am *not* his girlfriend."

"She called me to come pick her up, and I was a little late." Rasmus shook his head like he was commiserating with the guy. "You know how it is." He lifted his hands, oh so reasonable. "I was late, and now she's upset even though I told her I was sorry."

"That's a lie. I never called you." The stranger wasn't a screamer, but she was absolutely certain he was a mage. That meant she didn't know if she could trust him, but it didn't mean she couldn't use him. "Call nine-one-one. Please."

Rasmus raised his hands. "We had a misunderstanding. It happens, as I'm sure you know. It's late, and she needs to get home."

"There's no misunderstanding," the stranger said.

Rasmus muttered what sounded to her like nonsense syllables. At the end, he slashed a hand through the air from the level of his chest to his pelvis, and, swear to the heavens, a breeze lifted the stranger's hair.

"Rasmus Kessler," the man said. Paisley's heart froze solid in her chest. He lifted a hand, too. The breeze stopped. "You are not yourself. I suggest you leave before you get into serious trouble."

"For what reason should I listen to you?" Rasmus said in a voice of deadly charm. "You have no magehelds. You have no power to do me harm."

The man in the suit moved the first two fingers of one hand in a semicircle. "As it happens, mage, I do not need them."

A shadow appeared around Rasmus, so dark Paisley had to squint to see him. Within the bounds of that darkness, Rasmus didn't move. Once his magehelds were enveloped, too, they stood as frozen as the mage.

"Oh, my dear Lord," she whispered, retreating to the bakery door.

"Miss Paisley Nichols, I presume?" the stranger said. She nodded, and he stooped for her keys. "We ought to go before he works out a way to dissolve what I've done."

"Who are you?"

He tossed her the keys. Unwilling to take her eyes off him, she let them fall at her feet. "My name is Leonidas. Nikodemus asked me to keep an eye on Rasmus, and that task led me here in timely fashion."

Paisley wanted to believe him. She really did.

Leonidas smiled as if he understood her hesitation. He glanced at Rasmus, still enveloped in shadow. "We have a few moments. Perhaps you'd like to call Nikodemus to verify my bona fides."

"Can't." She pointed to the mass of melted metal that had been her phone.

"I have his number." He reached into the inside pocket of his jacket, but stopped when Paisley stiffened. "I am retrieving my phone." Slowly, he extracted a slim phone from his suit jacket. "You see?" He put it on the ground and pushed it toward her. It skittered on the pavement and stopped at the toe of her black clog. "You'll find him in my contacts."

She opened the phone, very much aware that you could label a contact anything you want. There was no guarantee the number wasn't going to a buddy of his. She found an entry for Iskander and called that instead. No guarantee with that number, either, but she'd know if it was really Iskander.

He answered the phone on the second ring. "S'up, mage?" There was traffic noise in the background. "I'm a little busy here."

She gripped the phone harder. "It's me."

"Just a sec." The noise muffled, and he came back to the call. "Something wrong?"

"Do you know someone named Leonidas?"

"Uh-huh."

She swallowed the lump in her throat. "Describe him to me."

"Greek. Dark complexion. Strong nose. Dark hair. Probably wearing a suit. You're calling me on his phone. Is he there? Where's the guy I sent?"

"Dead."

"Shit."

"What's a question I can ask him so I know it's him and not some other mage or friend of Rasmus's who stole this phone?"

"What happened, Paisley?" His voice was crisp. "Where are you?"

"Behind the bakery."

"Are you hurt?"

"No."

"Did Rasmus come after you? Is he there?"

"Yes. But Leonidas did something to him." She checked the stranger. He hadn't moved, and Rasmus and his magehelds remained enveloped in inky black. "I need to know if this is the real Leonidas before I go anywhere with him."

"Ask him where he first met me. I want you to repeat his answer to me. I'll tell you if he's right."

"What if he isn't?"

"Is there any place you can go? Back inside?"

She faced the back door and unlocked it. "Yes."

"Good. I'm on my way. I'll meet you there either way."

She relayed the question to Leonidas, who hadn't moved from where he'd stopped. The mage answered without hesitation. "At the home of the assassin Durian. In St. Francis Wood." She repeated the answer for Iskander and refused to think about the fact that Leonidas had so casually said the word *assassin*.

Iskander said, "Let me talk to him."

"Is it him?" she asked.

"Probably. Look, I don't trust him, all right? Not all the way. Put him on the phone."

"All right." She put the phone on the ground and shoved it toward Leonidas. "He wants to talk to you."

He picked it up. "Iskander." His eyes darted to Rasmus. "Immobilized for now. You have perhaps twenty minutes before he works free. After that, I will think of something else. Yes. Shall I wait here for you?" He listened for a while before he disconnected the call and put away his phone. "Iskander would like for you to please wait inside for him. You're to lock the door until he arrives. I'll remain here." He nodded in Rasmus's direction. "Keeping an eye on him. I advise you to do as Iskander has asked."

She didn't hesitate. Her heart beat a thousand times a minute even after she was inside with the door bolted and the alarm reset. She pressed her back against the door, weak-kneed but feeling better now that she was reasonably certain Leonidas was trustworthy and that Iskander was on his way.

The half hour it took for something to happen felt like an eternity. Her chest flexed before she heard a motor that cut off. It wasn't the Chevy; she'd have recognized the rumble. She held her breath, waiting as she faced the door, listening intently.

She heard voices, but they were muffled. After another bit, there was a soft tap on the door. Paisley stared at it, imagining all the ways this might not be what it seemed.

"Hey, Paisley." Iskander's voice was close to the door. "I'd call your phone but Leonidas says that asswipe Kessler melted it. It's me, and you have some work to do."

She punched buttons on the alarm so it would reset itself and opened the door. She halfway expected to see Rasmus standing there. When she saw Iskander, she walked straight forward and into his arms. He put his arms around and held her tight for a moment.

Leonidas said, "I took the liberty of calling Xia and Alexandrine to sever his magehelds. They are on their way. Perhaps another twenty or thirty minutes."

"Good thinking. You have him held for now, right?"

"At the moment," Leonidas said, "he's merely physically restrained."

Rasmus stared at her from within the remnants of the shadow that confined him and his magehelds. The spot on

her wrist flared so hot she jumped back, stumbling against
Iskander, who caught her around the waist. The darkness
surrounding Rasmus thinned to the point of looking more
like smoke than shadow. Paisley saw him move an arm.
He maintained his stare at her.

Leonidas made another motion with his hand, but it
was clear Rasmus would break free. Leonidas said something that wasn't English.

Iskander caught his hand. "Nikodemus will have your
nuts in a grinder if you do anything to hurt him. Keep him
like that until Xia gets here with Alexandrine. After they
take care of the magehelds, let him go. And make sure he
goes."

The mage motioned to the back door of the alley. "For
now, take her inside. I expect you'll know if I need you."
Iskander nodded at that. "Otherwise, I will call when it's
safe for you to leave."

Iskander pushed her toward the back door and let it
slam behind them. She reset the alarm. "Is there someplace we can wait?" he asked.

"Sure." She walked past him. "My office."

Office was an exaggeration. She took him to the closet-
sized space that contained a desk she suspected had been
there forever. They didn't make heavy furniture like that
desk anymore. Her laptop was there, closed and turned off
for now, as was the printer she kept tucked underneath the
desk. There was a mini-fridge so employees could store a
meal, snacks, or a drink if they wanted. A microwave sat
on top of the fridge. Mugs and a box of assorted teas were
next to the cheap coffeemaker on the corner of the desk,
for use when the café's espresso machine was off. Behind
the desk was a cheap office swivel chair. The visitor's

chair was black leather, a craigslist find like the fridge and microwave. That left about ten square feet to stand in.

Once both of them were inside, the room seemed even smaller. She did her best to ignore the way he took up all the space.

CHAPTER 24

Iskander looked for a place he could stand without crowding her, but there wasn't anywhere to go, unless he stood in the hall. Paisley's office was too small for the amount of crap in it. For someone his size, one step in just about any direction and he'd knock something over.

"I'm fine." She stood by the heavy wooden desk, rubbing her arms.

"You don't look fine." He did his best to crank down his sensitivity to her. She was leaking magic the way she had the night he found her near dying in her apartment. "Did Rasmus touch you again?"

"No." She looked drawn and shaky. "He just scared the heck out of me." She shrugged out of her peacoat and threw it over the chair behind the desk. She wore black jeans and one of her chef's shirts that didn't do much for her but that didn't hide her curves, either. He was in favor of her curves.

"I'm fine," she said.

"To me," he said, holding her gaze, "that sounds like

a lie." Felt like one, too, but he wasn't going to mention that just yet.

"It's not a lie."

"You sound tired and worn out." He looked her up and down, taking his time. "You look like it, too. No offense. Aren't you sleeping?"

"You know my crazy schedule." She tilted her head back to look at him in the cramped space. He liked the way his feelings about wanting her in his life meshed with the sexual hit he was getting from them being alone. Very cozy with him a decent amount taller than her and a lot bigger, and all his instincts about her going off. He was still plenty hot for her. Which was a record for him. "Want some coffee while we wait for Leonidas to give us the all-clear?"

"Tea. Herbal. What? I drink tea sometimes."

"That's fine for you, cupcake, but I can't drink tea. It'll make my nuts shrivel." He grinned because she liked it when he joked around with her, and he wanted to see her smile. He dug through the basket of supplies and found a bag of ground Peet's blend. "Or worse."

"Nobody's making you drink tea."

"I'm making us coffee."

"I want tea."

He turned his head to get a look at her. Her big hazel eyes were fixed on him, and his heart did that thing where it hurt without him understanding why. He'd watched Durian fall for the human woman, Gray, and all he'd ever thought was, *I don't get it*. He wished he did because then he might have a clue what to do about Paisley. "I'll make your tea first, all right? Where do you get the water?"

"Bathroom sink. Across the hall. I can get it."

"So can I." He grabbed the carafe from the coffee-maker and filled it from the bathroom tap. When he came back, he saw she'd taken possession of the swivel chair behind the desk and was now rocking the seat back and forth. Her hands were on her lap where he couldn't see them. He had no idea why she'd moved so far away from him, but the reason couldn't be good.

He prepped the coffee grounds and got the water started but kept enough to fill one of the mugs from the shelf above the mini-fridge. He stuck the mug in the microwave and punched a few buttons. "Fine," he said. Why would anyone drink tea? "You want tea, you can have tea. What kind do you want?"

"I like Chamomile."

When her water was hot, he dunked the tea bag into her mug. He looked around for supplies like fake sugar and creamers. Leonidas could finish out there any minute, for Christ's sake.

"Basket under the napkins," she said.

"Thanks." He could see her upper arm moving. "Is your wrist bothering you?"

"Some."

He added in the one sugar he knew she liked and gave it a stir before he handed it over. "Are you sure Rasmus didn't touch you?"

"Thanks. No, he didn't." Paisley gazed at him from over the mug. The words *Paisley Bakery* were printed on it in a paisley pattern on a bright yellow glaze. That mouth of hers never failed to give him dirty thoughts. What if she didn't want something regular with him?

The water was percolating through the coffee machine and into the carafe now. Coffee scent wafted through the room. He picked up his mug and switched it with the carafe.

"You're going to scald yourself doing that."

When the mug was full, he switched the carafe back without a drop spilled. He faced her with a smile. "I have skillz you can only dream about."

"Milk's in the fridge," she said.

He found a carton of organic half-and-half and loaded up. He stood there with his cup, breathing in the smell. She stared at his cup, and he smiled because he knew what she was thinking. The coffee was righteously good. He filled another mug with coffee and put in her sugar. Then he reached over the desk and took away her tea. "You don't need weed-flavored water. Coffee the way I make it, you can grow a pair even if you're a girl."

"Bless your heart," she said. But she took the coffee and drank some, too. "It's good."

"I told you. Skillz."

"Maybe you should be in charge of the coffee at home."

Home. Well, yeah. It was her home, too. So far, there wasn't any change in his reaction to the ambient magic. No phone call, either, so Rasmus and Leonidas were still out there. He sat on the black leather chair, but it wasn't made for someone his size. "I'm not doing anybody else," he said. Oh, shit. That came out all kinds of wrong. "Seeing anyone. I'm not seeing anyone."

"It's none of my business."

"Maybe it should be," he said. He knew two kinds of relationships: his failed one with Fen and his one-nighters. He wanted something else with Paisley.

She came out from behind the desk and topped off

her coffee from the carafe. He stared at her back until she leaned against the edge of the desk and took a big, long swallow. He arranged himself on the chair, a bit sideways, with one leg on the floor and the other thrown over the padded arm. He couldn't think of anything else to say.

She put down her coffee and ran her hands over her head and then kept them there. "Rasmus is getting to be a real pain in the behind."

He studied her as if his life depended on being able to recall every physical detail. The dark red hair, the pale skin. The blue shadows under her eyes. The way the corners of her mouth tensed. She looked unhappy, and that was at least partly his fault. He didn't know all that much about human women. Not nearly enough.

Did humans who couldn't make psychic connections on their own memorize faces and expressions and try to fit the physical whole of a person into some kind of representation of the person's interior life? He knew Paisley well enough to know she was stressed and tired and still dealing with the aftermath of Rasmus's attack. Every time the mage got around her, she ended up shaky like she was now.

"If I had my way," he said, "I'd end him right now."

"I know."

Hell yeah. He'd crush the mage's heart in his bare hand. He drank the rest of his coffee and set the empty mug on the floor. Then he held out a hand, and after a hesitation, she put her fingers on his palm. Their eyes locked and he could see the question there: *Should I?* As far as he was concerned, the answer was *hell* and *yes*. He drew her toward him and shifted so she ended up sitting on his lap, his arms around her.

"I wish everything could just go back the way it was. I want a normal life," she said as she settled against his torso. "Normal. I can barely remember what that's like."

"You can't have a normal life." Her eyes got big and hurt, and he felt bad for telling her the truth. "Besides, if you had a normal life, you wouldn't know me." He stroked her back, and when she relaxed against him, his heart went all funny again. Her ass was snugged up against him, but he played it cool.

He resettled himself, but there was no way she wasn't going to notice his physical reaction down south. He shifted them so he had his feet on the floor and she was across his lap with one of his arms around her upper back and her shoulder tucked in against his side. He pushed up her sleeve to take a look at her wrist. "Looks pinker to me," he said. All but one of the marks Rasmus had left had faded. One of the blisters on her shoulder had scarred like her wrist. "Does it hurt?"

"A little."

"Let me help." He set his hand to the back of her neck and spread his fingers upward, turning her head toward him so they were looking at each other. "Let me take care of you."

"You already do that."

"Let me help with this. Right now."

She wasn't acknowledging that he was touching her, but she also wasn't moving away. That had to be a good sign. But he was thinking about things he shouldn't be. Soft human skin, her curves, the taste of her, her mouth on him, his on her. And him. Possibly not even in human form. He stroked his fingers through her hair. He didn't know what to say to her, what words to use. They hadn't been necessary with Fen, and he'd never wanted more than a good time with anyone else.

"How?" she said.

"Let me in your head, and I can help with the pain." Iskander's phone vibrated in his front pocket. He ignored it and kept one hand moving over Paisley. He loved touching her. He wanted to do it more often. The contact calmed him, too, the way physical contact did between his own kind.

Paisley tipped her head back enough to stare at the ceiling. He swept his gaze downward and ended up looking at her chest and thinking impure thoughts. Her head came back to level, and by the time he realized it, there wasn't any hiding that he'd been ogling her. She put her fingers under his chin and pushed up. She was smiling a little, which was good.

"Are you talking about an indwell?"

"Not like that." He ran his fingers through her hair and ended up cupping the back of her head. "I'm not sure that would even work with you. I'm talking about a psychic connection between us. If it works, and it's okay with you, I can make it so it lasts a while. It would help me know when you're in trouble even when I'm not nearby. I could find you even faster than I can now. And you could find me, if you needed to. Sooner than you can now."

"I don't know."

"We don't have to." He touched her injured wrist. "At least let me help with this."

"Will it hurt?"

"It shouldn't."

"Lord knows aspirin never does any good."

He plucked at the shoulder of her white jacket, and they both looked at her shoulder. He said, "Does this come off?"

"Why?"

"Because," he said, and he put a whole world of longing in the word.

When he looked up and found her watching his face, he realized they were having a moment that had nothing to do with him helping with her wrist. The moment was about the two of them and the heat they were generating just from looking at each other.

"You were right," she said.

"About?"

"Sex with you."

"That so?"

"With you, it *is* better than chocolate." She unsnapped the fastenings of her jacket, and he helped her slip it off. Underneath she wore a white ribbed tank top thin enough for him to see through to her bra. He scooped her ponytail off her back and over one shoulder.

"Nice. Really nice." He wasn't sure where to touch her. Everywhere. Nowhere? "You aren't just a one-time thing for me," he said. His chest was tight, and he recognized the sensation as anxiety. About Paisley and whether she wanted anything to do with him the way he did with her. "It's different with you." He didn't like feeling this way— helpless. Uncertain. Wanting something he wasn't sure he could have and afraid he wouldn't get it. "I should have been bored after the first time, itching to move on. And I'm not." He kept his arms around her, as if that would keep her with him more than just physically and for the moment. "I don't know anything except I don't want you thinking this is just me having a good time."

She ran a hand up and down his torso. "I had a good time before."

"A good time."

Her hand wandered a bit more. "A very good time."

He let out a breath. "I guess that's better than telling me I'm lousy in bed."

"You are definitely not lousy in bed."

He stared at a wisp of red hair curling over the side of her neck. He imagined pressing his lips there. Maybe taking a nip. Enough to break skin. Reaching for her mind and making a connection there. And it wouldn't be fucked up the way things had gotten with Fen. He ran a finger along the strap of her tank top. "Jesus, you make me hot." He reached down to push off the black clogs she wore to work, but she toed them off, so he slid off her socks instead. They shifted on the chair again, and she ended up straddling him with her knees sliding deep into the cushions on either side of his legs. He put his hands on her ass, then slid his thumbs up either side of her spine. Her skin was warm through her shirt.

"Iskander," she whispered. "Lord, that feels good."

He drew her forward and breathed in. "I can't stop thinking about touching you. Not since the first time."

"You were pretty unforgettable yourself."

He repeated the slide of his thumbs along her back. She arched, and he prayed she wasn't going to be offended by the way he watched her breasts or the curve to her waist. "There's something else about this connection I should mention before we try it."

"Is it pervy?"

He laughed. "You seem like such a nice girl, but I think you're bad."

"Better than chocolate," she said. "So. Is it pervy?"

"It could be." He kept moving his hands over her and thinking about the way she kissed him, and how he wanted her to kiss him again. Jesus, he was hot for her. "If you think you'd like that."

Her eyes popped open when he slid his hands around her rib cage not quite touching her breasts. Then he did, curving his hands around her. Her nipples tightened, and he brushed the tips of his fingers over her. "It would do that other stuff, too. Like I was saying"—he drew in a breath—"it could be a gateway between us, and we could use it for this bullshit with Rasmus, too. But right now, I want it for us. Like this."

For a while, they didn't say anything while he touched her. Caressed her, got himself hot and aroused. Her, too, from the looks of things. The rhythm of her breathing changed.

Eventually, though, she leaned away, and because he didn't want to pressure her or come on too strong, he stopped touching her. He was dying to see her naked, to touch her skin. Dying to suck and nip and have his hands full of her. But without a link to her head, he had no way of knowing what she was thinking or feeling. "Tell me what you want," he said.

She cupped the side of his face with her palm, the side with his traceries. The contact sent a whole new surge of arousal through him. "Sometimes," she said in a low voice, "I want you so bad it hurts."

"Me too." He slipped his hands down the back of her jeans, reaching down, down, as far as he could, touching her soft skin, and at the same time he brought her toward him. She propped her hands on the back of the chair. Her eyes were wide open, her pupils pools of black surrounded by hazel.

She leaned in and pressed her mouth to his throat, the side of his jaw. "Make it stop hurting," she whispered.

He brought his hands up and underneath the bottom of her tank top, sliding along her spine until the tips of his fingers brushed the bottom of her bra. He leaned in and pressed his mouth to the spot where her neck joined her shoulder and was rewarded with a soft moan from her. She smelled like vanilla and butter, the way she always did when she came home from work.

His mouth stayed close to her skin. He brought up one hand and pulled down her tank top strap, taking her bra strap with it. Such pale skin compared to his. He already knew that if he took his true form, she'd look even paler by comparison, and he was thinking he wanted that again. He was dying to do more, but at the same time, this encroachment from almost-innocent touching to touching that wasn't innocent at all was worth the slow crank to out of control.

She didn't back away. Instead, she leaned closer. Close enough to put certain parts of her anatomy against his torso. Underneath her shirt, he palmed one breast, and when he processed the fact that all that full curve was in his hand, his mind kind of shut down for a minute.

"I don't have good sense where you're concerned," she said on a breathless gasp. "None at all."

"I'll take care of you," he said. He was aware his vow to protect her was behind some of his intense satisfaction in saying that. Fine by him. Even better, he had his hand on her naked skin, and she wasn't making him move it. In fact, she was breathing harder. Her nipple was hard beneath his palm, and he wanted her to feel the arousal more and more. "I won't let anything bad happen to you. That's a promise."

"Right now, all I want is for you to make love to me." Her words were warm breath against his ear.

"I would love to do that, cupcake." He struggled to get his thoughts straight, and even then, half his brain was detouring south while the rest dealt with the logistics of getting her naked. He pulled her hair free of its elastic band. Thick, soft hair, dark red and streaked with highlights of gold, spilled over his hands and down one of his arms. He pulled back enough for her to see his eyes, because he knew they weren't normal right now and she needed to know where he was at.

Paisley gazed into his face, into his eyes and into his heart. He watched her pupils get bigger and bigger when he flicked his fingertip over her nipple. He wanted in her head. He wanted to feel her reaction and know for a fact what she was thinking. He wanted her to know he was thinking about the taste of her skin, the shape of her mouth, and what might happen to them both if he touched her again.

His phone buzzed in his pocket again, and he ignored it again. A few seconds later, it vibrated, cut off, then started vibrating again. He dug it out and turned it off. He threw the phone onto the desk and tightened his hands around her. He wanted to do this. Hell, yes, he wanted to. "Even for just right now, you have to say yes, you'll let me in your head." He slid off the chair and knelt on the floor in front of her. She shifted to face him. He put his hands on her thighs, rubbing his hands along her legs. "You need to understand the risks before you agree to anything."

"I'm listening."

"One risk for you is that I do more than I say I will."

"Like what?"

He drew a breath and let it slowly out. "Assuming I can get past your resistance, things like take over your mind. Bind you over to me so your will belongs to me. I won't do that to you. I promise. But don't say yes unless you trust me not to, because it's something I could do." He studied her face while he slid his hands upward and around to her inner thighs.

"What about you?"

"I don't know what kind of power you have. Maybe enough to be dangerous to me."

Paisley gazed down at him. She touched the innermost stripe down his cheek and the contact flashed hot. Just as if she were a witch. He wondered if she felt the heat or if it was just him getting worked up and thinking ahead to more touching, more than what they were doing now. "You want me to say yes."

"Hell, yes." He curled his fingers around her wrist and drew her arm toward him, palm up. He traced the course of one blue vein from her elbow to her wrist. He bent his head over her arm and breathed in the scent of her, and all the while, the tip of his tongue followed the vein he'd traced before.

Her hand fisted but she didn't pull away. His teeth ached with the desire to bite, to make a breach in her skin through which blood would flow and he could taste her again. That rich, human coppery tang of Paisley. He pressed a finger against the pulse in her wrist and looked into her face again.

"Yes," she said.

He was a little lost without any mental connection to tell him what she was feeling and thinking. Then he lowered his head to her arm and bit her.

CHAPTER 25

Paisley felt the scrape of Iskander's teeth against the inside of her forearm and flinched. He had too firm a grip on her wrist for the reflex to break her free. He looked up, and she saw his eyes were cycling between blue and gold-flecked green. No one's eyes did that. No one normal.

Iskander wasn't human. She had to keep reminding herself of that.

He brought her arm up between them. The break in her skin hardly hurt at all, though a trickle of red zigzagged over the side of her arm. She knew she ought to be worried, but she wasn't. She trusted him completely. Without reservation.

"I'm going to try now."

She nodded. She longed to touch the stripes down the side of his cheek, or run her fingers through his hair, touching the blue that gleamed faintly there, too. But he was still on his knees on the floor, between her spread legs, and he still had his fingers wrapped around her wrist, and she didn't want to do anything to break the intensity of his gaze on her. He drew a finger through the blood on her arm, brought his finger to his mouth, and licked his skin clean.

The air around them rippled with a desert breeze and the scent of sunbaked sand. He went up on his knees and touched his fingertip to her forehead. Pressure built up at the spot where his finger pressed against her, and she could have sworn she saw his eyes change color again. Fully green, but not a green any human eyes ever were.

"Relax," he whispered. "Let me in."

Iskander would never hurt her. Not ever. Nevertheless, she was aware that he was holding her hand, and that she was squeezing his fingers, and that Harsh really was right about him. He was dangerous. She saw him in front of her, the stripes down his face, as perfect as ever. She let go of her instinct to keep herself separate.

She concentrated on not fighting the pressure, and then he was there, a presence in her head that hadn't been there before. Here. With her. His hand fell away from her forehead and landed on her thigh again. The pain in her arm vanished.

He scored his own wrist, swiped two fingers through the welling blood, and held them to her mouth. "Yes," he said, low and soft and honey sweet. Fever heated her skin when she took his fingers in her mouth. The connection between them strengthened. "Yes," he whispered. "Just like that."

Arid warmth spread through her, dizzying her, settling into her chest and inhabiting her very bones. Her sense of Iskander deepened, and with that came thoughts, reactions, and even memories that didn't belong to her.

He stood and scooped her into his arms when it turned

out she was too dizzy to stand on her own. He took two steps across the room and put her down on the desk. Quickly, he cleared most of the surface of the table. The coffeemaker went onto the floor, and he disconnected her laptop from the power supply and slid that under the desk. Her papers he stacked into a pile, and then he stepped between her legs and leaned into her, and just kept going until she was on her back and his hands were on her sternum. *Beautiful. Human.*

Anticipation.

The magic is there and can be touched.

Need. Desire.

His eyes were a different color again. Not blue but a dark green-blue that moved and swirled and made her think there was something alive there that was more than Iskander. She blinked hard but that didn't change. "I feel your magic," he said in a low voice. His hands remained on her sternum, one over the other. She felt . . . *something* flow from him and into her. The sensation set off a vibration deep in her chest.

And then.

Everything changed.

It was like a switch flipped inside her. The vibration turned into an electric hum that roared through her, and when it ended, her skin rippled with gooseflesh as ice-cold fingers danced up and down her spine and along the back of her neck, her arms, and even her legs. His magic echoed in her and entwined with her. She reached for him, clumsy because this was too new for her. They shared the same mental space—what he'd said would happen. He was telling her so without words.

"Paisley." He put his hands on either side of her face.

His eyes fixed on hers, and she fell into the wide pool of this new part of him. She disassociated with herself and briefly thought she must be looking in a mirror. She saw herself, her eyes open, a slash of red hair across her white tank top. She saw a stranger who was familiar to her. Herself, but she was not in her body. Her body was bigger. She had to be careful of her strength, of desires that spoke to her of dominance and bonds that would tie them together forever. One of her hands—no, that was Iskander's hand—rested on her upper chest, but the other slid down to the fastening of her jeans.

At one and the same time, she wanted him—Iskander, his naked skin against hers and their bodies intertwined— and wanted to unfasten Paisley's jeans and touch, touch that human body, stroke, kiss, taste the salt of her, hear the intake of her breath, show her what he felt and bring her to orgasm and tell her he didn't want anyone but her.

A moan slipped from her, and she did not know whose arousal she was feeling. Her own or Iskander's?

Then boundaries reappeared. She saw Iskander normally, but with the link between their minds in place. She reached for him, connected with his warm, smooth skin. She wanted him to touch her the way he had before, with all the tender attention that didn't hide his lust. Her body was primed for him. Ready for him. A fluttery sensation settled between her legs, a fullness, an aching longing for him, for the fullness of his penis inside her.

His breath came hard. He had his hands planted on the desk on either side of her head, and he lowered his torso to hers. "This is how I feel about you," he said with his mouth close to her ear. "Paisley, I don't know what the hell is going on with us. I really don't. But this is how I feel, and I say let's find out what that means."

She pushed up, mostly sitting. Iskander stood between her legs, his hands clasped on the top of his head, his body bowed back, his lower lip caught between his teeth. She put her hand over his erection. "Does this hurt?"

"Worse than you can imagine. Can you help me out?"

"I can surely try." She reached out and fingered the top button of his jeans, then pushed the metal button through the buttonhole. Her little finger slid along the side of his erection. "Is that better?" she asked.

He straightened his body but kept his hands on his head and his eyes on her face. His mouth curved up on one side. "Not yet, cupcake. Not yet."

Carefully, she undid the rest of the buttons on his jeans while he stood there, and then she scooted forward and got one hand down the front of his boxers to cup him and the other down the back. His skin was fever hot. The muscles of his backside flexed as he pushed his pelvis toward her. "Now?"

"I'm hurting bad."

"Maybe it's because your clothes are in the way."

With a growl that came from somewhere deep in his throat, he kicked off his shoes and stepped out of his jeans and his underwear. He stripped off his shirt, too, and Paisley could hardly believe he was here, ready, willing, and so wonderfully nude. Her awareness of his mental state hovered in her mind. She *felt* his arousal, too.

The blue stripes continued down his torso, and he stood unmoving while she touched all that lovely male body, that warm skin and taut muscle. He moved forward, then leaned in and kissed her. She put her arms around his shoulders, and twined her fingers upward to the back of his head. Her mouth opened under his, and their tongues met.

He moved his hand between them again and undid the top button of her jeans. He gripped the tab of her zipper. All the while, they were kissing like there wasn't going to be a tomorrow for them. He let go of her zipper and pulled up her shirt, higher and higher. They separated long enough for him to get it over her head, and he went for her bra. "I think I should help you, too," he said.

"Oh, please do," she said.

He put his fingers on her chest and slid them down, over the curve of her breasts, trailing across her nipples, pausing, teasing, oh, teasing until she was ready to let him do anything he wanted, then angling down to cup her. "Beautiful."

She lay back and he followed. His mouth on her breast was hot and wet, and if he hadn't slid her zipper down the rest of the way, she would have done it for him. The edges of her reality narrowed to Iskander and her. The electric hum continued to zing through her with every breath she took. He yanked on her jeans and she helped him get them off her. He was as desperate as she was.

"Let me see you," he said, peeling her arms from around his neck. His voice came at her, low and urgent and impatient. "All of you."

He looked at her, his hands stroking her, fingers dipping into and out of her navel and heading down, and each and every touch was like lightning through her. The entire time, he was there in her head, and that electricity in her wanted him, sought him out. She wanted him. She wanted his magic around her. Her mouth around him.

She pushed him back and slid off the desk to her knees and cupped his balls with one hand and found a sensitive spot on the underside of his penis. He wasn't circumcised.

"Oh, hell, yes," he said when she took him into her mouth. She loved the salty tang of him, the heat, the soft skin and hardness, and she loved his reaction. He wrapped his hands around her head. His fingers tangled in her hair and helped her find the best motion.

He pulled away before he came, then picked her up to set her back onto the desk. He lay her down again and brought her hips toward the edge of the desk, and Paisley arched her body while he thrust inside her, because it was wonderful, this sensation of his filling her, the slide of him in her, and she nearly lost her mind.

"You're who I want," he said. His words tripped over themselves. "You. This. Paisley, I want this with you." She clenched around him, and he threw back his head. "Fuck. Do that again."

She brought up her legs while he held her hips steady, and, Lord, but the way he moved inside her was heaven— a roll of his hips, a push forward. Inside her, there was a pool of electricity, the source of the hum that vibrated through her, and Iskander reached for it, skimmed along the surface and drew back. He did the same physically, too. She shared in his arousal, the pressure of her body around his, the desire for the magic that could be brought up and intertwined.

Her hands slid up and down his back, tracing the shape of his muscles and reveling in the warmth of his body, his skin against hers, the slide and thrust of him. Whenever she brushed the tattoos on his body, her skin tingled. He thrust inside her again, and his mind wrapped around hers, took her pleasure and opened himself to her, and his urgency sluiced through her. She came. Just like that. Harder than she believed possible.

When she opened her eyes again, Iskander's irises had changed from blue to brilliant green. He went completely still, and her heart about leaped out of her chest at his intense concentration. Her fingers tightened on her shoulders. "What?"

"Someone's here."

"I don't hear any—" The click of a door closing sounded like a cannon. Her head got cold.

"Get dressed." Iskander faced the door. She snatched at her clothes, shoving her legs into her jeans. She found her bra and got that on, then her T-shirt. Iskander found his jeans and put them on without fastening them. He was still erect, she noticed. He had not finished. He bent for his shirt but had to turn it right side out. Footsteps came down the hall, then stopped. Someone tapped on the door.

"Iskander? Is all well?" A man's voice. The door opened, and the mage Leonidas stuck his head inside. She ran her fingers through her hair and wondered if she was just making things worse.

The mage looked in Iskander's direction just as Iskander got his shirt pulled down. His eyes opened wide, and then he stared at something on the floor. Iskander's boxers were on the floor by his bare feet. His gaze slid to Paisley, who stood by the desk, and there really wasn't any doubt what she and Iskander had been doing.

"You didn't answer your phone."

"Oh, hey. Sorry about that," he said after he had his shirt adjusted. He stooped for his boxers and stuffed them into his back pocket. He smiled like they were meeting under normal circumstances. "I got distracted."

The mage looked at Iskander, then at her. "Are you all right, Ms. Nichols?"

"Yes, thanks."

He frowned. "Nothing occurred to which you did not consent?"

She knew she was turning about the same color as her hair. "No, sir."

Iskander picked up one of his shoes. "Fuck you, mage."

"Ms. Nichols, can I offer you a ride home?"

"No, thank you," she said. She still had her link to Iskander, and she knew just how angry he was at the mage's implication that he'd forced Paisley to do anything. "Besides, I live with Iskander."

The mage leaned against the doorjamb. "You might be safer if you did not."

Iskander had both his shoes on by now, and he stood straight. "Thanks for your help tonight. I really appreciate it." He put a hand out behind him and grabbed Paisley's hand. "I'll see you later. Right now, Paisley and I need to get home."

Leonidas ignored him. "I'll tell Nikodemus what happened here."

"You do that."

"And that I think she ought to be living somewhere else."

CHAPTER 26

11:00 P.M., *Vallejo Street*

Iskander opened the back door for her, then walked in after her. He threw his keys onto the table by the door. They clattered onto the wood. "I'm hungry. He dropped a kiss at the outer edge of her eye. "Is there anything to eat in this house?"

She pushed against his chest, relieved to have the conversation move to something she could deal with. "What kind of question is that? Is there anything to eat. Where do you think you are?"

They went to the kitchen and she took things out of the fridge and the freezer. A little later, they were eating saffron chicken with rice while they waited for the custard éclairs from yesterday to come to room temperature. He cleaned up in the kitchen as usual, and that was nice, not having to deal with the dishes afterward. Especially since he did a thorough job.

She put éclairs on a plate and headed to the living room. He grabbed her from behind and turned her around, pressing her back to the wall, the plate of éclairs between them. His fingers stroked her, a gentle touch; then he put both his forearms flat on the wall and leaned in as close as he could, drawing in a breath. "You smell great, Paisley. All butter and sugar."

"Iskander…" She couldn't think what to say because her head said not to let this go any further while her body had completely different ideas about how the next few minutes should go. She picked up one of the éclairs and held it to his mouth.

He took a bite and savored it, keeping his eyes closed until he swallowed. "Almost as sweet as you."

She fed him another bite. "You are crazy, bless your heart."

"Crazy for you, Paisley." He leaned in to get another bite of the éclair she held. "Crazy for you."

She leaned her forehead against his chest and knew she'd give in to him. Whatever he wanted, he would get because he was just too delicious, and she couldn't resist. She straightened, saw they were near a table, and put the éclairs on it.

He reached over and took another one, but he held this one to her lips. "Come on, it's fantastic. Have a bite. And don't give me any baloney about a diet. We're about to work off all those calories."

"Is that so?"

"Yeah," he said in a matter-of-fact tone. He took his phone out of his pocket, turned it off for the second time tonight, and threw it onto the table next to the éclairs. "No one's going to interrupt us here. If you're still interested."

"Are you?"

"What do you think?" He walked without letting go of her, backing her up again until her shoulders were pressed against the living room wall. He planted one forearm by her ear. His other hand rested lightly on her throat. His eyes glowed unearthly blue, and the longer she looked into them, the more convinced she became that something else was living there. Something very much not of this world. True, of course. His thumb pushed on the underside of her jaw so that her head tilted up. His touch was gentle, but she wouldn't have expected anything else.

"I love this." His smile could melt glaciers. His voice was turning her into a puddle. "I love when you get naked and touch me and let me touch you. I love getting blow jobs from you. I love giving you head. I love fucking you." He cocked his head at her. "Does it bother you if I use bad words?" She shook her head. "Good. That's really good. If you want to do any of that right now, don't be shy. I promise you, I will love it." His thumb swept along the line of her jaw, slower now. Loverlike. The backs of his fingers came to rest at the side of her face. "Your skin is so soft. I could touch you all day. I love that about you, too."

Paisley drew in a deep breath and let it out slowly. It wasn't possible to look at him and not think about how perfectly everything came together—the shape of his face, the lines of his body. His body radiated heat, warming her even where they weren't touching.

He kept smiling, but it was a different kind of smile than she was used to seeing from him. This one was full of secrets and edged with what struck her as madness, as if there were a whole series of logic threads he was following that were outside her ability to understand. That made sense, didn't it? Since he wasn't human. For all that his human form was so perfect, he wouldn't think like a human, either. Not really.

"What I want," he said, "is nasty and dirty and involves you and me being naked again." He held up the éclair. "You need to keep your strength up for what I want to do."

She took a bite of the éclair. "Hmm. It's still a little too cold."

"More."

"Later. When they're not too cold."

"We gotta do something while we pass the time." He finished off the éclair himself, then bent his head so his mouth was by her ear. "I want to finish us both right now. Here." He drew back enough to look into her eyes. Her stomach took flight. "That clear enough for you? You know what I want now, right?"

She licked her lower lip, and his eyes followed the motion of her tongue. "Yes. I suppose I do."

He moved a hand from the wall, and the next thing she knew, his fingers were sliding under her shirt, and her entire body felt like she'd been electrified. His eyes were half closed, his mouth soft. "You know what would be hot, Paisley? Let's do it here. Right here. Against the wall."

"Are you sure that's a good idea?"

"Hell, yes, it's a good idea. It's a brilliant idea. Genius idea."

She laughed despite herself.

"See? Already it's making us both happy." He slid his hand farther up her stomach. With his head bowed, he pushed her shirt up to the point where she had to either tell him no or lift her arms. At the same time, he kissed her throat, up near her jaw. He tugged at her shirt.

When he pulled her shirt up higher and just kept going, she lifted her arms. He reached behind her for the fastening of her bra and unhooked it. With his hands behind her holding the ends of her bra, he held her gaze. She melted. Between her legs she was wet and heavy. His attention flicked down and stayed there while he hooked his fingers through the straps of her bra and drew it off her. He did it slowly, too. Like he was teasing them both.

The air around them got warmer. Paisley wanted him to slick his hands over her. She wanted to see his body. To touch him. To lick and taste and hear the sharp intake of his breath. He cupped her breasts, and the moment he touched her, she drew in a breath.

"Oh, yeah," he whispered. "Do that again."

She was losing it, she realized. She was going to lose any and all dignity with him. Iskander was touching her, and she couldn't think of a time when she'd felt this kind of chemistry with anyone. Ever. He slid his fingers over her and she groaned. "I have spent too much time not staring at your chest when I talk to you, but hell, these are amazing. Did I tell you that before?"

He kissed her throat again, a little harder than before, a nip that made her jump and then settle against him. Not that it was unpleasant. Just surprising how strongly she reacted to his mouth there.

"You like that?" he said, drawing back a little.

"Yes."

He let go of her to peel off his shirt and drop it to the floor. He dipped his head in and kissed her there again, his mouth soft, then not as soft, fingers around her hips, thumbs brushing over her waist, his chest pressing against her breasts. He pushed her back just enough to unfasten her jeans. "I get to unwrap you like a present."

He had her zipper down and his hands inside her pants, shoving the fabric down her hips and legs. She left off her exploration of the most perfect male body she'd ever touched to shimmy out of her pants and underwear.

Iskander took a deep breath and shucked his jeans. The boxers he'd shoved in his back pocket fell to the floor. The blue stripe closest to the midline of his body went past his groin near to the dip into his thigh and continued down. She reached out and touched, running a finger from the dip of his hip upward.

"Let me in," he said. "Like before."

A pressure built in her head. She concentrated on Iskander, on relaxing herself, and then her chest flexed and he was there. Vivid. He brought her close and his kiss was hard and deep. His erection pressed into her belly. He had one hand on her breast and caught her nipple between his thumb and forefinger, plucking until she wondered if he was going to make her come just from that. The world was just the two of them, the heat of his body, the unbelievable pleasure and anticipation.

His palm slid along her hip to the underside of her thigh, bringing her leg up, and she felt cool air on her. He shifted his body and he was at her entrance. His mouth curved into a smile. "You're tall enough for this. Isn't that great?"

She pressed her hips forward, and he was there. Exactly what she wanted, after all. No regrets until tomorrow. He held the side of her face and made sure she was looking at him. With one hard thrust, he was inside her, stretching her the way he had before, amplifying the pleasure. He felt good. So good. A moan escaped her.

"Paisley." Her name rushed out of his mouth, hot on her skin. "Yes."

Then his mouth was at her throat again, that spot so close to her jaw. His hand hooked around her other leg, and he lifted her up so that the weight of his body kept her pressed against the wall, and she wrapped her arms around his shoulders and held on.

She rocked forward, trying to get him deeper inside. Her head echoed with the fever heat of his arousal and the sense of something else working its way through her. She closed her eyes and all she saw behind her tightly closed lids was blue. Dark, dark, fathomless blue.

"That's it," he whispered. "Let's get lost in this." Iskander lifted her up, pulled out, then set her down so her feet were on the floor. He faced her to the wall and spooned his front to her back. She saw his palm press flat to the wall. His other hand grabbed her hip. With a knee, he pushed her feet apart, and his hips were hard against her behind, and he tangled his fingers in her hair. He thrust inside her again, his pelvis and belly tight against her while his penis hit exactly the right angle. She braced herself hard against the wall so he could thrust harder and then harder again.

"Upstairs," he said, pushing her down the hallway toward the stairs.

He picked her up before she was halfway there. The next thing she knew, she was flat on her back on a bed—his bed—and he was covering her, sliding inside her. He pushed up on his hands.

His face was intent, and, God, she could just stay lost like this forever. "More," he said. His eyes were changing from blue to green, and she had the impression, quickly gone—hidden from her?—that he wasn't entirely in control of himself. "Paisley, I want more. Damn. Harder." He let out a gasp. "Please."

She wrapped her arms around him and then her legs and arched toward him. Iskander lowered himself to her, curled an arm around the top of her head, and they locked gazes. He wasn't smiling anymore. The look on his face was purely carnal, his mouth tense at the edges, his eyes blue-flecked green. He slowed his thrusts into her for a while, perfect, just perfect. With his weight on one arm, he traced a finger down the midline of her body. Heat settled into her where he touched her. His hips moved forward and stayed there. She wrapped her fingers around his upper arms and squeezed.

He dropped a kiss to the top of her shoulder. His lips stayed soft on her skin, and his tongue, Lord, his tongue traced a lazy circle toward her neck, and every so often he drew his hips back, then pressed slowly in again, and that went on, driving her mad. He slipped farther into her head, too, into her consciousness, and it was like touching a part of him he kept from everyone else. A groan ripped from him, and she had trouble distinguishing her pleasure from his.

He moved so they lay on their sides, facing each other, her outside leg over his hip. With his upper hand, he traced more lines along her body, and this time she was sure she saw tiny sparks leap between them. Her skin heated where those sparks fell.

When she blinked, she saw blue and green behind her eyes. Her sense of him in her head got bigger, and he made a sound deep in the back of his throat, and it was like he was flowing into her, enfolding her, and she knew him. She knew the oath that bound him to Nikodemus, the dark and terrible hole Fen had left behind, and the stark fact that he had willingly made oaths that required him to die if that's what it took to keep her safe.

Her arms tightened around his body. "No," she whispered, even though her throat was thick with tears. "Promise me you won't let that happen."

He kissed away her tears, and he made love to her, even if that wasn't what he called it. Iskander wrapped her up in pleasure and brought her with him when he came.

CHAPTER 27

The next day, 4:00 P.M., Paisley Bakery and Café

Paisley was in the back when Iskander walked into the café. The space was small, but it smelled great, like fresh bread. The young woman behind the counter gave him a long once-over before she left to tell Paisley he was here. He figured Paisley already knew.

The cashier came back, grinning. "She said to give you something to eat, no charge, and tell you she'll be right out."

"Thanks." The woman was good-looking, but he didn't have the slightest urge to hit on her. The old Iskander, the before-Paisley Iskander, definitely would have hit on her. "How about a couple of coffees to go? An extra strong cap for her, macchiato for me."

Today was the party at the home of Paisley's friend and mentor Ashlin Lau, given in honor of Paisley's ex-boyfriend Urban Drummond. The party was being filmed for his cooking show. Since he wanted to make a good impression on her friends, Iskander had turned to Durian for advice about what to wear. The assassin had come through for him in a big way.

He wore black pants, black loafers, and a blue V-neck cashmere sweater that Gray swore matched his eyes. Durian had hooked him up with a tailor to fit the pants and his suit jacket, and even he could tell the difference it made. He'd wanted to look good for Paisley and her friends, and he did.

The cashier placed his two coffees on the counter, and he fixed Paisley's cappuccino the way she liked it. He'd already downed half of his drink when Paisley came out from the back. She did a double-take that made him smile. *Thank you, Durian.* "Hey," he said.

"You look nice," she said. She walked into the customer area and put a hand on his chest. "Wow, Iskander."

He gave her a light kiss on the lips. Nothing hot, but not a *we're just friends kiss* either. He'd done the right thing, getting dressed up, because Paisley had, too. She wore a pair of slim trousers and a green blouse that brought out the green in her hazel eyes. "You look great, cupcake."

Her assistant baker came out of the back carrying some of the supplies for the party. He directed her to his truck. The Chevy was parked right in front of the bakery, and he helped load the boxes and the rest of the supplies. When he came back from that, Paisley was drinking her cap and had her coat draped over one arm.

"Let's go," he said. "I don't want to be late for all that food."

He helped her into the truck. With her looking all hot with her hair down and him in his fancy clothes, they were like any normal couple heading out for a date. Almost. There was no sign of Rasmus, and if there were any magehelds, Paisley would have let him know. He went around to the driver's side and started the truck. The engine turned over with a roar like the enormous 1968 Chevy motor it was. God, he loved this truck.

"Where to?" he asked.

She gave him Ashlin's Kensington address in the East Bay.

"Rasmus lives in Berkeley," he said while they headed for the Bay Bridge.

"I know."

"This isn't going to be Nikodemus's territory. Technically, Nikodemus's rules don't apply there. Magekind can do whatever the hell they want there."

"What about us? Can we?"

"You can. But not me. The kin don't mess with humans the way we used to back in the day. If something comes up, you do what you need to. And then so will I." With a clunk, the driver's side window fell down into the door. Air rushed through the cab. He looked over with a smile and raised his voice. "Ah, the air conditioning is on."

She sank down on the seat and pulled her coat around her. "My wrist hurts."

"Head?" Fucking Rasmus was still messing with her.

"The pressure's back." She touched her temple. "Like someone's trying to break in."

"I have never wanted to waste anyone the way I want to waste Rasmus right now."

Traffic always sucked this time of day, so it took longer than if the daily commute wasn't in full swing. But they made it. He found a place to park that wasn't too far from the house. Ashlin Lau, a tiny woman of Chinese ancestry, whose hair was just starting to go gray, opened the door to Paisley's knock. As he learned, she lived with Julia, her partner of the last thirty years. The guest of honor, Urban Drummond, famous chef and Paisley's former boyfriend wasn't here yet, but the television crew was.

Iskander handed a bottle of wine to Julia and bent to give both women a European-style kiss on both cheeks. They seemed to approve. He noted with some relief that his clothes fit in with what the other guests were wearing. He and Paisley transferred her supplies to the kitchen and then, with him holding her hand, they went to say hello to the people she knew. He reminded himself to keep a lid on his habit of saying whatever came to mind. These were vanilla humans. Not only did he need to pass, he wanted them to like him. For Paisley's sake.

Paisley made the introductions with Ashlin or Julia doing the honors for people she didn't know. The gray-haired man was a lawyer whose wife was a freelance food critic for the *San Francisco Chronicle*. Some of the people she knew from the days before she opened the bakery had new significant others, and there was also Renegade staff hired since she left the restaurant. Iskander thought he did a good job making small talk with them. He was good at passing for human.

The guests were gathered on the flagstone patio in the back, drinking wine and sampling cheeses and a series of canapés that kept appearing from the kitchen where everyone was taking turns sending out amazing food. Pretty soon Paisley would need to go inside to prep her desserts.

Before that happened, Urban Drummond arrived with

a pretty brunette on his arm who didn't look like she ate enough food to sustain her basic caloric needs. She was also a witch. What the hell was the guy doing here with a goddamned witch?

Iskander took an instant dislike to Chef Urban Drummond, and it wasn't just because he used to date Paisley or that he'd walked in here with a witch. He didn't like the way everyone applauded like he was some fucking big deal. He didn't like the way Urban smiled. He didn't like the way he ogled Paisley when he thought no one would notice. And he didn't like the way the guy obviously thought he could have any woman he wanted, including Paisley. The prick.

"I see parking is still impossible," Urban said after the round of applause at his entrance.

The asshole was handsome in a hearty way that made Iskander want to drop a wrecking ball on his head. Urban walked around and pressed flesh and slapped backs like he was running for office. The whole time he kept one arm around his date's tiny waist and his eye on the camera crew.

Iskander walked over to Paisley and took a stuffed mushroom off a nearby salver. "Oh, that's good," he said. He looked over his shoulder, then back at her. "So that's him?"

She nodded.

"He's pretending he doesn't see you yet." Iskander moved closer and lowered his voice while he took three more stuffed mushrooms. "Is the witch a screamer?"

"Yes."

She still had feelings for the guy; he could tell that from the way she was staring at him and the way her body tensed up when he looked her way. Iskander had the other humans blocked out, but he made eye contact with Urban, a second was all he needed, to survey the man's psychic state. He didn't make enough contact to put him afoul of Nikodemus, just enough to get a feel for the guy without breaking any rules.

No question about it, Urban was a confident bastard. He was basking in the attention, taking it as his due. What Iskander didn't get, which was a relief, was any sense that he was under a compulsion from the witch. Good. But he didn't like it at all that Urban had walked in here with one of the magekind. This had Rasmus Kessler all over it.

Paisley distracted him when she put a hand on his arm and told him she needed to go inside to get to work on her desserts. He gave a curt nod and touched her forehead. "Let me in? I'd like to be in contact even when I can't see you." She gave her agreement, and he made his link with her. It felt good. Right. "If you feel any magehelds, come get me, text me, call, yell, do something. I'll probably already know." He stroked his thumb across her forehead, viciously aware that Urban was watching him. "Just in case I've dropped out."

"I will."

He kissed her. Nothing over the top, just a brush of his lips over hers. When it was over, he had the satisfaction of seeing Urban acting like he hadn't been watching the whole time. The asshole.

Not long after Paisley went inside, servers brought out the first desserts. The cameramen set up shots of the trays as they came out. He stood under a grapevine arbor feeling jumpy about the witch and the fact that he might not know about magehelds until it was too late, but so far Urban and his witch were behaving themselves, and he wasn't getting anything worrisome from Paisley.

He caught the witch's eye. Maybe he was wrong about her. Not all the magekind were murdering bastards or bitches. Maybe Rasmus hadn't sent her. Maybe the witch was cool with his kind, notwithstanding she was a screamer. He winked at her so she'd know he knew what she was. She didn't make nice and smile back. All right, then. Now he knew where they stood.

Paisley came out to check the plates of tarts, and Iskander's skin rippled. The magic came from the skinny witch. She was directing all her magical attention at Paisley. So much for thinking this would be fun.

Ashlin Lau joined him and said, "Dear, dear Urban," in a disgustingly fond voice as the chef worked his way in their direction.

"Asshole," he said under his breath.

He didn't realize Ashlin had heard him until she dug her elbow into his side. "Hush now, he'll hear you."

He looked down. She didn't look horrified or insulted. In fact, she was trying not to smile. "Sorry."

"You're not sorry at all," Ashlin said.

"No." He liked this human woman. She was comfortable with herself, and she wasn't pissed off at him for his opinion about Chef Urban Drummond.

"It's true, of course," she went on. "He's only gotten worse over the years, but he is a genius in the kitchen. And amusing, when he wishes to be."

"Like that's an excuse." The top of Ashlin's head barely hit the middle of his chest. He liked older women. Someone like her, if she were into men, would be a lot of fun in bed. But it was just an observation, not something he would do. Before Paisley, he would definitely have taken a shot. He didn't like that Urban had been intimate with Paisley and obviously had fucked her over and was now wondering if he'd get some again. He was jealous of Urban for the former and pissed off at the latter, and he especially hated the guy for all the things he knew about Paisley that he didn't. "What the hell did she ever see in him?" he said out loud.

Ashlin kept her voice low. "He was unkind to Paisley, especially at the end, I'm sorry to say. We all knew the relationship would not last. As, indeed, it did not." She nodded in Urban's direction, but she meant the witch. "He's terrible to all the women he dates."

Urban the Asshole emoted for the camera.

"I'm not sorry their relationship ended," Ashlin said. "It means she's been free to find someone who won't treat her badly. Hmm?" Her eyebrows quirked. "Do you treat her well, young man?"

"As well as I know how."

She elbowed him again. For such a little woman, she was strong. "She's a woman worth having, Iskander."

He gave her a hard stare. If he said the wrong thing, she'd kick his ass.

Ashlin rolled her eyes. "Don't tell me you're one of those men who can't make a commitment. Foolish, foolish boy."

"That isn't it." Christ. He was always two steps behind this emotional crap. He watched Urban the Cooking Jerk move on to another introduction. The witch was still plastered to his side, but she wasn't watching Urban or even paying much attention to the people Urban was meeting. The witch was keeping a sharp eye on Paisley, who had come out of the kitchen again. A young man whose name he'd already forgotten was helping her set up a cake. He knew something about the process since he'd helped her out at that wedding.

"Then what is it?" she asked.

He turned his attention to his companion. Ashlin Lau was a latent, a human with magic she didn't know she had. Maddy would be interested to meet her. "I'm trying not to screw it up with her."

"I can't approve of such a conservative course. Be bold, dear boy. She deserves your best effort." Ashlin poked him in the stomach. "My God, there's not an ounce of fat on you, is there?" He shook his head and the tiny woman adopted an innocent expression that made him snort. "Look at you, you delicious man. No straight woman can look at you without thinking about what you'd be like in bed. I'm thinking about it, and I don't care for men that way."

"We've had sex," he said. "If that's what you're asking."

"Lord, I hope so."

"We have fantastic sex."

"I do like a man who can speak his mind." She rubbed her palm up and down his stomach. "One or two brilliant performances from you that include foreplay, my dear boy—tell me you know what foreplay is—followed by several thoughtful gestures and I think you'd be well on your way to giving her the effort she deserves from you."

He looked at Paisley again. She'd left off examining her cake to watch Urban and his skinny-ass witch working the party. He returned his attention to Ashlin. "I can't get her to tell me what kind of things she likes."

The woman lifted her wineglass in a silent toast. "Observe, my dear boy. What does she have in her home?"

He went back to watching Paisley. "She doesn't have

anything. She's staying with me until I have her apartment ready to live in again. It burned down in a fire." He patted Ashlin between the shoulder blades when her sip of wine went down the wrong pipe. "You okay?"

She coughed a few more times and then wiped her eyes. She lifted a hand to signal she was fine. "Recovered, yes. Thank you. Good heavens. A fire?"

"She didn't tell you?"

"No. She certainly did not."

"Her place burned down." Sort of. Close enough to the truth.

"When did this happen?"

"A while back. I told her I'd replace her things, but she won't spend my money. That's why I don't know what she likes. She needs everything. I could get her new dishes, but that isn't very romantic." He sighed. "Besides, anything I get her is just going to seem practical to her. Just replacing stuff she lost."

"Yes, I see the problem. Well, then, since she needs everything, you must do something impractical."

He couldn't kill Rasmus even though that would be a grand gesture. Nikodemus would have his head on a pike if he did that. "Like what?"

She was gazing at him with a thoughtful expression. "She's living with you, you say?"

"Yes."

"She could have stayed with friends. Me, for example. I'd gladly have taken her in."

He shoved his hands into his coat pockets. No way could he explain to her why that couldn't have happened. "I insisted."

"Before or after you became intimate?"

"Before."

She made an irritated face. "Oh, damn. Here comes Urban. And the cameras. Just when things were getting interesting, too."

With that, Urban the Food Cooker and his damned witch strolled over. The man spread his arms wide. "Ashlin."

Ashlin handed Iskander her wine and walked into the man's open arms to receive and return an enthusiastic hug.

Iskander and the witch gazed at each other. She didn't smile. Neither did he. "Fiend." She spoke in a low voice. "You'll regret your involvement here."

"Not tonight I won't." He lifted Ashlin's wine.

"Attempt to harm any of them," the witch said, "and you will end up as my mageheld."

He smiled softly. To keep up appearances. She was pulling magic through her, and that made his skin crawl, but so far he wasn't worried about what she could do. "Not going to happen."

"It's been too long," Urban was saying to Ashlin.

"Yes, it has." Ashlin, however, had caught the last word the witch had said to Iskander and looked with wide-eyed alarm at the woman.

"Let me introduce you," Urban said. He drew the witch against his side. "This is Freddie. Frederica Sylvester. She's works for my West Coast publicist." Frederica smiled and this time it was friendly. She was faking it. "Freddie, this is my beloved friend and mentor Ashlin Lau. She taught me everything that matters about sauces."

She held out a hand to Ashlin. Her nails were long and dark purple. "So pleased to meet you, Ms. Lau." The witch smiled, and it was a damn convincing act. "I've heard of you, of course."

"A pleasure, Freddie." Ashlin put a hand on Iskander's upper arm. "Allow me to introduce my handsome friend."

"Please do," Freddie said.

She did the honors and then got another baffled look. "What *do* you do, you dear man? Do you cook?"

"No." He gave Ashlin a big grin. "I eat."

By this time, Paisley was aware something was going on that involved him, and she walked over, looking as if she expected he would strip naked any minute. He knew from Paisley's grimace that the screaming from the witch was getting to her. He kept a smile, but he pulled his magic, because if this went south, he had to be ready. "I deal in antiquities."

"Do you?" the witch said. "Any kind in particular?"

"Sumerian and Assyrian, for the most part." He shrugged. "I invest, too."

"In?"

Iskander didn't fail to notice Urban's sudden interest at that. Odds were the guy was going to ask him to put his money into some venture. "Anything likely to turn a profit."

Paisley made it to them. At last, Urban acknowledged her existence. The cameraman backed up a bit and got a shot of Paisley shaking hands with Urban.

"Paisley. Honey, how are you?" Urban grabbed her by the shoulders and looked her up and down. "You look great."

Iskander didn't even have to reach for the man's thoughts to know he wasn't going to let go of the superior position he thought he'd established back whenever he and Paisley were a thing. Once an insensitive asshole, always an insensitive asshole.

She broke the contact, but after another sweeping glance at her, Urban pulled her in close for one of his patented hugs for hot women, meaning the embrace lasted a little too long and the hands wandered.

Ashlin poked Iskander in the stomach again. *No fucking kidding*, he thought.

The witch had to get in her dig, too. When Urban let go of Paisley, she held out a hand, gave her name, and said, "I've heard so much about you, Paisley. How's your little cake shop doing?"

"Very well, thank you." She reached for Freddie's hand.

Iskander felt the magic too late to keep Paisley from touching the witch, but he got a hand out in time to jostle Freddie and turn what should have been a firm handshake into more of a glancing brush of fingers. His skin prickled and a painful shock raced up his arm. Whatever she'd done, it was awkward and unsubtle, and exactly the kind of bullshit Rasmus was pulling with Paisley. He placed himself between Paisley and the witch. That magic-laden touch wasn't any accident, and it sure as hell wasn't innocent. "Sorry," he said. "Didn't mean to be clumsy."

He did a quick scan of the room for people who were reacting to Freddie's magic. No one was having any of the typical reactions when someone was stupid about pulling magic. No one was rubbing their arms, shuddering, or staring at Freddie with a puzzled expression. Ashlin, maybe, but she seemed to be the sort to play things close to the vest.

The witch tried again, and Iskander pulled his magic up through him until the witch had to be vibrating from it. Paisley reacted, too, but he already felt the echo from her, the tension and ache of the witch's attempt to use magic on her. She failed, of course.

"Hey, Paisley." Iskander touched her shoulder, and immediately he heard the screaming and got a full-on blast of the pain in her head, the sense of something attempting to pry its way in. Her eyes were losing focus. Shit. No, she was not all right. He slipped a hand under her forearm. "You've been serving up food long enough. I think it's time you let someone else do that."

She reached toward the witch. Iskander braced himself and made sure he was close enough to stop the witch if he had to. If he was careful and he timed things just right, he could take her heart before anyone knew what the hell was going on.

The witch didn't have a clue what was about to happen to her because she didn't do anything to keep Paisley from touching her. The woman pulled again, and there was no question in his mind that she intended to use her magic against Paisley. Paisley's hand touched the center of the witch's chest, and faster than the other times, she brought away her hand.

The witch gasped and her magic broke off. She staggered back. Urban, being clueless about what had just happened, caught the witch's arm. Paisley opened her hand and Iskander stepped in, giving the magic that flowed from her fingers a way to get home. It was her natural resistance, he realized, that kept the magic she'd taken from the witch from boomeranging into her, the way you'd expect with a talisman, for example. The woman had her hands clasped over her chest, gasping the way the other witch had done. If Urban hadn't caught her, she probably would have fallen.

"You bitch," Freddie said, low and ugly. She pushed away from Urban and lunged at Paisley.

Iskander stepped in to take the brunt of her attack. At the same time, he pushed Paisley back. He didn't hold back on the magic he pulled through him. He'd fry the witch here and now if he had to. He grabbed the witch's arm and released enough magic into her to scramble her brains for a bit. Her forward motion stopped abruptly. "Whoa," he said with a laugh. He looked at Urban. "My friend, I think your girlfriend has had too much to drink. Maybe you should get her a cab and send her home."

He let up on the witch just enough for Urban to take over. She was unsteady on her feet but aware enough to know she couldn't do anything here that vanilla humans wouldn't be able to explain away. All the same, Iskander kept himself between the witch and Paisley.

Her lips drew back from her teeth. "What did you do to me, you bitch?"

Ashlin drew herself up. "Iskander is right, Urban. You need to send the lady home."

She pointed at Iskander. "I'll kill you. Right after I kill her."

Iskander met her gaze and leaned in close enough to say, "If you have a complaint about me, take it up with Nikodemus. You know where to find him." He moved away. "Paisley, you ready to go?"

CHAPTER 28

The next day

Harsh called early the following morning, while he and Paisley were still in bed, because, yes, he was still more than interested in having sex with her, and he liked lying beside her while she slept. The phone woke her up, but he kept his arm around her while he answered.

"Hey, Harsh. What's up?"

Harsh said, "Meeting tonight. Seven o'clock. Bring Paisley."

"Bring the usual?"

"Yes."

The meetings were potluck, which meant Harsh cooked something fabulous and just about everyone else brought takeout. Iskander was in charge of desserts. He looked over at Paisley and grinned. She looked so adorably rumpled when she woke up. "Will do." He dropped his phone on the floor, rolled over to face Paisley, and told her about the meeting. "Can you bake some stuff? Something killer good."

"Sure. What would you like?"

"A cake. A really awesome cake like those ones you make for me. Chocolate with that bitching frosting you do. Brownies. Gotta have brownies."

"How about some tarts, too? Cookies?"

"Perfect."

"For how many?"

"Fifteen or twenty."

She pushed herself onto her elbow and brushed her hair out of her face. "Are they all bottomless pits like you?"

He laughed. "Yeah. Pretty much."

"What time is it now?"

"Little after six."

She snuggled back into the covers. "Good thing it's Sunday."

He turned onto his stomach and draped his body partly over hers. "You put in more hours than anyone else at the bakery. You should take some time off once in a while."

"I'm the owner. That's the way it works."

"Tell me how I can help you get more time." He was still racking his brains about what kind of things he could do for her that would show he cared. "If you need money, I have it."

Paisley frowned. "I'm not going to take money from you."

"Hire an accountant to do the books and payroll for you. Get a couple more bakers. Nikodemus has attorneys and accountants on staff. He'll hook you up with good advice."

"I can't afford advice that good."

"If he doesn't comp you, I'll call in some favors and

set it up at a price you can afford." He slid his arms under the sheets and pulled her close.

"I'll think about it."

"That's all I ask." He kissed her ear and then her cheek and worked his way lower. "What else can I do for you?" he said. He moved his hand between them and waggled his eyebrows at her. "Am I getting close?"

"You wicked creature, you."

"What's your favorite color? Do you like jewelry? Did you used to collect anything? What if we got a dog? Do you like dogs?"

She touched his face, sliding her fingers along his tats, and it felt good. Really, really good. "My favorite color these days is blue."

"What's your favorite flower?" But he never got an answer. She was too busy making him forget his own name.

At six o'clock that evening, her ponytail made a streak of dark red over the crisp white of her shoulder, mysterious with strands of mahogany and gold. He wanted to undo her hair and bury his fingers in it. The cake she'd made at his request was boxed and taped down so he couldn't peek at what she'd done. Three more boxes sat on the kitchen counter. His house smelled like a bakery, and it was awesome.

He took his time looking at her, thinking about peeling off her clothes and his and stretching himself out on top of that killer body of hers. She wore a black and white polka-dot dress and a pair of flat slipper-type shoes. She had a tiny purse under one arm and a jacket draped over the other. The dress was short. Or maybe it was just her legs were long. Plenty tight enough, though it looked to be made of a springy fabric.

"You look fantastic."

"Thanks." They loaded her boxes into the truck. The cake went on her lap and the rest of the items he put on the floor between her feet where they covered up the hole in the floorboard. Her dress hiked up another couple of inches.

He started the car and the engine about drowned out his words. "Ready?"

"Ready."

Fifteen minutes later, he parked the Chevy in Harsh's garage, next to Nikodemus's Reventón. Now, *there* was a car. He wondered if Nikodemus would consider trading. He got out and came around to help Paisley with the desserts. She reached for the boxes on the floor, and he tried not to look down her dress while she was doing that. The neckline didn't gape the way he'd been hoping.

She handed him the other boxes. Iskander balanced them on one palm while he helped her slide from the Chevy with the cake box firmly in her arms. Long, long pretty legs. Iskander thought of them with great fondness. With great lust.

She looked at the sleek black car and pointed. "That's a twenty-first-century car. Harsh must have some serious money."

"Probably, but that isn't Harsh's car." Should he buy her one? If he had the money, would that be overkill? What about insurance and maintenance? He'd have to cover that for her. Which he could get away with if let her think they would share the car. "It probably means Xia and Alexandrine are here. Xia is having some kind of affair with Nikodemus's car."

"Nikodemus." She shuddered, and he moved closer to her. "I can feel him. And others like you. Magekind, too."

"Carson, Alexandrine, Maddy. Emily. Leonidas. Maybe some of Maddy's wilders."

"And Harsh. I thought he was one of you."

"He is. Mostly." Well, wasn't that interesting? She was picking up on that about Harsh. He shifted the boxes he was carrying. "Just so there's no surprises, Rasmus Kessler is Alexandrine's father." Paisley's eyes widened. "They don't get along. He tried to kill her once. More than once."

"This is like walking into a minefield."

He kissed the top of her head. "No worries. I've got your back, cupcake."

Ashlin Lau was right. He needed to do something to prove to Paisley that he cared. He just didn't know what that was.

CHAPTER 29

Paisley took a good look around on the way inside. This wasn't a house. Harsh Marit lived in a mansion. An honest to goodness mansion. She happened to know the Gettys lived just a few houses down. She'd catered the desserts for a party there a couple of years ago when she was saving every penny she could in order to open up the bakery. Never once had she imagined she'd be a guest in any of these mansions.

If you had the ability to do magic that controlled other people and could do Lord knows what else, it must be easy to amass the kind of money that bought a house like this and a car like the one in the garage. Conversation got louder the farther inside the house they got, and her chest vibrated more. There were demons in there. Of course. Pretty soon the air smelled of curry and something cooked in garlic and butter.

Iskander led her into a living room full of people, and there was a dip in the sound level of the room. A sort of communal intake of breath. There was music playing, but it wasn't loud enough to cover the quiet. Most of them weren't people at all. Demons. They were demons. A few, very few, were magekind. There were no screamers here, thank God.

Maybe twenty people were here, mostly men but a few women. She'd met Carson before, but the other women were strangers. She stopped beside Iskander, holding the cake box with her purse squashed under one arm. They were going to have to walk the gauntlet all the way across the room to the table with food and drinks on it.

"Iskander!" someone said.

Iskander lifted a hand in greeting, not far because his arms were full, and headed for the table of food. She followed. The minute Iskander put down his boxes, a very tall and very big man clapped him on the back.

"Hey, Xia," Iskander said.

While she tried not to stare too hard, Iskander and Xia did that male hand clasp, back slap thing. They stepped apart when they were done. Iskander opened the top box, then looked around the room and said loudly, "Dessert's here!"

Xia rubbed his hands together. The ornately carved hilt of some kind of weapon was clipped to the side of his jeans. "Did you get those little brownies from the grocery again? I love those."

Paisley put down the cake box and shoved her purse into her coat pocket. She found a clean plate and, from the box of supplies she'd brought along, took out a bottle of chocolate syrup and piped a decorative swirl on the plate. She arranged her brownies and added a dusting of powdered sugar, also from the supplies she'd brought. She set out the first plate, then did another with the cookies and tarts from the other boxes Iskander had carried in.

Iskander took one of the brownies and handed it to Xia. "My friend," he said, "I have acquired the secret weapon of desserts."

"What's this?" From the corner of her eye, she saw Xia staring at the brownie he held with a deeply suspicious expression. She gave up arranging food to watch. She was always nervous when someone new was trying her food. There was, she knew, no accounting for taste, and some people flat out had none. He examined the brownie before asking in a worried voice, "Did you make this?"

"No," Iskander said. He rolled his eyes. "I did not."

"It's not my favorite kind."

Iskander glared at him. "This is better. Way better."

Her heart pinched a little at how fiercely Iskander responded.

The big man looked over his shoulder and called out, "Alexandrine, baby, if I die, it was for a good cause. I love you."

Alexandrine. Rasmus Kessler's daughter. And the woman was involved with a demon. She tried to figure out which woman she was. A tall blonde who didn't look anything like Rasmus except for the color of her hair seemed the most likely candidate.

"Try it," Iskander said. "And prepare for heaven."

Xia took a tentative bite. Good grief. He was almost as gorgeous as Iskander. She enjoyed watching the expression on his face go from worry to amazement to sheer bliss.

"Where did you buy these?" he asked Iskander.

Iskander jerked his thumb in Paisley's direction and grinned. "My secret weapon made them."

Xia's head whipped around, and Paisley was speared

by a pair of eyes too blue to be real. Nobody had eyes like that in real life. Neon blue. Not human. Her chest thrummed. He took a step toward her. She would have backed up if she wasn't already against the table. Xia was really big, and though she knew Iskander would never let anyone hurt her, Xia didn't look friendly. He jabbed a finger at her. "*You* made these brownies?"

"Yes, sir, I did." Her accent turned as thick as her chocolate syrup. She wiped her hands on a paper napkin and held it out. "Paisley Nichols. Pleased to meet you."

"You're Paisley Nichols?" His eyes went wide, and he did a quick check of Iskander. "The human woman Nikodemus was telling us about?"

She nodded. "I assume so, yes."

"You freed kin who were lost to us."

"That's her," Iskander said.

Xia ate another bite of brownie. "And you made these?"

"Yes, sir, I did."

While she watched in amazement, Xia went down on both knees and then bowed his head, the fingers of one hand pressed to his forehead. That got them some attention. The noise level in the room went down several more notches. Xia looked up and said, "For food like that, I'd swear fealty to you if I weren't already sworn."

"Good grief, get up." She shot a glance at Iskander, but he was no help. He was grinning like he'd made the brownies himself. "They're only brownies."

He stood, smiling like a kid. "What else did you bring?"

A petite woman with glossy black hair and a hooked nose that made her more beautiful rather than less, sidled in between Iskander and Xia to reach for a brownie. She wasn't the least bit afraid of Xia, and for a moment she wondered if this was Alexandrine. The woman slid a shoulder across Iskander's chest as she got between the table and Xia. She was magekind. "Hello, Iskander."

"Hey, Maddy." Iskander didn't do anything to avoid or end the contact. Plainly they were good friends. Then again, Iskander was friends with everyone. And a flirt.

"Cookies," Paisley said in answer to Xia's earlier question. She tried to ignore Iskander and Maddy and couldn't. "There's cake, too." She handed Xia one of the chocolate chocolate-chip cookies. "I brought strawberry custard tarts, too."

He looked at her from over the top of the cookie. "You made these, too?"

"Yes, sir."

He bit into the cookie. By now, there were several people crowding around the table.

Maddy fixed her attention on Paisley. She had a tart in one hand and the other on Iskander's chest. Her dark eyes went wide when she took a bite. "These are heavenly."

"Thank you very much." Paisley turned around and unboxed the cake, sliding the disassembled cardboard container from underneath. She had an awkward moment while she looked for a place to put the cardboard. She slipped it under the table. She was jealous of Maddy, which was stupid.

Oh, Jesus. She wanted to be the one who touched him like that. In front of everyone. She bowed her head. Somewhere along the way, her feelings for Iskander had gotten complicated. Or maybe it wasn't complicated at all. She pressed her hands to the table to stop them from trembling. Her first time meeting Iskander's friends and she was turning into a jealous bitch.

Meanwhile, Xia stepped up to examine the cake she'd made. White chocolate buttercream with white chocolate dots and sugared violets. Inside was chocolate and vanilla checkerboard, though the others didn't know that yet. Xia looked at her and back at the cake. "I fucking worship you."

"Paisley," someone said.

She looked and saw Harsh coming toward them. He wore a suit tonight, and for once she could believe he was a physician just from looking at him. "Dr. Marit."

Maddy gave her a strange look. She still had her hand on Iskander's chest.

"Don't you clean up nice?" Paisley reached up and touched Harsh's tie. He preened for her until she had to laugh. If Iskander could flirt with Maddy, then she could flirt with Harsh. Right?

"Thank you." He surveyed the cake. "That is too pretty to eat."

"No, it's not," Iskander said. He pushed his way closer, away from Maddy, who, Paisley was aware, was now regarding her with a curious expression. "Totally not. That's killer frosting right there—she made it specially for me—and I'm not passing it up because you're a pussy." He threw out a hand and grabbed a fistful of Xia's shirt. "Give me your knife."

"Fuck off. You're not cutting cake with my knife."

Iskander glared at him. Maddy had yet to stop staring at her, and that meant Paisley had to concentrate on not staring back just as rudely. A shiver took her, raising goose bumps up and down her arms. Something in

Paisley's chest flexed, and Maddy's eyes widened. The woman mouthed the word *ouch*.

"That shit's not going to work with her," Iskander said with a glance at Maddy. "She's a resistant."

"So I've learned."

"You want cake, Xia?" Iskander asked. "Or are you a pussy, too, and just want to look at it?"

Paisley didn't care for Maddy. At all. She was still standing too close to Iskander, for one thing. Xia unsnapped the weapon from the scabbard at his hip and handed Iskander a knife that didn't look like any knife Paisley had ever seen.

"Put that thing away," Harsh said. He made a brusque motion with one hand. "It's not safe in here and you know it." It wasn't clear to Paisley what Harsh meant by that besides what was obvious about a knife that wasn't made for cutting cake. Harsh said, "I'll get a knife from the kitchen." He glared at Iskander and Xia. "No one do anything stupid."

"Don't look at me," Iskander said.

"Maddy," Harsh said. "Don't let them do anything stupid."

"I make no promises," she said.

While Harsh went off, Maddy walked to Paisley and stuck out her hand. "I'm Maddy Winters. Nikodemus speaks very highly of you."

Paisley didn't want to shake hands but she did. "Paisley Nichols. Nice to meet you, too."

"How did you and Iskander meet?" She was being pleasant, but Paisley couldn't help thinking there was a note of something else in her words and in the way Maddy looked her up and down. Obviously, she thought Paisley was yet another in Iskander's parade of women.

She pasted on a big smile. "He's my landlord."

Iskander draped an arm around Maddy's shoulder, and the witch's arm slipped lower until only her thumb in his belt loop kept her hand from ending up on his ass. "I thought you knew. Rasmus scourged her apartment. She lives with me now."

Maddy twisted to look at Iskander. "She lives with you?"

"Yeah," Iskander said. Maddy disengaged from their embrace, and Iskander didn't seem to notice the look she gave him. Or the long and thoughtful look she gave Paisley.

"What have you two done?" Maddy said softly.

Iskander was oblivious. "We need to talk about our boy Rasmus Kessler tonight."

Harsh returned with the knife and a stack of plates, so Paisley didn't hear the rest of Iskander's conversation with Maddy. Harsh, she found, knew enough about the serious business of cake cutting to have brought a bowl of hot water and a towel.

"Bless you, Harsh."

"My pleasure."

She busied herself cutting square slices of cake. Harsh stayed next to her, moving plates of cake out of her way while she dipped the knife in the warm water and dried it off before she cut the next series of slices. The whole time, she was aware of Iskander and Maddy standing together. Close together.

Everything clicked into place. Of course. Iskander had been to bed with Maddy. She knew it. Absolutely knew it.

"They seem very friendly," she said to Harsh.

"Maddy and Iskander?"

"Yes." The knife hit the bottom of the cake plate with a *thunk*.

"He does some work for her from time to time."

Ka-chink. "Work." *Ka-thunk*. "How long did they date?" she asked as calmly as she could.

"I don't think they did." Harsh laughed. "But then Iskander doesn't date so much as commit serial sex. Maddy's too good for him."

She stopped cutting cake. "With all due respect," she said in a low voice, "that is bullshit." She lifted the knife between them, pointing it at Harsh. "Iskander is my friend. He is kind and caring and generous, so don't you dare go around saying he's not good enough for someone."

Harsh lifted his hands. "My apologies."

"Apology accepted." She kept cutting slices until Harsh wrapped his fingers around her elbow.

"Put away the knife, Paisley, and let me introduce you around before the meeting gets going."

She shot a glance in Iskander's direction. He was still talking to Maddy. The beautiful, very sexy, very-interested-in-him Maddy Winters.

Harsh said, "It's her business to know what's going on with the magekind in this territory. She's going to be interested in you, too."

"Isn't that just lovely?"

He walked her away from the table and started introducing her around. At least meeting the others was a distraction. She was shaking hands with yet another demon when a chill went through the room. It hit her, too. Just about everyone turned toward the main door.

A tall—most of these guys were tall—man with brown hair and light brown eyes came in with his arm draped around a woman so beautiful Paisley was in love with her herself. The two made a stunning couple. He was as gorgeous as the woman with him. "Wow," she whispered.

A strange thing happened, which she noticed because of where she was standing. First, the guy with brown hair, who was almost too adorably cute and had obviously dressed down for the party, paid no attention whatsoever to the fifteen or so men who faced him and touched their fingers to their foreheads as he passed.

He zeroed in on Maddy like he had some kind of radar. His hand, which was on the beautiful woman's shoulder, slid down to her waist, bringing her in tight. Maddy, who up to now had been keeping a more polite distance from Iskander—not that Paisley was keeping track—took one look at the guy and plastered herself against Iskander. Iskander looked like he'd been bitten by a rattlesnake.

The couple headed straight for Harsh. The man kept his arm around his companion's waist. When they stopped, she shook her long black hair over her shoulder and smiled. "Harsh, nice to see you. As ever."

Harsh pressed his fingers to his bowed forehead as the others had done. "Kynan," he said. "And, Emily. A pleasure to see you, too."

Kynan nodded like it was nothing to be greeted so formally. Then he looked straight at Paisley and said, "You're the new girl Nikodemus is so worked up about."

"Kynan," Harsh said, "this is Paisley Nichols." He drew in a breath and put a hand on her elbow again, as if he thought she needed to be steadied. From the corner of her eye, she saw Iskander striding toward them. "Paisley," Harsh went on in a smooth voice, "this is Kynan Aijan and Emily dit Menart."

Paisley stuck out her hand. "Paisley." She forced a grin. "The new girl. Nice to meet you, sir."

The man's eyes pierced her. He looked young, early twenties at best, but his eyes were a million years old. He stared at her, and she gazed back, taking in the ripped jeans and faded T-shirt and the eyes that belonged to a much older man, and her stomach curled up. Not in a good way. He swiped his thumb across her forehead like he was removing a smudge. While he did that, his eyes connected with hers, and for a minute she lost all sense of where she was in space. If Harsh hadn't been holding on to her, she would have fallen over.

She blinked a few times before things came back into focus, and even then not all at once. First, she became aware of the warmth of someone's fingers on the back of her arm, then the music playing and the sound of muted conversation. Kynan's eyes continued to bore into her. They were more gold than bronze, she thought.

"My friend, leave her alone."

"Iskander," Kynan said in a voice that sent shivers of cold up and down her spine, "what the hell were you thinking?"

"None of your goddamned business."

That was Iskander speaking. His arm steadying her. He didn't sound like his usual cheerful self. She looked up and saw that wasn't his usual cheerful expression, either. Maddy was beside him, though not touching him any longer. If looks could kill, Kynan would be a puddle on the floor. "And you will not interfere."

Another chill went through the room as Nikodemus strolled in. Carson went to his side. The room fell silent. Everyone bowed, even Kynan, fingers pressed to their foreheads. "Oh, good," he said. "You're all here." He looked around and waited a beat. "There's a mage coming in the next five minutes. A representative of the Russian Federation. Paisley, if he's a screamer, and I think he will be, you do your thing. I have a fucking point to make with the Russians."

CHAPTER 30

The Palace Hotel, San Francisco

His thoughts came into focus with a snap. There was no time for the breathless disorder that came with finding himself alone in his mind. He could not recall his name or where, precisely, he might be, but he was bone certain that if he had five minutes alone, he'd be lucky. Luck had not been with him lately. She would come. Fen. And he would lose even this moment of control.

He searched the pockets of his suit and found a cell phone and wallet intact. This was not his home but a hotel suite, an expensive one he gathered, since he was standing in a living room from which he could see through to the bedroom. Details registered in his mind with the speed of a desert tortoise. He found seven hundred dollars in hundreds and fifties in the wallet as well as three credit cards and a California state driver's license, all of them issued to someone named Rasmus Kessler. The license was inside a clear plastic sleeve. Kessler was an organ donor, he noted.

He found the bathroom and compared himself to the license photo. The face that gazed at him from the mirror was thinner than the one in the photo, and that man's hair was not braided as his was, but other than that, he appeared to be Rasmus Kessler.

The red beads worked into the dozens of braids clicked softly. The sound sparked a memory. The beads were rubies and they helped him somehow . . . The fragment of recollection dissolved.

There was, he noticed, a slip of paper tucked into the back of the sleeve that held the driver's license. He took it out and unfolded it to find a phone number written on it with the phrase *Nikodemus must be warned* scrawled underneath. The word *must* had been underlined several times, at least once hard enough to make a hole in the paper.

Warned of what?

He took out the cell phone and saw there was no list of recent calls and no phone numbers in the contacts. Whoever had used the phone last had wiped the device of any personal information. An interesting level of paranoia. Or wise. Very wise.

Rasmus dialed the number on the scrap of paper. His pulse raced while he listened to the ringing on the other end. Had he done this before? He strode out of the bathroom and into the living room just as a woman answered on the other end.

"Alexandrine speaking."

His breath caught. He grabbed a padded leatherette

binder from one of the tables near the sofa. The name of the hotel was embossed on the front. *Palace Hotel*. Underneath that, in smaller letters, was the location. San Francisco.

He still could not connect the name *Rasmus Kessler* to himself, though that had to be his name. In the same way, he knew he lived across the bay in Berkeley only because of the address on the license. Chasing down those thoughts did no good. His mind refused to offer up anything else. No assurance of his name. No memories of his house.

"Hello?" the woman said. "You still there?"

His skin prickled. Her voice was familiar, but there was nothing more beyond his certainty that he had at least spoken to her before. Words jammed in his throat. "Nikodemus must be warned."

"About what?" the woman said.

"I'm sorry," he said. "I do not know."

"Do you need help?"

"Yes."

"We can do that."

Someone in the hall outside the door laughed. The locking mechanism emitted a mechanized buzz. Fen. "It's her," he said to the woman on the phone. "If she discovers that I've called you, she will do worse than kill me."

"Who is this, and where can we find you?

"Rasmus Kessler. I am at the Palace Hotel."

There was dead silence on the other end. "Well, fuck you, Daddy."

The response made no sense to him, and there was no

time to figure it out. "I do not know what room I am in. You must warn Nikodemus."

Rasmus pressed the RESET button on the phone so that Fen wouldn't find out who he'd called. At least not from the phone. He dropped it into his pocket as the suite's door swung open.

CHAPTER 31

Broadway and Baker, San Francisco

Turned out the mage arrived in fewer than five minutes. Paisley felt the reaction thirty seconds before he appeared, and her reaction lagged behind most of others by a bit. Iskander moved closer to her as a florid man in a very expensive suit walked in with six men behind him. A screamer. She flinched and steeled herself against clapping her hands over her ears. The six men were magehelds. All six wore suits and all six had their hair buzzed short.

Iskander put a hand on her shoulder. Having him close helped. Everyone in the room tensed except Harsh, who went to the table and gathered a plate of desserts, which he presented to the man with a nod and a greeting. "Yevgeny. Welcome."

The Russian accepted the plate without acknowledging Harsh. He gave a tight nod to Nikodemus. "Warlord."

He spoke with a strong accent. "Please accept greetings from Bratislava Demitrova."

Nikodemus crossed his arms over his chest. "Yevgeny. I thought I made myself clear to both of you about who I'd accept as a representative in my territory. Was there a misunderstanding?"

Yevgeny handed his plate to one of the men with him and said something in Russian. The man took the fork and sampled everything on the plate. "These are dangerous times, Warlord. What you asked is not possible. To give up anything such as you ask." He lifted both hands. "Unthinkable."

"I don't give a shit what you can or can't think about. I made myself clear."

Yevgeny smiled and clasped his hands in front of his crotch. His magehelds moved in closer.

"Magekind in my territory cannot keep magic they killed to get. End of story. You shouldn't be here," Nikodemus said.

"If you kill me, Bratislava will not take it kindly."

Kynan, Harsh, and Xia moved closer to Nikodemus. There was enough magic in the room to make the air crackle. "We don't take kindly to being murdered."

"There will be war." Yevgeny took a step back. "No one wants that."

Nikodemus smiled. "I don't need to kill you. I just need to send you home with only the magic you were born with."

The Russian glanced at his magehelds. The screaming coming from him got louder, slicing through Paisley like a blade. The mageheld holding the plate of food put it down on a nearby table.

At her side, Iskander put a hand on her lower back. Paisley's heart about galloped out of her chest. This wasn't like the other times she'd done this. There hadn't been magehelds involved or a mage who knew what was going to happen to him.

"Give up the magic you stole, or it will be taken from you."

Yevgeny smiled engagingly. It was easy to imagine sitting down to drinks with him. His eyes were pretty, as blue as the sky and darkly lashed, with a sleepy look belied by the awareness there. "My answer is no."

"Paisley." Nikodemus gestured.

She swallowed once, hard, and walked toward Yevgeny and his magehelds. Iskander went with her. His body was loose, his hands swinging free at his sides. He was pulling magic, and it raised gooseflesh on her skin. Iskander wasn't the only one pulling, either.

"You swore your fiends would not attack me."

Nikodemus waved a hand in dismissal. "Bratislava knew my terms. She should not have sent you without you complying."

"An impasse, then." He kept a nervous eye on Iskander. "Can we not agree that she was wrong and have our discussion? There is much she wished me to bring up to you, Warlord."

"No."

Yevgeny looked Paisley up and down. The screams echoing in her head drowned out her fear. "Pretty girl. I will regret if she comes to harm."

"His job is to protect her, Yevgeny," Nikodemus said, hooking his thumb in Iskander's direction. "With his life, so be careful what you do when she's done."

When she was close enough, Paisley lifted a hand. One of the magehelds reached to block her. Iskander's arm shot out and gripped the mageheld's wrist. "Touch her," he said in a low voice as he pushed away the mageheld's arm, "and you will die."

The inside of her head filled with shrieks, and it was killing her to hear that horrible sound without cease. She lifted her hand again. The same mageheld moved to intercept her. Iskander's body became a blur. She didn't see how the mageheld died; she just felt it happen. In the space between her heartbeats, she touched Yevgeny's chest. Agonized screams rushed toward her, through her, like a hurricane. She yanked back.

Yevgeny shrieked.

She fell back at the same time two of the Russian's magehelds lunged for her. Iskander was there, impossibly fast. The two went down, and she was aware they weren't moving and that the Russian was still screaming. The other three stood, eyes wide, uncertain what to do.

She opened her fingers and the screaming in her head stopped. Blessed silence. At last.

On the floor, Yevgeny groaned, hands over his chest. He spoke in Russian again, and then in English. "Kill them all."

Out of nowhere, one of the men who'd been standing by Nikodemus appeared by the Russians. Durian, she thought his name was. The assassin. Magic poured from him. Iskander moved again, a blur of red mist blossoming in the air. Her hair blew in a desert wind, whipping around her face, blinding her and a booming sound echoed through her body. When she could see again, Durian was on one knee, his fingers pressed to his forehead, and Carson was stepping away from one of the magehelds.

Paisley blinked and tried to make sense of what had happened. Yevgeny was still on the floor, hands to his chest and breathing hard. Two magehelds were still alive, but they felt different to her. Both them were in various stages of some kind of convulsive collapse. She shivered, even though her skin felt hot.

The warlord approached Yevgeny, radiating enough power to heat the air around him. "I never make threats," he said. The Russian muttered something and Nikodemus shook his head. "Not here. Not in my house. Your magic won't work here." He leaned over the Russian. "I told Bratislava what would happen if she sent someone like you. Go home without your goddamned slaves and without our blood on your soul, and you make sure everyone you meet understands the terms I'm offering. Clear?"

Yevgeny growled.

"Harsh, see our Russian friend to the door, would you? Get him a cab if he needs one to get to his hotel. Xia and Alexandrine, go with him and sever any magehelds he left outside."

Harsh nodded. "Warlord."

Holding hands, Xia and the tall blond woman followed Harsh and Yevgeny out.

In the ensuing silence, Durian turned to Paisley. "I didn't believe such a thing was possible. What you did to the mage." He touched three fingers to his forehead. "Thank you."

Iskander bumped shoulders with Paisley, then caught her around the waist and pulled her close. From the corner of her eye, she saw Maddy cock her head. "That's my girl."

"Is it true you hear them screaming?" Kynan asked. He looked sickened by the possibility.

She held out a fist and slowly unfurled her fingers. "Until I let go."

"Jesus," one of the women whispered.

"If you don't mind," Nikodemus said to her, "I'd like a word with you. In private." He swept a hand toward a door to his left. Paisley felt a tug in her chest and exchanged a look with Iskander, who shrugged.

She went with the warlord to an office with a red leather couch, a red leather chair, and a bookcase filled with empty glass vases. Nikodemus took two bottles of water from a mini-fridge on one side of the room. He handed her one of the waters and sat on the desk. His T-shirt read *I'm with stupid.* "Have a seat."

"Thanks."

"Couple things." He opened his water. "First, good work out there."

"Thanks."

"I've cut a check to one Ashlin Lau, paying off her loan to you." He took a drink of water. "I thought about buying your current location but decided I'd wait to hear if you want to find a larger space. I paid the rent for the rest of your lease, so don't write any more checks to the landlord. If you have an auto payment, cancel it."

"That's generous of you. But it's really not necessary—"

He cut her off with a sharp gesture. "Not your call. I did it. I take care of my people, especially the humans." He swung his legs. "Maddy will give you a jingle and set up a meeting to go over your corporate structure, get you on the health plan and the 401(k). We do matching, by the way. Flex plan, health club membership. One of my accountants will get in touch with you. My advice to you is take advantage."

She opened her water. "All right."

He took another drink. "You should think about moving closer to the rest of us."

"Have you been talking to Leonidas?"

"My place in Tiburon has plenty of room. Lots of company, too. I know Carson wouldn't mind another woman in the house." He shrugged. "Or you could move here if you want. Up to you. Either way, you'd be safer from Rasmus."

"I'm happy where I am."

He met her gaze. "Yeah?"

"Yeah."

"If that changes, you know you have somewhere to go."

"Give him a little credit, Warlord."

"Oh, I do." He laughed. "I hope it works out between you two, I really do."

He didn't sound like he thought it would.

CHAPTER 32

Iskander was talking to Maddy and Harsh when Paisley came back from her meeting with Nikodemus. He put down his plate of cake and brownies. She was as pale as snow. Shocked, maybe, from what had gone down with the Russians. He didn't care if it was rude—he went to her and she walked into his arms and said very simply, "Please take me home."

"Let's go."

They left without saying good-bye to anyone. The drive home was quiet and air-conditioned via that god-damned window he was going to have to get fixed. Paisley wasn't inured to cold the way he was. At this hour, there wasn't much traffic, and they were home before he knew it. Home. His house, which he had so often struggled to make into a place he wanted to be, really did feel like home. Because of Paisley. That came as something of a shock to him, and it made him sad, too.

He wanted this to last, this feeling that he had a home and that everything was right and going to stay that way.

His life wasn't an easy one, and maybe Paisley had decided she couldn't deal with the violence. He wouldn't blame her if she just wanted to get far away from his world.

Inside, he threw his keys on the little table by the back door and stayed there, considering what to say. He came up with, "What?"

Genius, he thought. But she was being too quiet. Way too quiet.

She leaned against the wall, her arms crossed under her breasts. Her mouth was tense and his heart sank. He didn't expect a good outcome from this. She said, "Were you the one who told Nikodemus to buy out my lease and pay off Ashlin?"

"Is that what he did?" Her response to that was a roll of her eyes. Time to fess up, then. "I told him you needed business advice." He wanted to touch her, but he could tell she was angry about something. He just wasn't sure what.

"I wish you'd warned me about you and Maddy."

His stomach tensed up. "If I told you about every woman I've been to bed with, that's all we'd talk about."

"She isn't one of your one-nighters, Iskander. You two work together. You see her all the time."

"We're not seeing each other like that."

"You haven't slept with her?"

"We had a thing for bit. But that's over."

"Well, she obviously thinks you two still have a relationship." She balled her fists and looked away. "Listen to me." She let out a trembling sigh. "I sound like a jealous bitch."

"Hey." He closed the distance between them and touched her cheek. "Hey, cupcake. We had a thing, but we don't anymore. We both knew we were never good for the long-term."

She lifted her eyes to him, and even he could tell she felt miserable. "I'm sorry. It's none of my business. I shouldn't have said anything, but she's just so beautiful, and you were having a good time talking to her. And everyone likes her—I could tell."

"Yeah." He kept touching her, stroking her cheek. "She's smart and funny, and I like her a lot. But she's not you."

She rested her head against his chest and sighed again. "Damn," she said. "It's been a long day."

"No kidding. Come on. I know the perfect place for us to relax." He grabbed her hand and walked her toward a room at the back of the house. Durian had a similar room in his house in St. Francis Wood. Bare walls the color of midnight, a spray of copper stars scattered across the ceiling and falling toward the floor. He opened a drawer in a table he'd lacquered sunset-orange and took out a wooden box and a lighter.

Still holding her hand, he led her out back. She didn't resist, so whatever Nikodemus had said to her, whatever she thought about him and Maddy, she wasn't kicking him to the curb. Yet.

He took off his shoes and set the box down on the ledge. "Sit down if you want, Paisley. Or not."

She did, waiting in silence while he took the cover off the hot tub.

"You can ask me anything," he said. "And I'll answer you. You want to know about me and Maddy, okay. Or Fen. We can talk about her, too." He stripped off his shirt. His jeans were next, but he stopped with his hands on his fly. Her eyes were on him, and that was something, wasn't it? He dragged down his zipper. "So, questions for me?"

"A few," she said.

He shucked his jeans in one motion. Paisley wrapped her arms around her middle as he stepped into the hot tub and reached back for the box he'd brought with him. He proceeded to roll his own cigarette from the contents. "Water's warm, cupcake." He brought the hand-rolled cigarette to his mouth and inhaled.

Paisley sniffed. "What's in that?"

He let out a stream of smoke. "Bergamot-infused Turkish tobacco, cut with unrefined copa."

She shook her head. "Copa. What's that?"

"The kin use copa to relax." He lifted a hand in the air. "Commune with the greater world. The magekind found out it lets them use more magic, and a lot of them abuse. It's addictive to them. If they aren't careful"—he took another hit—"really careful, sooner or later they burn out their magic."

Paisley walked around to where Iskander had his arms on the platform. She sat down cross-legged and held out her hand. She wiggled her fingers. "What happens if I smoke it?"

"Tobacco is bad for humans."

"But not for you?"

"Nope. Demons don't get lung cancer." He snuffed the cigarette between his wet thumb and forefinger, then turned around and with one smooth motion, hauled himself out of the hot tub. Water dripped off him. He stayed where he was, letting Paisley look her fill. His stomach dropped off the world because she did look. From his head to his toes with a nice long stop at his junk. At the bench, he picked up the items he'd set there. He walked back with his hand open. There were two lumps of copa on his palm. "Pure copa. Take the smaller one. Don't let it dissolve in your mouth. Swallow it as fast as you can."

"Is it safe?"

"You'd have to take more than I have on hand to over-dose."

"Why?"

He knew what she was asking. "I want to see if it works on you. Maybe it'll take down some of your resistance."

"And?"

"And then there's nasty shit I want to do to you." He waited for her to tell him to forget it.

"What if nothing happens?"

He shrugged. "Then nothing happens, and I don't ever have to share my stash with you." She took the smaller lump from him. It was soft and a bit crumbly, the way high-quality copa should be. "Tastes like shit, just so you know."

"Thanks for the warning." She made a face when the bitter tang hit her tongue, though she did what he said and swallowed the stuff. Iskander put the larger clump of the copa in his mouth. "I'm not going see pink elephants, am I?"

"No." He slid back into the hot tub, sitting so he faced her. "Come on in," he said softly. "The water's fine."

Paisley stood up and pulled her dress over her head, and then, with Iskander watching her, she took off her bra and panties, too. Under the circumstances, he felt he didn't need to make an effort to look at her face. Her body ought to be illegal. She had killer curves and legs that went on forever, and, well, in all honesty, he was a boob man, and Paisley's were spectacular. He wanted to touch her everywhere, but especially there.

"Just so you know," she said, "I'm a total lightweight when it comes to drugs."

"I've got your back."

She blinked down at him and slowly nodded. "I know you do."

He held out a hand. "First question?"

She got in the hot tub with him and said, "Are you having sex with me because I have red hair?"

"No."

"Is it because I'm here and convenient?"

The copa was working on him, and he did feel less tense. But not less tense enough. "I'm sleeping with you because you're a beautiful woman."

"Is that the only reason?"

"No."

"What else?"

"You're human and that turns me on. You have magic, and that turns me on, too. I'm bound over to you, and that makes a difference. You're—"

"Are you in love with Maddy?"

"No."

"Why not?"

"She's in love with someone else, only it didn't work out, and that first night we hooked up—that was way before Rasmus scourged your apartment—she was looking to feel better." He didn't regret that night with Maddy. Paisley was right. It had been different with Maddy. She'd shown him that maybe there was something more he could have. "I'm good at making women feel better."

She sank lower into the water. "True."

"Funny thing is, when she knocked that night, I thought it was you." He stretched out a leg and touched her thigh with the side of his foot. Her eyes locked with his, and he got a straight shot of her psychic state. He smiled. Because, well, she didn't move, did she? "Hey, Paisley," he said softly.

She gazed at him, and damned if it didn't look as if her eyes were turning. "Is it only sex with us?"

He thought about her long legs and the way she felt to him the times he'd connected with her. She wasn't anything like the vanilla humans he'd been with. He moved closer to her. "No," he said. "It's not."

"Why?"

"I like you. A lot. You laugh at my jokes."

She waved a hand and blinked some more. "Some of your jokes are actually funny, you know."

"You work hard at the bakery. You're making a success out of it. On your own. You take care of me. You think about me. Nobody has ever done that before. And you're doing this thing for us, for the kin, even though it's dangerous. I'd respect the hell out of you just for that."

"Are you still in love with Fen?"

"No."

"What would happen if I said I loved you?"

His heart turned over. "Do you?"

"That's not an answer to my question."

"I'd be fucking scared to death, Paisley."

"Just so you know, I don't know if I love you or not." She wrinkled her forehead and blinked a few times, which made Iskander wonder if the copa wasn't affecting her more than a little. The drug did stuff to humans with magic that could affect vision, but that only happened with actual witches, not latent humans.

He moved through the water until he was right in front of her, straddling her with his thighs. They weren't far apart. He put his hands on the platform by her shoulders and leaned in to her. "You make me feel good, Paisley, and I want it to keep going."

She tipped her head back, exposing the length of her neck to him, and gazed at him. She didn't know what that meant to someone like him, showing him the pale sweep of her naked throat. Her eyes blinked a few times, slowly. In between he could see her pupils contracting. Her resistance thinned to just about nothing. Then she said, "You make me feel good, too. You're my friend."

What was he supposed to say to that? *I don't fucking want to be friends*?

"Urban and I were never friends. I think that's why we didn't work out. Well, one of the reasons. But you're my friend. We have a good time together."

Her eyes were a deeper green than they had been. While he watched, her pupils went from big to pinpoint small. Whatever Rasmus Kessler had done to her or had been doing over the last weeks had leaked magic into her. With her resistance thinned the way it was right now, he could feel the wide, deep pond that had been forming in her.

He grabbed her by the waist and put her up on the platform, and he took the time to drink in the sight of her wet, naked body. Her hands landed on his shoulders to steady herself. He reached past her for the copa and formed two more balls of the substance, working quickly so his damp hands didn't dissolve the stuff. He put one in his mouth and held the other to her. He placed it on her tongue when she opened her mouth.

"About those nasty things I want to do . . ." he said.

She made a face as the bitter copa dissolved in her mouth. "Mmm?"

"You on board with that?"

Her answer to that was a smile and a sultry backward lean against the hot tub.

"Then how about you let me in, Paisley." He tapped a finger to her temple.

"Yes," she said.

And he was in her head, easy and smooth. He put his fingertips on the upper part of her chest, just above the swell of her beautiful, gorgeous, human wet-dream tits. His slid his fingers down and made sure she was getting his reaction. Things got really quiet. His fingertips traced along her skin, slid over her nipples, and she drew in a shuddering breath. "Do you like that?"

She nodded.

"What if I used my mouth? Would you like that?"

"I'd like that a lot."

He circled her nipples, feeling her get hard under his tongue. He grabbed her hips and pulled her closer to him. The skin down his back rippled. He kept one hand on her hip and slid the other up to her breast again. Her sharp intake of breath turned a few cranks for him. She touched her palm to his cheek.

"Iskander."

He was so close. He moved his head to her shoulder and nipped her. With teeth that were still human. "I want a taste of you. A little blood. Can I do that? I can make it good for us both if you let me do that."

"All right."

He made a deeper psychic connection with her, and it was still smooth and easy. She was relaxed. Nothing invasive but enough for him to feel the magic in her and an echo of her fealty to Nikodemus. With one hand he grabbed her wrist, the one Rasmus had scarred.

Paisley drew in a long hiss, and it was all he could do not to take things too far. He brought her wrist to his mouth and let himself change. Enough. Maybe a little more than enough. He lifted his head and said, "Look at me and tell me what you see."

She did, but she was a little wobbly, so he caught the back of her neck and held her steady. Her eyes were jade green now, and he could feel the magic in her. And his oaths to her. She frowned. "I'm having trouble focusing."

"That's the copa working on you. It'll settle down in a bit."

"Oh."

"I won't hurt you, Paisley. Ever. I promise you that." He let the change take him the rest of the way. He was a thousand times more aroused that he'd been even with Fen, not because he hadn't loved Fen—he had before everything went to hell between them—but because Paisley was human and humans had that effect on his kind. And because he was with Paisley.

He watched her eyes. Her pupils were pinpoints of black in the jade of her irises. She squinted and then blinked several times. "This is what I am."

She put her hands on either side of his face, touching all the planes and angles that had changed, and while she did that, he touched her, too. "I know you," she whispered. "I know what and who you are."

He slid both hands around her waist and then around and up her back until his hands cupped her shoulders from behind. A growl rumbled in his chest. His breath hitched deep in his body. He made sure she understood that if he wanted to, he could take her over so she would understand all the risks. He wasn't going to, though. Instead, he let her feel his desire for her, his urge to be inside her. At the same time that pool of still magic came through to him and drove his desire higher yet. Not quite a witch. Something else. Something in between.

She sucked in a breath, and he looked down at her body, so slight and delicate compared to what he was now. He wrapped his fingers around her wrist and raised her arm to his mouth while he watched her face. His teeth broke through her skin, and her blood washed across his tongue, hot and sweet, and his body responded to the point where he forgot anything but the psychic connection and physical sensation. Warm water around them. Their wet, slick bodies, her skin under his fingertips. The scent of her, the taste of her, the sizzle of magic. His intense pleasure. Drugging pleasure.

Her reactions trickled through to him. Disbelief, a little fear, a big dose of arousal, curiosity. He drew back and brought his body back to human form and fought for control of his instincts. With his human hands, he drew his fingers along her waist, over the outside of her breasts, to her shoulders, her throat, her face.

She put her arms around him, touching him, stroking. "More," she said. "More."

CHAPTER 33

Paisley threw her head back and closed her eyes. She breathed in slowly as Iskander's tongue slid across her arm. The buzz that echoed back to her was beyond amazing. He pulled away, still holding her wrist, and made a shallow cut in the side of his throat. With his other hand, he cupped the back of her head and brought her forward.

Water sloshed around them as she moved closer to him. Her fingers slid along his torso, over solid muscle and sleek skin. The zing of the first touch of her tongue to his blood spread through her like fire. Iskander's hands tightened on her. The center of her chest flexed.

Heat flashed through her, a sensation that they were without physical support, floating. A weight settled in her, a pressure against her mind, and she had to concentrate on letting that pressure past and into her. Iskander's presence in her head became a brilliant heat.

They separated, though he continued to hold her. Her vision went crazy. Straight lines refused to meet at what ought to be corners, colors were more saturated, and there were shades she couldn't put a name to. With a great deal of effort, she forced her eyes to focus. The world came back to normal with a stomach-churning wrench. He peered down at her, still in her head. His face was recognizably human now, his skin the familiar brown. The muscles of his torso were as perfectly defined as ever. She touched one of the blue stripes on his torso and felt a buzz under her fingertips.

His expression was serious. That was different for him. He put a hand to her chin and tilted her head so she looked into his face. His beautiful, lovely, normal every-day human sensual face. She wanted him to smile because his smile always made her happy.

"Anything you want," he said. His mouth curved while his hand caressed the side of her face, and that sent shivers through her belly and to all the other sensitive parts of her body. She put her hands against his chest. His warm, naked chest. He brought her hand to his mouth and kissed her palm, then each of her fingers, and each touch of his mouth brought her closer to the edge. He straddled her, taking his weight on his thighs. "The copa's working."

"And?"

"Like I said, that's very interesting. For us both."

She moved her legs only to have him smile darkly and shift his thighs a little wider apart, an adjustment that brought his pelvis closer to the tops of her legs. He took her first finger and licked, and while he was doing that, she stared at his nearly closed eyes. One of the lines of his tattoo went down the center of his eyelid. His sooty lashes lifted, revealing irises that were an out-of-this-world blue. The middle blue line of his tattoo colored his sclera, too. How on earth had he managed to dye the white part of his eye?

He kissed her index finger and then pushed himself

back so that the water sloshed against the opposite side of the hot tub, but then he headed back. At the last minute, he slid his hands into the water and underneath her thighs; then somehow, her thighs were over his and his hands were supporting her bottom.

"Oh, my." She threw her arms around his shoulders.

Then he kissed her, and it wasn't the kind of kiss where she wondered for even a second whether he meant it. His mouth was gentle and then not, and one of his hands moved up to cradle the back of her head and pull her toward him. Iskander made a sound in the back of his throat that made her feel desirable and adored.

Paisley allowed the experience to slide over her, to inhabit her. She wanted to memorize every moment of this. He held her tight against his groin so it was impossible to miss his erection. He tightened his arms around her. With no warning, he picked her up and rose as if she weighed nothing. She wrapped her legs around him and held on tight. In two steps they were out of the hot tub, and he was walking inside the house with her.

"We're dripping water all over."

"It'll dry."

She nodded, and before she knew it, they were on his bed, and he was stretched out on top of her. He looked into her face and smiled. "Ready?"

"Yes, sir, I am." She smiled back. Her body was ready for him. Now. Right now. "For what?"

"While you're still feeling the copa, try to touch your magic. Because it'll be hot if you have some magic when we do it."

His gazed locked with hers. She wondered if she was hallucinating the brilliant color. He dipped his head and took her nipple in his mouth until she was moaning. When he stopped, his eyes were practically glowing, even after she blinked. "This is different," he whispered. "With the others it was just sex. But that's not us."

"We aren't having sex." She managed a grin. "In case you haven't noticed."

He smiled at her, that lovely, wonderful, sensual, incandescent smile. His hand trailed up the inside of her thigh. "You need to let me do something about that, then."

"Like what?"

"Like make you forget your name. Which I will do in just a minute." Her chest tingled where his palm lay on her skin. "Do you feel that?" She nodded. The sensation increased. "Hold on." He lowered himself to her and kissed the side of her throat. His mouth was firm, insistent, and the whole time the tingle in her chest intensified. When he drew back, he said, "I do this with Maddy's wilders all the time. Help them use their magic for the first time."

"I don't want us to talk about Maddy."

"We're talking about your magic, cupcake. Concentrate. Can you hold on to that? Like you're reaching inside and pulling hard. If you catch hold, don't let go."

The bizarre thing was that she could. She could touch the sensation quivering inside her and pull it through her, from nowhere to inside her chest. In her head.

Iskander's eyes opened wide. "You sure you've never done this before?"

"I've had sex before. More than once, too."

He laughed and his hand went between her legs and stroked her. God, she was so close. So close. "You're a natural. I've never seen anyone get it so fast."

She moved out of his embrace and touched him,

starting with that amazing torso of his. She got an echo back of his physical reaction to that, the arousal. Her fingers landed on two of those blue stripes that ran down his body. She felt the resonance through her fingertips, and the sensation seemed to move from there along her arm and into her chest. "You like this, don't you? Me touching you like this?"

His eyes flickered to dark, dark blue, and the tension of his sexual arousal raced through her. "What do you think?"

She took a breath. "Are you going to change?"

"I want to." He put his mouth at the crook of her neck, and his teeth nipped at her before he whispered, "Are you asking me to, Paisley?"

Was she?

"Maybe," she whispered. "Yes."

She felt the change in the size and shape of his body first; then he drew back, and she could see him, and all she could think was that he really was a kind of demon and that the centuries of human fear of creatures like him didn't touch her at all. He was Iskander and she knew him. She touched him, explored his body, and kept losing herself in pleasure.

After a bit, he pulled himself over her, positioning his body and using a knee to nudge apart her legs. His hide was warm leather against her skin. Not human, and she was going to let this happen. She wanted it to happen. Her body and mind were ready and more than willing. She shifted, tipping her pelvis to give him the access he needed. Her need to have him inside her seemed unendurable.

"Now. Iskander, now." She arched her back, and then he pushed inside her, slowly, his eyes locked with hers.

All the sensation in her body focused here, between her legs, inside her.

"You feel good." His pelvis rocked forward. "So good. Paisley, yes. " He drew in a long, slow breath. She could hardly believe this was happening, that he wanted her and that he was hard, and she was already at the edge of arousal and about to fall over, and, oh, God, he pulled back his hips and then pushed inside her again and this felt better than anything she'd ever experienced in her life.

He pushed up on his palms, taking his weight off her. But the pressure of his hips against her remained, his legs touching hers, and he was moving inside her, and he fit even though she could feel that she was tight around him. She was aware of him in another way, in the tingle that went down her spine and the resonance in her head, and she recognized that because he looked into her eyes and said, "Yes."

After a while, after their bodies slid and touched, and after she thought she would lose her mind, he pulled out of her and turned her over. He hiked her hips up, and his hands went around her waist. When she'd braced herself, he slid himself inside her again, and the difference in the angle made her groan with pleasure.

"Is this all right for you?" he asked in his rougher voice. "Tell me it is. Because it's better than all right for me."

The best she could do was gasp his name.

His nails were sharp; she felt them on her skin every now and then, once when his hand smoothed the length of her spine, another time when his other hand tightened around her hip. Her breath was tight in her chest and she responded to the way he held her. As they moved together, she felt him adjust the grip of his hands around her waist, and that worked for her. Her breath hitched in her chest. His skin was hot where he touched her, his body hard and inside hers. She rocked her hips in time with his, taking the roughness, feeding off it. Every stroke, every caress took her closer to mindless pleasure.

"Please," she said.

"Please what?"

"What you're doing. Lord, Iskander. Please."

He drew himself over her again, thrusting inside harder than before. She raised her knees, trying to take him deeper. He let go of her and withdrew so she could turn around, which she did. He bent his head to her chest, and his tongue flicked over her nipple. She knew from the touch of his mind with hers that he wanted things a little faster. Rougher.

He went still. "Is this all right?"

CHAPTER 34

Iskander let his mind slip around hers, finding the desire and letting her feel his and taking them both higher, and it was fierce and lovely, and he never wanted this to end. During a moment when he thrust hard inside her and then stayed there, buried deep, she arched against him, wrapping her legs tight around his flanks.

Her body shivered with incipient orgasm, and she pushed him onto his back and straddled him, leaning forward to get the best angle for taking him inside her while he lifted his pelvis toward hers as she came down. He knew she saw him, saw precisely what he was.

She leaned down and pressed her mouth to his torso. The touch of her tongue on him was exciting beyond belief. She ran her fingers along the muscles of his torso and belly, and he gripped her hips—he was careful of her because he was bigger and stronger like this and his instinct to procreate was edging out of control. He rocked up and deep into her, and he knew he was hitting exactly the right place for her, because her face got that flush of pleasure that always drove him crazy. He circled his arms around her and rolled them over so that she was on her back.

He could hardly breathe for looking at her. She obviously wasn't in the habit of sunbathing because her skin was the same pale, pink-flushed white everywhere he looked. No tan lines on her upper torso. He was familiar with the arousal that got fed by his magic; he felt it whenever he had sex with a vanilla human. He'd felt it with Maddy, too, but he'd never come close to asking Maddy to let things go this far.

He took her right hand in his and deliberately set a finger on the scar on her wrist. He scratched with a talon and watched the blood well. She picked up on his hunger and moaned. He might have done the same. This was like getting a direct line to her magic. She shivered. He brought her wrist to his mouth. The taste of her blood sent a shock through him. He got a tingle of magekind from her, and it was like a drug.

With his other hand, he stroked the length of her body. Hell, she felt so soft and smooth, and the whole time he touched the injury Rasmus had caused. It set him on fire, doing this, connecting with the place where so much magic had flowed through her. The fingers of his other hand slid down, touching her pubic hair, sliding past to the slick folds of her body and the spot that would break her apart for him.

Then her hand, her human hand, found his cock and held him just tight enough. Moved just enough. Fucking perfect. She got her other hand on him and let him know she wanted him closer to her, so he did that but without letting go of her wrist and without stopping the suction that kept the taste of her in his mouth.

She slid down his body so that she was the one on her knees, between his spread legs, a hand on his cock, and—

"Yes," he said. He let go of her arm. "Fuck, yes."

Her mouth closed over his dick, and her free hand cupped his balls. He put his hand to the back of her head and let her give him the best blow job of his entire life.

His orgasm just about took off the top of his head, because she worked him with exactly the right pressure but mostly because she was Paisley and not some woman whose name he wasn't going to remember the next day.

When he floated back to his body, he realized he had her wrist clutched in his hand, and when she looked up, he let her feel what he did—the visceral reaction to her scent, her skin, the anticipation of coming inside her, how all of it was tied up with his magic and hers.

"Feel that?"

She nodded, her eyes focused on him. After which he returned the favor and gave her head until she was writhing and calling his name and her breath was coming in short pants, and he made damned sure she came as hard as he had.

She made a tiny sound in the back of her throat when he thrust inside her, human this time. Both of them human so she'd be safe. She was slick and hot around him, and even though he was usually one to talk a lot when he was fucking, he didn't say anything because he didn't have the words for what he was feeling. He just did her missionary because he could watch her face and the arch of her neck and the way her mouth parted, and he could feel the way his cock was surrounded by her vagina. Her muscles gripped him, and her hands touched his shoulders and slid down his back, touching now and again the traceries alongside his spine.

Once, when that spot on her wrist brushed against the outermost line down his spine, it was like mainlining a shot of pure magic. Her hands cupped his ass, urging him on, and of course he was going to give her whatever she wanted from him. His own breath came in gasps, because he was heading for another climax.

His skin slid against hers, slippery with her sweat. He knew his eyes were changing, and he let her see that, the transformation threatening to take him again. In the back of his mind, he was hoping she'd tell him yes, that she was ready now for whatever happened. Only she didn't, so he held back because he didn't have her permission for that, and he didn't want her at risk of having a child she wasn't ready for or didn't want.

He hit an unbearable peak, when he was convinced he wouldn't break through to his orgasm, and he moved harder in her, faster, and she held him tight and then she came. She threw back her head and shuddered beneath him, and her throat was exposed to him, and the plain truth was that he lost it. Her body was clenching around him, and he dropped his head to her throat and bit hard enough to draw blood at the underside of her jaw. The moment her blood hit his mouth, he came.

Hard. And he held her there, feeling her coming still, his own orgasm separating his mind from his body, and hell, he just about died from the pleasure.

CHAPTER 35

Two days later

In half a daze, Paisley listened to Iskander's phone call. The room was still dark, but she didn't know what time it was because Iskander didn't have a clock. Early, though. It felt early.

"What's up?" he said in a low voice. Not at all sleepy. Because, as he'd told her, his kind didn't sleep. They just faked it if they needed to. He kept his body close to hers while he talked to whoever was calling him, though he didn't say much except at the end. "On my way as soon as you get someone over here to keep an eye on Paisley." He listened some more. "Yeah. He's good. Nine. She'll need a ride to work." He disconnected the call and kissed her shoulder. "Gotta go in a bit."

She rolled over. "I'll make you breakfast."

"It's four in the morning. You stay in bed."

She didn't, though. He'd eat leftover cake or brownies

for breakfast if she didn't make something decent for him. She grabbed one of his shirts and went downstairs while he got dressed. In the kitchen, she put on coffee and made a batch of buttermilk pancakes. Her mother's recipe and one she hadn't altered. She microwaved some bacon, too. He came down just as the first pancake was coming off the griddle.

When he was done eating, he took his empty plate to the sink and then paused, head cocked. A few seconds later, she got the vibration in her chest that meant his backup had arrived.

"Be careful, okay?" she said.

He kissed her. "Always. See you later."

She got the dishwasher loaded and some laundry started, and when that was done, she made the butter cookies Iskander liked. The rolled-out dough was chilling in the fridge when her sense of the fiend who was watching the house bubbled through her with painful intensity, then... vanished, followed immediately by a bang outside loud enough to rattle the windows. She held her breath, wondering if it was an earthquake and, if it was, whether the shaking would continue.

Her phone was upstairs and there wasn't any landline. The windows stopped rattling, but now there was a roar outside she couldn't place. A bonfire? That made no sense. Outside, somebody shouted. Other voices joined in. She walked to the front of the house. She still didn't feel the fiend who was supposed to be watching for Rasmus. Sirens wailed and instead of fading, got louder and louder. When she reached the front room, the lighting was all wrong for seven-thirty on an overcast morning. The smell of smoke wafted into the house.

Those were flames outside the window.

She peeked out, standing to one side so no one would see her. A car in front of the house was on fire. In the short time she watched, the flames shot higher than she could see. Heat pushed at the windows, and air around the fire rippled as if it were water. She wasn't sure but she thought she saw the outline of a body in the car.

A gray-haired man was fighting the fire with a garden hose, but he gave up and joined the knot of people backing away from the heat of the fire. Even Paisley leaned away.

The first fire truck arrived, lights filling the room with alternating flashes of color. The siren wound down to the point where she could hear the crackle of the radio. A patrol car rolled up. The gawkers backed farther away, leaving only one man in the street.

Rasmus.

He had his arms crossed over his chest, a familiar, satisfied smile on his face. His eyes met hers, and while she watched him, horrified, he made the shape of a gun with his finger and thumb and pointed it at her. He mimed pulling the trigger.

Paisley yelped and jumped away from the window.

She kept her body low and her head down and hurried back to the bedroom—Iskander's room—for her cell phone. Her fingers shook when she snatched it off the bedside table.

Rasmus had set that car on fire. She knew it. And now he was waiting out there, just one of a crowd of rubberneckers. No one would think he was stalking anyone. She didn't bother calling the police. She called Iskander and got voice mail. She left a message and dialed the other number Iskander had given her. There was a pop from downstairs, and the lights went out. The line on the other end rang and rang and then stopped.

The man who answered was annoyed. "What?"

She almost hung up. But she worked for Nikodemus, and she was in trouble, and they were all supposed to have her back. "It's Paisley Nichols."

"Kynan here." His voice gentled, and she could have sworn she felt something click in the back of her head. "What's up?"

"Iskander told me if something happened I should call this number." She was talking too fast and having a hard time getting enough air. She told him about how her sense of the fiend who was watching her had vanished, about the fire, and about how Rasmus Kessler was outside and had mimed shooting her.

"Is he alone?"

"I think so."

"Are you sure? If he brought magehelds, would you feel them?"

"Yes. I don't feel anything."

"I'm on my way. Don't do anything stupid before I get there. Sit tight—unless he sets the house on fire. Then get the hell out."

Downstairs, someone rapped on the door, followed by, "San Francisco Police."

Her pulse jumped into overdrive. "The police are here. I think they're evacuating the houses closest to the fire."

Kynan said, "I'll be there in ten minutes. Probably less. Wait for me." He hung up, leaving her listening to dead air.

The police knocked again.

Cell phone in hand, Paisley walked to the door. The

minute she opened it, the screams lanced through her. She would have slammed the door closed, but the officer, who looked like he was all of twenty years old, caught the edge of the door. Behind the officer, Rasmus smiled at her, his eyes jittering. She went on the offensive and pointed at Rasmus. "What is *he* doing with you, Officer?"

"Ma'am." The cop put a foot over the threshold so she couldn't shut the door when he held up a hand. His other hand curled over the butt of his gun. The holster was still latched. "He was concerned for your safety, ma'am." He did that looking-around thing cops did when they were assessing a situation. "And the safety of his residence."

"*His* residence?" she said. The fire trucks were still outside, and the firefighters were spraying water on the fire and the surrounding roofs. A nearby tree was on fire, too. The car, an SUV from the looks of it, was burning down to a blackened hull. The air smelled like chemicals and smoke. "He told you this was his house?

Rasmus's grin widened. "You shouldn't have started the fire. We could have talked about this the way I asked. Rationally."

She crossed her arms over her chest. She stared at the cop's chest and read his name off his shirt. "Officer Haines, whatever story he's told you is a lie. He's been harassing me for weeks. Please get him away from me. Now."

"You see, Officer?" Rasmus said. "Just as I said, she is not cooperating."

"Leave me alone, Rasmus."

"Do you mind if I come in?" the cop asked.

"Yes." She kept her hand on the door. "I do mind." Rasmus looked smug, and that bothered her. Why, when the law was on her side? "This isn't my house, for one thing."

"Of course not," Rasmus said. "As I said."

"The owner isn't home. And he"—she pointed at Rasmus—"doesn't live here. He never has." Her arm shook. There weren't any other cops that she could see, and the firefighters were still working on the SUV.

"Ma'am—"

"I don't know what he told you, but he doesn't own this house or rent it." She did her best to stay calm. Where was Kynan? "We never dated. We were never friends. He's a disturbed man, and all I want is for him to leave me alone."

"My love," Rasmus said. "Please calm down. Officer, my apologies. She's off her medication again. This happens from time to time. I'm sure you understand."

"Don't you dare pretend you know me." The screaming from him was horrific. "If he won't get you away from me, I'll call one of the officers who knows about my case." She lifted her phone and brought up her contacts. "This time they'll arrest you," she said. "And you'll go to jail."

Haines shot out a hand and slammed the door open. She had to jerk back to avoid getting hit in the face. He reached for her, and as he did, she saw a quarter-sized area of his skin on his wrist that shone bright pink. But he didn't go for her. He went for her phone and slammed it onto the landing. It shattered.

Her chest flexed and just like that, her phone was whole.

Rasmus muttered something, and Haines stomped on her phone, pulverizing it. He pushed the door hard enough to get her off balance and took a step over the threshold. At the same time, she heard something break at the back of the house. Her heart stopped, and a thrumming started up in her chest. Enough to hurt.

Rasmus gripped the side of the door, and something

above him gave out a *pop* that made Paisley's ears hurt. He yelped and jumped back, his eyes skittering madly. "Did you see that? She assaulted me." He got in the cop's face and spoke with emphatic clearness. "You will arrest her. Now."

"I wasn't anywhere near him." Behind her a dog growled. The sound made the hair on the back of her neck stand up. She looked around for Kynan. Anyone. And didn't see a thing.

The police officer reached behind him for his hand-cuffs. In the same motion, he grabbed one of her hands. His fingers squeezed her wrist hard. She locked gazes with him, and her stomach dropped to her toes. His eyes were devoid of life, but what terrified her was that his pupils were vibrating.

With eerie calm, the cop said, "Hands on your head, ma'am." At the same time he stepped forward and pushed her away from the door and into the house. Rasmus tried to follow, but there were several more pops. If she hadn't been restrained, she would have clapped her hands over her ears. The cop twisted her wrist behind her and pushed her outside with her arm up behind her. He snapped on the handcuffs.

Behind her, something clicked on the floor. She twisted around and saw a large brindled dog trotting toward the open front door. Bigger than any dog she'd seen before, its eyes glowed with a golden light she knew wasn't natural. The dog lowered its head and dropped its massive shoulders as it continued toward the door, snarling with its lips bared from its teeth.

Rasmus hooked his fingers into her hair. He pulled her backward toward the door and jerked her head hard to one side. The screaming was unbearable. He positioned himself just outside the doorway with Paisley in front of him. "Come even one step closer," he said, "and I will snap her neck." He gestured with his free hand. "Officer, shoot the dog. Aim for the head or it's no good."

The brindled dog kept growling. The air around her felt hot and sticky, and her stomach roiled to the point where she thought she might throw up. She flinched when the cop fired and hit the dog in the shoulder.

Rasmus reached for the cop and there was a flash of light. She smelled burning air. The mage shouted once in pain, but he yanked the police officer out of the house, bringing Paisley with him, and slammed the door shut.

In full sight of the neighbors and firefighters, the cop goose-walked her to his squad car and opened the rear door, pushing her head down so she didn't hit it on the car as he muscled her inside. She slid onto the hard plastic seat. The door crashed shut. There were no door handles and no locks. Rasmus got in the front passenger side and turned to look at her through the plastic and wire grill that separated the back from the front of the patrol car.

It wasn't him looking at her. Not really. It was someone else inside him.

The cop got behind the wheel, ignoring the dashboard laptop and the squawking radio. He started the car.

"The Palace Hotel," Rasmus said.

As the patrol car pulled away from the curb, she saw Kynan run out of the house. Blood covered the front of his shirt. He loped after them, closing the distance, keeping up. On foot. He had a phone clutched in one hand. He caught up and stretched for the door. Paisley really thought he was going to make it.

Rasmus turned on the front seat and leveled the cop's revolver at her.

Kynan stopped running. Rasmus said something urgent to the cop, and he hit the gas. Trapped in the back, Paisley turned onto her knees and stared out the rear window. The cop turned on the siren and gunned the car into traffic.

CHAPTER 36

San Rafael, California

Something was happening to Paisley.

Blood dried and flaked off Iskander's arms while he sprinted to Nikodemus's Reventón. His business here was done, bloodier than requested because he'd had to end things quickly once he realized something had gone wrong with Paisley. Inside the car, he grabbed his phone. He needed information. Blasting off without that might get Paisley killed, so he forced himself to calm down while he scrolled through the texts and e-mails that had arrived while he was busy.

Fifty-two texts, four voice mails, and a hundred and ten e-mails. He checked the text messages first. All the recent ones were from Kynan.

```
Where r u
Call me
```

```
F nkdms call
Mt ur hs urgnt
rk hz ur grl
call when u gt ths. Will updt
```

He switched to voice mail. On the face of it, there was nothing alarming in the list of messages. The oldest was from Alexandrine. There were two from Kynan in the last hour. He ignored them to listen to the one from Paisley that had come in about three hours ago.

His heart slammed against his ribs when he heard his fears confirmed. The fear in her voice made him want to punch someone. He widened his psychic link to her, but she was fucking resistant, and all he got back was a faint echo. He'd never get in without being closer. She wasn't dead, but she wasn't all right either.

He called Kynan next. Rasmus lived in Berkeley, but he didn't know for a fact that was where Paisley had been taken, and if he headed to the East Bay only to find out she wasn't there, he'd be screwed by horrendous commute traffic and two bridges. He squeezed the steering wheel with one hand while he waited for the call to connect.

Kynan answered on the first ring. "Where the fuck have you been?"

Taking care of Nikodemus's business. "Where's Paisley?"

"I have a line on that. Get back here, understand me?"

"I'm in San Rafael. Give me half an hour." He thought about Alexandrine's call and got a chill. "Wait a sec." He put Kynan on hold and listened to her voice mail. He switched back to Kynan. "He took her to the Palace Hotel. Meet me there by the registration desk." He called Durian next, got voice mail, and left a message. Gray was next.

"What's up, Iskander?" she asked.

"You anywhere near the Palace Hotel?"

"I'm not far from downtown. You need something?"

"I'm giving you a potential sanction. Nikodemus authorized me, but you can call him if you need to confirm." He switched to his Bluetooth so he'd have his hands free. He intended to drive like a goddamned demon.

"Not necessary. Nikodemus warned us you might call."

"Get a room at the Palace Hotel and text me your room number as soon as you have it." He started the Reventón and headed south to the Golden Gate Bridge. "Kynan's on his way. I'll meet you there."

"Who's the sanction?"

"Rasmus Kessler." He spoke over the silence at the other end. "Maybe Fen, too."

"On my way."

He checked the time. Nine o'clock in the morning meant the commute was barely winding down. The Reventón had some after-market work, illegal, that had removed the car's speed limitations for the U.S. market. He knew for a fact he could get it to one-fifty. At this time of day, there was a chance he could do close to that in the car pool lane for some of the drive into the city.

Twelve minutes later, his phone dinged with a text, and seven minutes after that he had the Reventón parked on the street in a red zone with a haze of magic over it to keep the police from noticing. Kynan was already heading for him. He read Gray's text while he waited for the warlord to dash across the street, found out she'd sent another one with a new room number, and without doing anything more than signaling to Kynan to follow, he went inside.

In the lobby, the hair on the back of his neck stood up. There was a fucking mage here, no question. Kynan made a low sound. Yeah. He felt Kessler's magic. His sense of Paisley got stronger, but she was still locked down tight. Every oath he'd made to her kicked in. Kynan had much the same reaction because she was sworn to Nikodemus, just like the rest of them. She was as good as kin, and important to Nikodemus. Good, because a pissed-off Kynan was a fucking dangerous beast.

They got into the elevator and went to the room Gray had reserved. She opened the door before they got there and stood aside to let them in.

"Smart," Kynan said. "Calling Gray."

True enough. Gray was a human woman who had, through a series of events that had not been entirely her choice, taken on the magic of one of the kin. She'd ended up training with Nikodemus's assassin, Durian, and though she didn't have the same set of skills as Durian, she did have an idiosyncratic and no less deadly set of gifts all her own. The fact that she was human and had something of a grudge against the magekind gave her an ironic edge when she got sent against a mage or a witch, as had happened once or twice.

The tall, slender woman shut the door after them. She wore black jeans and a black long-sleeved T-shirt. Her short hair was black. "Kessler's on the next floor up, three rooms over." She pointed at the ceiling in the direction she meant. "I changed rooms once I figured out where he was, then did some recon."

Kynan nodded his approval. "Excellent. Magehelds?"

"Eleven," Gray said. "Xia and Alexandrine weren't available, so Carson's on her way." She shot a glance in

Iskander's direction, but her next words were directed at Kynan. "I hope you don't mind that I called her."

The warlord shrugged. Everyone more or less knew that Kynan had once been ordered to rape and murder Carson. She was lucky to be alive.

"Good thinking," Iskander said. Carson would sever the magehelds, releasing them from their enslavement to Kessler.

"Last check," Gray said, "there were four in the lobby, two on guard outside the room. Best guess is five inside with Kessler and a human woman. I couldn't get close enough to be sure. She could be a witch. I assume it's Paisley."

"Yeah."

"What's the mental condition of the magehelds?" Kynan asked Gray. "Can you tell?"

"I don't know about the ones in the room, but the others are a bit off. Not insane, but off. Carson will have to be careful."

Kynan pulled out his phone and called Carson. He put the call on speaker and explained the situation.

"I'm parking at Minna Street. Should be there in less than five," she said. "Have Gray meet me in the lobby in case I need her to terminate any of the ones there when I'm done."

"On it," Gray said. She handed a key card to Iskander while Kynan disconnected the call to Carson. "Extra room key, just in case. I'll text you when Carson and I are done. You let us know where you need us next."

Iskander nodded and Gray headed out.

"What the hell happened, Kynan?" Iskander said. He was hyped up, looking to kill himself a few magehelds and, if he got lucky, a mage. And Fen, if Gray didn't take care of that for him. He forced himself to settle down so he could hear Kynan's recitation about what had happened to Paisley. When he was done, Iskander filled him in on Nikodemus's orders to keep Rasmus alive if possible. Not that he cared right now, but orders were orders and he didn't want Kynan in trouble if he could help it.

Kynan said, "He's already in a jam from a dead witch someone dumped on him. If Kessler goes down, too, he's not going to be happy."

"Asks me if I give a shit," Iskander said.

"You getting anything from Paisley?"

"She's shut down hard," Iskander said. "I can barely tell she's here."

"Then I guess we wait."

Ten minutes later, Iskander's phone buzzed with a text from Gray.

Clear. Where u at?

He texted back instructions to meet at the elevators on Kessler's floor, and then he and Kynan headed there. Once there, the four of them—Carson, Gray, Kynan, and himself—opened themselves to one another to minimize the need for words.

Kessler's suite was in the middle of a hall after a left turn. Carson and Gray took the point since they were going to deal with the magehelds guarding the door. Until they were inside the suite, all Iskander and Kynan could do was follow along and not fuck things up for whatever Gray and Carson had to do.

The magehelds were baffled about what to do with

the two women who both felt like magekind and therefore were not to be harmed, so they stood there like dolts until it was too late. Like taking candy from a baby. With Gray behind her, Carson strode up and touched each one in the center of the chest. The blowback was cold, but it was over fast. Both magehelds fell to their knees. One of them twitched uncontrollably while the other struggled to breathe.

With their bond to Rasmus severed, their link to the kin was restored. Iskander almost wished it hadn't been. The damage done to their minds was sickening. There wasn't much left to save. At a signal from Carson, Gray bent down and touched them both.

Done.

And done.

They weren't dead. They were both twitching. Gray had just scrambled their brains enough to take them offline. She straightened, did a quick hack job on the hotel lock, and opened the door.

Iskander pulled his magic and so did the others. The goal was to get Paisley back alive and safe. "Let me deal with Rasmus," Iskander told the others. "Kynan, back me up. Gray, once you and Carson have dealt with the rest of the magehelds, stay close to me in case I need you to terminate Kessler."

"Will do."

If he could help it, nobody but him was going to take the heat for killing Rasmus, but he wasn't going to risk Paisley's life if he thought Gray would do it better or faster. The suite opened onto a wide living room with a wet bar at one end and a door to the bedroom at the other. A mageheld shot to his feet when the door opened. Carson strode in like she had every right to be there. Gray was right behind her.

After that, things happened quickly. Carson severed the first mageheld, and Gray took him out. There were two more at either side of a closed door and another two moving toward Carson from a blind corner of the room. The two magehelds were just plain wrong. Iskander, Gray, and Kynan had all encountered magehelds like that, and the fact was, there was no point in severing them. Their minds were completely gone.

Iskander intercepted the first one, and pulling as much magic as he'd ever done before, he punched through its chest. When his hand whipped back, he had the mageheld's heart in his fist. He whirled in the same motion and did the same to the other. It was over before Carson had even moved from the middle of the room where she and Gray stood.

He faced the two magehelds at the door and grinned. The thought of solving his problem by taking their hearts, too, made his limbs light with anticipation. None of the kin liked to use their magic on a mageheld. You couldn't feel what they were doing for one thing. That hadn't stopped him before. It sure as hell wasn't going to stop him now. He lifted his hands and made a *come here* gesture with his fingers. They held fast to their places, as they must have been ordered to do.

Carson slid in front of him and severed the first one while Kynan immobilized the other. She did the other as well. Done.

It had been less than two minutes since the four of them had come inside.

Iskander opened the door the former magehelds had been guarding.

The first thing he saw was goddamned Rasmus Kessler sitting on the edge of a king-sized bed with Paisley next to him. He had a finger on her wrist. The magic in the room had sent a scattering of sparks into the air. Paisley was facing the door, and even from where he stood, he could tell her eyes were blank. Possibly, she didn't even see him. He didn't dare risk a connection with her. He didn't want to do anything that would break down or weaken her resistance.

He was aware, tangentially, of Carson, Gray, and Kynan behind him. All his attention was focused on Rasmus and Paisley. Gray moved closer but kept a safe distance.

Mentally, Paisley was fighting hard. Not many humans looked normal when a demon was fighting to indwell. He wanted to kill Kessler so badly he could taste it. In his mind, he saw himself punching a fist through the mage's chest, breaking through his sternum and closing his fingers around Kessler's beating heart. He wasn't just going to take the fucker's heart; he was going to rip out his spine, too.

"What the *hell* do you think you're doing?" Iskander said. Just to get something going.

Rasmus jumped off the bed like someone had set him on fire, but he moved without the grace for which he was noted. The mage's eyes shook uncontrollably, and Iskander recognized that as a peculiarity of Fen's. He couldn't feel her, but that skittering inability to focus her eyes had started shortly after she met Rasmus. He figured if he was seeing it in Kessler, then Fen was probably indwelling.

As for Kessler, though he was a naturally pale-complexioned man, his skin was ashen and his braided white-blond hair was damp around his forehead and temples. He extended a hand, palm out, as if that was going to stop Iskander from pulverizing him. In a tortured voice, he ground out, "Help me."

"Fuck you, mage."

Kessler's eyes closed and when he opened them again, his eyes were normal. "Come no closer." The words and their intonation, if not the voice, belonged to Fen. He knew her too well not to recognize that Rasmus was not in control of himself. It was Fen who was fighting for control of Paisley, not Rasmus.

Iskander took a step forward and welcomed the slip of his mind from his hard-won control. "Mage," Iskander said. "Are you there?"

Kessler's eyes jittered again, His mouth opened, and fuck all if Iskander didn't get a wave of despair coming from the mage. "She is no longer sane," he said. He ground out the words. "She must die."

The mage's head snapped back as if he'd been struck, and Iskander's brief contact with Rasmus Kessler shut down. Kessler had once been a mage of significant power, and Iskander didn't have any idea what effect his siphoning of magic into Paisley had been having on his magic. Did time restore his power, or was he permanently diminished by what he was doing to Paisley? Safer all around to assume he was in command of all his magic.

There was no telling what Fen would make Kessler do at this point, because Kessler was right: Fen was no longer sane.

"Fen," Iskander said. He had himself wide open to the psychic energy in the room, and now that he knew the difference between Rasmus when he was in command of himself and Rasmus when Fen was indwelling, Iskander could construct a sort of mirror image of his former blood-twin. He was, of course, intimately familiar with the madness that had nearly taken him, too.

He didn't bother hiding anything. Not the physical changes and not his boiling rage. At this point, thanks in part to Rasmus fighting Fen's indwell, Paisley was holding her own. He just needed her to hold on a little longer. "What is it you want, Fen?"

Rasmus smiled, but it was Fen's smile he was seeing, her cadences in Rasmus's voice, her mannerisms in the tilt of his head, the quirk at one side of his mouth. On the bed, Paisley's shoulders relaxed enough that he guessed Fen's attempted indwell had eased up while Fen concentrated on him and Rasmus.

"We need you back," Rasmus whispered in Fen's voice.

Rasmus Kessler had been in the business of fucking over the demonkind for more than his fair share of years, and now Fen had access to all the skill and knowledge he'd gained over the centuries. If she was in control of Rasmus, then Iskander had to assume all that magic was at her command. Except maybe it wasn't. Maybe Rasmus had realized the danger before it was too late, and by sending his magic into Paisley, he'd drained himself of power. He'd endangered his life by making himself less useful to Fen.

"Let him go, Fen."

"We love him, Iskander. He is ours."

The skin along his back rippled, but the magic he was reacting to wasn't coming from Rasmus. It was coming from Paisley.

"Please. We need you." Kessler held out his arms.

On the bed, Paisley's body went stiff. Her eyes rolled

back in her head, and in the interim, Kessler whipped his head toward Iskander.

"No!" the mage shouted.

Iskander crossed the room and grabbed two handfuls of Kessler's suit coat. "Let her go, Fen."

"Iskander—" That was Kynan, but Iskander ignored the warlord.

"I've helped her as much as I dare. Kill me," Rasmus said, low and hard. "If you don't, she will and it will be too late for us all."

Iskander reached out for his former blood-twin, but there was nothing there for him to touch. She was mageheld and her magic was bound up with Kessler's, and, as was the case for all magehelds with respect to the kin, he couldn't connect with her magic.

Kessler's eyes jittered madly. "If your human tries any more tricks, I will harm her, Iskander."

"Let Paisley go, and we'll talk." He moved closer to the bed but Kessler pushed back.

Iskander could take Kessler's heart now. He'd be justified. And Nikodemus had promised to take care of the fallout if that happened.

"I want your promise," Fen said through Kessler. His mouth twisted as he resisted her control of him. "Promise to come back to us. Promise us, and everything will be the way it should be."

"Let her go and we'll talk. That's the only promise you'll get from me."

Light refracted off the rubies in Rasmus's braids. Iskander glanced over his shoulder and saw Gray a few steps away. Carson and Kynan had come partway in, but Kynan had put himself in front of Carson, because, like most of Nikodemus's sworn fiends, he was ready to lay down his life to protect Nikodemus's witch.

"Gray," Iskander said. The assassin had enough magic to make her a witch. "Are you getting anything from Fen? Is she even there?"

"She's there."

"You're in Nikodemus's territory," Iskander said to Rasmus. "We can't harm the magekind, Fen, and that includes you. If you kill Rasmus, there will be consequences."

Rasmus held out his arms. "My love, my love, we miss you."

"One of Nikodemus's assassins is right here, Fen. If you don't let the mage go, she's going to kill you. You won't see her coming for you, and she won't let you live. Let him go, Fen. Before it's too late. Carson is here. She can sever you and you'll be free. Let him go. Before it's too late."

The jitter in Rasmus's eyes stopped. For an instant, Kessler, not Fen, looked out of the mage's eyes. He moved so that Iskander was left with a clear line of sight to Paisley.

Iskander's magic raged at him to be released, whispering in his head, burning through his blood. He would kill them both if he had to, Kessler and Fen. Before Gray had a chance to do anything.

His back rippled again and he shot a glance at Paisley. Her expression hadn't changed, though her eyes flickered to him. She sat in the same position on the bed. Her frozen stance was typical for an indwell when the human was putting up a strong resistance. Good for her, goddamn it.

He gave Gray a sign that she should do whatever needed to be done. He considered going into Paisley's mind and just taking over. He didn't doubt he could do it, but that might open up Paisley to Fen, and with Fen's sanity in shreds, he just had to hope Paisley continued to keep her out.

Rasmus made an odd motion with one hand, and then Paisley's head dropped back. Iskander pulled hard enough to send a shower of tiny sparks arcing through the air. He held up his fist, fighting for control of the magic raging through him. The mage's eyes fixed on his hand. He saw Gray slide close. Softly and with lethal grace.

"Do it," Rasmus said. "Please."

Iskander's skin rippled the way it did before he changed, and he embraced the onset. He was aware of Paisley leaning toward him, of the magic Kynan had pulled, of Carson and her magic, and of Gray positioning herself. But it was the magic coming from Paisley that seriously cranked him. If it was cranking him, then it was cranking everyone else, too.

"If you think I won't break the rules," Iskander said, "you ought to know Paisley is under my protection. I'll die for her. Right here."

Rasmus opened his mouth to speak, but nothing came out.

Now that Fen wasn't trying to indwell, Paisley could do something besides concentrate on keeping her out. She leaned toward Rasmus and reached for him, the air around her shimmering. Her palm touched the mage, and then she pulled back her hand.

A scream tore from Rasmus, shrill and piercing.

Iskander couldn't feel Fen's use of magic, but he could sure as hell feel the result. A barrier went up around Rasmus, but in the larger view of things, the barrier was fucking pathetic. He couldn't feel it magically, but he could see the physical effects. Iskander ripped through it like it was nothing. Which it was, to him. He grabbed Rasmus by the throat and lifted him up.

Never trust a mage. He ought to kill Rasmus right now and get this over with. Finally. Permanently.

Paisley lifted her hand and touched Rasmus's forehead, and what she did was pure magekind magic. More magic poured from her than he'd ever felt from her before. "Release the mage," she said. She was giving Fen a direct order, as if she were a trained mage.

Iskander held his breath. If this didn't work, if Paisley's order to Fen didn't work, he was going to kill Rasmus and take his chances with the aftermath. He pulled enough magic to turn Kessler's brain to fucking mush.

"Fen," Paisley said calmly. "You must release him."

Nothing happened.

The room was silent as death. Everyone waited: Gray, Carson, Kynan. Him. Part of him died inside. He drew on his magic, ready to let all of it release into the mage.

The mage's body went limp, and he crumpled to the floor, inert. Before him stood Fen, and there was not the least sign of sanity in her eyes. Her physical manifestation was no longer perfect. The shape of her face was off, and the contour of her body shifted. One arm too long, a leg too short.

Fen screamed, but no sound came from her throat. From his left, he saw Carson dart in and sweep a hand across Fen's chest. Fen gasped and her legs buckled. She fell to her knees. They all felt Fen strike back.

Kynan let out a roar and launched himself at Carson, putting his body between Fen and Carson. The magic that flashed out from Fen struck Kynan.

Paisley fell to her knees beside Kessler.

Fen struggled to her feet, ignoring the others. She reached for Iskander, and her magic crashed over him. For the first time in years, he felt her magic. For a heartbeat, everything was back the way it had been. He drew a breath and refused the push of Fen's attempt to restore their bond. That was over. Her madness shivered through the room in a sickening wave, and Iskander knew there was nothing left of the woman he'd once loved. Already she was losing her ability to maintain a physical form.

He pulled his magic and took her heart before it was too late.

It was his final act of kindness.

CHAPTER 37

Paisley walked away from Kessler's motionless body and went to Iskander. He was kneeling beside Fen's body, his head bowed, whispering. He looked up when she reached him, and he put a bloody hand to her cheek. "It's over," he said softly.

She put her arms around him and drew him to her. She wanted to cry but didn't dare. Iskander put his arms around her and held her close. His heart beat against his chest, in time with hers. While she held Iskander, Kynan Aijan knelt at Fen's side, too. He bowed his head and pressed his fingertips to his forehead.

Carson and then Gray did the same thing. Like the others, Paisley bowed her head, too. As the last of Iskander's whispered words faded on the air, Fen's body vanished.

Paisley shivered. Iskander's arms tightened around her and he held her closer, his head against her shoulder. She stroked his hair. "It's all right," she whispered. "It's all right."

He stood up, bringing her with him. "I thought Fen was going to kill you."

"She didn't, though." She managed a tremulous smile. "Are you all right?"

"Without you," he said, reaching for her again, "my life would not have been worth living."

Kynan stood, too. Blood trickled down the side of his face, and he held his left arm at an awkward angle. He extended his right hand to Carson and then Gray, and both the women were good sports about indulging the war-lord and pretending they needed help standing. "You're a fucking witch," he said.

Paisley shivered. She was cold inside and out. She turned her hand over. The inside of her wrist was bloody, and she was shaky with whatever had happened to her. At the end, she'd realized that all this time, Rasmus had been sending his magic into her, deliberately weakening himself and giving her at least a chance to defend her-self against Fen. If she hadn't turned out to be resistant, his plan might have worked much sooner. "If I am, it's because of Rasmus."

Everybody turned to look at the mage, sprawled on the floor, unmoving.

"Carson, if Paisley is still linked with Kessler, can you sever it?" Iskander pulled her tight against his side. He didn't want to let her go. Ever.

"I think so." She walked to Paisley. "May I?"

Paisley glanced at the mage on the floor. "Will it harm him?"

Carson glanced at Kessler, too. "Interesting question. I doubt it. It might end up trapping his magic in you. My guess is he intended all along to take it back."

"Never trust a mage," Kynan said, and there was an unsettling fire burning behind his words.

She looked at Iskander. "What do you think? Is it safe?"

"Probably not. But it's less safe to wait for Rasmus to wake up. Kynan's right. I say fucking do it."

"All right, then." Paisley nodded at Carson. "Let's do it."

"This might hurt a bit. Ready?" When she nodded, Carson touched Paisley's chest. The other woman's eyes fluttered open and closed several times. Heat flashed and twisted through her, and with Paisley's overloaded senses, she could pick out the heat streaking from her injured wrist to that pool of wide, still magic inside her.

When it was over, Paisley reeled back. Iskander caught her and held her steady. "You okay?" he whispered.

On the floor, Kessler's right arm flailed. His back arched once and his mouth opened wide then shut with a clack of his teeth. His body flattened out, and once more he lay still. His mouth went lax. She'd have thought he was dead, but his chest moved with a breath and then settled down into a curious nullity. No one moved against him, and she took that to mean they all thought what she did. Rasmus wasn't a threat right now.

Paisley fought for a breath herself, and if it weren't for Iskander's presence, she would have had a harder time of it than she did. She lifted her wrist. It was blistered and bloody, but it didn't hurt anymore.

"I think that takes care of that," Carson said. With a smile, she dusted off her hands. "Quite neatly, if you ask me."

Paisley put a hand to her chest and took stock of her condition. She no longer felt that sense that someone was waiting to take her over, and the low-level sense of unease that had been curled up in her belly for so long was gone. "What happens to him?"

Carson shrugged. "I don't know. I guess we'll find out, right?"

"How about you get her home?" Gray told Iskander. "You look like you both need a good long rest. We'll take care of cleaning up here."

"Sure." Iskander didn't release Paisley. "Somebody tell Nikodemus I'll bring his car back in a couple of days, okay?"

Carson waved him off. Her attention was on the mage now. Iskander slid a hand around Paisley's waist and led her toward the door.

"Paisley Nichols?"

She stopped at Kynan's sharp query of her name. "Yes?"

He bowed his head and pressed three fingers to his forehead. "Thank you."

She mimicked the gesture. "I'm the one who should be saying thanks to you. To all of you."

Twenty minutes later, she was in the passenger seat of a sleek black car with Iskander driving way too fast. They weren't heading home but rather north toward the Marin headlands. They took the first exit off the Golden Gate Bridge, and he gunned the car. She was sure they weren't supposed to be on this stretch of road, but considering the day she'd had, she didn't give a damn.

After a heart-stopping series of turns, Iskander parked the car up on the old Nike missile range. They got out to gaze at the distant East Bay hills and the dense fog that obscured all but the tips of the two red towers of the Golden Gate Bridge.

"I've been thinking," he said.

"About?"

"Maybe I don't want a tenant anymore."

"I hear they're a real pain. Always complaining about things being broken."

He shifted to get a better look at her. "Ain't that the truth. There's paperwork, too. Taxes and shit. Insurance. So here's the deal. I think you should just keep living with me."

She took Iskander's hand, and when he looked down, his smile broke her heart wide open. "Do you think you can stand to have me around all the time?"

"I'm not saying it won't be a trial," he said. "All that girl stuff in my house. But you're fantastic in bed."

She grinned. "You too."

"And you're okay in the kitchen." His smile slowly faded. He leaned in and wrapped an arm around her, bringing her in close. "I want you to stay with me," he said. "If you want to go down to city hall to make it official for your family and all that, I'll do it." He brought her closer. "I want you with me, kicking ass and living with me and putting up with me."

"We could do that." She touched his face. "I don't want to be your tenant anymore, either, and I surely do not need a landlord. They're a pain."

He drew in a breath. "I love you, Paisley."

The words settled around her; they were right and true. "I love you, too."

"All right, then. He lifted her hand to his mouth and pressed his lips to her palm. "Welcome home, cupcake," he said.

THE DISH

Where authors give you the inside scoop!

From the desk of Jami Alden

Dear Reader,

Whenever I start a new project, people inevitably ask me, "what's it about?" With BEG FOR MERCY, my answer seemed simple. This book is about Megan Flynn's desperate quest to get her wrongfully convicted brother off death row before he's executed. It's about a woman who is so determined she'll risk anything: her heart, when she begs Detective Cole Williams, the man who broke her heart when he arrested her brother, for help as she tracks down the real killer. And her life, when she herself becomes the target of a brutal killer's twisted desires.

But as I got further into Megan and Cole's journey, I realized that's *not* really what this book is about. Scratch beneath the surface, and you'll see that this book is really about faith. Not necessarily the religious kind, but the kind of faith you have in the people you love. It's also about the faith you have in yourself, in your gut, your instincts—whatever you want to call it. It's about listening to yourself and the truth that you cannot deny, even when the rest of the world tries to convince you that you're wrong.

No matter the evidence that points to her brother's guilt, Megan knows, deep down in her core, that her brother is not capable of the kind of brutal murder for which he was convicted. Nothing will convince her otherwise, her belief in her brother's innocence and faith in his true nature is absolutely unshakeable.

It's so strong that it can even convince a skeptic like by the book, just the facts ma'am detective like Cole Williams to put aside everything he thinks he knows about this case. It will drive him to risk a career that means everything to him in order to help the woman he loves.

Megan and Cole's journey to happily ever after isn't an easy one, but nothing worth having comes easily. I hope you enjoy their story, and as you read, ask yourself, how deep is your faith in yourself and the people around you? How far would you go for someone you love?

Enjoy!

Jami Alden

www.jamialden.com
www.facebook.com/jamialden
twitter @jamialden

♥ ♥ ♥ ♥ ♥ ♥ ♥ ♥ ♥ ♥ ♥ ♥ ♥ ♥ ♥ ♥

From the desk of Carolyn Jewel

Dear Reader,

Paisley Nichols, the heroine of MY DANGEROUS PLEASURE, is living her dream. She owns a bakery in San Francisco's financial district, and she's making a go of it. It's hard work and long hours, but she loves what she does. I had some real life inspiration for her character. When I was a kid, my mother baked from scratch; bread, cinnamon rolls and delicious cookies, which my siblings and I took for granted. It wasn't until much later in life that I realized that not every mother baked like that. Now I bake goodies for my son, and if I have to taste test what I bake, well, that's a sacrifice I'm willing to make.

My youngest brother worked as a pastry chef for a while (he now does catering on the side) and there was a time when he was training when he'd drive up from Santa Barbara where he lived, spend the weekend at our house, bake up a storm and leave us with a refrigerator full of whatever he was practicing at the time; creme brulee, chocolate soufflé, chocolate mousse and what have you. When he got married, the restaurant threw a party for him, and if you've never been around a slew of professional chefs, let me tell you, you are missing out on great food and lots of fun.

With my brother as an example, I got more ambitious

with my own baking. He taught me that quality ingredients make an enormous difference in the outcome, but there are also any number of little tips and tricks that get left out of many recipes that can transform a dessert from great to amazing or from decent looking to professional looking. For example, when making pie crust, use ice water, not room temperature water. Not even the *Joy of Cooking* mentions that crucial fact. Suddenly, my pie crusts were a success! I've also picked up and shared lots of recipes and tips from people on Twitter (I'm @cjewel).

Lest you think my story is nothing but sweetness and 70% (or higher) pure cocoa chocolate, Iskander, the demon hero of MY DANGEROUS PLEASURE, has a very dark side to him. He's been tasked with keeping Paisley safe from the mage who's stalking her, and when she develops some unusual magical abilities, his job gets even more difficult. There are people after them both, and they aren't very nice. But in between the enslaved demons and magic using humans chasing them, Paisley and Iskander do find the time and place to indulge themselves with delicious sweets and each other.

Enjoy!

Carolyn Jewel

www.carolynjewel.com

♥ ♥ ♥ ♥ ♥ ♥ ♥ ♥ ♥ ♥ ♥ ♥ ♥ ♥ ♥ ♥

From the desk of Laurel McKee

Dear Reader,

I have a confession to make—I am totally addicted to dark, brooding, tortured heroes with complicated pasts! I blame *Jane Eyre*. This is still one of my all-time favorite books, and I first came across it when I was ten or eleven years old. It was a battered, old paperback copy from a box of books from a garage sale, and I stayed up all night reading it. I was shocked by the wife in the attic! And when I had finished, I started reading it all over again. I then snatched up every Gothic romance I could find. I guess I've never gotten over the "Mr. Rochester thing."

When I started writing the second book in The Daughters of Erin series, DUCHESS OF SIN, I had planned for Sir Grant Dunmore to be part of a love triangle in the story, who would probably die in the end. But as I wrote his scenes, he showed me that he was much more complicated than that. His scenes with Caroline seemed to take on a life of their own, and I wanted to find out more about him. I wanted to see what would happen between Grant and Caroline and where their unexpected attraction would take them. The answer became LADY OF SEDUCTION. And their passion for each other caused a *lot* of trouble for them, and fun for me!

I've loved spending time with the Blacknall sisters and their heroes, and I'm sorry to say good-bye to them in this book. But I'm very happy they've all found their happy-ever-afters. For excerpts, behind-the-book information on the history of this era, and some fun extras, you can visit my website at http://laurelmckee.net.

And if you'd like to put together your own Irish feast, here is a recipe for one of my favorite dishes—Shepherd's Pie! (The first two books featured Irish Soda Bread and Sticky Toffee Pudding, all great when served with a Guinness...)

Ingredients

- 1½ lbs ground round beef
- 1 onion chopped
- 1–2 cups vegetables—chopped carrots, corn, peas
- 1½–2 lbs potatoes (3 big ones)
- 8 tablespoons butter (1 stick)
- ½ cup beef broth
- 1 teaspoon Worcestershire sauce
- Salt, pepper, other seasonings of choice

1 Peel and quarter potatoes, boil in salted water until tender (about 20 minutes).
2 While the potatoes are cooking, melt 4 tablespoons butter (½ a stick) in large frying pan.
3 Sauté onions in butter until tender over medium heat (10 mins). If you are adding vegetables, add them according to cooking time. Put any carrots in with the onions. Add corn or peas either at the end of the cooking of the onions, or after the meat has initially cooked.

4 Add ground beef and sauté until no longer pink. Add salt and pepper. Add Worcesterchire sauce. Add half a cup of beef broth and cook, uncovered, over low heat for 10 minutes, adding more beef broth as necessary to keep moist.

5 Mash potatoes in bowl with remainder of butter, season to taste.

6 Place beef and onions in baking dish. Distribute mashed potatoes on top. Rough up with a fork so that there are peaks that will brown nicely. You can use the fork to make some designs in the potatoes as well.

7 Cook in 400 degree oven until bubbling and brown (about 30 minutes). Broil for last few minutes if necessary to brown.

Serves four.

Enjoy!

Linnel McKee

♥ ♥ ♥ ♥ ♥ ♥ ♥ ♥ ♥ ♥ ♥ ♥ ♥ ♥ ♥ ♥ ♥

From the desk of Katie Lane

Dear Reader,

There's something about a bad boy that's irresistible, something about a man who lives on the edge and plays by his own rules. And whether it was the time you caught the teenage rebel checking you out in your new

Christmas sweater—or the time the tatted biker sent you a blatantly sexual look as he cruised by on his custom bike—a run-in with a bad boy is like taking a ride on the world's biggest roller coaster; long after the ride's over, you're still shaky, breathless, and begging for more.

No doubt a portion of the blame lies with our mothers. (It's so easy to blame Mom.) Maternal warnings always include the things that turn out to be the most fun—wild parties, fast cars, and naughty boys. (All of which got me in plenty of trouble.) But I think most of our infatuation has to do with our desire to take a break from being the perfect daughter, the hard-working employee, the dependable wife, and the super mom. For one brief moment, we want to release our inner bad girl and jerk up that sweater Aunt Sally gave us and flash some cleavage. Or hop on that throbbing piece of machinery and take a ride on the wild side.

Even if it's only in our fantasies—or possibly a steamy romance novel—we want to throw caution to the wind and fearlessly proclaim...

MAKE MINE A BAD BOY

Katie Lane

www.katielanebooks.com

Find out more about Forever Romance!

Visit us at
www.hachettebookgroup.com/publishing_forever.aspx

Find us on Facebook
http://www.facebook.com/ForeverRomance

Follow us on Twitter
http://twitter.com/ForeverRomance

NEW AND UPCOMING TITLES

Each month we feature our new titles
and reader favorites.

CONTESTS AND GIVEAWAYS

We give away galleys, autographed copies,
and all kinds of exclusive items.

AUTHOR INFO

You'll find bios, articles, and links to personal websites
for all your favorite authors—and so much more.

GET SOCIAL

Connect with your favorite authors, editors, and
other Forever fans, and share what's important to you.

THE BUZZ

Sign up for our monthly romance newsletter,
and be the first to read all about it.